The Voices Arrive

The Voices Saga

Volume II

William L Stolley

iUniverse, Inc.
New York Bloomington

The Voices Arrive
The Voices Saga Volume 2

iUniverse books may be ordered through booksellers or by contacting:

iUniverse
1663 Liberty Drive
Bloomington, IN 47403
www.iuniverse.com
1-800-Authors (1-800-288-4677)

ISBN: 978-1-4401-7574-9 (pbk)
ISBN: 978-1-4401-7577-0 (ebk)

Printed in the United States of America

iUniverse rev. date: 10/01/09

Dedication

I WOULD LIKE TO EXPRESS my thanks and gratitude to Anitra Louis. Ms. Louis is a freelance writer and editor with a BA in English from Greensborough College and a Masters from NCCU. She assisted me with the grammar and punctuation of this novel. I would like to acknowledge Dr. Milton Gipstein, Kevin Kelly, and Elaine McKeough for their continued friendship, support, and inspiration. I also wish to express my sincere appreciation for my mother, Annamary Stolley. Her valued input helped to shape the final version of the novel. Finally, I wish to express my undying love and respect for my wife, Lori, and my son, Michael, whose understanding of me create an ideal environment for writing.

"If and when humanity discovers intelligent life on other planets, we may find that aliens have been telepathically connected to other species on different worlds long before our awareness of them." WLS

"Not one shred of scientific evidence exists that explains the phenomenon known as being "psychic" is real in any measurable shape or form," Professor Li Po Chin, Harbin University, April 1967 from his address to a Chinese symposium entitled – "Fallacies and Myths of paranormal activity inside the human brain."

Contents

From whence we came 1
An ideal setting 10
Appraisal 23
Night search party 32
Moving day 41
Ancient rhythms 53
Taking over. 67
Adjustments 75
Chou Lo's historic journey 79
A highway to the stars 92
Worlds upon worlds 107
A price must be paid 121
As did Ruth. 127
Invasion 137
Long overdue 143
Intimate revelations. 151
A most magnificent dream 164
Altering Rollo 175
Friendship betrayed 189
Preparations 203

The Voices Arrive 219
Awkwardness 230
An excuse for harm 239
Departures and arrivals 256
A troubled flight 264
Paree 272
Event horizon 280
Crossed wires 290
Flight to Hades 299
Abandon ship 308
Chou's churners 312
An end and a beginning. 322

Chapter One

From Whence We Came

The townspeople of Rollo had turned off nearly every light by 10 p.m. that July evening. The last bit of twilight in the summer sky had barely faded from the western horizon. A few streetlights and the old-fashioned incandescent light bulb over the front of Baker's general store on Main Street remained lit. A person could stand at any place in the village, tilt their head back, and gaze up at a myriad of stars overhead – a feat impossible in large cities such as New York, London, or Beijing. Out here on this flat Midwestern plain, isolated far from the rest of humanity, life came to a screeching halt every evening about this time with little else for its residents to do but tune into their personal electronic devices or sleep.

Into this silent little hamlet, nestled between the rising western hills of Colorado and the flat southwestern Kansas plain, an extraordinary event took place that would transform this forgotten slice of humanity into the most unique and yet most secret of all places in the world. A semi-translucent bubble of psychic energy, visible only to a select gifted few, settled onto a grassy field. Not one of Rollo's sixty-plus residents could hear or see a thing. Only those possessed with an extraordinary ability could visualize the corporate jet when it set down. The large, yet invisible aircraft within the special sphere of influence could quietly move about unseen.

Why did this jet land here of all places? Why did this incomparable group of extremely gifted and incredibly unique individuals bother with an out-of-the-way, dull, ordinary, and lonely place like Rollo, Kansas? Why come to America at all? Surely they could find isolated places in the world other than one located in the heart of the United States, with its paranoia for invasion, and its massive military/spy complex that guards over its protected borders. Why not live on some remote island in the South Pacific, or create a special niche in the middle of the Brazilian rain forest, or perhaps begin some secret habitat within the vast Siberian wilderness?

Twenty hours earlier, these very special people began a trans-Pacific flight that would have frightened most people to death. The incidents that surrounded the start of that trip nearly killed them. During what seemed like a year instead of a day, this gifted group nearly perished before they started out life together. A guided missile aimed directly at their private jet almost blasted them to smithereens as they streaked across the south end of the Yellow Sea. Their aircraft dangerously skimmed over the surface of the water traveling at seven hundred knots as they sought to escape the confines of China in search of a permanent home.

Flying low to avoid radar detection, Villi (pronounced vee-lee) piloted a jet aircraft which the group took from an unscrupulous general by the name of Xing. They thought they could escape the country undetected, but unfortunately that would not be the case. From the start of this harrowing flight, they used their mental prowess to deflect military fighter jets sent to destroy them. They also convinced coastal radar installations that their jet did not exist. However, when confronted with the bridge of a nuclear submarine set on a collision course against their escaping jet, Cecilia had trouble when she tried to navigate her psychic ability through the dense seawater. Between the speed of the jet aircraft and the submarine's location, she could not convince the emotionally heightened crew to ignore the perceived threat. In their own defense, the Chinese submarine fired a missile at the fleeing psychics unaware of their benign intent.

"They fired a rocket at us!" Cecilia cried out a warning to the others.

"Master Li!" Michael Tyler urged. "We need your help!"

Michael turned to the group's leader, a short, slender, elderly man with thinning white hair, and piercing gray eyes. His name is Li Po Chin (lee poh cheun). He had once been a professor at Harbin University. Michael first named him "master" when he begged the venerable old man to teach him what he knew regarding his formidable psychic power. After a terrible confrontation with a rogue psychic in Shenyang, Cecilia and the rest of the group confirmed Li's status as their master, too. Whether Li wanted it or not, the others called him Master Li.

As the missile shot out from the submarine, Master Li ignored Cecilia and Michael's pleas. Instead, he focused on the group's most recent acquisition: Han Su Yeng. Fortunately, this group chose to add one final member before setting out from China – strategist Han Su Yeng, a twenty-eight-year-old civil servant from Beijing. Han's strategic insights convinced Li that the civil servant played a key role in their future, although he had not contributed to the group effort.

Li confronted Han as the seconds ticked down toward the time of impact.

"Han, we need you to apply that brilliant mind of yours to this problem," Li urgently requested. A shrill warning from the cockpit filled the cabin's interior. "We need a solution now!"

The alarm and Master Li's pleas shook the young man awake. As a seasoned strategist and statistical analyst for the state, Han could sift through mounds of bureaucratic data. He had the capacity to tie seemingly random facts together and then quickly form pertinent conclusions. He turned to the group and addressed them in those final seconds.

"Open your minds to me," the normally meek Chinese man requested of the eight other psychics aboard the jet.

In a blinding instant, Han found that he could separate their trivial memories into distinct categories. He understood all he needed to know to make the right choice. The voices of Galactic Central once surrounded Michael and Cecilia with a protective bubble of psychic energy while the couple lay unconscious on the floor of a fishing trawler as it crossed the Sea of Okhotsk. Master Li discovered the uses of this application and made the group practice this technique. They worked to perfect the technique as they journeyed through China. In this instance, the other psychics did not see its strategic use as Han did.

"We must form one large psychic bubble around the jet using our combined energy!" he informed the group via a mind link. "If we unite our power, the bubble's field should contain sufficient energy to repel any blast!"

Master Li watched with absorbed amazement as the group opened their minds and linked. They brought their energy together united in thought and purpose. Li speculated that they either acted out of instinct for self-preservation or by mutual cooperation through friendship. Either way, this moment represented a first for them.

With only seconds remaining, the jet and rocket flew in an unavoidable head-on collision course. The ballistic missile rapidly bore down on their advancing position. Its blunt, round, head and fierce jet trail zoomed through the air ready to unload an enormous force of destructive energy.

The psychics on the jet took the completed image from Han's mind. Their energies melded together into one large unified field. A shimmering form engulfed the speeding jet aircraft in the form of a large translucent sphere filled with psychic energy. At that precise moment, the missile struck with tremendous impact. The explosion shook the craft with terrible force. A ball of hot, fiery, destructive gases engulfed the psychic sphere. Yet, the jet moved on with sufficient forward kinetic energy. It sailed through the impact zone without so much as a scratch. The passengers only experienced a momentary rumble as the aircraft continued on its flight. Somehow, the bubble repelled the blast while allowing the flow of air to pass through its membrane. This passage of air maintained the aircraft's ability to fly.

The moment the psychic bubble formed, the jet disappeared to all visible eyes. Its timing was perfect. Inside China and aboard the submarine, it appeared as if the missile destroyed the stolen jet. A few moments later, the aircraft passed over the submarine's position. It did not fire again. The group did not detect anyone scanning their position. Everyone in the cabin cheered. As the danger passed, the group turned to Han. While he had not contributed to the creation of the bubble, his strategic value suddenly became apparent to everyone. Yet, before Michael or anyone could offer their thanks, Master Li turned toward the front of the plane.

"Villi," he linked to the pilot. "We are invisible to all radar. Take the jet up to a safer altitude. Stay on this course until you clear the Yellow Sea. Be mindful to avoid collisions with other aircraft as they cannot see us," he said and then added. "Remember to keep your focus on the bubble."

"Yes Master Li," Villi replied as he used his mind to increase the engine's thrust.

The aircraft soared up through the troposphere into the stratosphere. They left the dark ocean water off the coast of China far behind them. Breaking through the cloud level, the jet popped out into clear night sky where it leveled off. Villi could sense other jets cruising at this level, though miles away from their position. He had been a pilot for about eight hours. A download from Galactic Central gave him both experience and knowledge.

"This isn't easy," Villi mumbled. "I'm trying to fly a jet, watch for traffic, and keep up this bubble."

"Just do the best you can," Li advised.

"No privacy either!" Villi complained.

"Use your block!" Li shot back.

"That's easy for you to say Master Li," the young Russian muttered. He shook his head. "Next, you'll want me to fly blindfolded!"

Master Li turned his attention to the man who had rescued them from death.

"We owe you our lives Han," Li linked as he bowed slightly. "Congratulations on your quick thinking master strategist!" he added with a slight smile.

Everyone relaxed and breathed a sigh of relief. They joined with Master Li in thanking Han. He humbly accepted their gratitude and nodded his acknowledgement to each person. The bubble, along with the links to his fellow teammates, was a new phenomenon to him. Therefore, he could not help them form the psychic bubble.

Only a few hours had passed since he lay on the tarmac of the emergency airstrip outside Tianjin. He awoke to find the group standing over him in a circle just after his conversion. Prior to that moment, he never heard of a psychic being or a place called Galactic Central. Unlike the other members of their group who had time after their conversions to adjust, no one had the time to instruct Han on psychic basics. Li hoped that when the aircraft cleared Chinese airspace either he or a member of the group could begin Han's initiation.

"Can everyone keep their focus on the bubble?" Li asked. He tried to appear calm as he glanced about the interior space at the eager youthful faces.

The young psychics inside the jet's cabin nodded or gave visual reassurances back to Li. Only moments before, the psychic group separately used their mental power to alter the minds at radar stations along China's coastline. They used their power to dissuade pilots who intended to shoot them down. In a moment of crisis, they became one powerful force. Li marveled at their ease to act in unison.

"Good," Li replied relieved. "Then I suggest we remain… uh, camouflaged all the way to, uh… by the way, Michael, just where are we going?" Li wondered when he addressed the tallest young man in the cabin.

Michael Tyler, the slender young American and the world's first psychic convert, suddenly realized he did not have any specific place in mind and that he did not thoroughly plan what would happen after they initially formed a group. He always assumed their destination would be America. Although as he thought about the group's members, the majority of them were Chinese. He then considered other destinations such as Canada, Australia, or even Mexico would suffice as a place they could settle. He liked all of those places.

"The group should decide," he privately thought. "If I ask for suggestions, I might appear unplanned and foolish," he reasoned. "Perhaps I should field questions first."

Michael forgot that when he helped to create the bubble that surrounded the jet, he had no block over his private thoughts. His personal trepidations leapt into every receptive psychic mind nearby.

Cecilia groaned while the others clicked their tongues. Even Han rolled his eyes.

"Michael, you are in a room where everyone knows your thoughts," Master Li reminded him. The young man shrugged and grinned. "Since we see you had no specific destination in mind, we should try to find a consensus before we go too far in one direction. Agreed?" Li offered and searched their minds for confirmation.

Of the nine psychics aboard the jet, Han was the least experienced and yet seemed the most relaxed. He silently agreed to acquiesce any leadership position to the other more dominate psychics. Instead, he assumed a supportive advisory role.

"May I offer a suggestion or two?" he linked while Li awaited feedback.

"By all means master strategist, proceed," Master Li responded.

"I believe we can eliminate China as a destination," Han began, "seeing as we have fled that country with a large piece of stolen property too difficult to hide." The others quickly murmured their agreement. "I assume that also excludes Russia as a possible site because we would not appear to conform to any normal standard of behavior in a country with virtually no privacy. Would you agree Villi?"

"A large group of Chinese psychics would attract attention in most Russian cities. People might ask questions," the big Russian pilot replied. "We could not remain anonymous for very long."

Han shrugged his shoulders. "Instead of trying to pick over a list and argue the assets of this country or that, we should simply head straight to America," he suggested. "It is the most logical place for us to start a settlement. We don't need identification to move about locally or to make most purchase transactions, especially if we obtain enough cash to spend," he offered.

"Go ahead Han, continue," Li urged. "I wish to hear more of your analysis."

Han stood up and faced the younger crowd.

"My life's work has been to gather seemingly random facts and apply analytical formulas to support my hypotheses," he told them. "I use the same logical progression in most instances." He cast his eyes down for a second, as if he were silently making some swift calculations in his head. "I will make the case for America," he said as he looked up. "I feel we can better blend with the general population. They refer to their nation as the melting pot – a mix of people from a variety of cultural and ethnic backgrounds. America has large Asian communities in several cities."

"So we are to be a Chinese group?" Zhiwei eagerly spoke up. He found the prospect delightful.

"Most of us are Chinese," Han replied as he pointed out the obvious.

"I suppose that leaves Michael, Cecilia and me out of the group," Villi spoke up from the cockpit. "Can't we find a mixed neighborhood in the nation known as a melting pot?"

"We are to live in another city?" Su Lin linked as she added her opinion.

"Don't you want all the conveniences of a city nearby?" Chou asked as he turned to confront her. "We'll have access to public transportation, stores, schools, sporting events, entertainment…"

"Yes and no," she interrupted. "While it's true that a city has many public conveniences, it has many draw backs too, such as a lack of privacy. I thought we performed well as a group when we had the house in the country," Su Lin tried to explain her position. "We relied on each other. Moreover, we began to work together as a team. We didn't have the intrusive psychic interference of the city."

"Living in that country house did give us structure and cohesion as a group," Zinian agreed. "Su Lin is right."

Cecilia glanced over at Michael. She knew he spent nearly a year living in New York. She thought he should speak up and assume more leadership.

He shook his head and privately linked, "Not now."

"Hmm," Han pondered. "I see. I hadn't thought of that. You lived in a house before we met and stayed there for nearly a week, too. Perhaps if we isolate our group away from humanity we could function more effectively."

"Are you talking about living in the suburbs?" Michael finally spoke up. "Suburban communities are large. Every city in America has them. Perhaps we could find a large house with several bedrooms…"

"Are you suggesting that all of us live in one house?" Villi questioned. "If you thought privacy was an issue in the city, imagine what would happen if we lived together day after day, week after week in the same house. We could hear each private thought of the other eight in our group. I'd go crazy!"

"Villi's right," Chou spoke up. "Currently, we get along just fine. But we've only been at this for less than two weeks. Eventually, each of us would need to find his or her space. We all need privacy whether our minds are open or not. Besides, the house in Shenyang served as a temporary place. We had only just gained our new powers of perception when we stayed there. If I had to know every thought in their heads…" he jerked a thumb toward Zhiwei and Zinian. Before he could continue, Cecilia cut him off.

"The suburbs are out of the question as well," she pointed out. "We'd have the same problem living in the suburbs as we would in the city. American suburbia is too well populated," she stated. "The houses are close together. Eventually someone would see flying objects through an open window. Nosey neighbors provide too many witnesses to unusual events. We'd attract the wrong kind of attention."

Master Li linked over to Han.

"Do you see how your analysis sparks debate?" he privately linked. "Cecilia and Chou are right," he openly linked to the group. "Neither the city nor the suburb are the types of places where nine psychic people of our caliber should start a new life. We must begin our community in a place away from humanity's prying eyes. Perhaps we could find a village with enough infrastructures already in place, homes ready for us to occupy. We cannot start out by building a new town in some wilderness."

"The American west is full of small towns," Michael offered. "We could… take over one of them…"

"…and do what with the residents," Han interrupted. "Would we kick them out?" The idea of using their power to oust someone from their home struck him as being callus.

"We would give them the same kind of compensation we give everyone," Villi suggested.

"It better amount to more than blank pieces of paper," Cecilia linked. She referred to the how she and Michael used a mental trick to trade blank pieces of paper with merchants instead of currency.

"Before we start squabbling over details, I believe Michael has made a very constructive point," Master Li observed. "By taking over a small isolated town with less than a hundred occupants, we could offer them a better life in some other location. Perhaps they would prefer an ideal setting that we obtain from their mind. We could then tap Michael's trust and fulfill those desires. We could occupy what they leave behind as a place to start."

"That's it?" Villi squawked. "Your plan is to find a place for just the nine of us to live in some little isolated village and not have other people around? I'm not certain about Zinian, Zhiwei, or Chou's feelings in this matter, but I like to interact with other people," he voiced. "I don't want to be stuck in some prairie town with no other people but us. Can't we find a location where we could take over part of a village or somehow integrate with an existing one?"

"Villi's right," Chou added quietly. "Zinian… Zhiwei…" he said as he indicated the other two university students. "We are young men Master Li. While it's true that I didn't have a wife in Jilin, I did have a date now and then. We don't have psychic mates waiting for us when we arrive. Please don't take offense Villi or Michael."

"None taken," Michael replied. "Believe me, I understand."

"That's not to say Villi or Michael will have an unconditional mate either," Su Lin spoke up. She saw that Cecilia supported her.

"This variety of perspectives presents new problems for us to consider," Master Li responded as he pondered their comments. "Therefore, based on our discussion I'm assuming that we should find a place where we can isolate our group from massive crowds and yet have understanding neighbors. Is such a place possible?"

"Wait a minute," Han spoke up. "First we need to make some basic decisions. I believe we should decide if we are going to America. Second, we should look for a small isolated town or village in the American west that lies within a comfortable distance of a major city. Are we agreed?" he asked while he glanced around the jet's interior for approval.

"We should vote," Li requested.

"What if someone objects to this idea?" Han queried and turned to Li as their unelected leader.

"We reconsider all ideas until we find mutual agreement," Li offered.

"Will we always require a unanimous vote Master Li?" Su Lin wondered.

"I leave that to the group to decide. I am not some officiating judge, nor should you expect that of me," Master Li explained. "I am only here to offer guidance."

"I suggest we vote," Chou linked.

In the silence that followed, the nine members of the psychic group relaxed into their soft leather reclining seats. They contemplated the roundtable discussion as the jet cruised at an elevation high above the clouds. Since no one objected to America, Li took that as a unanimous "yes" to the last suggestion.

"Set your compass for North America, Villi," Li linked to the pilot. "We're heading to the United States of America!"

Chapter Two

An Ideal Setting

VILLI STRETCHED OUT HIS LEGS and yawned, reaching back with his big, long, muscular, hairy arms. The Russian ex-police officer worked the tension out of his muscles before he sat forward to set a new course for the western coastline of the United States of America. He placed San Francisco in the center of those directional crosshairs.

"America," he sighed. "I've always wanted to go there. I read where they line the grocery store shelves with hundreds of products to buy, always fresh, always wholesome," he softly uttered. "America is the land of abundance. I understand beautiful women wearing bikinis cram the beaches of southern California. Ha! I can hardly wait!" he grinned while he rubbed his hands together.

The aircraft banked around the southern tip of Japan and headed out over the Pacific Ocean as fast as Villi could push its jet engines. Once he reached cruising altitude, he throttled back to ride the jet stream heading east. Yet, as he gazed out on the vast flat ocean that spread before him, Villi realized that the jet had to cross the widest ocean on the planet. He glanced down at his fuel gauges and quickly computed their consumption. He began to consider major airstrips between their current location and America.

Aviation fuel was not only very expensive in 2016 but a rare commodity in that fewer private airstrips stocked large quantities due to its high cost. However, as he computed the necessary amount for the trip, he noted an anomaly. The sleek, large, private jet seemed to meet less wind resistance with the psychic bubble surrounding them. However, even with the bubble in place, they would not be able to make the trip nonstop.

"America is too far away," he thought as he stared down at his figures.

He had enough fuel to take them over the mountains into India, or to the coast of Australia, or even make it to northern Russia; areas he originally presumed would be their destination. However, this jet did not have the capacity of a large jumbo jet, able to circumnavigate nearly half the globe before refueling.

"Master Li," Villi linked. "I want to advise you of our status."

"Go ahead," Li linked back.

"We do not have enough fuel to reach the western shores of North America," Villi informed him. "We must either go to some alternative place, or refuel between here and America."

"Go on," Li linked.

"If you insist on American then…" he glanced down at the electronic map display. "Checking the system… I would say Hawaii seems the logical choice to refuel."

"Try a private airstrip Villi," Michael broke in.

"Why there?" Villi retorted. "A private airstrip may not have fuel."

"Less traffic than a military base or a commercial airport, also less security," Michael told him. "You'll have fewer minds to manipulate. Take offs and landings will be easier. Plus, wealthy people like to have everything they need in abundance. Look for one that caters to large private jets. They'll be certain to have an ample supply of jet fuel."

"Thanks Michael," Villi linked back.

"Well done," Cecilia whispered as she sat next to him.

She squeezed Michael's hand. It was the first time the two psychics made any personal contact since they took off from Beijing. Her hand felt warm and inviting to Michael. He squeezed back and glanced her way. Their eyes met. Neither had kissed since that day at the house in Shenyang. The couple separated when they busily carried out the plan to obtain Han for the group. Cecilia inched closer. She decided it was more private to whisper than link.

"By the way," she spoke. "I thought your idea of using a small town brilliant."

Michael gazed into those deep blue eyes. He took in every detail. He had turned away from the aisle toward Cecilia. Just as he felt confident enough to kiss her, a hand touched his shoulder.

"Hungry?" a feminine voice asked.

Su Lin stood behind Michael. His head snapped around startled by her voice. She held out a sandwich tray.

"I made turkey…," she pointed.

"You made?" he asked.

"I had some extra time before we boarded in Beijing. I made them especially for the American and Canadian onboard," she kidded. "I knew you wouldn't like the Chinese snack food we packed."

"I didn't see you get up," Michael said as he twisted around in his seat.

"I would say you were… preoccupied," she pointed out. "Master Li says I must serve the team first," she said. She nodded her head in his direction before she turned back to Michael. "Try the chicken salad. I made it from a recipe that I found in your mind while we raided the military mess hall for supplies. They were surprisingly well stocked."

"Yes, but there's only one commercial mayonnaise," Michael started to object.

"Don't worry," she smiled. "They had it."

Michael took the chicken salad and unwrapped enough plastic to take a nibble.

"Mmm," he linked as he chewed. "This is good!"

"She's a great cook," Villi commented from the cockpit.

Cecilia noted that Su Lin removed some of her outer garments. Her partially unbuttoned blouse revealed an ample figure she had yet to display. This surprised the Canadian. She glanced up at Su Lin, half-smiled and made an hourglass move with her hands.

"Some sexy stewardess," she commented. She reached over Michael, grabbed a sandwich off the tray, and took what she presumed was a can of orange soda with Chinese characters on the outside. "What brand is this?" she questioned.

"Sweet and bubbly, made for tourists," Su Lin smiled back. She turned the can to the front label. "Don't look at the ingredients. It'll make you sick; though perfect for you dear… sexy indeed!"

"Meow!" Chou chirped from the back.

The two women glared at him, which made him squirm.

"May I help?" Han offered to Su Lin.

"That's very considerate of you Han," she answered. "I can manage."

Su Lin returned to the galley at the front of the large private craft. She purposely swung her hips back and forth, which prompted catcalls from the entire group this time (except Han and Master Li, of course). Everyone laughed which seemed to break the tension hanging over the group since they departed Tainjin.

"Hey!" Villi called out from the cockpit. "That's not fair! I can't see!"

"Don't worry," Su Lin ducked her head in behind him, "you get the private show later. Here, I hope you like it, roast beef with a slice of onion and horseradish sauce on a poppy seed roll." She ran a few fingers around his face and placed the hefty plated sandwich in his lap. Her very touch sent Villi's senses tingling.

"My favorite!" he grinned as he held up the monstrosity.

"Don't expect a kiss after that," she warned and pointed at the sandwich.

"I don't have to eat," he smiled.

Su Lin laughed. She returned to the main cabin and brought a special tray to the Chinese passengers. She knew they would not eat American-style sandwiches. She took out the specifically targeted tray loaded with the Hsia fan (period of grain) or Chinese noodles as Zinian, Zhiwei, and Chou were accustomed to from their northern diets. She tossed the cooked noodles with some vegetables in a wok and packed them into separate servings while Master Li as General Xing changed into his flight uniform.

"Here are your chopsticks," Su Lin added after handing each his container.

"Su Lin… this is wonderful," Chou gratefully stated glancing up.

"Yes, thanks Su Lin," Michael and Cecilia agreed as she passed.

"Su Lin, this sandwich is great," Villi piped in from the cockpit.

"It's just like you could…" Han started.

"Read their minds?" Su Lin finished.

Her comment brought smiles and chuckles around the plane. With everyone's mind open to maintaining the unified sphere, the entire group could see into each other's thoughts.

"How can Villi eat? I thought he was flying the plane?" Han asked, concerned.

"I have the jet on autopilot," Villi stated. "Don't worry, Han. I downloaded a very good flying lesson!"

"You've only had one flying lesson?" Han gulped as the others nearly choked on their food.

Zinian and Zhiwei poked each other and pointed at Han. The rest of the group smiled.

"Believe me my cautious friend," Master Li reassured him. "What Villi learned in that download would take ordinary humans decades to learn."

Hearing that news from Master Li, Han wondered what he could learn during such a process. The possibilities of his psychic connection with Galactic Central intrigued Han. As he stretched back, he finally noticed the exquisite comfort of the jet's interior.

"We only steal the best!" Zinian chimed into Han's thoughts.

Zinian, Zhiwei and Chou sat together at the back of the luxurious cabin. The aircraft was originally designed to seat fourteen corporate passengers. General Xing ordered four seats removed to expand the front galley and install larger seats that converted to beds. The cream-colored reclining seats also had wooden tables that pulled out from the wall. A passenger could manipulate the tables into various positions. The three students sat on a curved bench seat that surrounded a beautiful polished wooden table. The opposite wall had a cocktail bar with a sink and a refrigerator; near the aircraft's tail, a full bathroom.

"I'll have tea for you in a minute Master Li… Han," Su Lin said as she headed back to the galley.

"Oh by the way, have we decided on a final vote about this village?" Villi asked. He thoroughly enjoyed his roast beef sandwich.

"I believe we are past that," Han indicated.

"What did we decide?" Villi wondered.

"A small town in western America… displaced but compensated citizens… a small community that we can mold into our own. It should give us a fresh start away from humanity's prying eyes. Am I right?" Han turned around.

The group linked common agreement. No one spoke as their mouths were full of food.

"Master Li?" Han asked as he turned to the man sitting across from him.

Han looked over at the elderly white-haired man who appeared to relax in the large leather seat. His small slender body sank into its soft plush surface. Li held his eyes closed, deep in thought. He did not respond to Han.

Master Li's mind traveled elsewhere. For the first time in his life, he was high in the air. He had never flown in a jet airplane. From this perspective, he could circumnavigate the globe with his power. His thoughts rippled out beyond the confines of the speeding aircraft, past the Islands of Hawaii and the west coast of the United States, over the broad plains of that nation's interior and beyond the Atlantic Ocean. On the opposite side of the planet, Li felt new voices rising, specifically three individuals: an African man and woman along with a tall, slender, and beautiful French woman. Those three seemed poised to evolve their psychic ability soon, probably by the start of fall he guessed.

"Funny," he reflected, "all in their early twenties…"

Unlike the other psychics in their group that utilized a portal inside their mind, Master Li had the capacity to send an ethereal body outside the boundaries of Earth's atmosphere. It zoomed into the far reaches of space, far beyond the Milky Way Galaxy. After crossing the universe at speeds that defied reason, he arrived at the large planet of the voices. Their thousand-kilometer high, bullet-shaped, silvery column thrust upward from the planet's surface is known as Galactic Central.

"Master Li!" they called to him as they mimicked Michael's label.

"My planet is on the verge of emergence," he told them. "Do you sense them?" he asked as he approached the first available voice. He indicated the trio of new psychics he sensed in Europe.

"We do," the voice closest to him answered for the collective.

"I feel these three will need conversion soon by your measurement of time," he linked to them.

"We will find their corresponding voices," it replied.

"Within seven cycles of your three moons," Li added, "I cannot assist now… I am… preoccupied."

"Understood Li," the voice said before it returned to its duty.

He glanced about the enormous space as he floated amidst the whirling boxes of light that flew to the millions of workstations within the gigantic tall structure. Something drew his attention to the top of the spire. A force started to pull his ghostly body in that direction.

"I cannot go to that place at this time," he considered, "I must return." He dismissed the attraction. He had to return to his physical body still aboard the jet.

Han could no longer feel Li's psychic presence, which alarmed the new psychic.

"Master Li?" Han asked again.

With a time differential present inside Galactic Central's spire, only a few seconds had passed between the first time Han inquired of Li and his follow up request for attention. In the blink of an eye, Li's energy returned to his body. He took in a deep breath. Han sensed his energy return and felt his power join the others maintain the psychic shield. This surge gave everyone a break from the strain.

"What is it Han?" Li wondered as he rubbed his tired eyes.

Li quickly reached out to Japan as a source of energy.

"While Japan is still in range, I want everyone to recharge their energy levels," Li warned.

"I can pull psychic energy?" Han asked.

One by one each person dropped out of the bubble and drew energy to fill their reserves.

"Observe and repeat the group's techniques," Li advised. "Do as they do."

Han did as Li requested. He followed the group's example. He absorbed a fresh supply of psychic energy. He filled up on its vitality as if he took in some rapid-acting form of nourishment. Content with his restored state, he turned back to Master Li. He wished to ascertain why his energy level apparently dropped to zero and then abruptly returned.

"Did you leave the plane?" Han accurately guessed via a privately link.

Li glanced over his shoulder. He wanted to make certain no one overheard his soft verbal reply.

"Other pre-psychics urgently need our help," he privately indicated.

"What other pre-psychics?" Han questioned. "These are psychics that are ready for conversion?" Han asked, to which Li nodded. "Where are they located?" he inquired.

Master Li knew that Han loved to manipulate statistics. Han spent most of his life studying data regarding his analysis. He often made his own charts and graphs along with averages that showed him trends. He was the perfect bureaucrat.

"Statistically speaking, where should we see emergence?" Li challenged him.

Han enjoyed solving problems that involved statistics. "I would say that since we found all or most of the pre-psychics emerging in China," he thought, "India would logically be the next location followed by Russia, perhaps Mexico or even Japan."

"All large population centers," Li commented. "Those were my thoughts, too." Li shifted in his seat. "The newest voices are in France… well actually, two of them are from Africa, only one was born French. However, all three currently live in Paris."

"You can sense pre-psychic beings that far away?" Han asked.

Li smiled at Han's naiveté regarding the nature of his power.

"My dear Han, I don't mean to sound patronizing, but I can sense many things you cannot," Li informed him. "Like you, I was born pre-psychic. However, I am different from any other psychic creature in the universe. For a reason that no one knows, I possess greater capacity to manipulate psychic energy than anyone," he said.

"Why did it take Galactic Central years until they performed your conversion?" Han wondered. "Why don't they simply enter the mind and change it?"

"They can't," Li explained. "They must not interfere unless the world in question accepts their help," he said.

"So that is why they asked me before my conversion, if I knew what I was doing," Han commented. "I supposed I ignored my voice like the rest of you."

"I would not listen to my own voice either," Li smiled. "I was completely stubborn and intransigent. They tried to speak to me many times. As I child, I envisioned an invisible companion. I learned to tune that voice out after a traumatic event convinced me to ignore it. Recently, I assumed I heard my ancestors calling me. Galactic Central knew that by Earth's standards, I was near the end of my biological life. They realized that an outside intervention from some other party would be necessary to convince me. Of all the pre-psychics, Michael Tyler met their criteria... if he would listen. He was the first person from the planet to take the voice seriously. Despite other psychics located closer, he had the best chance of convincing me. He possesses extraordinary psychic ability. He may be the second most powerful psychic on the planet after me. We're very fortunate he set out in search for us. We owe him a debt that none of us can ever repay."

"He set out for China on his own?" Han asked.

"He eventually had help from Cecilia and Villi," Li explained. "However, none of us would be on our way to America if Michael had not desired to form a community of like minds."

Han glanced over at Michael with renewed interest. Before Han could question Li further, the two men noticed Su Lin approach with a tray.

"I have hot tea, won ton soup, a small bowl of rice, and a small plate of thinly sliced steamed vegetables," she told him. "I believe this was your favorite meal as a child."

Master Li rubbed his hands together in excited anticipation. "Isn't it early for breakfast?" he wondered.

"You haven't eaten in hours," Su Lin said. She practically scolded him. "Besides, I picked this meal up from your thoughts... when you used to be freer with them," she quipped. "I would have made it sooner, given the chance. I used the military's mess hall before we boarded in Beijing..."

"Thank you," Li said. He rose from his chair as he reached for the tray.

Su Lin pulled it back. She teased Li and kept the tray just out of reach.

"Han pestering you with questions?" she tilted her head.

"He is our newest member. Naturally he is curious," Li said and tried to grab the tray.

"If it's too much food," she began. She pretended to turn away. "I can take it back. Perhaps you'd like a sweet roll..."

"No! No, I would love to taste it," Li eagerly stated. He smelled the delicious and familiar aroma.

"What would you like to eat?" Su Lin asked as she indicated Han The tray lifted out of her hands and floated over to Master Li.

The floating tray put a look of astonishment on Han's face as he followed it through the air.

"Just tea," he stated with his mouth open. "No wonder Michael called you Master Li," he uttered before Su Lin grabbed the cup of tea from the tray and handed it over to Han.

"Oh, we can all do that," Su Lin said as she spun around. "You can too with practice," she told him. She headed back to the galley. "Let me know if you and the wonderful, magical, Master Li need anything else."

Li smiled. "I appreciate the compliment, if you intended one," he retorted.

"I did… sort of," Su Lin chuckled as she made her way back.

"Any seed cake for later?" he asked in an open link to her.

"Unfortunately no, Master Li," she answered respectfully. She returned with a different cup of Master Li's favorite hot green tea made with lemon and honey as he preferred. She handed over his cup before she offered Li a compromise. "I really do have some sweet rolls," she suggested. She held one up with some tongs.

"That will do," Li thanked her. He held out his saucer to place the roll along the side.

"Han?" Su Lin turned with another sweet roll ready.

"None for me thanks," Han linked as he sipped his tea. "I have some thinking to do."

"Busy with strategy already," Su Lin commented before she moved on.

"I'm always busy with strategy," Han mumbled under his breath.

"We appreciate it Han," Li linked. He was ready to enjoy his meal.

"Is there any way to maintain one's privacy in this group?" Han asked as Li held out a won ton in front of his mouth.

"Haven't you tried blocking?" Michael broke in.

"Blocking?" Han queried back. "What is that?"

"Master Li, if you don't mind," Michael spoke up. "I believe I should drop from the bubble. Han needs some basic practice contacting Galactic Central, telekinesis, and blocking," Michael suggested.

Making up for Michael's absence would require his utmost concentration. That meant he would need to delay his meal. Li glanced down at this tray. He saw all the little touches that Su Lin put there. General Xing did live a life of luxury onboard his private jet. Su Lin provided real porcelain Chinaware, a white linen napkin wrapped around silver chopsticks and a sparkly leaded-crystal goblet filled with filtered ice water, all from the general's generous cupboards. Everything appeared so perfect on the polished wooden tray. Li had only begun preparations when Michael interrupted. With the chopsticks in his hand, he poked at the hand-made wontons floating in the rich, dark broth. His mouth drooled to taste even one of them. He pulled out the cloth napkin he tucked under his chin and deeply sighed.

Master Li could not be his all-powerful self, support the bubble and eat at the same time. "I want to enjoy the meal," he thought. He motioned for Su Lin to return and remove the tray.

"Very well, Michael," Li told him. "Han's instruction is paramount. I will help hold up the bubble while you assist Han as he explores his new abilities. It is only proper. Go ahead, Su Lin, take my tray…"

"Are you going to eat that soup?" Chou called out from the back.

"I can warm it up," Su Lin said as she bravely stepped between them. She glanced down at Master Li. "Everything will keep."

"Where did you get the crystal goblet and silver chopsticks?" he asked her.

"Evidently General Xing had extravagant tastes," she informed him. "I found everything aboard the jet except the food, which I had the military privates stock before we boarded. We have a week's worth of meals… just in case. I did not know our destination. Let me know when you are ready to eat," she said as she turned back to the galley. "I promise it will taste just as good later Master Li," she nodded reassuringly.

After Han completed some lessons to Michael's satisfaction, Han eventually returned to his seat and Michael joined the group's effort. Su Lin did as she promised. She returned the tray to Master Li with the soup just as warm. He finally sampled her marvelous meal and sighed with relief at the end after he devoured more than he should.

The group made one pit stop in Hawaii to refuel. The translucent sphere kept the jet hidden from the Hawaiian tower until Villi convinced the ground crew to bring the fuel truck into their proximity. He parked the jet inside one of the hangers. The group released the bubble and took a break. Villi went outside, dismissed the ground crew, and refueled the jet from the tanker truck alone.

Many hours later – as the day passed behind them and the sun sank lower into the western ocean – the jet aircraft flew over the west coast of America and headed inland toward the Rocky Mountains. As the terminus of night approached, the jet passed deeper into the nation's interior. They flew over numerous small towns in Utah. None seemed to fit the bill. The mountain ranges rose up, which forced Villi to fly the jet at higher altitudes.

As much as they might try, no one could agree on any village or town to stop and conquer. They found some flaw, some fatal fault that made them pass and move on. Each place they spotted seemed slightly too large, too remote, or too primitive to meet their criteria.

"I'm tired," Su Lin spoke up. "My mind is frazzled."

The others muttered in agreement.

Villi flew the jet onward into the darkening sky. He had to rely on instruments and occasionally locate landmarks with his mind. He was afraid if he used the satellites to pinpoint their location, it would alert the American government to their presence. He practically flew the jet blind while he tried to avoid the mountain peaks and keep the aircraft on some sort of easterly course.

"Descending out of the mountains," Villi informed them. "Master Li…

we're running low on fuel," he added. "I could also use some psychic energy. Any suggestions?"

"I sense several major cities to the north – Pueblo, Colorado Springs, and Denver. Try to absorb some energy from those sources," he advised. "They should offer some respite."

"That's a relief," Han put in. His first psychic experience had turned into a marathon.

As the jet left the Rocky Mountains behind and headed out over the great plains of North America, the group pulled psychic energy from the large metropolitan areas to the north. This time when they tried to draw in energy, the process seemed even more difficult than previous efforts. The psychic energy they found was not enough to make up for the group's physical fatigue.

"Michael," Master Li indicated. "I'd like you to drop away from the bubble. Reach out with your feelings. Search the land ahead. See if you can sift through the maelstrom and find some town that would meet our overall criteria."

"I'll try Master Li," Michael replied.

The group felt his energy pull away. For a moment, the bubble actually wavered until Li pumped in more energy. The energy Li drew from Denver spread like a warm blanket over their chilled skin and gave the group temporary relief. Master Li knew the group was tired and exhausted. He felt rather helpless in this foreign land.

Town names like Pritchett, Walsh, Campro, Manter, and Richfield came to Michael's mind as they neared the Colorado and Kansas' state line. Yet, none of them seemed suitable for Michael. They did not meet that elusive ideal the rest of group expressed earlier in the day.

"I've searched town after town Master Li," Michael linked after nearly twenty minutes. The others felt his hopelessness. It drained them. The psychic bubble around the jet wobbled and nearly collapsed. Master Li tried to bolster their spirits.

"Steady," he told them. "We must keep the bubble intact for at least another hour." He desperately turned to his star pupil. "Think Michael," he put to him. "Where would we fit in? Where would we find sufficient resources to make this work? A small town with just the right qualities for us must be out there. Please try again," he encourage.

Michael's mind roamed back over the approaching countryside. Suddenly something jarred him – a spark, a tiny psychic spark shone from a rather isolated spot ahead. The moment he sensed it, Master Li felt it too. Michael narrowed his senses in on a small community of houses not far away from the spot where he felt the brief spike in psychic energy. He found a very small town, more like an isolated village.

"Michael's found it," Li told them. His words brought sighs of relief from everyone. Master Li filled in the details. The town was about a hundred miles from a major city with sixty-four people living in two dozen houses to relocate. The small community had enough existing infrastructure in place for a new start.

The group actually perked up when Li piped through the news. A light started flashing on the screen in front of Villi which pinpointed the precise landing coordinates. Villi realized that Master Li changed the guidance computer to help direct Villi to the spot.

Villi reached forward with his tired mind and searched for a place to land. Soon he slowed their speed and dropped their altitude. With the bubble around them, he could use far less runway than he would otherwise need – a fact he discovered during their landing in Hawaii when he only used three hundred meters of runway.

"Buckle up," he instructed as he lowered the wing flaps to their maximum drag position.

"Nice work," Cecilia said. She sensed Michael's low energy level and lent him some energy. He could only lean toward her, grateful for her generosity.

Villi cut his engines and dropped his landing gear. He spied a wide grassy field just north of the small village that Master Li indicated. The field was located along the eastern side of a long, narrow two-lane highway that skirted the town's western edge.

"After I land on the road, I'm going to put the jet in an open field just north of the town," he told them.

Li slowed or sped traffic along the narrow ribbon of highway to make the road clear. With the bubble in place, no one in the town could see or hear the jet aircraft landing right next to them. The highway only had a short patch of road without the bothersome power or phone lines that ran along its side. Villi did his best to avoid them as he brought the craft down hard and quickly applied the brakes. The moment he came to a halt on the two-lane flat highway, he turned the jet around. Villi craned his neck to see as far right and left as he could to avoid entangling the wings.

"We just landed in America," Chou whispered.

His simple statement reverberated with Zinian, Zhiwei and Su Lin. While they tried to better their life in China, the whole world knew that the real land of opportunity was America with all of its freedoms. They looked at one another and nodded as if to say; "We made it!"

Michael and Cecilia did not see it that way. They saw nothing special in being home. They knew that America had problems just as any country has.

"I'm exhausted," Cecilia pleaded.

"Can we take a break?" Michael asked.

Master Li turned and looked up the aisle. Every face appeared worn out. He called out to Villi.

"Villi find a place to park the jet," he requested. "Shut down the engines and turn off the outside lights."

"Just a minute longer Master Li," Villi linked back. "The terrain here is uneven. Hold onto something," he warned.

At that moment, the nose of the aircraft dipped and dropped down. The sharp downward angle caught everyone by surprise. Cecilia let out a squeak. However, the jet soon leveled off a moment later. Villi shut the engines down and turned off the landing lights. Li indicated it was time to release the shield.

"We'll be visible," he told them. "But I don't believe anyone will spot us without our sensing it. Ok," he indicated, "release the bubble."

The entire group let their long held concentration go. As if they had been holding their air in their lungs, they breathed a communal sigh of relief at finally being able to relax.

Master Li unbuckled and stood up. He faced the group.

"Welcome my friends to Rollo, Kansas, our new home."

Chapter Three

Appraisal

For a moment no one moved. Everyone stared at Li for answers. He bent his head and briefly glanced out the window. His eyes seemed as dreary as their spirits. No one challenged Michael's wisdom on choosing this innocuous obscure location. Yet this improvised plan seemed too spontaneous. No one knew what to do next. Master Li decided to take the lead.

"I suggest we spend the night on the jet…" Li began. His suggestion met with immediate groans.

"What?" Su Lin objected. "Why can't we take over at least one house?"

Her question echoed a shared sentiment. They all wanted to sleep in a bed. The group joined in a chorus of protests. While the jet had a beautiful plush interior, Cecilia wanted to take a real shower.

"We can't kick people out of their homes on our first night here," Li told them. "That would be extremely inconsiderate. Do we wish to start our community by depriving others of their possessions?"

Knowing he spoke the truth, they collectively shook their heads.

"Good," he said. Li sounded like his old persona of schoolmaster. "I believe we would later regret that decision."

"Master Li," Michael spoke up. "Perhaps we should make taking over the town our top priority. We need to find the current occupants suitable housing right away."

"That is the kind of thinking I hoped to hear," Li told him. "This takeover of Rollo may require days of preparation and a great deal of money. Do you still intend to use your trust?"

"Trust?" Han questioned. "What is this trust?"

The others tried to dissuade Han from asking further questions.

"Be patient Han," Li broke in. "I'll brief you on the details later," he reassured him. Li returned his focus to Michael.

"Can you access the account?" Michael asked him.

"I believe so. Is it still located at the Santa Fe Bank in Simsbury, Connecticut?" Li questioned.

"Yes," Michael replied as his eyes started to droop. "I'm sorry Master Li," he apologized. "I'm trying to help but I can't think. I'm very tired."

"We're all tired," Cecilia chimed in.

"You aren't the only ones exhausted by this trip. I am tired too," Li spoke to them. He turned in his seat and faced forward. "Here I am over seventy and they are complaining of stress, hum," he muttered, although it seemed no one listened.

Su Lin unbuckled and went to the galley. She tried to make a mental inventory of their resources. She spotted six blankets and pillows earlier in a storage space. That was not enough for everyone. They had restroom facilities and running water, for a while at least. She knew they needed to conserve that limited amount of fresh water. She would dissuade Cecilia from taking a shower. She hoped they would find permanent shelter soon.

Li closed his eyes and leaned back while he raised his feet to be comfortable.

Han sensed his presence leave the jet once more. He tried to follow Li this time, but found that Li's psychic energy moved with lightening speed, faster than his thoughts could follow. He decided to focus on the group's needs instead.

"If spending the night on the plane is too difficult, may I suggest we find a hotel or hostel," he offered.

"Well you won't find one of those here Han," Villi linked as he left the cockpit. "I thoroughly scanned this area before we landed. This area doesn't have a hotel room for two hundred miles in any direction. Now here's the bad news," he continued. "We will have to find a permanent place to live soon. The batteries on the jet cannot support our activity longer than eight hours at the most. The internal power will fade by morning unless we start the engines back up and burn what precious little fuel we have left to cycle air."

"How much fuel is left Villi?" Michael asked.

Villi shook his head. The others could see the disappointment on his face.

"I estimate we might have enough for a short run to Mexico if the American military somehow spotted us. But we'd only just make it to the border. The obvious solution is to open the doors. If we do that, we can expect an invasion of local mosquitoes and flies. This is summer. I figure we have enough oxygen in the cabin until six in the morning. After that, we'll start building up too much carbon dioxide in here."

"I'll set my cell phone alarm," Chou stated.

"You brought your cell phone?" Zhiwei asked. "You can't get service here!"

"Why not?" Chou shot back. "I had it the whole time we moved around China?"

Chou glanced around the room. He did not understand that the government could trace his whereabouts with his cell phone on.

"Is it on now?" Zhiwei asked.

"No," Chou said as he dug for it. "I shut it off outside Beijing to save the battery."

Zhiwei held out his hand.

"It was a graduation gift from my mother!" the young man protested.

He saw the disapproving glare from the others including Han. Chou reluctantly handed his expensive phone over to Zhiwei. He glanced over at Michael and hoped to receive a reprieve. Instead, the tall American closed his eyes and shook his head. Zhiwei stepped on the phone and crushed it underfoot. The pieces floated up into Zhiwei's hand. He discarded them into a waste receptacle. Chou realized that he made a major mistake.

"I'm sorry Chou," Zhiwei explained to his friend. "Things have changed. Our lives, everything we do from this moment on, must be different. We are no longer like them in any way, shape, or form," he linked as he gestured toward the window. "We are here as a group to start a new community. The rules will be different because you and I are different, my friend. Besides, if you attempt to use it, the NSA might pick up the signal and narrow in on your foreign cell," Zhiwei explained. "They would send someone to investigate."

Chou nervously swallowed hard. The idea that the technology he relied on in the past would no longer be relevant startled him. Even something as simple as a cell phone would need to change. Like Han, Chou realized at that moment that his first priority would be to contact Galactic Central about adapting Earth technology for psychics.

"In case you hadn't noticed, we're in this country illegally," Zhiwei went on sanctimoniously. "The Americans do not take kindly to foreigners flying their private jets into their country unannounced. If someone alerted the authorities or if their military defense system somehow detected our entry, we could all be in big trouble. By the way," he said and turned to Michael. "How are we supposed to hide a jet aircraft? When the dawn comes up, any passing car from the highway will see us."

"We must camouflage the plane," Han suggested.

"What about the residents? Suppose someone goes out for a late night stroll tonight and spots the jet sitting in a field. The police are just a phone call away," Zhiwei observed.

"We'll have to go out and explore the community… tonight," Han suggested.

Zinian, Su Lin and Cecilia groaned in response. They wanted to sleep. Zhiwei and Han both agreed to each other's proposal.

"Before we strike out on expeditions, does anyone mind if I say a few words?" Michael asked as he stood up.

He first glanced down at Master Li. When the venerable man did not move and Michael heard no objections, he continued.

"I'm not trying to pull rank," he started. "As far as I'm concerned, we're all equal. That goes for every person here," he glanced over at Han.

"We understand that Michael, what's your point?" Villi added.

"Master Li pointed out our strengths in China," he reminded them. "Well, I've been making some observations of my own since we started this journey. I'm not a psychologist," he said. "My point is this: after I've observed you, listened to your thoughts, your wishes, your desires, your dreams, your hopes, ambitions, and fears, I feel as if I've come to know you. I also know that you've read my mind, too. A psychic community has little to hide."

"Go ahead, Michael," Villi urged. "We'd like to hear what you think…"

"Yeah," Zinian spoke up.

"Me too," Chou added, while the rest nodded their approval.

"To begin… Zhiwei," he turned to the straight-faced young man. "You've just demonstrated your proclivity for security. Every time we get into a dangerous situation, you think of our safety first. That's the job of a security officer. I believe you intended that as a career. Therefore, you should take charge of our security. Do you agree?" Michael asked him, glancing around the room for consensus.

"You hit the mark, Michael. I'd be honored to hold that position," Zhiwei said affirming the choice.

"If that is the case, I would suggest you start by considering how we can maintain our security and raise questions regarding what we need to keep us secure," Michael pointed out.

"Ok Michael," Zhiwei stated. "I'll start right away."

The rest of the group found Michael's approach not only refreshing but also helpful. Michael acted as natural leader, at least in this instance. Cecilia beamed proudly in his direction. He tried not to let it distract him.

"Great, let's move on," he continued. "Zinian, your task will be buildings and construction. I believe you wanted to be an architect. I would add that subject and materials management as subjects for Galactic Central the moment we get settled," Michael requested.

"I'll need supplies, a crew, I can't build houses alone," Zinian stated.

"We'll work it out, Zinian," Michael put to him. "As you walk around, appraise every building, large or small. I'd like you to make a complete inventory. Use your ability to probe every structure. Try to give us a complete picture of what we have, and what we'll need to get started. When we schedule our first meeting, share with the group a detailed report, infrastructure, projects, cost analysis, everything."

Zinian's lips turned up as he, too, nodded back to Michael and glanced sideways at Zhiwei. He jerked his head toward Michael, and linked; "This man has it together."

Michael next turned to Chou. The young man in glasses squirmed when the tall twenty-one-year-old American focused his eyes on him.

"Chou, you were easy to read from the start," Michael noted.

"Am I supposed to be grateful for that comment?" Chou shot back.

Michael chuckled, "I simply meant that you usually have one thing on your mind. You'll be our expert in technology. You love to dabble with electronics and devices. Why don't you make being a technology expert your vocation in life? Remember that promise Master Li made to you back at Jilin University? You won't have to attend a university to be the smartest man on the planet. Galactic Central has access to the most advanced technology in the universe. The moment you settle into a house, expand your mind with a few downloads. Don't bother to think about anything else. Come to me with a list of anything you need. I'll see what I can do to satisfy your requirement. We may need some alien technology to give us an advantage."

"Ok, Michael," Chou nodded. "Sounds like fun!"

"To some," Villi mumbled behind Michael.

Michael turned next to the diminutive and shapely young Chinese woman.

"Su Lin, I noticed how much you love food, yet you keep so stylishly slender," he told her.

"Careful," Villi cautioned.

She blushed slightly when he said it.

"Find out what kind of resources this town has," Michael offered. "Go house to house if you must. Present an inventory so we can evenly divide the resources. We need to know if delivery trucks arrive once a week or daily. Search their minds, get the information; it will be vital to our survival."

"This isn't exactly what I had in mind as an avocation," Su Lin responded. She was in her second year of college with a major in education. She wanted to be a teacher.

"I know your first love is education," Michael added, which caused her to brighten. "Once we separate into houses, I suggest a few trips to Galactic Central as well. We could always use a good teacher. Make us wise Su Lin, and keep us honest."

"If I can somehow teach…" she tried to express.

"I'll import kids if I have to," Michael promised.

He turned to Cecilia.

"I know you better than anyone in this room and yet, I know of your aspirations least of all. I suspect you wish to become a doctor. Am I right?" Michael asked.

Cecilia eagerly nodded. She did desire it.

"To accomplish this goal, you will need both a clinic to practice and medical supplies. We do not know if they have a doctor here," he pointed out. "I would be surprised if they did have one. So, after pitching in to help tomorrow, I suggest some intensive medical study at good ole GC, the best alma mater in town," he smiled at her and she nodded back.

"Han," Michael turned toward the front.

Han wondered how he would fit into the scheme of things.

"Outside of Master Li, we will depend upon you most of all," Michael pointed out to him.

"Me?" Han's eyebrows rose.

"You have both life experience and analytical knowledge," Michael stated. "Like Master Li, we will look to you for guidance. Your emphasis on strategy will help steer our new community in the right direction. After the locals start to leave, check with Zinian and assess the various locations he's scouted. Then I'd like you to assign houses to us as you deem fit. We will all heed your advice, right group?" Michael said as he turned to the rest.

Everyone agreed with Michael. This made Han feel truly part of the ensemble.

"That leaves you," Cecilia said as she looked up at him.

"I will do what I've always done best," Michael offered. "I'll facilitate. You tell me what we need and I will try to get it for you… for us. Any questions?"

"What about money?" Han quietly wondered.

"I have practically unlimited funds from my family's trust…" Michael began.

"The moment you access your money, they would know you are living in southwest Kansas… the government could trace every penny back to us," Zhiwei objected.

Michael had not considered that aspect.

"We can't have the government suspicious of Rollo," Michael agreed. "I'll arrange a connection via my voice or through Master Li," he considered.

At that moment, Li opened his eyes and sat up, as if he rose from a nap.

"Excuse me for interrupting," he started. "I've made some arrangements on my own during your eloquent speech Michael," he informed them. He stretched his arms and yawned. Li noticed that the entire group stared at him with baited breath for his report. "Where to begin… The families of the Baker's, the Walker's, the Miller's, the Frank's, and the Henderson's will be leaving in the morning," Master Li told them. "I arranged for limousines to come from Oklahoma and Wichita. They should arrive at first light," he explained.

"How many minds did you enter to make those arrangements?" Zhiwei asked.

"I lost count after fifty," Li quipped back. "By midday, seven more families should follow. We may be able to evacuate Rollo in two days or less."

"Have you considered their feelings?" Han questioned. "I thought this was supposed to take days?"

"It's funny that you should first address their feelings strategist," Li retorted. "I sifted through the mind of every man, woman, and child in Rollo. I feel confident we will fulfill everyone's dreams and aspirations," Li told him. "Did you think I would just run everyone out of town?"

"I only meant…" Han countered.

"Han, we trust Master Li's instincts and judgment," Michael intervened. "You must learn to trust him, too."

Han realized at that moment how much Li could easily accomplish in such a short time span. He wondered what else the elder psychic could accomplish, if he wanted. He feared Li's power more than the younger psychics who admired him.

"I've scheduled the remaining families and individuals to leave as fast as I can find accommodations for them," Li continued. "Although I may be sick of them before that, and simply run them out of town."

Cecilia burst out laughing, but the rest were too tired. She stopped when no one else laughed. Master Li, however, shot her a wink.

"I transferred a large amount of money from the Tyler Trust to two regional banks," Li continued. "One is in Oklahoma and the other in Wichita, Kansas. I'm making the transfers in small, intermittent amounts via banks in Chicago and Kansas City to avoid electronic tracers."

"What are…?" Han started.

"The treasury puts tracers on all large money transfers," Michael explained to Han. "Tracers spot trends related to illicit money launderers, such as drug smugglers or gangs."

"Those funds are not for us," Li continued. "They will cover the moving expenses and set up the residents in new homes. Michael will inform the trust tomorrow that he is now living in West Palm Beach, Florida and running a new business model from there. Part of that model will include the purchase of real estate and small business ventures. That will explain the sudden increase in withdrawals and transfers. Michael's new enterprise will also apply for a business license in Florida and other states," he commented. "The transfers will only maintain a ghost company. Your voice, Michael, at Galactic Central can shuffle funds from bank to bank as we need them. Neither the government nor the trust will suspect that Michael is living in Rollo, Kansas."

"You did all of that in the past twenty minutes?" Han asked, flabbergasted.

"Go ahead, Michael, continue your organization plan," Li stated briskly, ignoring Han.

"Thank you, Master Li," Michael acknowledged.

At that moment, Li leaned back and closed his eyes. His breathing slowed and his head slumped to one side. Han assumed he fell asleep. Michael and the others did not focus on Li, rather the tasks they had to finish tonight.

"I can see that we have a little more work to do before we sleep," Michael said. "I suggest we form two scouting parties," he requested. "I'd like Zhiwei, Zinian, and Han to come with me. Cecilia, take Su Lin and Chou with you. Find whatever resources you can scrounge this evening. Remember to use stealth," Michael directed. "Assess the town as you move along. Make certain you do not disturb anyone or their pets. Does anyone have a comment or question before we start?" Michael asked.

"Mind if I tag along?" Villi suddenly cut in. His link startled Michael.

"Villi!" Michael declared as he spun around. "I'm sorry, my friend, I forgot you were behind me. I missed your assignment."

"Isn't it obvious, Michael?" the big man spoke casually. "I'm good at transportation. I'll set up a garage to handle the maintenance and care of all vehicles, including the jet aircraft. That's the job I would like, if I can have it."

"It's yours," Michael said, pleasantly surprised.

"Great," Villi calmly replied. "I'll search tonight for some kind of cover for the plane. Tomorrow, I'll arrange to have some of the cars left behind, with Master Li's permission, of course," he added as he glanced down at the supine white-haired man. "I'll try to find a truck or two for Zinian and one for Chou to haul around equipment."

"I'd like one, too," Zhiwei linked in.

"I'll see what I can do, Zhiwei," Villi nodded back. "Do either of you want a car?" he put to Cecilia and Su Lin. Both women shook their heads with Cecilia mouthing, "Later."

"Thanks, Villi," Michael privately linked. He felt grateful that he did not anger his friend or hurt his feelings.

"Don't worry about hurting my feelings, Michael," Villi privately linked. "I made a decision a long time ago about our friendship. Let's just say, I'll always be on your right flank," he told him. He put his hand on Michael's right shoulder.

The two men stood eye to eye, both equal in height and stature.

"I'll always look for you there," Michael shot back. He allowed a brief smile to cross his stern lips as he placed his hand on Villi's arm. The two men broke off when Michael turned around. "Am I leaving anything or anyone else out?" he asked.

Master Li linked back in, his powerful surge unmistakable.

"You've forgotten one important detail, Michael," he told the young man.

"What is that?" Michael wondered.

"The spark… the one you felt… the one that led us to this place," Li said. His face showed no expression.

"Yes?" Michael asked.

"The citizens of Rollo are not alone," Li told them. "To the south and west of this town live another isolated group of people… a tribe if you will," Li explained. "I shall go to assess their living conditions in the morning."

"A tribe?" Michael questioned. "You mean a tribe of Native American Indians?"

"A small group of *Comanche* Native Americans broke away from the main group in Oklahoma many years ago," Li relayed. "Since then, their group has suffered from neglect. The time is right for us to intervene on their behalf. I want Cecilia to come with me in the morning."

"Me, Master Li? Why do need me?" the teen spoke up.

"You want to be a physician?" Li asked her.

"Yes?" she replied.

"You need to see what poverty, isolation, and lack of proper medical care has done to destroy these people," Li commented.

When Han tried to search Li's mind for the details, Li blocked him and the others from learning what he discovered only moments before. The people of Rollo did not call out to the psychics, the signal originated with the Comanche.

Chapter Four

Night Search Party

Michael's group quietly slipped from the plane and headed out into the warm, humid, evening air. With few streetlights, stars filled the clear night sky horizon to horizon. Zinian and Chou paused a moment. The two teenagers stared up at the twinkling dots of light with a sense of awe.

"I grew up in the city. I've never seen so many stars," Zinian commented.

"I wonder which one is Galactic Central," Chou asked as the two men stood together.

Just as Michael started to point to the general area of sky, a tiny flash of light around one faint star revealed the location to all five men simultaneously.

"Did you do that?" Han turned to Michael.

"The voices tune into our thoughts…" Michael pointed out. "They did the same thing to me about a year ago in Mississippi," he recalled. "The same gesture convinced me they were real."

"How far away is Galactic Central?" Han wondered.

"I only know it is measured in hundreds of millions of parsecs, give or take a few hundred million," Villi sighed. Michael and Cecilia shared their mutual trip to the silvery tower when the voices took them on a virtual trip. "Michael and Cecilia went to Galactic Central."

"Went there?" Han questioned.

"We didn't leave…" Michael started when Villi cut him off.

"It happened when they made the first discovery of psychic manipulation. They infiltrated the mind of two tourists and made them dance off to their room," he told Han. "The voices decided it was time the two psychics put a face on Galactic Central. They brought the couple to Galactic Central by way of a special form and took them inside." Villi joined Zinian and Chou looking up. "Have Michael share the memory sometime."

Michael was tired and wanted to end this quick romp.

"Let's start our search over there," he linked as he gestured toward the nearest house.

The heat and humidity in the air remained from the hot summer day. The air hummed with nature's sounds from crickets to the pestering buzz of mosquitoes.

"I can't afford to have any of you sick. We don't know what an insect bite will bring," Michael cautioned. "Follow my example," he told them. Instead of a sphere, Michael raised a psychic shield close to his body.

"Nice control," Zhiwei noticed.

With concerted effort, the other men followed suit by copying his method. The psychic shield would prevent mosquitoes from biting and also give them invisibility. Han struggled at first as he tried to create an individual field for the first time.

"Let me help," Michael offered as he lowered and raised his shield slowly a few times until Han finally managed to create a large enough sphere to place around him. "Excellent work Han," Michael told him. "You did that twice as fast as Villi."

Villi started to open his mouth when Han very uncharacteristically laughed. Michael and Villi both looked at Han and smiled as the young strategist seemed more relaxed around them.

"Keep up your levels," Michael reminded them. "Pull energy from the residents."

The five men absorbed enough psychic energy from the locals to sufficiently raise their levels. They silently moved through the grassy field until Michael put out his hand near the back of a house. The group stopped and watched for his signal. He sensed activity inside.

"What is the local time?" he asked Villi. He assumed Villi probably noted the time from the jet's computer when they landed.

"Just after twenty three hundred hours," he linked back.

"Most people should be in bed," Han guessed.

Villi and Michael gave Han a quizzical expression.

"What did I say?" he replied unable to penetrate their feelings.

"If you are sixty, you go to bed before eleven o'clock," Michael quipped.

"Or have nothing to do," Zinian piped in.

"Most Americans stay up very late and watch television," Michael told him.

"Or they use the Internet," Zhiwei spoke.

The isolated Han seemed like the outsider once more, when at that moment, Zhiwei sensed danger as he suspected Michael did, too.

"Dog," he warned via a link. He froze while he waited for someone to make a suggestion.

Michael had some experience when he put a dog to sleep before he took a man's car on the Kamchatka Peninsula.

"Observe," Michael linked to him. He showed Zhiwei and the others how to enter the creature's mind and put it into deep sleep.

"Very useful, thanks Michael," the new security chief stated. "We could all use the practice," he directed.

Zhiwei made a sweep and found other animals scattered about town in other houses. For a few minutes, the group took turns as they entered pet's brains and put them asleep.

"That will keep the town quiet tonight," Han said.

"A little too quiet, some might become suspicious," Zhiwei added.

"I'm sensing Master Li thought of that," Michael told them. "I believe he's having most of the residents retire early in spite of their desire to stay up."

Zinian's mind swept over the house for important structural information. Michael, Han and Villi read the minds of the people inside before they moved on to the next house.

Block by block, street after street, they walked through the small town and thoroughly assessed each house, the current condition of the structure, and any usable supplies.

"Scanning refrigerators makes me hungry," Villi stated while he walked.

"Especially the last house… homemade apple pie," Michael sighed.

"Cut it out you two unless you're going back to get that pie!" Zinian joked.

The group quickly discovered that most of the houses were in poor condition at best.

"What's up the street?" Han asked.

He pointed toward a small one-story building with a large plate glass window in the front. A metallic light fixture hung down over the entrance. Its old-fashioned, dim, yellowish light bulb shone down on an old iron park bench that had wooden slats in the seat. They walked toward this building on Main Street, which was closest to the highway.

"Baker's Store," the sign over the front said.

"The last of the independent grocers," Michael mumbled. "You can take off your shields gentlemen," he added. "I don't detect mosquitoes here and I believe anyone is awake."

They stood before the patched up one story building. Zinian noted that someone attached a few rooms onto the back. He briefly scanned over the structure and rolled his eyes.

"I can't save that place," he linked. "This is a disaster waiting to happen. The walls are in extremely poor condition. The substructure is riddled with wood rot and insects. It would be best to tear it down."

"That may be our only source of food for a while," Michael cut in.

"…plus what I stocked on the plane," a voice spoke into their minds. It was Su Lin.

All five men turned when they felt Su Lin, Cecilia, and Chou moving toward them.

"I see your sweep through town didn't take long either," Cecilia openly linked.

"Yeah, you can jog around the whole town in five minutes," Villi added.

"How did American civilization pass this place by?" Han wondered aloud. "Rollo has no chain fast food places at all, just this store," he pointed out and jerked his thumb toward the ramshackle building.

"Not economical," Michael offered.

"Changing the subject," Cecilia broke in. "Chou and I entered a few houses."

"You actually walked inside?" Han spoke up.

"It seems someone put all the dogs to sleep," Chou linked as he glanced over at Zhiwei.

"We found some spare bedding in the house of an older couple, blankets and sheets," Cecilia explained.

"Stealing Cecilia?" Michael questioned sarcastically.

"They won't miss them," Su Lin cut in, as it was her suggestion to take them. "They had a cedar chest filled with that stuff under a pile of stacked boxes," she linked.

"They had ten extra pillows in one of their closets. I ask you, what do you do with ten extra pillows?" Chou added.

"Jump off the roof into a pile of pillows?" Zinian wondered with a smile.

"That sounds awfully dangerous…" Han interrupted.

"He's kidding Han," Su Lin spoke up. "Most of us are acquainted with the crazy thoughts that come from Zinian's head," she added.

"Chou, tell Michael about Rollo's technology," Cecilia requested.

"They have very little in terms of usable technology," Chou reported. He gestured toward the collection of old wood-frame houses. "A satellite dish or two, some game systems and television sets – except as a diversion, I found nothing I would consider worth keeping."

"I could use a satellite dish to tie into the nation's communications systems," Zhiwei suggested, when Michael interrupted him.

"Before you make your attempt, let Galactic Central show you how to do that Zhiwei," he said as he turned to him. "They can tap into anything via your portal."

"Really?" he said as he gazed at Michael.

"Place a computer near a satellite dish and your voice can break into any system, military or otherwise," Michael explained. "They don't follow the Internet, they follow the current."

Michael manipulated the markets in New York for months before he left to find them. He seldom discussed his past life. He moved away from the group and stared up the road away from Rollo. He could feel another psychic presence, albeit a strange one. The moment he sensed it, the rest of the group felt it too. His sensation immediately changed the subject.

"What's down there?" Villi spoke up as he walked up next to him.

"Too far to walk," Zhiwei observed.

"As Master Li told us, he'll find out in the morning," Michael thought dismissively as he turned around. "Do we need anything from the store tonight?" he wondered.

"Let's see what we can find," Villi stated. He walked up to the entrance and touched the door. The locks unlatched and the door swung open.

Han's mouth hung open wider than the door. When he saw how easily Villi gained entry, he realized he had much to learn about psychic manipulation.

"Watch the others and follow their example," Chou indicated in a quiet private link to Han. "The rest of us have had a couple of weeks to practice. Allow some time for adjustment, Han. Your powers will develop."

He gave Han a reassuring expression that put the older psychic at ease. The entire group proceeded to walk inside and pilfer the shelves for things they needed. They collected items in bags as if they were shopping. Master Li targeted the owners, Judith and Seth Baker, as the first to leave Rollo in the morning with an extremely generous benefit package.

"Won't those things be missed?" Cecilia suggested.

Before Michael could answer, the lights in the room switched on.

"What's going on?" a gruff man's voice spoke.

The group stopped to face an elderly man with a shotgun in his hands, His excited nervous emotion kept the psychics from penetrating his mind, mostly from lack of experience. Cecilia acted first. She shoved Han back out the front door and ducked down.

"Are you robbin' my store?" he asked Michael, Zinian, and Villi. The barrel of the gun was shaking as the man clearly telegraphed fear facing three men much bigger than his five foot eight height. "You'd better get out before I call the police or somebody gets hurt."

His old crooked finger twitched on the trigger.

Michael, Zinian, and Villi acted at the same time. They cast psychic bubbles that would make them invisible and protect them from any bullet. From the man's perspective, they instantly vanished. Zhiwei and Su Lin chose that moment to move behind opposite shelves.

"Hey!" the man cried, "What's goin' on? Where'd you go? How'd you do that?"

Suddenly, something yanked the shotgun from his hands.

"Hey!" he shouted. "Give that back to me." He tried to reach forward, but a mysterious force held him back.

The gun floated out into the air in front of him, and then it vanished. Startled, the restrained man could only stare at the space where he once saw his gun. He reached out at the empty air, running his hand through it. He hoped he would meet up with his shotgun.

"I… I…" he nervously stuttered. "Judy!" he called to his wife for help. "Judy, you'd better…"

He stopped speaking. His eyes rolled back into his head. He twirled around and started to go down.

"Oh," he groaned as he started to fall.

Michael materialized with his arms around Seth Baker.

"What's going on?" a feeble female's voice spoke. The older woman's footsteps creaked as they crossed the wooden floor.

The man's wife walked out from their bedroom in the back of the store where the couple lived for many years. Every head in the psychic party turned toward the sound of her voice.

"I've got this," Villi said stepping forward past Michael.

"Seth?" the portly woman called out. She stood before them in her flowered dressing gown and pale pink slippers.

She stopped and stood still for a moment, just staring at the air. She pivoted around and headed back to bed with Seth close behind her. He had his eyes closed with his limp body seemingly supported by a ghost. He slid back under the covers by an unseen force.

When Judy did turn over in bed the following morning, she thought something might have happened to her husband. Yet, Seth lay next to her and behind him she saw his shotgun propped up in the corner in its usual resting place. Seth woke up and blinked his eyes. Instead of saying anything, the elderly man first rolled over onto his back and stared up at the ceiling.

"You know what I'm thinkin'?" he finally wondered aloud to Judy as he rose. He scratched his chest and pulled up his suspenders as he walked out of the bathroom. "I'm gettin' pretty sick and tired of Rollo…"

"That's funny," Judy said as she sat up in bed. "I was thinkin' the same thing this mornin'."

Just as their eyes met, they heard a bell dinged inside the store. That sound indicated a customer pulled into the fuel lane out in front.

"Land sakes," she said as she quickly rose from bed and pulled on a robe. "Can't they see we ain't got the sign on yet?" she commented referring to the "open" red neon sign.

The elderly couple hustled toward the front of the store to find a large black luxury car parked next to the fuel pumps, the kind of car that did not require liquid fuel. A driver stepped out of the fancy vehicle and yawned as he looked around. He was a young man dressed in a pressed gray business suit. He wore a white shirt and black tie. He strode up to the screen door and knocked. Seth and Judy hesitated and exchanged glances before they moved to unlock the door.

"Seth and Judith Baker?" the tall young man asked.

The couple only nodded in reply. He handed Judy an envelope. Along with a formal paper whose letterhead appeared very official, a brochure fell out. Judy looked down at it and frowned. The color brochure displayed the kind of place reserved for the wealthy. She turned her attention to the letter. It stated that as part of an insurance settlement, a company offered to pay all of their expenses if they moved to San Antonio, Texas. Further it stated the company would "sustain them in a lifestyle befitting a person of their fine stature for the rest of their lives." Attached to the letter was a check to "assist with any extra expenses." It was made out to Seth and Judy Baker for $250,000. She fell backward and grabbed her chest. Seth caught her.

"Who died?" he asked as he anxiously glanced over her shoulder.

"You ain't gonna to believe this," she told him and handed Seth the letter.

Seth read the details: a major chemical company settled with Rollo's residents in regards to the poison in the groundwater, "no longer fit to drink." Attorneys with the company offered this relocation as settlement. The EPA would take over the town in a week and close it down "until further notice."

"Is this on the level?" he asked the driver.

"I practically drove all night sir," the young man said as he stifled another yawn. "It better be!"

Speechless, Seth glanced up from the letter at his wife of forty-one years. They burst out laughing and hugged each other.

"Guess we'd better pack," Judy started.

"That won't be necessary," the young man told them. "Did you read the rest of the letter?"

Seth turned the letter over. On the back, the document specifically stated that everything would be provided for them in San Antonio. They would be given a country club condominium fully furnished complete with new appliances including food, clothes, and transportation.

"...consider everything you possess in Rollo as contaminated," the letter stated.

Judy and Seth exchanged looks and realized this was a new start for them.

"What about Rollo... our neighbors?" Seth wondered.

"I believe everyone in Rollo is being given the same offer this morning," the young man said.

"Did you hear that?" Seth said. "We're being scattered to the four winds... our friends." For a second, Seth nearly destroyed their moment of joy. Judy took him by the arm.

"They'll be fine and so will we," she told him. "Besides, Rollo is the most god-forsaken place in the world," she added. "I'd just as soon forget it!"

... and so they did. Master Li placed a time-delineation suggestion in each resident's mind. After a week, they placed their earlier memories of Rollo in some other location. As far as Rollo's previous residents were concerned, the place never existed.

On the way back to the jet after their encounter with the Baker's on their first evening in America, Zinian and Zhiwei walked slower than the rest of the group. Whether they were tired or simply wanted to exchange thoughts, the two friends could not say. After a few blocks, Zinian broke the silence. Between the two lifetime friends, he usually initiated their ideas.

"Do you realize this will be the first time since we gained our powers that we will be independent?" Zinian linked to his friend.

"What did you have in mind?" Zhiwei linked back.

"Let's grab one of those cars and drive to Kansas City for a good time!" Zinian declared with a smile. "Can you image the kind of girls we could have if we placed in their mind..." He glanced over at his friend but noticed Zhiwei did not smile back. "What's wrong?" he asked.

"I don't think he would like it," Zhiwei nodded with his head toward Master Li.

Zinian turned in time to see that the rest of the group had stopped outside the jet and turned their way. Master Li stood in their midst in front of the aircraft's door. He stared right at Zinian with a dour expression. The big Chinese man sheepishly smiled and shrugged as the two teenagers joined the others.

"I am only eighteen, professor," he told Li.

"Is that the excuse you'll use to abuse your power?" Li privately pondered to Zinian. "What will your excuse be next week when you attempt to take over the country?"

"I only wanted a date..." Zinian mumbled as he shuffled past Master Li.

"Obtain one through legitimate means, not perverting one with your power," Li told him. "Besides, with your fine physique, I doubt you'll have any problem finding a date when the right woman comes along."

"Let's hope that doesn't take too long," Zhiwei added for his friend.

"Funny thing about the future," Master Li told them, "the possibilities are numerous."

The psychic burglars having ransacked the town moved onto the jet with their bags full of loot: some brought back snack food items, while others had bottled water, batteries, flashlights, microwavable dinners, pillows and blankets. They shared their observations with Master Li. He listened and nodded, not speaking until the last person finished their report.

"Great work team," he told them as they settled. "Don't worry about compensation," he added. "Every person in Rollo will be well provided. I believe we're off to a good start."

That reassured Cecilia and Han, as the taking of things from the houses and the store upset the two. Michael always blindly trusted Li. He knew that whatever happened, Master Li would find a way to make things equal in the end. Villi turned off the power to save the batteries. In the dark and silence of the jet's passenger cabin, the group quickly fell asleep. Even Li was too tired to hold a lonely vigil.

Chapter Five

Moving Day

Rollo, Kansas is very a small town located in the flat, dry, southwestern corner of Kansas just off Highway 55, a two lane blacktopped road with few travelers except local farmers and occasional trucker. Had any passing motorist looked carefully from the highway toward the large metal barn on the north end of town, they would have spied the tail portion of the jet, visible above the tall reeds that surrounded the dried-up pond where Villi unknowingly parked the aircraft last night. Otherwise more of the fuselage would be present. For a few minutes, the rising orange rays over the Kansas plain reflected off the metallic skin. After the sun rose higher, the eggshell-colored plane partially blended into the bland obscurity of the dry landscape.

"Huh? What the…" Master Li stirred, suddenly aware that he overslept. "The jet!"

He immediately sent out his psychic senses to assess his surroundings. His mind reached down the highway into motorist's minds going north and south. To his utter surprise, he did not sense that a passing motorist detected the jet, nor did anyone in the village, at least not yet.

As he gathered his thoughts for the day, Li checked the progress of last night's work. The limousines were already on the road and headed for little Rollo. With them they held special letters and documents. Last night, Master Li had forced individuals out of their beds to make special arrangements. Bankers opened their banks. Lawyers drew up special papers. Couriers ran from place to place. Phones rang all over Kansas, Oklahoma and Texas waking strangers in the night to make ready for this morning's radical changes. No one thought it strange that they should do this at such a late hour. Li made dozens of plans for hundreds of people on a scale that defied imagination in a matter of time impossible to describe.

"Everything and everyone is on schedule," he thought.

Of course, no one in their group would ever know the extent to which Master Li could perform these feats and he doubted whether he could ever again perform such an amazing feat in the same manner as he did last night. He leaned back in his seat and stretched his old creaking limbs before he picked up some energy from a passing motorist. The entire group inside the cabin lay fast asleep. He decided to rouse Zhiwei first.

"Zhiwei," he quietly called to his mind.

The security conscious man nearly leapt from his seat. He looked around and realized that it had been light outside for more than an hour. He was certain someone had called the authorities to report the jet.

"I'm sorry Master Li. I fell asleep. I failed at my…." the new security chief sputtered as he scrambled to sit up.

"Zhiwei," Li broke in. "Calm down. We are safe. Nothing in regards to our security status has changed. Michael did us a great service choosing this location. This town is indeed in the middle of nowhere. Plus, Villi parked us far enough from the road and low enough that most of the jet is obscured. However, I need your assistance," the older man requested.

"Yes Master Li," he perked up.

"I'd like you to secure our perimeter," Master Li requested. "I must monitor the operations outside. After all, these people have not had days to prepare for moving to Wichita, Guymon, and Woodward," Li related. "I purchased every vacant house or condominium in those cities that I could find. Most of the residents are moving to a new house. Some of them will go as far away as Oklahoma City, or Austin, Texas," Li finished.

"Why so far?" Zhiwei asked as he sat up and straightened his electronic chair.

"I tried to find what each person felt was the ideal place to live. Some had relatives in those cities they wished were near; others simply wanted to retire in some nice planned community," Li quietly explained. "Tyler Trust will spend a great deal of money on this first part of Michael's plan."

"I'm not sure I know American currency that well, do you mean…" Zhiwei started.

"Millions," Master Li linked back.

"Mill…" Zhiwei started, grappling with the concept.

"That's right, millions of dollars," Li told him.

"Does Michael have that kind of money?" Zhiwei asked.

"Right now, Michael's trust is worth billions of dollars," Li calmly stated, "give or take a few million. Some of those assets are what we call liquid or available as cash. The trust also has investments in venture capital, index funds, real estate, corporate boards, research associates, advertising firms, law firms, medical boards, government bonds, foreign banks, and seats on stock exchanges…"

Zhiwei sat there nodding his head as Li rambled on about the extent of Michael's holdings until he realized something.

"If you don't mind me asking, who was Michael's father? I never heard anything about that part of life," Zhiwei wondered.

"Anthony Tyler?" Master Li contemplated. "The team of Tyler Architecture and Engineering created bridges, ships, roads, buildings, mostly for government projects, but also for private contractors, such as banks and factories. The Tyler Corporation existed for nearly two centuries."

"You say that in past tense," Zhiwei observed. "What happened to the company?"

"Anthony and Jessica Tyler died when a drunk driver struck their car in a head on collision," Li continued. "At the time of the accident, they had already committed Michael to an institution for delusional adolescents. Without Anthony's leadership, Tyler Industries broke up. Only the trust remained, which Anthony set up for his heirs. Upon his parents' death, Michael's psychiatrist, Dr. Hami, took the sixteen-year-old before a judge and had Michael declared mentally disabled and incompetent to take over the Tyler fortune. However, Anthony's lawyers carefully constructed an airtight trust that protected Michael and the trust for as long as the boy lived despite his condition. Unfortunately, Burt Loomis, the Santa Fe Bank's manager, became the default executor of the will and the trust. Even after the state emancipated Michael when he turned eighteen, Loomis kept most of the funds away from Michael and used every excuse he could to alienate the troubled young man. Loomis privately pilfered the trust for his own gain," Li told him.

"You see… it was his Galactic Central voice that drove Michael mad," Master Li quietly explained. "Every time it spoke, the ten-year-old boy lashed out in anger. He mistrusted the alien that only sought to help him. He spent eight years in that asylum. In his mind, the voice betrayed him. It took away his life at home, and then his mother and father. With his parents gone, he felt utterly alone. That's when he turned to wine and homelessness."

Zhiwei stared over at Michael's sleeping form.

"I can't believe he didn't give up," he linked to Li.

"He nearly did," Li pointed out. "This was a difficult period for him. He nearly took his own life. However, once he experienced his conversion, he realized his true worth. After a year, he regained his trust, and set out on the quest that brought us together."

Zhiwei cocked his head, "His face is so pure… he doesn't look like an ex-alcoholic…"

"That is because Michael's voice showed him natural skin rejuvenation techniques," Master Li interjected. "Now, if you will secure our position…"

Master Li tuned out Zhiwei as he monitored preparations for the day.

Zhiwei rose from his seat and headed into the galley. He took out several tea bags and opened bottled water to make a fresh pot of tea.

"Pardon me Master Li, I don't mean to interrupt," he linked. "How many properties will vacate today?"

Li grumbled as if aroused from sleep. He glared at Zhiwei a second before he answered.

"I suspect most will leave sooner rather than later," he said as he frowned at Zhiwei. "They will be easy to convince once the rumors spread regarding contaminated ground water. I hope to evacuate Rollo by the end of the day."

"Wow!" Zhiwei exclaimed. "That means we can sleep in a bed tonight," he reasoned.

"I would assume that to be the case," Li told him. "The limousines are on their way. The families have started to rise. I must focus my power…"

However, Zhiwei spoke yet again.

"Michael said he sensed another psychic presence south of town last night," Zhiwei linked to him. "Would that source be located in the village of Native Americans?"

"That group has roused my interest," Li replied. "I'm sorry Zhiwei, but you must excuse me," Li said as he closed his eyes. "I have many details to attend and little time left."

Zhiwei noticed that Master Li drew a large mass of psychic energy into his body before his presence flew out of the plane and scattered about the small community at speeds he could not follow. As he made his hot tea, he watched Li's eyes moved back and forth under their lids as if he was in the middle of an intense dream. Zhiwei reached out his thoughts and monitored the minds of people nearby. No one had seen the jet as Li informed him. He scanned for any traffic and discovered very few vehicles moving at this hour.

Villi woke up and saw Zhiwei in the cockpit drinking a cup of tea. He rose and silently poured out a cup of tea on his own while Zhiwei looked over the cockpit controls. His fingers ran over the various indicators.

"Do you know what it is you want?" Villi intruded.

Zhiwei nearly jumped out of his skin. He spun around and looked up at Villi.

"Just curious," Zhiwei muttered.

"I'm curious about security," Villi said, "but you won't find me fiddling with your equipment."

Zhiwei started to say something sarcastic when Villi read his mind. The two men burst into laughter. The Russian reached over to reassure Zhiwei it was alright to be in the cockpit when he noticed an unusual odor. He'd forgotten that it had been nearly three days since he had bathed. He sniffed his armpit and wrinkled his nose.

"No wonder Su Lin is stand-offish," he declared.

"When was the last time you took a shower?" Zhiwei asked him.

He started to say when he glanced out the front window of the jet.

"Unless I'm mistaken," he said, "the sun has risen. We need to hide the jet. Otherwise, we are visible to everyone and everything," he said. He emphasized his last word by pointing up.

Zhiwei knew he meant satellites.

"What do you recommend?" he replied to the pilot.

"After this tea, let's you and I search for some cover..." Villi started to link.

"We can't just cover up the jet," Zhiwei pointed out. "The shape will still be too obvious."

"True," Villi agreed. "I saw a large barn not far away, possibly large enough to hold the jet, or at least part of it," Villi said. He gestured to an area across the field. They could just make out the top of a large metal two-story barn. "I'll have to fire up the engines to drive it over there. That might wake every person in the village," he linked.

"We'll have to surround the jet with another bubble," Han suggested. He overheard the end of their conversation. "We should move quickly and wake the others." He stretched, yawned, and rose to search for a cup.

"I'm up," Zinian linked as he rubbed his eyes.

He reached over and tapped on Michael's chest. The tall young man rose and looked over the seats at Master Li.

"What is Master Li doing...?" Michael started when Zhiwei held up his hand and pointed.

"Li arranged things with the locals this morning," he explained. "It took a lot out of him. I believe he's in recharge mode."

Su Lin rose and moved into the galley to prepare a light breakfast for everyone. Chou and Cecilia took turns washing their faces in the back sink. Su Lin thanked Zhiwei for making tea. Villi checked over the instruments and hoped he had enough battery left to start the engines.

About ten minutes later when the group absorbed sufficient psychic energy, they gathered near the cockpit to form the bubble barrier around the jet.

"Are we ready?" Michael asked. The group returned a unanimous confirmation.

Without a word, the translucent form of pulsing energy surrounded the aircraft. Safely encased, Villi started the engines. The vibration from the engines alone caused the jet's wheels to rise into the air above the ground just a few inches as the craft seemed to defy gravity. Unanchored, the aircraft began to drift.

"How is it doing that?" Han asked.

"I'm not sure," Villi linked back. "It didn't do that yesterday."

Slowly the jet rose above the depression made from the dried lake bed. Villi used the pulsing power of the engines to steer the hovering craft toward the large metallic barn.

"Will it fit?" Chou asked. He stood behind Villi and tried to assess the barn's narrow opening.

"I hope so," Villi linked back while he watched his fuel gauges.

Before he took the jet into the barn, he used his mind to open the sliding front doors to their maximum width.

"I'm not sure it will be wide enough," Chou stated as he peered over Villi's shoulder. "Perhaps we should…"

At that moment, they felt a shudder pass through the bubble.

"What's going on?" Chou asked.

Villi glanced down at the instrument panel. He had no indicators out of alignment. He twisted in his chair, only to see Master Li standing in the doorway with his eyes closed, braced against the doorframe with his arms outstretched.

"Look!" Chou pointed ahead through the window.

The metal doors on the barn shook on their runners and began to push back even further until they fell off in opposite directions. The metal frame surrounding the opening to the barn made an odd noise and started to flutter, no longer stiff. It seemed as flimsy as paper blowing in the wind. The metal made a groan and began to bend. In one swift movement, the sheet metal bent back and curled up like a piece of aluminum foil. This made the rectangular opening even larger to accommodate the wings of the jet.

"It's gonna be tight," Villi said as he kept his hand over the engine controls.

The nose fit in along with part of the fuselage. Just as the wing tips approached the opening, the sheet metal curled back even further until the wings cleared the sides of the opening. Master Li sucked air into his lungs as if he'd been straining and holding his breath the whole time. Cecilia sensed his imminent collapse and rushed forward. He fell into her waiting arms. She pulled him over to his usual front seat. Michael, Zhiwei, Su Lin, and Zinian all turned to their right. They quickly entered the minds of every person attracted to the sound of the twisting metal. One after another, they took the occurrence out of their memory and sent each person on his or her way as if nothing happened.

"Master Li!" Villi declared with both amazement and alarm.

The moment the psychic teens turned their attention on the town, the bubble around the aircraft collapsed. The jet gently plopped back down onto the ground. Villi shut down the engines. The nose of the aircraft nearly rested against the back of the building.

"Whew!" Chou sighed. "I didn't think it would fit!"

"You'll have to erect something over the front opening," Han advised while he watched Cecilia tend to Li. "How is he?" Han asked her. What he witnessed amazed him. Yet this was but another feat he had witnessed in the past two days that astounded him.

"How can he do such things?" Han wondered. His unguarded thoughts cascaded to the others.

"He's Master Li," Cecilia said as she cast Han a quick glance. She brushed the matted hair from his sweaty brow. "He does this sort of thing before breakfast," she confidently linked.

Han marveled at how well the rest of team took his prowess for granted.

"The limousines have arrived," Michael noted. "Each driver bears a special note and a… check?" he questioned.

"That's some bonus!" Villi pointed out, "they get a new house, a new car, and a nice chunk of cash!"

Michael looked down at Li, shook his head, and smiled. "I'll have to make some money for the trust this month it seems," he chuckled.

Pandemonium seemed to break out as a fleet of limousines began to pull up in front of every house in Rollo with drivers bearing messages of new fortune. Surprisingly, no resident argued with the plan. Some families received bonus checks larger than the Baker's had.

"I thought he said a few families would move," Zhiwei observed.

Master Li stirred in his seat and glanced up at Michael and Villi standing over him.

"I decided it was best for Villi to have his own shower, rather than spending another night with him in this cabin," he weakly linked.

The group roared with laughter. For the first time in his life, Villi actually blushed. Michael slapped his friend on the back. However, Li's energy level concerned Cecilia.

"Please don't link for a few minutes," she quietly spoke to him. "You need to rest and gather up additional energy. I don't have a hospital nearby should your normal body functions require medical care."

Li smiled at her. "I'm confident that in your hands I'll recover," he uttered aloud.

Su Lin stepped forward and placed a cool wash cloth to Li's forehead as Cecilia palpated a pulse.

"Thanks," Li said as he glanced up at her.

Villi felt partially responsible for Li's present condition as he had not considered the size of the wingspan.

"Master Li," he started to apologize. "I'm sorry about the entrance..."

Li rolled his eyes toward Cecilia. She understood their meaning without Li having to link.

"No need to apologize, Villi," Cecilia quickly responded. "Master Li understands you had the best intentions. He simply tried to help. It took a great deal out of him. He must rest for a while. I suggest we all leave Master Li in peace and do whatever it is we should be doing this morning."

"I intend to walk around," Zhiwei informed the others. "I'll use psychic energy and be invisible," he added with a note of pride in his voice.

"Don't run out of energy," Michael advised, "or you'll suddenly pop into view and pass out!"

"Mind if I go with you?" Zinian put in. "I'd like another look around in daylight."

"Come on," Zhiwei waved.

The two friends hopped off the jet only to stop just outside. This was the very first time they had a chance to use their powers on their own and explore without some directive hanging over them. Like adolescents in possession of a new toy, they delighted at the prospect of independence. They started to laugh and took off at a sprinter's pace. Just as they emerged in the sunlight, they vanished.

"Watch where you step," they linked back over their shoulder, "you'll find animal droppings..."

"You're in the country," Michael commented. He glanced over at Villi. "I agree with Han, I think we should find a way to cover the opening," he suggested. "Want to explore with me?" he put to him. Michael had an impish tone to his request.

Villi knew he was up to something. "Let's go," the big Russian nodded.

Michael and Villi casually left the confines of the jet and the barn. They ventured across the field together and started to jog – stride for stride each man was equal in height and stature.

"You must share some of your memories about being a cop," Michael requested as he and Villi crossed the field.

"I'd rather share memories about my time living near the university," Villi told him as the group's thoughts faded into the background. "I learned so much when I used to frequent the coffeehouse…"

Villi sensed a change in Michael's focus. The two men stopped jogging. Michael scanned one of the houses that bordered the field ahead. He found some items that would be useful for their purposes. However, a playful streak ran through the American's mind. Villi caught it.

"I can see that we are going to be good friends," Michael said as he shared some of Villi's enthusiasm.

The two men broke into a sprint as they raced across the field to see who would be the first to arrive. When Villi started to pull ahead, Michael put his martial arts knowledge to the test. He dove in front of Villi to knock him off his feet. The Russian leapt into the air and flipped over Michael's head. The American countered and quickly twisted around. He reached up and grabbed Villi's shirt. Villi reciprocated. The two men fell to the ground. They tumbled over and grappled until the two landed on their sides as neither could dominate the other.

"We're off to a good start," Villi said breathing hard. He pulled and pushed on Michael.

"If you think I'm going to yield…" Michael began as he strained for a dominant position. Villi strained equally hard. Suddenly, the two men stopped and stared at each other. They realized at once their abilities were matched. Both men burst out laughing and helped the other to his feet.

"For being an American, you are stronger than I thought," Villi stated.

"For being a Russian, you learned faster than I realized," Michael smiled. "Come on," Michael said as he extended his hand. "The contents of that basement need liberating," he said to his friend as he nodded toward the house.

The two invisible friends jogged over to the horizontal outside entrance to the cellar. It opened on its own as they approached.

Chou stood at the jet's doorway. He thought about what he should do first. No one would want to analyze electrical grids, power fluctuations, or load capacities. He wondered what kind of raw chemicals he could find. He had never used his psychic ability to make scientific observations. Making precise analytical measurements might require assistance from his Galactic Central voice. Therefore, he decided to go solo this morning.

"I suppose I could try to contact GC," he thought. "I could also use a lab… a place to evaluate data." He wanted to search the houses for probable locations to set up a new laboratory and to determine if he could use any tools or equipment in the village.

Han wanted to try the psychic bubble on his own. As he patiently stood behind Chou, he decided he would mix with the locals in daylight traveling incognito.

"We could save energy by joining forces," Han offered Chou.

"Sorry," Chou shook his head. "I'd prefer to walk around and think. You go do your strategy thing," he encouraged. "You'd find my observations of power lines boring."

"You're right about that," Han agreed. The two men wandered off in different directions.

With the departure of Michael, Villi, Zinian, Zhiwei, Chou and Han, only Cecilia and Su Lin remained on the jet with Master Li.

"Michael suggested I check on supplies," Su Lin linked to her friend. "Do you mind if I look around on my own?" she requested. As with the others, she was as eager to use her power in solo mode.

"Don't worry about us," Cecilia linked back. "We're fine," she said reassuringly. "He's quite stable. I'll watch over Master Li," she offered.

Su Lin stepped from the aircraft. In seconds, a glimmering field of energy surrounded the beautiful young Chinese woman. She could feel her own power surge through her body.

"I believe I'm going to like this," she noted.

She sprinted off in the direction of the general store that was already vacated by the Bakers. She jogged across the meadow in seconds and hummed a tune, as her psychic energy made her feel buoyant today. She took a jump and landed some twenty plus feet from where she leapt in to the air.

"Wow!" she declared and smiled at her new ability. She then ran and hopped the remainder of the way to the store.

With Su Lin gone, the two remaining psychics sat in silence. Cecilia rose and poured out another cup of tea while she kept a wary eye on her patient. Li held his eyes closed and breathed slowly. She sensed he did not sleep.

Cecilia went to the jet's door and stared out of the barn across the flat plain of Kansas. This scene seemed all too familiar to her. Being alone for the first time in weeks, she contemplated the fact that she was back in North America and not that far from where she grew up in Canada. She pictured her mother rising each morning, going to work every day, and worried about her daughter's whereabouts.

"Funny," she thought as she stared down at her tea. "When Michael and I left Battleford, I pictured us living together on some exotic tropical island. Now, here I am, right back on the flat boring plains of the Midwest where I grew up."

"You miss your mother. Don't you?" Li's thoughts suddenly intruded.

Cecilia turned around and gazed into those gray penetrating eyes of

Master Li. She smiled when she sensed he had partially recovered from his exertion.

"To be truthful," she began, "I miss her very much, Master Li," she linked as she brought her focus back to her patient. "Patient," she echoed the thought. "Do you realize that you are my first patient?"

"I can't think of a better physician to treat me than Cecilia Beaton," Master Li replied.

"Cecilia Beaton-Tyler," she corrected.

"Let's wait until the formal ceremony," Li reminded.

"…which I hope will be soon," Cecilia continued. "I don't like living in shame."

"You have no reason to feel shame," Li commented. "I consider you as my children. As such, my children are clean of mind, body, and spirit," he told her. "I am proud that each of you has independently taken the high moral ground."

Cecilia laughed. "Me? Your child? Hardly," she cynically stated. "You have your experience with older 'children' as you call us. I can tell that you never raised a teenager," she added. "Oh, we're cute when we start out, and as college students most of us are eager to learn. However as teenagers we can be defiant, stubborn, and argumentative!"

Li shook his head and took in a deep breath.

"You may be right," he sighed. "Anyway, I'm feeling much better… doctor," he casually let slip. "Let's you and I explore as the others are doing," he said and paused to evaluate the young woman seated next to him. He only had to think on the problem for a moment. "I do have physical limitations, despite my power. I cannot walk as briskly or as far as you can… therefore, we must find a ride."

"Master Li," Cecilia began, "finding a car at this hour might be…"

Cecilia heard loud squeaks and rattle sounds approach the barn. She leaned out the jet's door but could not see the source. After a moment, she saw a very strange, old, domestic truck whose model year must have been in the 1940's. It heavy steel frame had large rounded brown rusty fenders, a missing hood over the engine compartment, and a big, wide, chrome bumper crusted with corrosion across its front. The vehicle bounced toward them along a duo-path "tractor road" that led from the north end of town to the barn. The old decrepit truck slowed down as it neared the barn. She noticed no driver behind the wheel. She turned back to Master Li. She knew he had manipulated the vehicle's path.

"Where did you find that piece of junk?" she wondered.

"I found it behind a house," he told her.

"Another appropriation?" she inquired.

"Call it… a donation to our cause," he put to her.

She turned back to look at the object once more. It resembled more junk that any recognizable make or model. She shook her head and smiled at Master Li.

"Let's hope our cause is a just one," she commented.

Chapter Six

Ancient Rhythms

Master Li rose up off the comfortable leather seat effortlessly. Cecilia eyed the aging psychic with suspicion.

"I feel much better," he linked to her. "Thank you."

Cecilia still wanted to support him. Li waved her off as he had seemingly recovered. Despite her initial misgivings about his swift restoration, she did detect his power levels rising. As a matter of courtesy, he appreciated and accepted her help down the steps from the aircraft to the barn floor. He gestured ahead toward the truck as he and Cecilia headed out of the barn.

"I never knew they made trucks like this" she linked to Master Li as the ancient vehicle silently pulled up to them.

"The 1947 Chevrolet truck – an American classic," he observed.

"I didn't know you knew anything about automobiles," she linked to him.

"I do now," Li said with a half-smile. "Here come the Olympians."

He pointed over the field at two figures in the distance. Focused on the old truck, Cecilia realized she missed Villi and Michael walking toward them. With the summer heat rising, the two men had removed their torn shirts. Half-naked, they strode side by side with the morning sunlight glistening over their moisture-laden lean muscular chests. She noticed that the two men dragged several sections of huge dark-green tarpaulin across the field toward the barn. They seemed to move easily with the large heavy sections.

"I'm amazed at how everyone is digging up old things today," she commented to Li. "Where did you find the tarp?" she linked directly to Michael.

"We found five of them," he linked back to her. "A man had a stack of World War II tarpaulin packed away in his basement that his grandfather purchased from an Army Surplus store in 1955!"

The two men grinned at her as they approached.

"You're in a good mood," she noted.

Although Michael and Villi pulled the five heavy tarps with their power, she could tell they had done something that worked up a sweat.

"Michael and I are testing our… skills," Villi declared. He shot his friend a quick glance.

"We've been trying out martial arts moves and ended up nearly tearing each other's head off!" Michael smiled and waved as the two men passed them on their way to the barn. They seemed to thrive on the physical exertion. Cecilia could tell that privately, they were engaged in an intensely linked conversation about philosophy, football, and girls.

She chuckled and waved back. In that moment, she noticed the outside of the barn. She paused to appreciate Li's psychic strength, clearly apparent in the light of day. Nothing short of a massive bulldozer could bend the sides and top of the door frame into a twisted and curled hunk of metal. She jumped into the air and pulled down on the metal with her whole body. It did not budge an inch.

"If you think it's difficult moving that metal with your body, try bending it with your mind," Li quipped to her as he strode ahead.

She smiled at his comment, dropped down, and headed for the truck. Li climbed into the passenger seat. Cecilia looked inside the old truck made around the time her grandfather was born. The floor had three pedals.

"I've never driven a truck with a clutch," she noted through the driver's window. The interior had a distinctive musty odor.

She grabbed the door handle. The rusted hinges groaned and squeaked when she pulled hard to open the door. She watched as the torn black leather seat resealed its rips before she sat, the edges magically pulled together and melded. A swift wind blew through the cab and pulled out the odor of decay from the inside. Cecilia shook her head. She knew that Master Li did everything. She still frowned at the clutch pedal while she thought about driving. That is when she realized the ignition had no key.

"Michael didn't know how to drive a clutch either on Kamchatka," Li commented. "Somehow you continued to the coast. Never fear. I will help us out today," he told her.

Before Cecilia could grab the truck's steering wheel, it began to move.

Silently, the truck backed up into the field, pulled around and headed across the crude two-path field road toward one of the side streets in town.

"What is it, electric?" she asked not hearing the motor.

She sat so far back from the dashboard that she could not see the engine. She leaned back and decided to let Master Li do the driving. She bounced up and down on the springy seat with a higher view of the surrounding area than she was used to from a car. She turned her head this way and that to see the north end of town as they headed south out of the field.

"I'm curious about a feeling I've had ever since we landed," Li informed her, as Cecilia propped both feet on the metallic dashboard. She was content to let Li manipulate the truck. "Let us investigate this feeling of mine together. Shall we?" he offered.

"Lead the way Master Li!" Cecilia declared as she smiled at the day.

They headed west for the highway. The ride smoothed out so well that Cecilia doubted they were moving at all, if not for the scenery that passed.

The truck silently moved past two old men walking up the street just before Li and Cecilia turned south on the highway. The two white-haired men dressed in bid overalls watched as the truck passed them on the street. Their heads turned to follow as the rusty antique headed out of town.

"Isn't that your old truck?" the first one said calmly.

"I believe it is," the other man replied softly. He stared with the same disbelief as his friend did.

"When did you put a motor in it?" the first man said.

"It doesn't have a motor in it," the second replied. "The grandkids used to play at driving years ago. It's been rusting behind the house for over fifty years!"

The two men's eyes followed the truck out to the highway. Their mouths hung open aghast. For a second they blinked, stared at one another, and then the two men returned to walking in the direction they originally headed.

"No motor!" Cecilia gasped when she overheard the men's conversation before Master Li silenced them. She sat up and tried to see over the massive dash. She had not noticed the engine compartment, or the tires for that matter. "Master Li what if we…" she started.

"We don't have to worry about running out of fuel, do we?" he said. His eyes peered toward the southern horizon.

Cecilia shrugged and returned to her previous posture. She knew Master Li would take care of the details.

A group of psychics huddled together in front of the general store to compare notes on their travels through Rollo this morning. They had been linking when the rusty old vehicle that moved on tires which could not possibly hold air, passed by them as it headed south on the two-lane highway.

"Isn't that Cecilia and Master Li?" Zinian pointed.

Su Lin, Han, and Chou stood with Zinian and Zhiwei outside the general store. The group watched with curious amazement as the truck silently drove by Main Street. Cecilia and Master Li waved as they passed.

"I wonder how he does that," Su Lin linked.

"I wonder where they're headed," Zinian thought.

"I wonder how they're getting there. That truck has no..." Chou spoke.

"As you've so frequently pointed out," Han interrupted. "He's Master Li."

"They must be going to investigate the Native Americans who caught Michael's attention last night and led us to this place," Zhiwei pointed out. He tipped his head back and took a long drink of cold bottled water.

"Do they have any Chinese food inside?" Han asked as he pulled open the old screen door.

"Mr. Baker has great Chinese food," Zinian casually remarked, "if you like canned chop suey."

On hearing that comment, Zhiwei choked and spit out the water he'd been drinking, all over the curb. A little boy standing across the street thought it strange to see a sudden mist of water burst out of nowhere. Frightened, he turned around and ran up the street. Zhiwei did not bother to alter his thoughts. He knew no one would believe him.

The old truck silently moved down the road leaving Rollo behind.

"Where are we going?" Cecilia wondered. She had not used her power to scan the area ahead.

"I must show you the true face of medicine," Master Li replied. "It is neither glamorous nor elitist. In the world of the country doctor, you must be the emergency department, obstetrics, pediatrics, geriatrics, surgery, and diagnostician. You will see humanity at its most basic, often its worst. You must cope with having no assistance but your wits, because you will be on your own. Here is your hospital doctor," he gestured at the surrounding countryside, "and these are your patients."

"I had to ask," Cecilia said as she shook her head.

The flat, bald, and torn remnants of tires on the old truck miraculously stayed inflated as the two psychics drove only a few kilometers south from Rollo before they noticed several aging and dilapidated trailers in a group off to the right. A small dirt road led into a trailer park with one, small, proprietary house in very poor condition located at the front. Yellowish dust rose up from the dry roadbed and surrounded the truck when they turned onto the driveway. Several curious people stuck their heads out. Visitors seldom stopped at this place. No one ever received a package or mail here.

They picked up general delivery from Baker's store once a week where they cashed their support checks and usually spent them in the store.

"These are the Comanche?" Cecilia questioned.

"What's left of them," Li informed her. "Many years ago, these people broke from the main tribe in Oklahoma. They refused help from the main tribe, although the state of Kansas did offer some assistance fifteen years ago. That is how some received these trailer-homes."

"You call these trailers a home? They're in terrible shape," Cecilia pointed out.

"They were surplus units from the American government that the state purchased at a rock bottom price. They sat in a large lot for over ten years before they were moved here. No one else wanted them," Li explained. "A variety of man-made poisons fills each mobile home. Their troubles don't end there. Most of the men are unemployed. The nearest place that will accept an uneducated Native American is over fifty miles away. To commute those distances is very expensive for people with few resources. The government delivers remittance checks for financial support. Otherwise, they have nothing."

"America seems like such a wealthy nation, Master Li," Cecilia began.

"It is for a small percentage," Master Li answered. "The privileged class is always comfortable. Many others, like these poor souls, must struggle to live."

His thoughts traveled from trailer to trailer. Cecilia could sense that Master Li examined the living conditions inside each one.

"Long ago, things were different," he linked to her.

The roads and trailers disappeared. Wooden structures covered with bundles of grass stalks and animal furs took their place. A great, organized village appeared. Half-naked men trained on horseback, while women worked the land, and children ran in the distance. The sun arched across the sky. Night fell on the placid scene. An old man seated next to a campfire slowly beat on a drum. His painted face sang out a sorrowful tune. The entire village sat around the fire and listened intently to his song.

"I-ee-ah, aa-ee-oo-ah," he cried as he pounded the leather with a stick.

He told them stories as he sang… of the great plains… of buffalo, deer, and beaver… of the wind and storms… of the change in seasons… when to plant… when to harvest… even when to mate. The village listened and learned from his songs. Cecilia watched the fire's smoke curled upward. Her eyes traveled up as the vision of tune and smoke faded into the pitiful, crumbling, government-issued trailers. She looked over at Master Li. She wondered how he knew about this history.

"Two hundred years ago, the North American Native American lived in an abundant country that gave them so much while they took so little," Li explained. "Look at how they live now – in abject poverty. They cling to unemployment checks. Their minds are aimless, their spirit broken and forgotten, while their community rots."

Li slowly manipulated the truck between two trailers. It rolled to a stop. He shook his head as he glanced about him.

"The water is unfit to drink, but they drink it anyway," he quietly linked to her. "The quality of food is disgusting, but they eat it anyway. The houses are falling apart, but they live in them anyway."

"Why didn't the people of Rollo help them?" Cecilia asked.

"The people of Rollo cannot help themselves, let alone these desperate people. I do not blame Rollo for this," Li commented.

Li looked at the dents and scratches, the peeling faded paint and rusty nails that scarred the exterior metal walls of the trailer. The front screen door had holes in it, as did the screens over the small side windows. Every small window was wide open, which still did not allow air to circulate properly. A sleeping, misbegotten, mongrel of a dog lay on the ground, chained to a metal stake. It did not stir when the truck pulled up. Cecilia wondered if it was even alive, though it did have a bowl of water on the ground next to a makeshift doghouse.

Broken toys, pop and beer cans, food wrappers along with a variety of discarded debris littered the yard. An older model car sat parked next to the trailer had four flat tires. Weeds grew up around it. Its condition described the owner's current state of affairs.

A heavy, dark-skinned woman with a large nose and white hair stared out one window. She wore a flowered housecoat that snapped up the front and used her fat stubby fingers to pick at something in her teeth. She revealed her crooked stained teeth when she snarled her lip in quiet disdain over the approach of strangers.

Master Li stepped from the truck while he still surveyed the scene.

"Where are you going?" Cecilia asked. She seemed a little frightened to move.

"I want you to come inside the trailer with me," he requested.

"Inside?" she replied. She stared with dismay through the truck window at the decayed structure. "We don't even know these people."

"Please," he indicated. He motioned toward the trailer. "Cecilia, this is day one of your new life, time to use this special gift for good. You must let nothing stand in your way. Do not fear any fist, knife, pistol, or any threat that might come between you and your work," he reassuringly spoke. "They cannot harm you. Let no rude comment, or possible threat from a bullet, halt your mission. You have a duty to perform," he linked as he indicated the trailer's front door.

He went to the front door and politely knocked. The heavy woman they saw in the window came to the door. However, she only opened it wide enough to reveal her eye.

"Yes, what do want?" she demanded while she peered at them through the crack.

"I am here to see your granddaughter," Li said. He started up the step.

"You can't come in. Go away," the old woman ordered.

"Sorry, that excuse will not stop us today," Li said. He gently yet firmly pushed the door open with his mind. "We have urgent business," he said with command in his voice. "Step aside!"

He backed the woman up as if she had no resistance to him. She glared as Li stepped into her home although she did not protest. Cecilia moved in behind Li. She was uncertain as to what would happen next.

"Master Li…" she started and stopped short of entering. "I… I…"

She could hardly breathe from the assault on her nose. A strong foul odor hit Cecilia's nostrils before she had a chance to check out the inside of the house. The still, heavy, warm air inside the trailer held the strong scent of cigarette smoke, stale beer, along with putrid smells of urine, feces, and rotting garbage. Master Li had to push trash aside with his mind to open the door wide enough for the two of them to enter. Cecilia could not go past the front door as nausea gripped her insides.

"Cecilia you must come inside," Li said. He twisted half around.

"I can't," she responded. She turned her head away. "I'll be sick."

"You want to be a physician?" Li asked her.

"I do," she said as she struggled to keep her stomach contents down. "I don't know if I can handle this, Master Li."

"You must gather courage to face what is ugly about the world," he advised. "This is the world of the indigent. Disease neither looks nor smells pretty." He reached back and pulled Cecilia into the small cramped space of the trailer.

Litter and filth covered every inch of living space. No one had dusted anything in the house in a long time. Cobwebs hung in every corner. A broken television sat against one wall. A small table and plastic chair sat by the window. A worn deck of playing cards rested on one corner. They signified the hours that the woman played solitaire to pass the time.

Cecilia struggled with her mounting nausea.

"I can't take this anymore," she gagged. "I need some fresh air," she pleaded.

"You cannot leave," Li told her. "You haven't seen the patient."

He pulled her further into the filthy room. Cecilia knew it was futile to resist. When Li turned toward the hall, the old woman saw her chance. She raised her arm to strike Li when he turned his back. Cecilia flinched when she caught the action from the corner of her eye. Yet, when she glanced back again, the woman stood completely still, frozen in mid-movement with the same expression on her face.

"This way," Li said as he tugged on Cecilia's hand.

Li navigated the debris field and gently guided Cecilia up a narrow cluttered hallway to a little side room. The trailer's interior had only the amount of light coming in through its small windows. The dark filthy corridor frightened Cecilia, as if any moment a monster might jump out from somewhere. She wanted to flee. She changed her mind about being a doctor.

"The monster is in here," Li indicated the side bedroom. He chided Cecilia for conjuring up a fantasy monster image from her imagination.

Cecilia pulled her hand free. She straightened her shoulders and mustered a modicum of courage. She took in a slow breath through her mouth and followed Li.

Inside the little bedroom, a small young nine-year-old girl lay on a narrow bed covered with a bright multi-colored spread. The cover had several yellowish and brown stains on it. The odor of feces inside the room smelled twice as strong as it did at the front door. Cecilia reeled back from its effrontery. Li released the old woman's speech center. He wanted to speak with her.

"Stay out of that room!" her voice blurted. "What do you think you are doing? Stay away from her!" the old woman yelled.

She could not move. Her feet remained glued to the floor. She was unable to stop Master Li from his determined purpose.

"Where is your help this morning?" Li called out while he allowed the woman time to respond.

"She's not here yet!" the woman spoke up. Li knew that she made excuses for her absence. "What I mean to say is… well, this is her morning to be here… but she's late!"

"No time to wait… we must act," he insisted.

Master Li placed the old woman back in stasis.

"Who is she talking about?" Cecilia asked. However, the odor and the sight were too much for the inexperienced young girl from Canada. Her head began to swim. Her blood pressure dropped and little objects appeared to swim in the air before her eyes.

"Another woman comes by four or five times a week to clean the trailer and take care of the girl…" Li explained as he focused on the girl. "The woman helps them in an endless cycle of thankless rituals."

He bent down and took hold of the covers. With one swift movement, he yanked them off. A large pool of liquid brown stool surrounded the girl's bottom and backside. It appeared as if someone dumped a bunch of mud around her. The smell of excrement flooded the room. Its pungent scent wafted up from the bed.

"Force your mind past the elimination wastes," Li linked to her.

When she did not respond, he glanced over at her. Her lashes fluttered as her eyes rolled back. She nearly toppled over and began to reflux. He quickly reached inside her mind. His energy moved into the chemoreceptor trigger zone of the fourth ventricle. He blocked neurotransmitters, vagal stimulation, and calmed her reflux status.

"Easy Cecilia," he said while he assisted with her control. "Follow my pathways, you can do this to your own mind," he linked as he helped her overcome her nausea.

Gradually, Cecilia returned to a conscious state. She no longer focused on the odor but on the girl's condition.

"Thanks," she sighed. She wiped sweat off her forehead and focused on Li's eyes that gazed back at her with affection.

"Time for your first anatomy lesson," he told her. "Follow my thoughts into the young female's body," he requested. "I intend to make a thorough examination."

"I'll try," she told him.

The little girl on the bed stared up at the two people standing over her. Eyes were wide with fear while beads of sweat broke out on her forehead. She grunted and moaned. Sores covered her pale skin. On a stand nearby, Cecilia noticed a washbasin and some towels hung on a wooden rack to dry, a large cake of white soap rested next to the basin.

"Note the central cavitation," Li linked as he gestured to the girl's spine. "Also note the reduction in the subarachnoid space and the abundant abnormal cells…"

"Spinal tumor of unknown etiology?" Cecilia guessed. She began to see how her interactions with her voice on subjects such as anatomy and physiology were paying off.

Master Li nodded his approval of her diagnosis.

"Very perceptive," Li stated. "Notice that with so much spinal cord damage, she has experienced an increased loss of feeling that has spread throughout the lower extremities. Loss of bowel control has led to secondary incontinence which resulted in skin ulcers that formed from lack of hygiene and contractures from insufficient range of motion exercises. She also experiences excruciating pain in her back from the tumor and the ulcers. The constant severe pain and lack of communication has resulted in madness for the little girl. To escape reality, she is lost in ideation. Her mind drifts in an endless world of fantasy." For a second, Master Li could not link due to emotion. "This is a most pathetic case," he finally whispered.

"Master Li... I'm sorry that I..." Cecilia struggled to find the words to match her emotions. She felt shame for not having the courage to help someone so obviously in need.

"You did well to recognize the tumor," Li said as he turned to her. "Consider this your very first case, Dr. Beaton. By the way, I expect subsequent follow-up visits," he said as he turned back to the girl. "We are not only physicians; we are sociologists, psychologists, and nutritionists as well. What would be the usual treatment in this case?" Li asked her while he awaited her response.

Cecilia paused as she considered her limited medical knowledge.

"Surgical consult, chemotherapy, wound care, physical therapy and prescription pain medication?" she speculated. "She could also benefit from a psyche consult."

"Excellent Dr. Beaton," Li pointed out. "This young girl could benefit from skin grafts, too. Unfortunately, everything we've suggested takes a complex medical facility, an excellent surgeon, a neurologist, an extended hospital stay with a very good attentive nursing staff along with physical therapy and lots of money, something this family does not possess," he pointed out.

"What will you do for her?" she asked him.

"I will attempt to perform the impossible," Li explained. He closed his eyes and reached out with his psychic senses.

Cecilia could feel him gathering the abundant psychic energy present in the residents of the tribal village. What they lacked in nearly everything else, Cecilia noted they exuded an inordinate amount of psychic energy. Using his mind, the tumor shrank and disappeared. Then he instigated repair of the bone, nerve tissue, spinal discs, close the fragile broken skin, and fill-in the ulcers. Muscle and skin cells rapidly began to replicate. The girl cried out in pain. Master Li opened his eyes and gazed down at the young girl.

"Melissa," he spoke softly to her mind. "Look at me."

The young girl shook with fear. She stared up at the strange white-haired oriental man. The moment their eyes met, a feeling of calm spread through her as pain and discomfort left her body. Melissa began to cry and whimper with grateful relief. Cecilia's eyes welled up with tears as she could sense Melissa's feelings of gratitude, which she could not verbally express. Master Li also sensed her grateful emotion, yet he felt the sadness in her twisted mind.

"Cecilia," Li linked. "Would you mind cleaning the trailer? Do what you can. First, take over control of the old woman. I find it difficult to maintain her quietude while I work on the patient. I need to focus my power here.

I'd like you to use your skill on the surroundings, if you will, please," he requested.

Cecilia applied Li's control to the older woman in the front room. However, she paused before leaving to carry out the remainder of his request. She watched with fascination as Master Li entered the girl's spinal column, destroyed the cancerous cells, and actually accelerated the growth of new nerve cells while at the same time rapidly reconnected their parallel strips, and made thousands of tiny bridges inside her spinal column.

He worked so fast that Cecilia could not keep up with his efforts. He sped up replication of skin, muscle, cartilage cells, connective tissue, hair follicles, and sweat glands. He accelerated their growth and filled up the gaping holes in the girl's shoulders, elbows, buttocks, and ankles. The sores on the skin rapidly vanished. The spinal column refused and reformed which allowed full body sensation to return.

Next, Li cleaned the bedroom. The urine and feces that saturated the bed sheets lifted up out of the soiled linen and flew out the open window, along with a dark yellowish cloud of dust and odor that clung to other items in the room. All of it flew over the plains as if shot from a catapult. It landed on distant sandy spot that held no vegetation or animal.

"Eeeiiihhhh!" Melissa yelled not from pain but out of fear. Li gradually straightened her legs with his mind. The return of sensation in her legs frightened the young girl.

"Melissa," Li whispered to her mind. "Do not be afraid." His calm thoughts washed over her like a warm blanket. "You are no longer ill. You are well. I want you to rise from the bed and move about the room. Start by moving your fingers, your arms, your toes, and your legs. Please try," he encouraged.

She cautiously moved and stretched her arms and legs out. She wiggled her fingers and toes. She reached down to feel her legs for the first time in over a year. Her hands found her face. Her fingers lingered around her throat. Master Li entered the speech center of her mind. He untangled the mess he found that would allow her to speak. He straightened out her psyche as best he could without damaging its delicate chemical structure and returned her mind to a sense of normalcy.

Her eyes locked with Master Li's. Using his power, her body rose up from the bed and Melissa landed on her feet. Li held her steady by grasping her hands. She tried to bear weight, but her legs were very weak. She seemed like a newborn calf. Unsteady, her pale thin body trembled as she attempted to stand before him.

"Th... Th..." she tried to speak, although her mouth had never uttered truly intelligible speech that she could remember. "Thank you," she finally managed. She leaned forward and nearly collapsed on Master Li.

"You're welcome," Li said while he squeezed her hands.

Li held her up by her hands until Melissa finally managed to use the newly formed muscles in her body. She took one step and then another. She smiled at Master Li as he fought to control his emotions. She openly wept unable to express her gratitude.

Clothes leapt out from an old dresser drawer. Puffs of yellow soap flew out of the material. The clean fresh clothes magically slid down over her body. Li lifted her into the air as underwear slid up her legs. Gently using psychic energy, Li pulled the dead skin and body secretions from her hair and scalp. Her hair fluffed out. A pair of scissors glided through the air and flew around her head while they snipped and styled her hair. She turned and floated down in front of a dirty mirror. With a thought, Li removed the surface dirt and cleaned the mirror. The startled girl looked at a reflection of a beautiful young person. The sores on her face were gone. Clean, clear, healthy skin stared back at her. Grateful tears streamed down her face. Master Li said nothing. He bowed and backed away.

"Welcome back to humanity Melissa," he said as he backed out the door.

Master Li heard a great commotion coming from the rest of the trailer. Cecilia performed the same "cleaning technique" she noted that Master Li used in Melissa's bedroom. She gathered up old vomit stains, cat hair, dirt, dust, and spider webs. She pulled soiled matter from the entire room and let it fly out the window as she worked around the old woman still frozen in place.

Master Li emerged from the room to join her work on the trailer. He repaired the screens, fixed the leaky faucets, and tightened the plumbing. As a last minute gesture, he turned toward the television. The old screen came to life. It showed a program in progress. Li nodded silently toward Cecilia content with their work. He tipped his head toward the door. She caught on and headed in that direction.

When the two psychics walked from the trailer, Cecilia and Master Li stopped in the front yard and turned around.

"Nicely done!" she declared.

"Not quite," Li added.

Next, he turned his attention to the family car. Li took in a deep breath, gathered some more psychic energy and went to work. The flat tires filled up and the engine started up, revved for a few seconds, and then stopped, fixed. The nearly empty tank needed fuel to run. Otherwise, he fixed the car. He turned to Cecilia and nearly toppled over when she reached out to steady him. He briefly smiled at her.

"I used up a little too much energy," he stressed. "Our work here is finished… for now. I might also add that we left a significant calling card and perhaps made an impression. We will find out later what kind of impression we made. Do you feel up to being a country doctor?" he asked her.

"Master Li, with you as my guide, it will be my pleasure," Cecilia replied.

He held out his elbow, which Cecilia took as the two walked back together to the truck. Moving around to the passenger side of the truck, she opened the door with her mind this time, and helped Master Li step in. She gave the rusty door a shove shut with her hip. Li reached out and absorbed more power from the village.

"I only ask one thing," Cecilia added as she got in the other side and closed the door.

"Let me guess," Li quipped. "You want me to find a car with a motor," he offered. "That would be nice, but isn't my way of traveling quieter?"

"Much," she smiled and shook her head. "I simply wanted you to drive," she added. She leaned back and put her feet up on the dashboard, while Master Li took them back to Rollo under his power.

As the old truck silently rolled away, a young girl cautiously moved out of her bedroom door. She stood in the hallway, unsteady and frightened to walk.

"Grandma?" Melissa called out.

The elderly woman – made to stand motionless and stunned for the past several minutes – blinked her eyes awake. She thought she heard the sweet voice of a child. She tried to focus her eyes on the hall in front of her.

"Grandma!" the girl cried out to her.

The old woman screamed as a young girl ran to her, threw her arms out and hugged her.

"Oh, grandma," the girl sighed as her thin arms wrapped around the big woman's waist.

"Melissa?" she cried. She held the young girl away from her body to see. Her tired old eyes searched the young girl's face, a face she washed a thousand times. "It is you…" she said as her throat choked up with emotion.

Tears ran down the old woman's face as she bent her body down to one knee and put her arms around the child. Sobbing, the old woman could not speak.

Outside the spruced up trailer, a middle-aged woman sporting a large felt hat with a gray ponytail that protruded from underneath cautiously approached the front of the trailer in time to witness the miraculous reunion through the freshly-repaired screen door.

"Melissa… oh, Melissa!" the old woman sobbed as she hugged the young girl. "How is this possible?"

"Yes," the middle-aged woman outside the trailer repeated. "How is this possible?"

She turned around to face the highway. Her questioning eyes followed the silent truck as it drove north up the highway toward Rollo.

Chapter Seven

Taking Over

As Master Li intended, Rollo's residents left most of their worldly possessions behind. They took only those personal items, which mean so much to most people… pictures, mementos, memorabilia, collections and so forth. Family after family left the isolated little town as if fleeing for their lives. The limousines arrived and drove families away all day to different destinations. When the first day ended, Rollo's residents left behind a deserted town.

By the time Han finished his rounds with Zinian, the two men found that Rollo consisted of twenty wood-frame houses in a variety of conditions that ranged from poor to very poor. The community also acquired three adjacent farms and farmhouses on its periphery, one to the north, east, and south. Each of these had a barn and some other small buildings in stages of deteriorating physical condition. When the sun finally sat like an orange ball on the western edge of the Kansas plain, the psychic group gathered once more at the jet aircraft, now partially camouflaged with tarps strung together.

Michael turned the group's attention to the man in charge of designing the new town.

"Well Zinian?" he inquired.

Zinian did not know where to begin. When he last walked through Rollo with Han, debris littered Main Street from one end to the other – scattered clothes, odd pieces of forgotten things, and dozens of other items dotted every lawn.

"I'm afraid it's worse than we thought," he said as he stared down at his clipboard. "Nothing is salvageable. Most of these houses are older than thirty years and in extremely poor condition," he informed him. "Sooner or later, we'll need to replace every single dwelling that is currently standing… within the next two years, if we can manage," he stated the grim news. "Even if we chose to live in the current houses, I'll need to replace pipes, wells, power lines, and restock every house with new appliances and furnishings. I'd roughly estimate that this overhaul will conservatively cost between ten and twenty million dollars give or take a million."

"Is it really that bad?" Michael asked.

"Rollo needs help and needed it yesterday," Zinian told him as he flipped up his summation paper on his clipboard. "The town has no central sewage or water treatment plant. The wells and septic are obsolete. Chou placed water filters on every tap to ensure that our drinking water is up to standard. Master Li's fabricated story about poison in the water isn't that farfetched."

Zinian flipped another page over.

"This leads me to conclude that eventually we'll have to gut or destroy every house in Rollo and start over."

Michael nodded in total agreement with his master builder.

"We will do what we can, Zinian," Michael calmly replied. "Let me know what you need. Give me a list. I'll start ordering construction supplies. Don't hold back. Tell me whatever you need, from tools to supplies."

"I need everything!" the young man threw his arms into the air. "Construction tools for a start, from power saws to nail guns, you name it. I'll also need new doors, siding, roofing, flooring, paint, stain, nails, calking, insecticide, fungicide, windows, insulation, boards of varying thickness and length," he read from his list. "Most of all, I need a crew. I can patch up some of these houses. I can't do this alone, Michael."

"Please Zinian," Michael pleaded. "Just give me a list and some time. I'll see what I can do. Delivery may take a few days until we establish organized supply lines," he said as he turned to another group member.

"I'm next," Su Lin said. She also had a clipboard in her hand. "Are you ready for my report?" she asked.

"Go ahead," Michael sighed.

"The general store provided packaged food with very little in the way of fresh…" she started to explain. "Most of the fresh items – fruits, vegetables, eggs, and the like – came from local farmers. It will take some time, but we'll have to change the delivery system."

"Make me a list of what you need," Michael requested. "I promise I'll try to find a good distributor from Wichita. Villi," Michael linked in with his friend.

"Michael," Villi nodded back.

"What about our transportation needs?" Michael asked.

"I examined the ground fuel tanks," Villi said as he wiped sweat from his forehead. "They've been using one of the old bio-fuel blends that will be difficult to find or manufacture. I estimate the tank at the general store has enough fuel to run two cars and three trucks for about eight weeks, if we ration the stuff. I'll still need to look over their engines," he said and paused. "How many lists do you have?" he asked.

"Including your list?" Michael tilted his head and glanced around, "that would make nine." The group could see the fatigue on Michael's face. He tipped his head back and turned a water bottle upside down over his mouth. "Thought we'd better put these up soon," he gestured toward Su Lin. Two large placards floated out with big letters "no fuel" printed on one side. "If you would, please, Su Lin. How did your day go, Cecilia?" he asked the next person.

The mood had remained positive with everyone until Cecilia related the story of the little girl in the trailer. She went on to explain what Master Li did for her. When a psychic relays a memory, the group shares everything as if they were physically present. The story quickly swept away the playful mood from a moment earlier.

"That's so sad," Su Lin stated as she set down her drink.

"I'll skip dinner tonight," Han muttered. He closed his eyes as he sucked in fresh air to keep from passing out.

Villi walked up to Master Li. The tall man bent in half and gave the shorter elderly man a big hug.

"You are a great man Master Li," Villi said as he bowed down.

"Thank you, Villi," Li replied as he glanced at others, "I wondered how you felt."

"Are we going to help the Native American village?" Cecilia questioned.

Michael glanced around at the nodding heads.

"I believe the answer is unanimous," he responded. "Therefore, we should split our focus on development between the two communities, since both will require basic work on housing and infrastructure. As of now, they are the only supply of psychic energy," Michael openly linked, "and possibly a crew?" he added as he glanced at Zinian.

He turned his focus back to Villi.

"Is it possible to keep the jet aircraft, in case we need it for some future venture?" Michael asked.

"It's possible," Villi began, "yet exceedingly difficult to maintain without a proper ground crew. Would you like my true assessment of the situation?" he pointedly put to him.

"Go ahead," Michael relented, "we may as well face every the truth this evening."

“The barn is hardly a hanger,” Villi stated as he gestured around them. “Zinian and his mysterious crew will have to tear down this barn and raise a building meant to house a commercial jet. We can use the highway as a temporary makeshift runway, however, I’ll need a large tank to hold a supply of aviation fuel just for take offs,” he explained. “I’ll also need a long list of parts, maintenance items, tools, a well-equipped workbench, and at least two hearty helpers to whip a program into shape. Other than that…”

“Spoiled sport,” Michael quipped. “Thanks for your honesty Villi. I expect more of the same in the future. Ok?” he said to his friend, who nodded back in the affirmative. “Don’t hold back next time!” he joked. “We’ve heard from Cecilia, Zinian, Villi, and Su Lin,” he said as he turned, “Zhiwei?”

By the firelight coming from the pit that Su Lin created to cook dinner, the new security chief appeared more haggard than the rest. He spent nearly the entire day walking through Rollo, altering minds, scanning minds, observing passing motorists and changing their minds, too. His task of being the lone security person seemed daunting, if not impossibly overwhelming.

“Security is haphazard at best,” Zhiwei mumbled. “So many people were coming and going. I found it difficult to keep track of all the cars that passed, as I watched over the chaos in town today. Hopefully, things will improve in a few days…”

Michael saw the strain on his face. He wanted to tell everyone in the room that they did a good job that day, for the group accomplished a great deal since their arrival last night – Master Li performed the most difficult tasks of all. He closed his eyes took in a deep breath and finally turned to Han.

“That leaves the assignment of our living quarters,” he began. “What do you say, master strategist? You’ve been going in and out of houses all day along with Zinian and Chou. May we sleep on a bed in our own house tonight?” he put to Han.

Han glanced down at his pink-colored clipboard with little pink daisies on it – the only one he spotted. The dark-haired, slender, twenty-eight-year-old Chinese man scratched his temple with the eraser of his number two pencil. He held a crude diagram of the town that had names next to boxes erased several times.

“After Zinian and I compared information, we determined that the community built the best houses in the center of Rollo along Main Street,” he commented. “Fortunately for us, Master Li chose to empty these houses first, which gave me time to inspect them. Each one has sufficient furniture, linen, and supplies, thanks to Chou and Su Lin. They helped me shuffle last minute items around this afternoon.” He glanced down at the hastily drawn plan. “I tried to place members in close proximity based on friendship and how they could best serve the community.”

He held up the simplified chart he made and pointed to it.

"Michael will take the first house at the far eastern end of Main Street, the last house on the south side. It's probably more room than you need, however, this will place you in a good spot."

"I know that house," Michael interjected. "Thanks Han."

"Don't thank me yet. We didn't have time to clean up or make the bed," Han told him. "Master Li told us not to bother," he added.

"Master Li…" Michael started to protest, but Han continued.

"Villi, you'll have the house directly across the street from Michael," Han pointed to the picture. "The jet's hanger will be a straight shot out your back door. If you stood on Main Street facing back toward the highway, you'll be on Michael's right. That is where you wanted to be, isn't it?"

Villi smiled slightly acknowledging Han.

"I located Su Lin's house next to Villi on the same side of the street," Han said as he pointed to the next symbol.

"Convenient," Su Lin commented. She gave Villi a side-glance.

Han cleared his throat, "I placed Cecilia in the house next to Michael on the south side of the street opposite Su Lin."

"Yes, very convenient," Cecilia noted. She glanced over at Su Lin instead of Michael. "We're all neighbors, how cozy," she linked to them.

Han continued, "I put Zinian and Zhiwei in the two houses after Su Lin's on the north side of Main Street with Zhiwei closest to the highway. You are on a block alone Zhiwei," Han pointed out, "with a street between you and Zinian."

Zhiwei frowned disapprovingly at the suggestion.

"You disapprove," Han noted, "however, as chief of security your home positions you closer to the town's main access road. I placed you between the highway and the rest of us. This assignment finishes out the good houses available on Main Street," Han indicated. "In the next block to the south, I put Master Li and I together in the large three bedroom house behind Michael's house. He and I agreed to this arrangement before the meeting. I placed Chou in the next house on the same side of the street. I chose that one because… well, you've been inside and requested it," he said to the young man.

"Yes," Chou spoke up, "it has a finished basement and a workbench, perfect for working on experiments."

"Master Li, I have a personal request," Cecilia linked in. "I'd like to move in with Michael," she boldly stated, "if you don't mind."

Michael glanced over at Cecilia and then over at Master Li. Cecilia shifted her eyes back and forth between them. No one spoke but tension filled the air. Li cleared his throat and sat up.

"Yes… well… I'm not really in favor of cohabitation before marriage," he began. "However, these are not exactly normal circumstances. Since I've already been lenient with your relationship in China, I'll allow this exception… and only this exception," he indicated to the rest of the group.

Villi and Su Lin exchanged worrisome glances. Before Villi could open his mouth or thoughts in protest, Su Lin used her hands and signaled him to be quiet. They made a brief private communication and agreed that since they were next door to each other, crossing the fence would not be a problem. Therefore, Su Lin did not make the same request Cecilia did.

"We're adults," she linked to him. "We'll behave as adults," she added.

"I'd like to offer my house to Chou instead of the one you chose, Han," Cecilia continued. "That would place you next to Michael's house on Main Street. That house has a larger basement than the house you intended. Doesn't it?"

"It does!" Chou linked and brightened. "Thanks, Cecilia."

Han then turned back to Zhiwei.

"Then I would suggest you take the house next to Chou's across the street. It is inferior to the first choice. However, we would all be grouped together."

"You don't have to draw me a picture to see the advantages of that layout Han," Zhiwei linked. "I'd like to review job assignments," his link expressed concern. "The task of watching for intruders is mounting," he explained. "I will maintain security as Michael suggested. But, I am only one person. I cannot cover every end of Rollo at the same time. If you notice a car or truck slowing down to enter Rollo, we must divert those people before they stop," he suggested.

"We'll all try to help each other out," Michael pitched. "I'll be glad to help you Zhiwei. Everyone will."

"Zinian," Master Li spoke up, "it's become painfully obvious that we need the tribal village in more ways than as a source for psychic energy. You'll need a work crew – men and women motivated by the lure of having a steady job. In order to train a crew, you'll need experience. Take a couple of days in downloads to bring up your skill level. Then visit the tribal village and speak to any of the older teens or young men interested in construction work. It will be a difficult sell at first. Offer them cash payments at the end of each week's work," he suggested.

"Yes, Master Li," Zinian replied.

"Cash?" Michael questioned.

"You'll have to keep a large amount of cash nearby for emergencies," Li suggested. "Go through your voice and have a security truck make the delivery here, only have the record show that the delivery was made to our account in Witchita," Li linked to Michael.

"How much cash?" Michael asked.

"At least fifty to a hundred thousand or more to start," Li instructed. "Oh and Zinian, when you go, do not speak to anyone else in the village," Li told him. "If anyone else approaches you, such as a middle-aged woman wearing a large hat, do not respond to her."

"Very well Master Li, if you insist," Zinian responded.

"I do insist," Li said using a professorial tone. "Our relationship with our neighbors is precarious at best. Also, starting tomorrow, every member of our group not directly engaged with some immediate need should interact with their Galactic Central voice. We need knowledgeable psychics running things."

"Master Li," Chou asked, "how should I address my Galactic Central voice?"

He regarded the young man's considerations for only a moment.

"Why don't you ask them what they would consider the most indispensable knowledge regarding technology that someone on Earth could comprehend," Li suggested. "You might be able to apply some advanced technology to our benefit."

"I couldn't agree more," Michael interjected. "I will help patrol the city during the day. If Han could remain on Earth and offer his strategic analysis…"

"I'll rise early," Han put in.

"Then I believe our first official meeting is over," Michael linked to everyone.

"Before we leave," Cecilia linked, "I would like to demonstrate a technique that I learned today," she added. She shared the moment when Master Li pulled the soiled material from the linen and how they tidied up the trailer. She suggested the group do the same in their prospective homes. The meeting broke up with each person having to clean and straighten homes left in relative mayhem.

As Michael and Cecilia turned to go, they realized they had one destination in mind. For the first time, they would spend the night in the same bed, a significant act not lost on Villi. He stared at the other couple as they gazed into each other's face. Su Lin read the disappointment on Villi's face and crossed over to him.

"We might be able to understand one another clearly," she quietly linked, "but even a psychic needs a moment of privacy. Come on lover," she suggested as she took his arm.

Master Li watched as Michael and Cecilia left together. He could sense Villi's jealousy over the other couple's intimacy. He hoped he had not sparked a rift that might widen over the coming weeks. He could not picture the two, Michael and Villi, squaring off and having some sort of psychic power duel. Yet, if he were not here, things might have turned out differently. He scratched his chin and thought about his choices as he and Han made their way across town.

"I wonder if we've made the right decisions tonight," he considered.

CHAPTER EIGHT

ADJUSTMENTS

WHEN MICHAEL AND CECILIA ARRIVED at their front door, the house interior brought reality back to the starry-eyed couple. The previous owners left the place in total chaos. Neither one had the opportunity to visit the house prior to stepping through the front door for the first time.

"What happened?" Michael said as he noted the disarray. "I don't know where to start," he wearily stated.

Cecilia rolled up her sleeves and started to clean as Master Li showed her in the trailer. Michael, too tired to assist, watched as things flew around the room. Trash flew into garbage bags and clothes folded into a pile. After a few minutes of this, he diverted her attention. He reached out, grabbed her wrist and pulled her toward him. He wrapped his arm around her waist.

"Can we work on this tomorrow?" he requested via a link, his lips pressed against hers. "This day has drained all of my energy."

Cecilia shrugged. Objects in mid-flight dropped to the floor.

"...all of your energy?" she questioned.

"Oh, I could muster some physical energy," he added.

"I thought so," she confirmed.

Cecilia laughed and tore from his grasp. She flew up the stairs with Michael in hot pursuit. The two laughing teens skidded to a halt at the master bedroom door. Someone left trash all over the room including a soiled bed. Michael groaned at the thought of using more psychic magic. Cecilia shook her head. She was tired, too.

"I take that back," she sighed. "Certain things – like a clean bed – will not wait."

Cecilia closed her eyes and concentrated on the bed. A cloud of yellowish dust and soiled particles rose up out the linen and the mattress. Michael opened a nearby window to allow the debris cloud easy exit to the night air. Next, the mattress vibrated and another debris cloud emerged that also flew out the open window. What remained were completely clean albeit slightly worn sheets and blankets with no trace of human skin cells, hair, or excrement in them.

"Works better when we cooperate," Michael mused.

"I need to change," she told him as she wondered off to the clothes closet. He said nothing in reply. Instead he went into the bathroom. He flipped the light switch and stared at his own image in the mirror. He felt more nervous about this night than he did when they first made love in China. He found a new unopened toothbrush next to the sink along with a tube of toothpaste. He started to brush his teeth when a hand slid over his shoulder that nearly made him jump.

"Did you find the supplies?" Cecilia asked as she brushed past him.

"Supplies?" he questioned.

"Han went through the houses this afternoon and stocked them with new items," she indicated his toothbrush. "He wanted to make certain we had our own personal items for hygiene."

When she opened the cabinet above the sink, Michael noticed new razors, deodorant, pump soap, tampons, and shave gel along with two new electric toothbrushes. Michael glanced down and noticed the toothbrush he'd been using came out of an open box.

"I hope they didn't use that to clean the toilet," she said and wrinkled her nose.

Michael spit toothpaste everywhere. He dropped the toothbrush and stuck his head under the faucet. He filled his mouth with water and repeatedly rinsed. He heard Cecilia laughing behind him. She knew that Han personally placed those items next to the sink as extras. When Michael caught the image in her mind, he spun around in time to receive a pillow in his face. When he pulled the pillow away, he saw Cecilia lying on the bed in the shadow. He turned off the light over the sink and lay down next to her on the bed. The two teenagers stared at the ceiling.

"Exactly one month ago you walked across a street in Battleford and into my life," she whispered in the dark. "Did you ever think we would end up here… like this?" she wondered.

"It isn't much," he began as he thought about the poor condition of the house. "For all of our power, this is hardly the kind of life I expected to live…"

He turned toward her and waited for a response. Cecilia said nothing. "I suppose… any place with Villi, Su Lin, Zhiwei, Zinian, Chou, Han and Li will feel like home to me," Michael whispered.

"What about me?" she asked. "Where do I fit in?"

"Right here with me," he said and moved closer, "as we build a new town together."

At that moment, a bubble of translucent energy surrounded the couple.

Master Li and Han took the old rusty truck back to their new residence one block south of Main Street. Li used his power to guide the silent vehicle. Moments after they stepped from the truck, it clunked down hard on the pavement when Li released his influence.

As the two men started up the front steps, the front door opened and lights turned on. Han marveled at the elderly man's controlled use of psychic power. He held back and allowed Li to lead the way. When Han chose the house for them, he did so for selfish reasons. The back of the house had a moderately sized living room. Books lined one wall with a fireplace on the opposite outside wall. This room pleased him for aesthetic reasons. A fireplace represented more than a cozy feeling to Han. It stood for the heart of the house that spread not simply heat but contentment. Surprisingly, he discovered those same feelings in the man the others called Master Li. He had not yet grown accustomed to using that title.

"I like the house," Li commented as they crossed the threshold. "Thank you, Han."

Across from the front door, an uncarpeted wooden staircase rose to the second floor where the two main bedrooms faced one another across a common hallway. The second floor also had a smaller third bedroom in the back with the bathroom across from it. Han manually cleaned the house earlier and put out clean linen. Now, he wished he had waited until after the meeting. He did not know about the "clearing" technique. Li saw that Han still had reservations about him.

"I appreciate the way you cleaned the house for us," he told him.

Master Li put his hand on the railing at the bottom of the stairs and turned to Han as he gathered psychic energy. "Do you see the strategic advantages to the Native American's proximity?" he linked. "This community will prosper thanks to everyone efforts."

"…and yours," Han added. "What profit will your efforts bring?" What did he have to lose by confronting Li with his fears? "Your use of power overwhelms me. Why bother to have them do anything? Why not just do what you want and be done with it?"

"I will not be here in the future, Han," he quietly spoke aloud. Li knew why Han confronted him. "My task here is limited. My true calling is elsewhere... off this planet. I can't expect you to understand my purpose. I am here to help. When that time is finished, I must go."

At that moment, Han realized the magnificence of Li and that Li had acted out of selflessness. He did not seek power. Yet he chose to wield his might with delicate precision. With surprising deftness, he watched as Li rose up the stairs with seeming little effort. When Han started to walk up the steps, the wood groaned under his weight. He was not a heavy man by any means. He stopped on the stairs and thought that his approach to this entire change in his life had been a naïve one. He had a lot to learn and that Li was probably the person who could be teach him. He reached out to the village south of town and absorbed energy. When he put his foot down this time, the stairs answered with silence. Han smiled as he made his way to his bedroom.

South of Rollo, a lone shadowy figure appeared in the road. A middle-aged woman walked up the quiet highway toward the sleeping little town. She wore a tattered, wide-brimmed, cloth hat that covered her small, gray-haired head, and drooped down over part of her face. She carried a shotgun in one hand and a Bible in the other. When she arrived in Rollo, she walked onto Main Street, and faced the row of houses. She watched as the last lights went out in each home. She then walked over to the general store and sat on the bench in front. A dim, yellow safety-lamp glowed with enough light for her to read the precious book. From her backpack, she produced an insulated container with hot tea. She sipped the brew and read her favorite passages.

Master Li suddenly sat up in bed. His action forced Han to follow suit. With their bedroom doors wide open, Han stared through the dim light at Li's silhouetted form across the hall.

"What is it?" Han asked. He listened intently. He tried to tap into Li's thoughts, but Master Li would not let him.

"Nothing," Li said as he lay back down on the mattress. "I'm tired Han. I'm going to sleep. Goodnight." Han echoed the sentiment. In the darkness, Li stared up at the ceiling. His mind had not yet settled. "Stuck in a little town on the flat Kansas plain in the middle of nowhere – how boring," he thought. "What could possibly happen to us here?"

Chapter Nine

Chou Lo's historic journey

Early the next morning, Master Li woke refreshed and ready for a new day in the new town. He drank a quick cup of tea and left the house on his own. He wanted to stretch his legs and take in the scope of the task before them. He strolled to the western end of Main Street and looked up the street to where the bizarre woman from last night sat in front of the store. She returned to her home before dawn. Li knew he would have to return to the Comanche Village soon and confront her, but he did not have time today. Too many team members would be off world this morning, which left the group vulnerable.

He saw a figure out jogging around the town's perimeter. He waved and Zhiwei waved back as he trod along at an easy pace.

"Morning, Master Li!" Zhiwei linked.

"Morning, Zhiwei," Li linked back.

He wondered how Zhiwei missed the presence of the woman last night.

"Zhiwei have been as tired as the rest of us," Li thought. "Still, it's odd that he wouldn't feel her presence." He remembered that Han didn't sense her either. "She is a bit of an enigma to me."

Li continued his mental scan around to the other houses. He noted that Su Lin spent the night in her own house. He knew that the tense situation between Villi and Su Lin would not endure. They would need to express their love via their physical attraction. He wondered how long the other men would remain chaste when women from the Comanche village started to invade their little town. He sighed that life presented more complexity than it had yet to reveal.

"So, Chou will be our first ambassador," he thought as he passed the young man's house.

Until this moment, no member of their group had traveled off world to any destination other than Galactic Central for packets of basic advanced knowledge. While Michael communicated with his voice during his nine months in New York, he did not have the sophisticated level of psychic ability he currently possessed. His voice downloaded a great deal of information to his mind, yet it did not connect Michael to any psychic on another world.

The privilege of being the first person from earth to meet another intelligent life form, other than the voices at Galactic Central, fell to Chou Lo.

Chou rose early that morning. After he finished his breakfast, he found a comfortable chair that leaned back. He took in a deep breath, closed his eyes, and opened the portal in his mind. He heard the now familiar metallic voice that guided him after his initial conversion.

"Hello Chou Lo," the voice responded to the contact.

"I wish to make an off world contact today," Chou requested.

"For what purpose," the voice inquired.

"To learn about technology," Chou replied.

"You should speak to the technologists on Ziddis," his voice directed. "They have dedicated their lives to the advancement of technology. You are fortunate Chou. The day rotation of their planet faces Galactic Central at this time. Since this is your first visit, you will speak with a low summoner until your name and reputation rises in rank. That is the custom of Ziddis. You will enter (his) mind and be part of (him)."

Some of the voice's translations were implied as they reached Chou's mind.

"When will this visit happen?" Chou asked. The idea of being inside another person's mind began to unnerve the young man.

"Now," the voice responded.

All at once, Chou felt as if the voice pulled his entire body through space at an alarming rate of speed. He could not see, hear, or feel anything. The physical sensation of lying on the reclining lounger in Rollo vanished in an instant.

His head began to hear thoughts in another language, a strange series of chatters, barks, and hisses. He thought he landed on an animal planet and would have to deal with some bizarre species, when the sounds quickly turned to words in his mind.

"... can loosen them if you turn your tool ninety degrees to the..." the creature thought and then paused in his sentence. "Who is in my mind?" it asked.

"Galactic Central," the voice spoke. "This is a first contact, requesting level seven," Chou heard his voice say. Naturally, the voice had begun to translate what Chou first heard as sounds into something he could easily comprehend as language.

"Is this a formal honor?" he heard the alien reply. The alien's voice seemed personal with intimate emotion attached unlike the cold machine-like Galactic Central voices.

"It is a formal request," his Galactic Central voice indicated, "a first time visit to any planet in the collective," the voice indicated.

"The off-worlder's request is granted," the alien replied. "As a first visit in the Intergalactic Psychic Collective, this is a great honor for me that you have chosen the world of Ziddis. Since you have made us first choice, this will also be noted in the log of logs. Who calls on me?" the alien requested. "Please state your name and the planet of origin."

Rather than answer as Chou tried, the voice still controlled the communication.

"Chou Lo is the name of the new candidate," his voice responded. "He is species human from the newest colony in the collective, Earth."

"Earth?" the alien questioned. "No wonder you phrased your request so carefully," the alien stated with a note of disappointment. "The Earth creatures are primitives! We've seen pictures of them – hairy animals that make violence on each other with crude weapons. They have no technology to share with me. This connection has little value and cannot help my team to rise."

"The Earth person wishes to learn from Ziddis," the voice stated its case. "He considers it a great honor to address and learn from your level, summoner."

"That is why you contacted me," the alien wondered, "to rob Ziddis of our ideas."

"We of Galactic Central invoke rule seven," the voice added, "the exchange of code."

"I see," the alien responded. "Then, according to the collective agreement, I must initiate first contact protocols and prepare to share with Earth as we have shared with others in our collective. Does it know of contractual agreements?"

"What agreements?" Chou started to ask.

"The usual non-interference clause stuff," his voice told him as if it were trivial. "I will explain the details later."

Chou began to wonder how much detail he should know when the alien jumped back into the thought process.

"I will ask the Earth human for a price first, perhaps a new code…" the creature requested.

"Transfer of codes is not acceptable first protocol practice," the Galactic Central voice reminded.

"I am aware of galactic law," the alien cut in. "I will not request the transfer of a forbidden code. Oh, very well…," the alien stated, "begin protocol contact. Come forward, Chou Lo of Earth."

"Need I remind you of courtesy," the voice said in parting. "This is the planet of Li Po Chin."

The alien did not respond as Chou seemed to move out of the darkness and discovered he stood upright. He could see what the alien saw and feel what the creature felt. Where the creature's eyes followed a line of sight, so did Chou's vision.

The creature's eyes glanced down. A strange slender appendage stuck out from its body. Chou realized it must its hand. It ran its long slender grayish fleshy digits over a screen in front of him. The surface of the object not only changed colors, but sounds and other strange audible frequencies alternated. Chou could feel them, too. This time the voices did not interpret what Chou saw. The alien busily moved its "fingers" over the flat surface as symbols, colors and pulses flashed. Chou noted that its flesh was not entirely gray, but had subtle differences in color and texture, just as his skin had.

"This is day one Chou," the alien's voice calmly spoke. "Consider this interaction as your first lesson in dealing with aliens. You must assume that I have eyes as you have. That is how we gather information just as you do. Now observe my (fingers). We tune into our (instruments) as you tune into your (electronics). We use symbols, color, and intensity of current to communicate," the alien explained. "Our technology is tuned to a wide spectrum of frequencies and a variety of energy types. In our most basic device, we convert energy to matter by polarizing atoms into alignment which form a key matrix. We build up additional atoms on those matrixes into larger structures. We increase their density by manipulating a pulsing energy field. This allows us to create solid forms from any energy source including (starlight). Perhaps one day you will have this capacity. For now, we must work with you on a primitive level that you can emulate."

"You seem to know about Earth's current level of technology," Chou thought to it.

"Do not interrupt human," it curtly stated. "I am not here to review or compare our technology to Earth's. Time is precious to us. Observe, learn, and recall all you see and hear. We of the Intergalactic Psychic Collective know of many civilized planets with a variety of technologies. We constantly search new planets for ideas in advancing our level of technology. Once your planet turned sentient, we linked with voices familiar with your level of civilization. We found nothing we could use. By saying this, I cast no aspersions on your species."

"I am here to learn," Chou linked succinctly.

"Then let us begin," the alien stated. "As I mentioned, our most basic instrument is capable of creating physical material out of pure energy or inert matter. This instrument then transforms the by-product into whatever shapes and materials we can imagine. For example, take the transition metal known as aurum, which you call gold. You considered this substance a rare and valuable element on your planet. Your species prizes this malleable metal. Here on Ziddis, we have no rare elements, as we can rearrange atoms into many stable alignment configurations. We can make whatever quantity we need out of the nearly 300 known elements."

"300!" Chou exclaimed. "That's impossible! The periodic table of elements…"

"Your unrefined measuring devices cannot possibly detect all the elements that exist for fractions of seconds," it cut him off. "We can create energy fields that stabilize these elements and keep them in existence for longer periods of time. You will find that our most basic alignment mechanism will be useful to advance your level of technology, especially when you begin to use a device called the (reader)," it said.

Chou understood the alien as his Galactic Central voice translated its language instantaneously, although at times the voice delayed for a fraction of a second in deciding the proper word to use in English.

"I would like to orient you to your new environment," the alien linked and made a sweeping gesture. "Presently, you are in my home," it stated. "You will travel with me, as I must arrive at my work station today. My work cycle begins soon. The way we travel will seem disconcerting to your sense of movement, human. Therefore, you should prepare."

The alien stood up, which made the floor move away at an alarming rate. Chou estimated the alien must be quite tall. It walked over to a garment on the wall and attached it around its middle. Its appendage or arm reached out and touched the wall. Judging from the narrow opening that appeared, the alien must be slender, too.

"My (living space) is on the fringe of the city, since I am (less of stature). Only those of higher rank may live near the center. That will change as my position rises," the alien told him with a hint of pride.

Chou was not certain why the creatures grew so tall. He knew nothing of Ziddis or its planetary system. He would have to determine these details later from his voice.

"I am facing the (wild jungle)," it said. "Note the boundary line," it gestured.

The boundary line to which the creature referred consisted of a wide wall, yet not too high. Beyond that, he noted a wide, deep, mote-like pit and a tall wicked fence covered with sharp spikes beyond that. No crawling creature could either jump or cross such a barrier. He also noted an occasional white spark in the air. He assumed a force field of some kind existed to deal with flying creatures. Chou saw a vast array of densely growing plants that stretched out far beyond the specific outline of the city. This area seemed as untamed as the city was specifically organized – a clear demarcation between the two.

While the jungle had an enormous variety of plants with lush dark green foliage, the flowers glowed around their edges with bluish-purple light. The sky above the creature's head appeared yellow near the horizon yet pinkish directly overhead. Chou noted that despite the daylight, he saw more than one visible star in the sky with one larger star nearby, similar to Earth's sun.

"You wonder about the color of the atmosphere," the alien interrupted his line of thought. "My eyes perceive different spectra of light than yours do. Although our molecules share a common origin, creatures develop differently on other planets. I can see partly into the ultraviolet range, which you cannot," it stated. "Oddly, the chemical composition our atmosphere is very similar to Earth's, a combination of nitrogen and oxygen endemic to the development of our species."

It paused in its deliberations and moved toward a strange white platform that glowed violet around its edges. This structure varied in that its material took on a glow that other structures did not. That distinction made it stand out.

"This place is where I travel to the (city)," the alien stated. "We live in organized cities just as you do. Our laws and codes do not permit us to travel into the (country). It is a very deadly place. I must go to (Techno-World) – the company responsible for all technology on my planet. Our business creates devices to sell for profit, our business for about ten thousand of your earth years."

"Ten thousand years!" Chou thought.

"Silence please," the creature insisted. "I must concentrate."

The creature moved into the travel station not far from his living quarters. He carefully stepped on one of several small devices lined up in a row. Chou could see three other creatures on similar devices before him, waiting for their turn. He felt something grab the creature's lower extremities.

"Travel on Ziddis can be disconcerting," Chou's voice privately instructed. "If you experience nausea, I can pull you out."

Suddenly, the being flew up into the sky on what appeared to be a guide wire that disappeared. Chou noticed that the catapult device timed the release so precisely that they easily mixed into a constantly moving formation. During the initial launch, the alien narrowly avoided thousands of other flying beings of varying height and description. Nearly every creature possessed the same features – tall, thin, grayish-skin with a head, arms and legs. Each was dressed in some flimsy colorful outfit that flapped in the breeze.

When their riding device began to lose altitude, another rotating catapult grabbed them – along with everyone else in front of them – and threw the creature's machine further along its intended course. Occasionally, another rapidly descending arm reached out and snatched someone out of line, which diverted them onto an alternative path. Chou also noticed that certain colors indicated rank, as some aliens rode in large machines with additional amenities that flew at higher altitudes. These creatures wore sparkling clothes.

"You wear clothes to distinguish your rank?" Chou questioned.

"Very good human, you observe correctly," the alien noted. "We only wear coverings when we go outside. Once we enter a structure, we discard them. We determine rank by other means inside the office."

"You must lack modesty," Chou concluded.

"Is this a query into the culture of our mating rituals, or do you seek knowledge of technology human?" the alien asked Chou point blank.

"Sorry," Chou apologized. "I am not aware of what I may or may not address," he stated.

"Your act of humility is not required," the alien replied. "Confusion between cultures is acceptable during the first few visits to Ziddis. After that, your host may consider it rude and terminate your connection. Be warned Earthling. Do not question the social practices of an alien culture if you wish learn a particular subject. Besides, clothes do not offer our bodies protection as they do on your world. The (people) in our (cities) are not exposed to hazards such as insects, communicable diseases, or changes in weather as your world has."

"Understood," Chou replied.

Chou took in an expansive view of the city as they flew along. He saw an enormously complex yet finite city with extremely tall buildings that not only went up very high, but also sunk deep down into the planet. These were supported by the largest, most elaborate system of crossing bridges he had ever seen. Great canyons opened into the planet's interior. Arching clear tracks held sky trains that moved hundreds of the tall creatures into the highest structures. Some of these "trains" rose from the city's depths and rushed upwards toward the surface at tremendous speed. Chou noticed that they stopped at various levels and let out hundreds of passengers while taking on as many.

Individual flyers, such as the one he rode, encountered congestion as they entered the city center. The alien's device moved onto a guide that slowed his progress. Chou noticed rows of aliens who stood and waited to move into a variety of buildings. Each alien, whether large or small (he surmised the shorter ones as children) had a device on its forearm that the citizens of Ziddis used for diversion or work. Chou noticed thousands interact with these screens as they slowly advanced.

"This happens when stocking days coincide with work days," it spoke with a saddened tone. Chou discovered that waiting to the creatures of Ziddis represented a terrible waste of their precious time. Before he could question their longevity, it continued. "In case you haven't noticed, this form of travel is not the best way to move around the city. Today, I am fortunate. We will enter the work building directly without waiting in line. This is low census day, when most of us do not work. I must address presentation issues with my team. Therefore, I must work until the problems are fixed. I am trying to look at everything for your benefit."

Chou expressed his gratitude to the creature and felt odd with its civil and calm psychic interaction, which barely possessed any attached emotion. After searching its mind, Chou discovered the creature was a male of his species.

A huge spherical building with hundreds of floors similar to the rings of Saturn appeared before them. The colorful semi-transparent rings on the outside were actually levels that rose and fell through other levels. Nearly every rail guide and tram-path in this area focused on this gigantic central structure.

"Wow!" Chou declared as he took in the fantastic sight. "I've never seen anything so beautiful or complex!"

"Behold Earth-creature; this is (Techno-World's) headquarters. Of all the cities on Ziddis, none is like this one. It is entirely devoted to the development of new technology. From this place, all the creatures of Ziddis benefit," he proudly stated.

Chou could only appreciate the enormous scale for a matter of seconds as they flew head long at breakneck speed toward one of many tall slender slits in its side. A machine whisked off the alien's clothes as he slid through the narrow long opening. The male creature reached up and grabbed a variety of items before it flew out into the huge open interior.

The creature, still on its platform, flew through the most amazing world Chou ever witnessed. Different floors, located as rings around the interior, gradually rotated up and down. Each floor was transparent with changing color to identify rank. Brighter colors rose toward the top, while darkening or fading colors fell toward the bottom. Some beings walked between floors by moving to permanent structures inside the central shaft system.

On each floor similar creatures worked on a variety of products. As these products entered the market place and sold, the team rose in height and prosperity. As products sold less, that team's floor fell and caused those workers to double their efforts to improve their products and make their floor rise. When a floor went up, each worker's salary went up with the opposite also true.

Chou discovered that production chiefs along with department managers dwelled on permanent structures in the middle. They did not have preferences. They simply wanted all products to sell. They did not care who brought them new inventions as long as they had market potential.

"Management," the being pointed out as he passed one station. "You don't want one of those jobs."

"Why not?" Chou asked.

"They have lower risk, but less profit," the alien explained. "Managers can never achieve rank or live in the city center. I've made ten times what my managers have made. I've also lost profit at times, mostly I've done well. I am currently on the red floor. We are rising. We should make level six soon. When our team achieves yellow level five, I can move back to the city center. I very busy today. This connection with Earth will not profit me. I cannot profitably contribute to my team unless I break contact."

"I will terminate," Chou suggested and he started to withdraw.

"As a first contact, I will not allow you to discontinue without potential profit sharing. That would bring shame on my position," the alien linked. "I can also make profit by a rise in diplomatic status, which I can share with my level. Status is not contingent on sales but also on prestige and ideas. Contact with Earth may have potential future value. The market will determine that with time," the alien explained. "Simply by interacting with you, I will raise my team's potential. In appreciation of this honor, I will reward you with a special (business contract)."

"Can anyone rise in status?" Chou asked before the alien moved on.

"Of course, what kind of system would not allow that?" he stated.

"I can think of several," Chou thought back.

"We must go to the (Hall of History)," it said.

Its platform zoomed past the interior and lashed upon another guide wire. The creature then entered another slit that turned into a very long series of passages before he emerged into a large open area with many devices on display, similar to museums on Earth. This time the platform slowed down and remained attached to a guide.

"A (business contract) consists of sharing information or products to the mutual benefit of both parties," the Ziddis being said as they moved along. Chou marveled at thousands of devices as they moved through the multileveled structure. "This is our (history museum)," the alien informed him. "I am taking you to our very first and most important device – one that changed our world and has changed many others too. Intergalactic code allows us to share the knowledge in regards to this basic device, providing..."

"Providing?" Chou interrupted.

"We will not simply hand over advanced technology to a society not prepared to understand it, Chou," the being stated. "If you can create a similar device on your world with your level of technology, then you belong in the advanced group. Then you may transmit complex codes to other worlds in the collective. The Intergalactic Psychic Collective codifies everything in the universe by its structure and purpose, whether it is a device or a living object. If you fail to produce this device, then according to Galactic Law, we cannot share our advanced technology with Earth."

With all the restraint he could muster, Chou kept his thoughts clear. He held back any feelings or opinionated thoughts in response to the alien's obviously brusque remarks.

One device stood out alone at the very end of this incredible room. The creature slowed down until it stopped before a large display case.

"This is $#*%^@#&!" it said. It gestured toward a cubical representative model.

The symbolic speech the creature used to describe the device came through as gibberish to Chou's mind. The Galactic Central voice intervened.

"Since this is your first visit to Ziddis, I must explain," his voice privately broke in. "The device does not have a name that corresponds with anything on Earth or in the English language. I give you permission to add this new name to the Galactic Earth dictionary."

"What does it do?" Chou asked his host.

"It uses a concentrated, dynamic, electromagnetic energy field to re-align atoms into any form or configuration. A reader device can input code data to its stasis field. The interior field manipulates inert material and rapidly creates molecular matrixes controlled by exterior forces on the stabilized field. The result resembles any structure or element, including organic molecules," the creature explained. "This device is considered the core to advanced technology on any planet in our collective. Without this device, Earth may not send, receive, or share code with other planets in the collective.

"I see," Chou replied as he considered the device's accomplishments. "Duplicator sounds dumb," he thought. "Someone already took the name of replicator," he added. "I would call it the Ziddis, only I believe that would lead to confusion," he rambled. He recalled a piece of history in the world of electronics, one made by a man who was part scientist and part dreamer. "How would it be if we call it the *fusor* as a tribute to good ole Farnsworth?"

"What is a Farnsworth?" the voice asked.

"Not what, voice, in this case, whom – Philo Farnsworth helped to invent television," Chou explained. "He also conceived of a theoretical mechanism for nuclear fusion. I'm certain this alien device would most certainly have fascinated the scientist. Therefore, as a tribute to his genius, we'll call this new device the fusor in his honor."

"As you have indicated, Chou," his voice responded. "Henceforth we shall translate the name of the technology in question as a fusor. You may continue your contact," the voice linked. It resumed the two-way communication.

"Chou?" the alien called out.

"I apologize for the interruption," Chou replied.

"I assume Galactic Central gave you private instruction?" the creature asked.

"Yes," Chou replied. "It had a problem with naming the object."

"I see," the alien said. It understood his dilemma. "I must have used a term it could not translate into your language. They do that sometimes, very frustrating. At any rate, this is the (fusor)," he linked to Chou and gestured toward the large cubic shape. "At its heart is a special energy field which we call a stasis field. With it you can manipulate inert atoms fed through this chute," the alien pointed out. "Your fusor will be different when you attempt to make your own, due to the elemental formulas that you must employ to achieve the same effect."

"Different?" Chou questioned. "What about radiation leakage?"

"That will be contained in a stable field," the alien told him. "If you can keep the field stable, that is. Otherwise, some risk is possible."

Chou thought a basement would work best. If this device did leak radiation, the thickness of the surrounding ground should help stop gamma radiation from harming others in Rollo. His exposure was another matter. He would need to address the safety issues before he instituted such a powerful open field.

"You do not need containment," the alien replied to his thoughts.

"I'm sorry, I didn't realize…" he began.

"No need," the alien quickly cut him off. "I understand your concerns. Radiation will not leak because the field is contained within this application. The structure forms the external forces that create the internal field. You'll see once we start your downloads. This is only a scale model," the alien told him. "Using Earth's current level of technology, you can duplicate this device in approximately two decades of your time, if you are diligent and work steadily. Do you have many assistants?" he asked.

"Two decades!" Chou responded.

"We do not assume you have the mental capacity to remain focused long enough to complete the task," the alien threw at him. "Of course, our team of scientists accomplished this feat in less than one solar cycle (a year). We do not expect Earth has an equal intellectual ability."

Chou struggled to keep his composure despite the insults.

"Before you begin, you must receive (multiple downloads) from Galactic Central on the creation and use of (minus one hundred twenty-two degree Celsius superconductors), how to maximize power generation, electromagnetic spectrum manipulation through external force fields, stabilizing power fluctuations, microburst magnum capacitors, applying field alterations through rapid micro-switches, and finally how to create a stable (stasis field)."

"I could use computer chips to control micro bursts," Chou stated.

"No computer chip you currently possess has the capacity to carry such heavy loads of electrical current," the alien told him. "Perhaps you can invent a new one," the alien related. "I will arrange for your information relay in a few moments. This is the end of my participation in your first contact. I must ask as a matter of diplomacy... did you (enjoy) your visit to Ziddis?" the male creature asked.

"I enjoyed Ziddis," Chou replied and added, "and I appreciate your help."

"A (nice feeling) to meet you Chou," the alien told him. "May we meet on a higher level. Now, here is your first of many (downloads)."

An hour later when Chou woke from his instructive bombardment, he noticed Master Li sitting in the shadows nearby.

"Master Li?" Chou asked as he rubbed his eyes and stretched his limbs. "What are you doing here?"

The elderly man did not move. He linked his thoughts and feelings instead.

"Do you realize your importance in history Chou Lo, eager student from China?" Li asked him. "You are the very first person from the planet Earth to speak with an alien species and make first contact," he quietly linked. "I would say you did well, Chou," he said, rising. "This is only one of over a hundred intelligent worlds, which are part of the collective."

Chou leaned up on one elbow. His eyes filled with water as the enormity and gravity of the moment sank in. He gazed up at Master Li.

"Were you watching over me?" Chou asked him.

"I wanted to make certain they treated you kindly on Ziddis," Li told him. "The creatures on Ziddis are brilliant technologists but lousy conversationalists!" he exclaimed with a raised eyebrow. "By the way, I can't wait to see what a fusor does... when you build it."

"Oh, Master Li," the young man struggled to speak. Tears streamed down his face. "I know so much about everything. You were right when you tried to explain it to me that first day in the hotel. No one on the planet knows what

I know about physics, mathematics, chemistry… I feel I know everything! You have fulfilled all my hopes. What I knew about technology a few hours ago pales to what I know now," Chou said as he wiped off his face. "I owe you my life."

"Just think what you'll know by next week," Master Li said while he moved toward the door, "and how you'll feel then! Welcome to your future, Chou Lo, technologist extraordinaire!" Li smiled as he left Chou to ponder applications for his new level of knowledge.

Chapter Ten

A Highway to the Stars

Only three days passed since their arrival and Chou took his first journey yesterday. During that time, the team worked long, hard hours to make this new community a success. Michael urged everyone to take advantage of this opportunity. As the group met that evening inside his home, he encouraged everyone to travel the cosmos. While Chou had visited a planet, the others simply took downloads to increase their mental capacity and understanding. Michael wanted more from the group.

"Stay home," he suggested, "explore other worlds via Galactic Central. Master Li and I will monitor Rollo."

"What about you?" Han asked Michael. "Why don't you go off world?"

"I have plenty to do Han," Michael replied. "I'll take some trips later. For now, Master Li and I would like the group to raise its knowledge levels and goals. Go to other planets. Learn from them. Return enlightened with new ideas, new projects, and new visions to share with the rest of us," he told them. "Chou's journey to Ziddis is the perfect example of what I had in mind. When he shared his experience with us, we saw a planet filled with technological wonders."

"Not my idea of paradise," Zinian muttered under his breath. "When you come across the planet of buxom women, let me know," he spoke up.

Zhiwei chuckled. Even Michael smiled. However, as their official leader, he continued with his unflinching inspirational rhetoric.

"I encourage you to explore other worlds," he added. "Let their wisdom become our wisdom."

"Boosting morale I see," Master Li privately linked to Michael as the tall young man sat down next to Cecilia. Their hands entwined by their side. "Good job, Michael."

Michael leaned over to Villi.

"You've been strangely silent of late," he privately wondered about his friend.

"Gets rather lonely out at the barn, away from everyone else," Villi grunted in a private link. He was still envious over Michael's present living arrangement. Michael sensed his resentment.

"Have you and Su Lin..." Michael kept his link private.

"Not yet..." Villi privately linked back. He cut Michael off. He did not want to reveal too much of his envy. Villi once told Michael that he found "plenty of action around the university." Having to mind his manners around Master Li made Villi feel as if he were back in middle school.

"I didn't mean to pry..." Michael linked back.

"Are we not psychics? If you prick us, do we not bleed?" Villi parodied the famous Shakespearian phrase.

Michael half-smiled because he understood his friend's frustration.

"I don't believe that you wish to be pricked," Michael quickly shot back.

This time the Russian turned to Michael and smiled broadly. His friend's humor lifted his depressed spirits, albeit temporarily.

Su Lin and Cecilia scowled at the two men. The women suspected that they were the subject of their private blocked discussion. Cecilia leaned closer to her friend.

"They're probably talking about sex," she linked to her friend as to why their boyfriends were so secretive.

"That's how it is with all men," Su Lin linked back. "Women never think about sex that much..." she linked, then glanced over at Cecilia.

Both women burst out laughing which made Michael and Villi wonder what they were linking. Their sudden laughter also made Zinian and Zhiwei jump. The two young friends had discussed the young Native American females they spied at the village south of town. Han felt left out of every conversation. He sat alone and thought about where he would like go for his first journey.

Chou seemed the most content in the group. He was pleased with his first contact, his progress, and his newly acquired level of knowledge to the point where pride overtook his accomplishment.

"Perhaps you may not find a planet as technologically fantastic as Ziddis," Li told the group. "Still, I want you to know that each planet holds its own mystery, beauty, and surprises. The collective contains a wide variety of civilizations. Go to your voices… they can help guide you," he encourage.

Chou's over-exuberance worried Li. He wondered about the implications involved in placing such a heavy burden on Chou's shoulders. The young man was nineteen-years-old with hardly a year away from home. Li felt he did not have enough experience to create something as complex as the fusor. Granted, Chou expanded his general knowledge after his journey to Ziddis – more knowledge than any university professor on the planet possessed. Yet, this fusor took their community into areas none of them ever considered. Its affects had the potential to reach far beyond the borders of Rollo. Li pondered this and other possibilities as he watched and listened to all of their thoughts.

At the end of the meeting, Chou handed Michael a long shopping list that the group's leader promised he would somehow obtain for his friend. When Michael looked over the list, he realized that many items would be difficult to locate.

"Chou, some of these things may take me days, if not weeks to provide," he told eager young man. "I mean… superconducting magnets made from gallium ceramics, high-speed max-current isolated microcircuits, high density compressors, insulated cooling blankets, high torque motors, tanks of liquid nitrogen, tanks of liquid oxygen, two thousand meters of four centimeter diameter copper tubing, six hundred meters of seven-gauge gold wire, amphorous metal beams, six portable high-output electrical generators… nuclear fission material? Chou, this is not exactly your every day shopping list. I'll need a lab to create some of these items!"

"Can you get them or not, Michael?" Chou asked with a pleading tone. "I can't start on the fusor without them… these components are critical to its success…" he said.

Michael thought that the tone Chou broadcast bordered on fanaticism.

"I'll see what I can do," he replied.

The group's organizer gave out his usual exasperated sigh and thought he would put his voice on the task right after the meeting. Perhaps, with the help of Master Li he could remotely manipulate a few minds to create some of the stuff. Chou's thoughts, however, rambled on as if he was speaking to someone. It reminded Michael how he must have appeared to others in his youth. Chou walked past the rest of the group and headed over to his house. Zinian hand signaled to Michael that he would follow Chou. Michael tried to end the meeting on a high note.

"If Chou can have that kind of experience, imagine what can happen to the rest of us when we explore Galactic Central with an open mind?" he linked to the others.

"Yes, we'll all be mumbling idiots," Zinian linked to Zhiwei.

Michael's platitudes rang hollow with Cecilia and Su Lin. They noticed the change in Chou as did Zinian and Zhiwei. Michael had other considerations on his mind than Chou's mental state. However, Zinian had grown to appreciate Chou's contributions to the group.

"Whether Michael wants it or not, I'm watching out for that geek," he said privately to his friend, Zhiwei.

He and Zhiwei followed Chou back to his house from the meeting. Along the way, the two privately discussed how Chou had changed since his encounter yesterday with Ziddis. Zinian seemed more concerned than Zhiwei was. He noticed that Chou lost his cheerful joking attitude and seemed too focused on adapting this alien technology. It worried the big Chinese man. He had grown to like Chou and felt like a big brother who looked out for a younger sibling, despite the fact that Chou was actually a year older.

"What would happen if Chou created a chain reaction from his fusor with so much destructive force, it destroyed America," he commented.

Zhiwei was too tired to counter his large friend. He broke away and went to his house. As Zinian headed over to his house, he decided it was in the best interest of the group to keep his thoughts focused on Chou during the day and to monitor the young man's progress as he tried to build this fusor. Zinian stopped before his front door before he opened it.

"What if he actually builds the thing and it works?" he questioned. His mind began to consider the possibilities of the fusor's applications. "If Chou was correct about what the fusor could accomplish, I could completely remake Rollo." He wondered how he would reshape Rollo if he had such a tool at his disposal. A new plan began to form in his mind.

After the meeting, Michael went into another room to speak privately with Li. He sought the sage's advice on a range of topics. The two men discussed some of the problems and solutions to obtaining items on Chou's list and other difficulties present in the community. By the time he retired to his bedroom about an hour later, he found Cecilia asleep.

The following morning, Michael scanned the community to check on his friends. He first looked in on Villi. The big Russian decided to take the morning off to explore other worlds. He wanted to learn the mechanics of all engines, including many not of earth that other species could reveal to him. He opened a portal to his voice.

"Good morning!" he linked in his casual fashion. "I'd like to…"

"Visit the planet of buxom women," his voice linked in.

Villi chuckled. "Not fair…" he linked back. "I had no idea your species knew humor. You've been speaking with Michael."

"As your community leader, he does link with other Earth voices," Villi's Galactic Central voice responded.

"I was not aware of that," Villi linked back. "Actually, instead of visiting other planets, I would like to expand my practical knowledge and boost my understanding of physics, mathematics, and possibly mechanical engineering, too if you can squeeze it in," he put to his voice.

"Perhaps you could review airplane mechanics, jet engine assembly, aerodynamics, flight control, automobile engines, that sort of thing?" the voice suggested.

"You read my mind," Villi put to his voice.

"I am certainly glad we share a sense of humor, Villi," his voice stated.

"I'm glad you understand it!" Villi shot back. "So, how about bringing up my learning curve," he requested.

"Easily done," the voice told him. "Relax. Your lessons will start in a moment."

In a relatively short time, Villi returned to consciousness from his intelligence upgrade. He possessed total proficiency in the repair and building of aircraft or automobile engines. In fact, Villi could assemble or repair any engine that produced power, including electrical engines. The voice also instilled knowledge that utilized their support systems. Villi practically sprinted out to the barn, eager to start applying what he learned.

After the download, Michael sensed Villi's exuberance. He was glad that the community's top mechanic took the time to achieve some personal satisfaction by developing his mental prowess. Villi's recollections of his university days impressed Michael. He admired the way his friend quickly adapted new information into knowledgeable applications.

"Perhaps this will keep his mind off sex," he thought, "at least, for a while."

Michael continued his rounds. He checked on Su Lin's Galactic Central contact. She expressed interest in expanding her level of general knowledge, since she strived for an avocation in teaching. Her voice transported Su Lin to the vast libraries on Artane, the most extensive collection of knowledge in the universe. The libraries of Artane derived information from every world that participated in the Intergalactic Psychic Collective.

Satisfied with those two contacts, Michael pressed on to the next Rollo psychic. Architects on three worlds privately instructed Zinian on the applied uses of materials based on Earth's gravitation. His lessons included an extensive catalogue of techniques in structural engineering that showed Zinian how to create a building as both a function of structure and art.

Michael noted that Zhiwei discovered a new world meticulously concerned with maintaining various levels of security. By connecting him to these worlds, his voice addressed Zhiwei's concerns to monitor and maintain the safety of the Rollo group.

With everyone happily busy off-world, Michael finally turned his attention to Cecilia. She had a late start this morning after she took the time to make some designs for a medical clinic. She prepared a place to lie down and relax after breakfast. Michael already knew her destination, although Cecilia did not. He checked with his mentor last before he looked in on his future wife.

Over at Master Li's house, the venerable psychic assured Han that he would not need him today for security. Han then interacted with GC to find a world suitable for his first visit. Michael, having quickly scanned the town's residences, expressed his pleasure to Master Li that the group engaged in constructive activity.

"Everyone is away," Michael informed him.

"Good," Master Li responded, "glad to see them busy."

"I'll stop by their houses with food and drinks later," Michael linked to Li. "First, I have one final person to help settle."

"This will be a most interesting journey," Li noted.

Michael turned his attention to Cecilia. He hoped to fulfill a promise he made to her a long time ago. He put Cecilia's career on the fast track by contacting Galactic Central prior to her first off-world visit. He requested that her voice assist the young Canadian become a physician. Cecilia had only begun to relax when Michael walked in the front door and headed to the kitchen instead of their bedroom, where she lay on the bed. She could sense him below.

"I'm here for tea," he linked to her. "Begin your link to Galactic Central," he told her. "I'll monitor your progress as I make rounds today."

Without a responding thought, Cecilia closed her eyes and opened her portal. Her voice immediately spoke via the conduit that made such energy transfers possible.

"You wish to expand your knowledge of medicine, am I correct, Cecilia?" her voice responded.

"I could never hide anything from you," she linked.

"Anticipating this moment," it tactfully stated, "I approached several worlds where this practice has reached a zenith. We feel you should attend the medical school on Tegixil, considered the finest in the collective. It is located in the community of Sverchun. The instructor, Professor Tsi, awaits your arrival. The class is set to begin any moment."

This news flustered Cecilia's response. She hated to be late for anything.

"It's the first day of class and I'm already late for the start of her lecture?" Cecilia squeaked. "Take me there at once. I must apologize to Professor Tsi."

"No formal apology will be necessary. Every psychic has time differentials, since no two planets are the same size with the same rotational rates. Time is measured differently throughout the cosmos, which can vary from system to system."

"You're confusing me," Cecilia countered. "I'm not ready to make an analysis of time differentials. Please take me to… Tagstell?"

"Tegixil," the voice corrected. "You are now on Tegixil."

When a psychic arrives on another planet via someone else's mind, the feeling is disconcerting. Chou could easily attest from his first experience. Hearing one's thoughts intermingle with another creature's thoughts, and trying to clarify them, troubled Chou from the start. It took him several minutes to adjust.

Cecilia's journey differed greatly from Chou's. She did not arrive inside the head of another psychic. She fell like a thud into darkness. Her thoughts bounced around an empty vessel as if the voices stuck her inside an echo chamber.

"Wait… I can't orient…help!" she cried. The initial experience made Cecilia want to leave before she started.

"You must focus your psychic energy on vision or you will go mad inside your shell… human," a feminine voice of considerable power advised. The voice spoke to her aloud.

"Vision?" Cecilia questioned. Her thoughts only echoed. As she tried to concentrate, the panic she felt initially began to subside. "I could hear that voice…" she reasoned when she started to feel dizzy. She suddenly felt a strong urge. "Uuuhhhh!" she sucked in a deep breath. "I can breathe!" she thought.

Cecilia did not anticipate this level of realism. She extended her arms. Her hands felt something solid in front of her. She opened her eyes and blinked. Bright light shone through her fluttering eyelashes as she attempted to orient her vision. She glanced down and saw a table within the grasp of her trembling hands… human hands.

"Steady," she thought. "This is very different from Chou's experience."

She cleared her throat and blinked her eyes once more. She moved her head to gather in a wider view. To her astonishment, she discovered that she sat in the middle of a large sloping auditorium that curved off to her right and left. She saw hundreds if not a thousand of tables/desks similar to hers. All kinds of creatures sat behind them. Some rested on different seating devices, while others were contained within artificial environments wrapped around them. She took in another deep breath of air. She could feel her bottom resting on a chair beneath her. She happened to glance down and discovered…

"My word! I'm naked!" she cried. She stood up and struggled to cover her bare flesh with her hands.

"Do not be alarmed," the feminine-sounding voice spoke once more. "Please sit down." It startled Cecilia that the feminine voice spoke in English. "None of us are clothed. We are presented as we are as a species. That is because we will study each other's anatomy and physiology. During one class we will look at your shell too, human."

The thought of a thousand other alien creatures staring at her naked body unsettled Cecilia to say the very least. She did not scream but she felt like it. Yet, no one seemed to notice or even care about her appearance – not even the creatures closest to her. In fact, they behaved as if she were not there at all.

"I'm sorry for the disruption," Cecilia said apologetically. "I feel rather exposed."

She resumed her seat while she nervously glanced around. Still, she noticed that no other creature ever looked directly at her. They remained focused forward toward the great stage at the bottom of the large amphitheater-style auditorium.

She tried to focus her new eyes in the same direction. A beautiful creature stood on an elevated platform with several light sources aimed on her brilliant iridescent scales that defied description. She had the relative shape of a human being with no visible sign of sex, although Cecilia suspect she was female. Her long flowing scales seemed to float and undulate as she moved as if she were in water. Her golden eyes glistened in the bright light as she lifted her head and looked up toward Cecilia.

"That is not your body, human," the creature spoke. This time, her thoughts leapt into Cecilia's mind. "After we examined the DNA structure of your species, we created that shell for you to inhabit. It has no memory of living. It is a construction made for your comfort. It never had a thought until the moment you occupied its brain. You brought your memories and your abilities with you. When you leave, it will return to its former state. It is a biological construction that we call a shell. It is your shell, which we provided for your use."

Cecilia ran her hands over the body of a rather voluptuous woman. While her Earthly body had curves, this woman had grossly accentuated curves.

"While you are here, you must possess a body," the feminine instructor's voice continued. "This is a classroom, not some random visit to another planet. We do not allow psychics to occupy the mind of others in the classroom. That would be considered cheating," she firmly spoke. "You will adjust to the body in time. If you are curious about your appearance, your table contains a large mirror, normally used for dissection. Use your mind to open your control center and extract the mirror. You can view your shell if you feel the need."

The professor resumed her lecture. She addressed the large gathering of a thousand different creatures.

"Since the human from Earth, Cecilia Beaton, is the last to arrive, we shall begin your first lecture," the creature stated. She moved toward a covered table. "You may start your recording devices if you need to recall this lecture for later reference."

"How do I…" Cecilia started to question.

The moment the thought sprung into her head, her table lit up in one area and displayed controls with strange symbols at first. The symbols quickly reverted to English letters. One said, "Devices." She touched the panel and something pierced her skin. A microscopic-sized needle shot up from the table and then withdrew after it poked her skin.

"Ow!" Cecilia responded.

"Species, human," her table spoke, "Identified subject occupying shell's brain as Cecilia Beaton, medical student from the planet Earth. Day one. Proceed."

Uncertain what would poke her next she timidly reached out again. This time a column of choices lit up with colors that made sense to her. She touched the red "record" button. It turned green.

"Recording lecture for future reference, day one. Proceed," the table said.

She touched a second tab labeled "secondary devices" that sent out a long list with tabs, one marked "dissecting mirror."

Meanwhile, the scaly professor continued her lecture.

"You wish to be healers on your planets," she spoke to the gathering, "commendable and noble. On this first day, you will understand that where you find intelligence, you will also find complexity. You are the flowers of the universe, each unique, special, and beautiful. Your planets – spread throughout the cosmos – have produced highly intelligent creatures capable of crossing the gulf of space via Galactic Central. You arrived here to learn the ancient art of healing. Together, we shall discover how to maintain optimal health. The first lesson is meant to impress upon you the importance of both life… and death," she said.

She yanked back a cover sheet to reveal the fleshy carcass of a deceased creature. This made the class collectively gasp including Cecilia.

The Canadian girl chose this moment to glance down at the mirror that rose out of the table. As she adjusted the mirror's angle, she saw a rather strange being in the reflection. She had an oval face with big round blue eyes, puffy lips, high pink cheekbones and broad shoulders. She had a large head of curly, bright, blonde hair that flowed down her back. Going further down the body, she noticed large, round, perky breasts that stuck out without any droop, as if they defied gravity. She had a narrow waist with long slender muscular legs. She flexed her trim arms.

"Gross! Some man designed this woman," she thought as she moved closer to the mirror. "My lips and breasts are much too big," she commented. She shook her head in disapproval. "How is my..." she thought and twisted to see her behind. She saw a round, tight, bubble butt, which made her giggle. "All of my clothes would have to be tailored. I couldn't wear anything off the rack with this curvy body," she thought.

Cecilia lowered the mirror and faced forward just as Professor Tsi picked up an instrument while she moved closer to the bluish corpse. The professor lifted a limp appendage with one of her fin-like arms that had articulating digits at the end. Those digits grasped the device she held.

"When you perform surgery," she instructed, "you will use this instrument more than any sort of crude device on your planet. This is the most sophisticated form of invasive technology on any planet, including any found on Ziddis. They may have constructed this device, but we hold the rights to its design," she smiled.

As she moved the instrument toward the creature's flesh, a white screen opened in the air just above the instrument. A large screen appeared over the professor's stage that drew most of the creatures' attention upward.

Out of the desk in front of each student, a hand held device appeared, similar to the one the professor held. As Cecilia took hold of hers, the physical sensation of grasping something seemed very real to her. The light-weight device immediately melded with her hand, which made it very easy to hold. She noticed a similar tool appeared for the other creatures over their tables with slight variations to fit their particular species. Her desktop opened again and this time, a part of the creature identical to the one that Professor Tsi examined, appeared to take shape.

"Make your first incision here," Tsi instructed. "Hold your tool thus," she angled it. "This will give its sensors time to scan your subject before you enter."

A red dot on her table flashed over a part of the specimen. Cecilia advanced the instrument and held it as Professor Tsi did. As she performed this movement, the device carefully but rapidly extended hundreds of tiny wires that created a crevice between cells. The wires separated the skin until it created a narrow slit like opening. The wires worked with amazing speed. Cecilia also noted that due to its delicate nature, no anesthesia was necessary. Nor did the device require skin prep since the sterile probes did not bring bacteria from the exterior to the interior. Several tiny snake-like instruments entered the alien's appendage. A small bright screen hovered in the air, which gave Cecilia a view inside the creature's corpse. When the tiny wires withdrew, the skin on the outside closed around the telescoping probes that continued to snake inside the body.

For a second, Cecilia's hand shook when she realized that her thoughts controlled the instrument.

"Stay focused, Cecilia," the professor's voice came through. "How is your shell operating?" she asked.

"My shell… we call them bodies, professor," Cecilia responded. "My body is working as it should, I suppose."

She felt the presence of the professor start to withdraw, when she spoke up.

"Do all of my body functions… work normally?" she wondered.

"Yes, it is a normal human… body," the professor told her. "It only lacks a mind of experiences. Otherwise it functions as your body does on earth."

"Then I will need nutrition to maintain my brain function," Cecilia said uneasily.

"That will not be necessary," the professor informed her. "To activate the control for nutritional supplements, simply think about what you need, and it will perform that function. Should your body require sustenance; the mechanism will provide it. Should you need to eliminate wastes; the mechanism can perform that function as well. Treat your shell… your body well, Cecilia. Later, we will dissect it," the professor said. She linked with such perfunctory frankness that it startled the young girl.

"You're going to kill me?" Cecilia wondered.

"That body is not you, nor is it anyone else," the professor explained. "It is not a person. It is a construction and nothing else. It has no purpose, no family, nor does it think. It is a shell… merely a body and nothing more. Do not think of it as a person," Professor Tsi told her. "Besides, you will not be in the sh… body when we perform surgery and later dissect it. You will be in my mind. That lesson will be for you alone."

"Oh, I see," Cecilia responded. "I must learn to adjust as Chou did," she thought and swallowed hard on the news that this body would later be the subject of dissection. "Nutrition," she thought. She watched with captivating terror as a protruding snake emerged from the side of the table. Its sharp pointed end sought out a large vein in her arm. She closed her eyes and braced for the impact. When the point stabbed her arm, she felt no pain. She glanced down and noticed some strange purplish fluid pumped directly into her vein. Her hunger pangs subsided at once. Not only did she feel better, she could focus with greater clarity. She did not wish to know how to eliminate wastes. She felt exposed as it was, sitting naked in her classroom.

"I'm glad that's over!" she said and straightened.

She moved the instrument's probe further into the imaginary corpse on her table. She found the construction of the creature's anatomy fascinating, while the screen rattled off fact after fact regarding its functions. Once more, the voice of the instructor spoke in her mind.

"Good! You use your instrument correctly, Cecilia," Professor Tsi told her. "Continue your internal probe of the body. This is an autopsy. Your task is to find the disease process that killed this being. This should be easy, even for a human," the professor stated.

"How is it you can speak to me personally, when this class must have several hundred…" Cecilia began to consider.

This time Cecilia distinctly felt Tsi's presence withdraw before she could ask a question.

"Which pupils have found the disease process?" Tsi addressed the assembly.

Cecilia realized that Tsi probably had the capacity to keep her communication with all of the students simultaneously, a task even Master Li would find daunting.

Several desks lit up, as students indicated their accomplishment of the first task.

"You are at the site of origin," Tsi's soft voice chimed back in.

Cecilia finally spotted the cause: Necrosis of the Setil, a vital part of the creature's sensors, due to toxins from its environment. She reached out with her mind and her desk lit up, joining the others around her.

"I expect better results from you, Cecilia," Professor Tsi piped in the moment she turned her light on. "You humans possess more than ten times the psychic power compared to three quarters of my class. Put that power to good use and take the time after class to perform at least three downloads today. These headings include: 'How to recognize and diagnose human diseases,' 'Human anatomy with physiology,' and 'Earth microbiology.' Make good use of your time," her instructor added.

After the professor reviewed the functions of the probe and its properties, Tsi called on every student to recite the physician's oath (a variation of the Hippocratic oath), never to use their knowledge to promote death, disease, or destruction. Absorbed in every aspect of what happened around her, the class seemed to pass quickly for Cecilia. Yet, Professor Tsi left the stage and cut the psychic connection without any formal goodbye. Cecilia sat up in bed and tried to reorient to her bedroom. It seemed strange to return inside her "normal" body.

"Good heavens, its one o'clock!" she cried when she saw the bedside clock – five hours had passed.

She felt a tugging sensation. She realized that she still had her connection to Galactic Central open.

"This download will take a long passage of your time," her voice cautioned. "May I suggest a break before you proceed?" it suggested.

"I'll return after lunch," she thought. She terminated her connection.

On her way into the restroom, she glanced over at the full-length mirror in the bathroom.

"I like you the way you are," she spoke to the image in the mirror.

"I'll go along with that," Michael said behind her as he came up the stairs.

Startled, she spun around to find Michael entering the bedroom.

"What's up?" she wondered.

"Chou's first trip took him three hours," Michael commented. "You were out a long time. How did yours go?

"Professor Tsi is amazing," she told him. "I must share what we did with you sometime," she started.

"You mean watch dead alien corpses get poked? I don't think so," Michael acknowledged.

"How did you…" she questioned.

Michael winked at her and touched his temple.

"You were there?" she asked.

"Zinian had a short trip," he explained. "He said he would go to the village soon and recruit a crew of young men, if they were willing to join us. We decided on cash payments at the end of each week and offer them a bonus at the end of a month if they stayed."

"If they stay, it won't be for the money," Cecilia said as she turned from the mirror and moved over to Michael. "I have a feeling the best will stay for friendship. True, money generally helps in any impoverished society. But I believe that once they get to know us, Zinian, Zhiwei, Master Li, Han, you and the others… they will help us form a new community in which they can participate."

"Perhaps you are right," Michael agreed.

"Join me for lunch?" she asked.

"Sure," he said. He waited while she used the restroom. After she washed up, the couple headed down to the kitchen. "What's Tegixil like?" he asked.

"How did you know the name of the planet?" she linked and quickly probed his mind as the two descended the staircase.

"I told you," he answered. "I looked in on your lecture. I was worried about your first day."

At the bottom of the stairs, Cecilia moved up on her toes and kissed Michael.

"That was sweet," she told him. "Learning makes me hungry. I'm famished. Let's make sandwiches," she suggested as she turned toward the kitchen. "I didn't see much of Tegixil, or even the city of Sverchun where the university is located," she continued as they headed up the hall. "I only saw the inside of this great lecture hall… an enormous space, larger than any lecture hall I've ever seen on Earth."

"That's because it was a lecture hall based on ones you knew from Earth," he explained.

"What?" she stopped and spun around.

"Your voice said that what you saw and heard was an elaborate illusion except for your shell body," he told her. "They do that to new students to make them feel at ease and more comfortable with their surroundings. You wanted to see strange creatures from other worlds that were also going to school. They put them there. You wanted to sit behind an elaborate desk. They provided you with one," he explained. "The surgical tool you held and the feeding tube were real. Everything else was an illusion, including Professor Tsi whom I understand is very busy. She never meets individually with students. You interacted with a computer program inside a holographic tube that fed information wired directly into the shell. It tapped your thoughts the moment Galactic Central connected your portal. Sorry to pop your bubble."

Cecilia stared at Michael for a moment. She knew he spoke the truth, although it disappointed her.

"I wondered about all of that," she thought. "So that's why none of those creatures looked at me! How silly!" she smiled. "When the professor kept popping up in my thoughts and spoke so personally, I thought she must be as powerful as Master Li."

"I don't think any psychic creature is as powerful as Master Li," Michael commented. "They speak of him throughout the collective with reverence."

"Professor Tsi did mention something strange about humans possessing more psychic ability than other members of the collective," she commented. "Still, whether it was an illusion or not doesn't really matter I suppose," she thought as she walked into the kitchen.

"What was it like being inside the shell?" he asked her.

"Trust me," she said with a knowing smile, "you don't want to be there on dissection day!"

"I understand you were a female?" Michael asked.

"Oh, the shell was overtly female," Cecilia answered. "You would have loved her," she shook her head as she looked into the refrigerator. "What man wouldn't?"

Michael closed his eyes a moment while Cecilia perused items for lunch.

"Mm," he hummed and opened his eyes. "I think her lips are too big," he commented, unexpectedly.

Cecilia spun around and shot him a suspicious expression.

"You searched my mind and saw me… as that… thing?" she correctly guessed.

"I think you were kind of… cute, in a cartoonish way!" he smiled. Cecilia frowned back. "Compared to the other aliens, I mean." He tried to throw up a block but Cecilia saw right through it and knew his thoughts. "Well, you have to admit, Cecilia," he added. "She does resemble one of those voluptuous females in nudie magazines, if you over emphasized the parts males like best."

"Do you like her?" Cecilia asked as she pulling out a cold turkey breast for slicing.

"I like the arrangement I see right here," he said and crossed toward her.

"After my download, I could be persuaded into a private anatomy lesson… if you don't mind me playing doctor," she teased as the couple moved closer.

"Private lessons are preferable to downloads," Michael said softly as the two embraced. "The kind of medicine this patient needs."

"Then I'll prescribe your dose as PRN," she told him. Their heads moved closer.

"PRN?" he questioned as their lips nearly kissed.

"Pro re nata… as needed," she linked when they closed the gap.

Chapter Eleven

Worlds upon worlds

Han Su Yeng quickly settled into his new American life. Despite the radical change in cuisine and lifestyle, he adjusted to living with Master Li. Only four days ago, he lived alone in Beijing and managed a large section of Chinese governmental bureaucracy. He ordered hundreds of subordinates to perform multiple tasks. His department turned out dozens of reports every month that often exaggerated low pollution levels or high productivity outputs. Ever since his wife passed away four years ago, he never once took a vacation day. After his conversion, that burdensome past lay behind him. Han thought that he could now concentrate on other tasks and anticipate a brighter future.

One improvement came from Michael, Villi, and Zinian in the form humor. They taught Han how to laugh again. He learned to accept their sarcasm and insults as American-style humor and threw them right back. He slowed his energetic pace and actually joined the others in morning jogs around Rollo. When he returned on the third morning, Master Li waited at their front door.

"I have a humble breakfast for you," he offered.

When Han entered the kitchen, he found that Li made two bowls of congee (or jook) and a fresh pot of tea. Han topped the concoction with ground peanuts and a drizzle of honey. He quietly but eagerly ate a bit of homeland as he listened to Li.

"I can't make it as well as my wife could," Li apologized.

"Mmff," Han mumbled through a full mouth.

"I'll take that as approval," Li commented.

Master Li tapped the side of his head with his finger and winked.

"Oh," Han linked, "I forget. Actually, this is delicious. Thank you, Li."

Master Li allowed his bowl to cool while he spoke with Han.

"I know you are probably bored being in a place like this. Kansas is far from Beijing," Li began. "However, the Intergalactic Psychic Collective has over a hundred worlds that you can vicariously explore. The time has come for you to broaden your horizons. I want you to join with the others in taking a private journey," he suggested. "I believe you will find the experience very… enlightening."

"Will it seem real?" Han asked him.

"As if you were there," Li stated. "You will employ all of your senses as you explore the world you visit through the mind of a native psychic. This perspective is unique. For he or she can impart new emotions you may have never experienced. Each world is as subtly different as a snowflake or a human being."

Han put down his chop sticks.

"I'd like to see all of them," Han told him.

Master Li smiled.

"I suggest one at a time," he offered. "You may want to savor each experience."

"…to discover the culture of another civilization never seen by man and immerse my mind in their languages, their histories, art, and nature… it would be the answer to a prayer," Han wistfully told him.

Again, Master Li smiled that slight knowing smile while he linked no thought or emotion.

"I suggest you go this morning, right after breakfast," Li linked. "Go into your bedroom, lie down, and reach out to Galactic Central."

Han finished the rest of his bowl in silence and then walked upstairs to his bedroom. He laid on the top of his comforter and closed his eyes.

"Relax," he heard Li's voice. "Open your mind to your voice."

He wondered if other worlds resembled Earth… green plants, blue skies, a variety of animal and insect life. Were they possible on other civilized planets?

Han stretched out his legs and opened his special portal to that distant point in space hundreds of millions of light years away. He made an instant connection to his Galactic Central voice. The connection felt strong today.

"Han Su Yeng," the metallic-sounding voice addressed him. "Would you like to visit a world different from Earth?"

Somehow, the voice disappointed him. He hoped he would see a world similar to Earth. He quickly realized that Master Li must have prepared his way.

"Certainly," Han answered. "Take me to one of your worlds."

"Let us start you out with a planet that has the most psychic beings of any in the collective," it stated, "over a million at last count."

"A million?" the fact amazed Han, "on one planet?"

"The Vstl's of Uthx, a famous family of creatures similar to a mammal species on your planet," his voice explained. "They are warm-blooded creatures, whose entire body is covered with short hair, and have stretchable, leathery skin. Similar to humans in size, they see their environment with binocular vision, breathe air that consists of oxygen mixed with nitrogen, and use a sophisticated system of language."

"How is that different from Earth?" Han questioned. "Everything you've described sounds exactly like Earth."

"I can assure you that these creatures are very different from humans," his voice explained. "While they tolerate the presence of other psychics, some Vstls consider the occupation an intrusion. They may try to switch you to another mind. If this happens, you can ask to pull out," the voice informed him.

"Very well," Han said. That news disappointed him. Perhaps he should visit some species other than the Vstl's of Uthx. His voice spoke up before he could change his mind,.

"If you are quite ready to begin," it requested.

"Yes, I am ready," Han informed his voice.

He took in a deep breath and prepared to make the transition.

"One last important detail," the voice added. "Do you have acrophobia?"

"Not really," Han replied. "Why?"

"They fly..."

"Fly?" Han responded.

If he had any apprehension, he did not have time to react. All at once, a new point of view came into sharp focus. He was very high in the air, soaring through the atmosphere of this planet, higher than most clouds. A clear, blue sky overhead with nothing below him but a vast ocean of calm, dark green water that stretched out to the distant horizon. Han sighed with relief at its familiarity. Yet, the sensation of flying was both liberating and frightening at the same time.

The creature banked to one side and then swiftly dropped down through the atmosphere like a rocket toward the water. Han thought he would experience nausea as he dove straight down. Instead he felt excitement and exhilaration. The surface of the water rose faster and faster until Han could make out huge waves not apparent from his previous height.

Suddenly, the creature folded in its wings and plunged straight into the warm water. It flexed its body and pushed through the water. It opened its mouth and grabbed a large swimming crustacean in its teeth. The creature swept its powerful limbs out and pushed down on the water with tremendous force until it sprung out of the water and leapt into the air. With water dripping off its wings, it stretched out its large limbs to catch the air. With a few mighty thrusts, it slowly gained altitude. For a brief moment, it struggled to catch a head wind while it held the wiggling prey in its mouth.

Han practically gasped for air when the creature burst from the water and then struggled to gain height. He felt and saw everything the creature did. Slowly the water moved further below him. With one big snap, the flying creature clenched its teeth and broke off the useless parts of its prey with the expertise of a chef deboning a filet. Its teeth crunched down through bones and shell. Using its tongue, it discarded the waste as it worked the tender fresh morsel into its gullet. A feeling of supreme satisfaction spread through the flyer.

At that moment, Han sensed the creature to be male. The flyer stretched his large wings and used the wind to gain additional height. Effortlessly, it flapped and pushed down on the air as it skimmed only a dozen meters above the churning waves. The giant bat-like creature caught a headwind that lifted him into the air. He banked around until Han could see land on the horizon, not visible until now.

A shudder of apprehension passed through the flyer. He glanced down and saw movement in the water. A gigantic shadow swiftly followed him beneath the waves. With amazing speed an enormous creature rose from the murky depths, its great jaws opened to reveal a wide gaping mouth. Rows of sharp boney teeth bore down on them. At the last second, it writhed and cried out as if in pain, its mouth clamped down on air, and barely missed the flyer before it shrank back into the sea.

"The mindless Wlk," the flyer thought. "They always want to attack us, when we couldn't possibly offer it a proper meal. They never learn," he thought. "Wait! I sense the presence of another psychic. Who is in my mind?" he asked. "Your timing is lousy! I am trying to harvest."

"I am Han Su Yeng… of Earth," Han timidly replied.

"Urth? I never heard of Urth," he said. "Where is Urth?"

"It's Earth, not Urth," Han corrected. "Our planet is near the outer rim of a spiral galaxy called the Milky Way," he began to explain.

As Han exchanged his linked thoughts with the creature, he noticed that a large body of land drew nearer. It must have been behind the creature when he first entered his mind.

"I am a human, a bipedal creature that walks upright on two legs," Han added.

"A land-dweller?" the flyer asked of his mental visitor.

"Yes, that's right," Han told him. "We are new to the collective. We recently converted," Han inform him.

"How many legs do you have?" the male creature asked.

"Two…" Han began. "We have arms on our upper bodies."

"To reach your destination, you must walk on the ground, do you not?" he asked him.

"Yes, we cannot fly," Han told him.

"Pity, flying is much faster than walking. Did you say your name?" he asked. "Or do creatures from Earth run about calling to each other, hey you, human, come here!"

Han laughed at this. He was not expecting humor.

"You laugh, human," the creature spoke. "That is good… for we all love a good joke now and then, don't we… Han Su Yeng, Chinese human of Earth."

"You know me?" Han asked, surprised.

"You are in my mind as I am in your mind, bipedal human," he informed him. "Bipedal indeed," the creature scoffed, "as if that were a significant attribute to make one intelligent!"

Realizing that an equal exchange of thoughts existed, Han timidly probed his host's mind and instantly discovered many things about this creature as it flew deeper inland over a vast forest of immense plants, whose size and shape resembled huge trees, yet they were very different. Their fronds opened wide and tapered to a tip until the creature flew close, at which time they snapped closed and resembled huge spikes to ward off predators, or so he assumed. Han wondered how they could land in such a tree when he recalled that this flying creature could land anywhere and be safe.

Han deciphered from his thoughts that the flying creature is a Vstl named Patr, an organizer of the Vstls. He was responsible for feeding two younglings, hence the fishing expedition. His mate's name is Fete, a young beautiful Vstl, daughter of Isl, elected Supreme Ruler of all Vstls. This pairing elevated Patr's status from a member of the First Guard to Prince-in-waiting. He could possibly be the next Supreme Ruler within his treetop colony, if chosen by his peers.

"Have you perused around my brain long enough to know me?" Patr asked of Han. "It is considered rude on Uthx to enter the mind of another and stay among one's personal thoughts uninvited. Your voice warned us about humans, that we should throw you off to another."

"Yes, but he... I mean, it... well, I suppose what I mean to say is..." Han struggled, trying to make a good first impression.

Patr let out a great roaring laugh that shook his body and startled Han.

"You must forgive me Han," Patr told him. "As a human, you are rather shy. I doubt that Master Li would be so timid."

"You know Master Li too?" Han wondered.

"Every psychic creature in the collective was aware of Li Po Chin from the moment of his conceptualized existence," Patr informed him. "Are you typical for an Earthling? I sense you are a strong psychic for being a ground-dweller."

"I don't find the term 'ground-dweller' accessible..." Han began before Patr cut him off.

"Ground-dwellers on this planet tried to destroy my species," Patr explained, "before a great war between us ended by a strange quirk of fate. In their eagerness to rid the planet of my species, they became a victim of their own aggression."

While Patr briefly explained his history, Han's mind filled with stories about an entirely new culture, its way of life, its idioms and its quirky nature. He marveled at this creature's complex mind yet simplified needs compared to human ones.

Patr began to slow his descent.

"Look below," he said. He tipped his head and angled his flight for Han to see. "Behold! The great city of Materly!" Patr declared with pride.

From this distance, Han could make out the tops of gigantic trees that grew into amazing shapes. These plants were very different from those near the coastline. Massive biological structures with enormous wide trunks twisted to form a variety of rising shapes. Han noted the bark on the outside had a sheen that resembled iridescent fish scales which caught the sunlight and dazzled the eye.

"Materly," Han repeated with awe in his tone. "I have never seen the like..."

"...and you never will Han," Patr added, "on any world."

As they grew closer, Han noted a solid wall of tree trunks that rose up from the forest floor to form a natural barrier against intruders. In the middle of the city, a flat living boulevard bordered by a variety of dwellings, specialty shops and other buildings sprung from the same plant material. Thousands of Vstls walked around the city, whose details Han could barely make out from this distance. They moved upright instead of flying – bipedal indeed!

Han surmised that the Vstl's used their psychic influence to create Materly.

At the center of the boulevard, he noted a crowded village square with a great water fountain at its heart. At the back of the square, huge spires covered by flowering vines of different colors rose higher in a series. He assumed these columns were probably for decorative purposes.

"I've never seen anything so magnificent," Han noted.

"Don't let the weapons alarm you," Patr told him. "We have not used them since the war with the ground-dwellers ended," Patr linked as he indicated an enormous battlement along the outermost wall.

Han noted their decayed condition, as if this war took place many years ago.

"How did you make these plants grow like this?" Han questioned.

"Do not plants respond to your power where you live?" Patr asked him.

"I've only just begun to apply my ability," Han replied in a quiet manner. "I shall try to coax our plants into growing faster."

"Faster, taller, into a variety of shapes," he began and then paused. "You must forgive me Han. I am being a terrible host. I will fly over the city to offer you a better view."

Patr swooped down and flew right through the heart of the city. Many Vstl raised his or her head. They waved up at him or arched their heads as he passed.

"Patr!" they called to his mind or "Prince!"

Han noticed that this planet's dominate flying creature had appendages – short arms that had digits at its end similar to fingers. The Vstl used these to fashion certain intricate tools from which they create delicate woven material. It did not take much imagination to see how a flying creature that worked in teams could create yards of material for all kinds of uses.

Han also discovered that Vstls around the planet communicate from colony to colony with their minds in tandem. They flew great distances if necessary to visit or help other communities.

"The planet holds well over a million Vstl," Patr explained, "with several tree top cities like this one located around the planet's equatorial region. Each colony holds approximately ten thousand Vstl except Materly," he linked. "This is the capital city. We have about fifty thousand Vstl here."

Han detected great pride in his thoughts.

"The word Materly means 'mother on high' in our language Han," Patr replied when he sensed the question in Han's thoughts. "I must pause. We have arrived."

Patr landed on a perch high above the city. No one greeted him. Han did not notice a sentinel, a guard or any security. He realized the Vstl had no threat from the air and probably none from the ground, at least not any longer.

They placed these special landing and take-off platforms high above the rest of the city. Han presumed take offs were difficult for the large creatures.

"When we move about in the city, we must robe," it stated. It then pulled on a brightly-colored, shimmering, woven cloth that hung nearby in the same place where Patr left it when he took off to fish. Han did not see anyone else with "robes" as fine as these, whose weave and color indicated rank as well as a practical covering.

As Patr glanced down, Han saw how several enormous trees twisted together to form tight formations. The branches flattened and made wide gradual steps for Patr to walk down. Han then assumed the Vstl had feet.

"I am a bi-pedal creature..." Patr began. He sensed the question in Han's mind.

"Yes, but one that flies, a major distinction," Han pointed out. "I see why you made fun of me when I said I was a bi-pedal creature. You were right to point out that particular quality is not a distinction of intelligence."

"I believe you are beginning to understand us at last Han Su Yeng," Patr said as he adjusted his robe.

At the bottom of the turning staircase, a side avenue led them toward the main thoroughfare. Patr walked past a series of dwellings, so intricate in design that Han could only describe them as "storybook-cottage" in construction. A vast concourse spread out before him on the main thoroughfare. He saw sculptures created from living plants scattered about a grand courtyard, large decorative pools of water, flowering plants and a variety of "perches" where Vstl could ascend to fly. An enormous multi-tiered fountain, which sprayed water from a variety of plant shapes, rose up in the middle of a great courtyard.

"A fountain requires pumps to bring water up from below and piping," Han questioned.

"Remember, psychic energy manipulates our surroundings," the creature thought to him.

"What did you say?" a Vstl standing next to Patr snapped at him. The creature turned its head and then recognized the color of robe. "Oh, I am humble to you Patr," it said and bowed. "I was in deep thought when you intruded."

"No apology is necessary. I am occupied by a creature from Earth," Patr explained. "He wishes to learn our way of life."

"May I speak with him when you are done?" the Vstl requested.

"Perhaps," Patr said as he moved on. "I am currently busy with his first visit," he proudly stated.

"As maintainer of the lower city, I would make a better tour guide," the other fellow opined. "If I am not mistaken, he asked how water is pumped from below. Kindly explain that the trees form conduits when they squeeze the ground with their roots. They also filter the water, remove impurities, and push large volumes to the top of our colony. This allows us the opportunity to bathe and drink…"

Patr stopped for a moment and regarded his fellow citizen.

"All that you say is true Feto," Patr countered. "You are wise in the mechanics of our colony's operation. I do not know why the voices chose me for first contact," the prince concluded.

"You say you are his first contact? He is the first of his planet to ever visit us?" Feto asked.

"Yes…" Patr began.

"Then it is I who must beg your pardon Prince. I should not slow your progress. You must be on your way to the…" Feto stopped. He gestured toward the other side of the courtyard.

"Yes, I was headed in that direction," Patr concluded.

"Ah then, the human is quite fortunate indeed. I will not cause any further delay, my beloved Patr," Feto said. He bowed respectfully again.

"Good thoughts to you Feto," Patr wished.

"Good thoughts to you also Patr," Feto said and added, "and to our new guest!"

As Patr walked away, Han challenged the previous information the voice shared with him.

"I thought the voices said you were rude, that you would toss me about from mind to mind," Han stated. This misinformation upset him.

Patr chuckled. His laughter shook his body.

"You must forgive me Han," the prince told him. "That was my intended joke. We Vstl enjoy humor and use it to disarm those who make first contact," he spoke his thoughts kindly.

"I… I didn't know," Han tried to recover.

Patr continued. "If you must know, we are as curious about you as you must be about us. Unlike you however, we have an open psychic society that has evolved over many of your centuries. We do not block our private thoughts. We share every thought, every emotion and every feeling. As a result, many Vstl around me can hear my conversation with you."

The princely Vstl stopped and turned his head. Han then noticed heads turning toward Patr. He bowed and acknowledged each Vstl as he passed them. That included little children who peered from doorways as he made his way up the square toward the main fountain. In this way, Han finally saw what other Vstls resembled, as he could not see Patr.

Very tall and slender in their overall shape, about three meters in height, each Vstl has leathery wings and elongated heads. Their arms and hands extend forward out of stretchable fleshy skin when they fold their wings behind their backs. Their wings then tuck into a large groove that runs down their spine.

Han marveled at the details within the city as they passed "house after house" constructed from the fabric of the trees around them. Han could see in through each open door. Tables and seats grew up from the floor, though what they called a "chair" would hardly be fit for human use.

The walls grew elaborate decorative perches where they slept. The children slept in suspended nets that resembled hammocks. Matter shot out from the walls of dwellings into a matrix of complex shapes. When he considered the bodily construction of the Vstl, Han thought the perches would be very comfortable for sleep.

As more Vstl's passed by, Han realized that the robes, which Patr donned earlier, were fancier and more elaborately woven with a particular pattern than the robes of others walking around the city. Patr sensed Han's curiosity and held out his sleeve.

"We did not make these with our (hands)," he explained. "The plants intertwined fabric and infused them with natural dyes," he told Han. "Each house spins a unique cloth pattern."

"You can speak to the plants?" Han wondered.

"In a very crude sort of manner," Patr told him. "Over many centuries, we formed symbiotic relationships which began thousands of solar cycles ago not long after we first joined the galactic collective. As stewards of this planet, we allow all species of life to flourish," Patr told him, "whether on land or in the sea. Only the ground-dwellers chose to burn, cut and destroy. Since their extinction, life is abundant and plentiful."

"Yes, however I see one flaw… without the ground dwellers, where do you obtain your psychic energy?" Han wondered.

"We never took energy from them," Patr said.

"Where do you get it?" Han asked.

Patr looked up. "From the stars… I thought all worlds did."

Han did not volunteer the source of abundant psychic energy on his planet. He kept those thoughts suppressed. As he observed the world through Patr's eyes, Han did not see one insect until he noticed something akin to a beetle emerge from a crack. Three Vstl children dove for the floor and fought over it.

Many Vstl tried to inquire about the Earthling as Patr made his way down the thoroughfare. It suddenly occurred to Han that Patr could easily have landed at his destination instead of this march through the city.

"You did that on purpose?" Han questioned.

"Of course," Patr said with pride. He bowed to more Vstls as he passed. Han could see that Patr headed toward a large structure at the far end of the square where he saw the towering columns. "I am proud to be the bearer of the first human to visit our planet, a distinction and a great honor Han," the prince explained.

As they passed the central fountain surrounded by large fruit trees and plants with beautiful colorful blossoms, Han read from Patr's mind that the Vstl came to the fountain to snack on fruit, drink water and to groom their fellow creatures in social groups. He also noticed their lack of close personal interaction, despite several-paired Vstl who gingerly treated each other with minimal contact.

"We are fragile Han," Patr answered his thought. "Our bones are hollow. We make love in the air... and do so very carefully."

Back on Earth, Han's face broke into a grin. Even Patr laughed at his own joke, as did several couples that picked-up on their conversation.

At the opposite end of the concourse, the top of an enormous structure stretched upward. The colorful columns he noticed earlier rose like great spires into the sky. The columns grew straight and branchless with huge round smooth trunks. Their white exterior had a living sheen that reflected in the sunlight, similar to the exterior walls. They towered high above Materly. One trunk bent to form a proscenium-arched entry to a structure whose intricate detail astonish Han.

"I... I...I can't believe what I'm seeing," he marveled.

A series of wide steps led up to a large open entrance at the base of this great structure. Patr walked between rows of Vstl who stood along either side of the steps. Each Vstl bowed as Patr passed. Han began to hear the sound of voices – a chorus of voices. Their high pitched tones rang out in perfect harmonious chords. Han felt as if he were ascending the staircase to heaven.

"What is this place?" Han asked.

"This is the heart of my people," Patr informed Han. "This is the leadership pavilion where the Supreme Leader and his council live. It is open to all Vstl at any time of day or night."

"What has he seen?" a powerful voice boomed into Patr's head. The voice startled Han.

"I've been fishing for Tsra and Nibl," Patr replied.

"Have you fed them?" the powerful voice asked.

"I wanted to wait until after the ceremony," Patr confessed.

"Then right after Patr, while the istr is still fresh. Has it seen..." the voice began.

"Has *he* seen," Patr corrected.

"Has he seen the city?" the great voice beckoned.

"Some father, not all," Patr humbly replied.

"Father?" Han's thought broke in.

Patr stepped through a very large archway. The floor and walls inside the massive hall seemed like a work of art to Han. Parts of trees blended into a mosaic of patterns that resembled three-dimensional pictures and sculpture. These living scenes were meant to honor those great Vstl of the past. Scenes depicted the building of the tree cities, the battle with the ground-dwellers and the triumph of the Vstl. These finely crafted reliefs ran along the walls of the massive chamber. A group of special larger statues that were dedicated to the leaders sacrificed in the attempt for peace, stood off to one side. Their kindly faces appeared saint-like to Han. He marveled at the exquisite workmanship and miniscule details such as fur on the skin.

"She is a great artist, isn't she?" Patr thought to Han with pride in his tone. "That is the work of Fete, my wife. She just completed the statues to commemorate the one thousand cycle anniversary of Materly."

Han did not have time to react, for Patr stood at the entrance to a great wide room filled with a variety of Vstl dressed in colorful robes. They turned to Patr and a great cheer broke out.

"All hail Han Su Yeng, the first human from Earth to visit Uthx!" the room cried out. They did not shout as voices, these cheers came through mental links into the Patr's head.

Hundreds of protruding thoughts flooded into the mind of Patr, as if Han stood inside a room with many people all glad to meet him, all patting him on the back, all giving him incredible feelings of well being. Moved by this shared community experience, he could not link back to them. Overwhelmed with emotion, Han choked on his thoughts of gratitude and humility.

"He thanks you," Patr linked back to them on Han's behalf. "He also likes the palace."

At the opposite end of this incredible interior space, bright light shown down from above, illuminating a central dais with several figures who stood higher above the crowd. Patr started to move toward the central figure. Instead of being a shade of brown like the others, white fur covered this single Vstl adorned in a shimmering silver gown that flowed down to his feet. Standing nearby, gray fur covered a few others that gathered around the central figure. Their blue robes sparkled in the light. The white Vstl wore a beautiful crown made of blue jewels set in a dazzling ornamental metal that sparkled on his head.

Patr approached this figure and bowed.

"Father," he said to this Vstl. "Mother," he said as he bowed to one of the gray Vstls that stepped out. Her blue garment, trimmed with yellow and green flowers, seemed to have a light of its own. "Fete," Patr linked as he turned and acknowledged his mate. The mother of his children, a dark brown creature to their right, stepped forward. Unlike Patr's flashy colorful robes, she wore a glittering robe of silver and red, singularly unique.

"Your highness," she bowed back.

Han learned that once a mating takes place, the mother and father of the mated daughter or son adopt the spouse into the family. They kept the daughter while gaining a son, which they did not have, prior to Patr. He would be next in line for succession, if the council elected him. The vote was never one of competition but humility. If the council elected Fete instead, he would be her huta or supporter. Either would be happy with the choice, as being ruler is such a heavy responsibility that the fur of the ruler turns white and hastens their death – shortening their lifespan.

Fete's search for a mate led to Patr after several cycles of friendly competition and mating rituals. She chose him, not the other way. Han could sense their love and admiration for each other.

The white-haired Vstl with the jeweled crown approached Patr. He cast a warm and loving eye down on his son, who had been fishing for his grandchildren's supper – it still resided in Patr's belly. Patr cast no aspirations for the crown, a certain sign he would be the next leader, for he possessed great humility. He stared up at Isl with both love and admiration. Isl ruled over all of Uthx for many cycles. He was very old and would soon pass that privilege on. Han never felt such closeness in a family unit. The emotion they expressed and the feelings they shared overpowered his senses.

"May I have this honor?" the large white-haired Vstl requested.

Patr again bowed.

"I share this honor with one greater than me," Patr thought. "I present to your honor, Han Su Yeng of Earth, oh great Isl, leader of all Vstl."

Han felt Patr leave his presence as he did indeed switch over to the Vstl leader, Isl. All at once, Han could see Patr for the first time. His eyes beamed with pride as he looked upon Isl. The leader looked back at his son with love and acceptance. He gazed out on the gathering. He spread his arms wide.

"All hail Han Su Yeng!" they cried.

Isl bowed to the assembly. He turned and bowed to the elders on his right. He turned and bowed one final time to the elders on his left, as the crowd cheered once more. Han could hardly bear the adoration heaped upon him. He linked his feelings to Isl.

"Great Isl," Han spoke with humility, "I am honored by your presence."

"As I am yours Han, friend of Master Li, the wisest of us all," Isl stated.

The room quieted to a hush. Han noticed that every head in the hall bowed when Isl mentioned Li's name.

"Your visit here, while brief, is welcome," Isl stated. "We treasure your company. You must come back soon," the leader pointed out. "Many here wish to share their stories with you, including Feto, whom I understand is eager to show you the undercity. That is a fascinating place. For now, we bid you adieu," the leader spoke. "Goodbye Han."

"Goodbye Han!" the others in the hall cried out.

Han's last view showed Fete bringing out two baby Vstl, one female and the other male. He wondered which one would succeed Patr when the image faded.

Han was not sure why they were dismissing him so soon. He wanted to stay. He wanted to see the feeding. He wanted to fly about the city again. He wished he could find Feto and see the inner workings of the city from below. No sooner had the leader Isl uttered his farewell thought when Han's connection via Galactic Central cut off. His voice pulled him away from Uthx and Han felt the connection with the planet grow cold.

Just then, he felt Master Li's presence back on Earth. Li had just entered his bedroom. Han blinked his eyes open. He lay on the bed in his small bedroom inside a rather mundane dwelling compared to the grand hall on Uthx. His disappointed eyes fell on Master Li who stood in his doorway.

Han started to sit and tell Master Li of his experience on Uthx, when he noticed Li appeared to be shaken. The older man breathed heavily and clutched at his shirt. He looked at Han with a most serious expression. Han opened his mouth to speak, when Li brushed his hand through the air to dismiss his attempt.

"How did you like your journey to Uthx?" Li asked him. He tried to avoid Han's probing stare.

"I found it exhilarating," Han told him. He wanted to add "and far too short."

"Good," Li replied. "Worlds upon worlds await us, Han. It is a glorious adventure that I wish all of earth could share… unfortunately, they cannot."

Li sought the comfort of Han's reading chair. Han noticed how he nervously glanced about as if preoccupied with a troubling thought.

"What is wrong?" Han asked.

The elderly white haired Chinese gentleman leaned back in the chair and stared up at the ceiling. He took in a deep breath and closed his eyes.

"We are no longer unknown…" Li linked to him.

Chapter Twelve

A PRICE MUST BE PAID

From the very first day the psychic group took possession of the small town up the road, the forty-year-old woman with the careworn face, the tattered wide-brimmed hat, and long gray ponytail, returned to her nightly vigil at the general store with her shotgun and Bible. Sometimes she brought a container of hot coffee as she would sit on the wooden bench and stay awake all night while she watched the road. She had not decided whether she brought her Bible to ward off the evil of these strangers or to read it for inspiration. To her, this book represented the views of Christianity and Judaism, not the beliefs her people clung to for centuries.

Unfortunately, she could no longer recall the set of tribal principles that she once knew as her religion. Nor could she envision the stories her father told around countless campfires when he recited the legends that his grandfather passed to him. Like many of her fellow tribespersons, she forgot most of the old ways, the ways of the medicine man, of being attuned with nature and how to call on her ancestors. She could not remember the Shoshone chants her father and his friends made when they danced or meditated. She was too young then. Too many years passed since those events happened in her youth, events that no one in their tribal fragment practiced for decades.

Her father died when she was just sixteen. The man who took her father's place divided the community. He persuaded several people to give up the old ways and follow him back to a more civilized existence in Oklahoma on the Comanche reserve. Torn between this man's promise and her father's dream, she made an impassioned plea in regards to her father's last wish.

"My father believed in the Comanche ways," she said to them. "Please stay and carry on his vision!" she begged. Enough people trusted her and remained, which split the group.

At that time, an older man came forward to her defense. She looked up to him as she did her father. Soon, the man took the relationship to the next level and he moved in with her. Those were the golden days of her life, despite his struggles to find work and keep food on their table, they were happy. She eventually gave this man a son, followed three years later by a daughter. She could not see how their severe struggle to survive wore away at his spirit. One night after working in Wichita on a five-day stretch, he blew his brains out in the family truck. His abhorrent act left an emotional scar on her mind that never truly healed through the years.

The village seemed to go downhill after that until the condition grew so poor, she knew she had to act. Two years after her mate's suicide, she went to the Kansas state legislature in Topeka and asked for assistance. When she met with resistance, she erected a tent and vowed to sleep on the steps of the capital until they helped her people. They put her name in all the papers and her cause on television. Sympathy money poured in. The state purchased cheap government trailers, but they were better homes than the shacks they had. Temporarily at least, they prospered. Yet, as time passed, their group once more faded into obscurity, forgotten, discarded, and abandon. She used up the money from her husband's life insurance policy to keep the village alive. When that ran out, they turned to welfare and food stamps.

Many years passed. Those who stayed in southwestern Kansas eventually suffered for their decision. Isolated and forgotten, their resources dwindled. Many resorted to alcohol and drugs. The young girl, now an aging woman with a family to feed, felt responsible for the rest of the village. She took over the leadership position. She worked hard on a daily basis to keep her people together. Lately, the grown children, those of her son's age, began to slip away.

Too proud to ask the Comanche tribe in Oklahoma for help, she turned to faith and prayed for deliverance. She nearly gave up hope, when the strangers arrived. They seemed a godsend, or so she thought at first. After a few days, however, she feared the strangers' new power. Instead of relying on her tribal beliefs, she relied upon the white man's holy book to ward off evil. Whether it worked or not, she could not say.

On the fourth morning after she finished her nightly vigil, she walked home along the two-mile stretch of highway – a weary woman. From the moment these strangers arrived, she experienced very little sleep at night. The new residents of Rollo filled her mind with worry.

She secretly watched with uneasy anticipation, when the little white-haired oriental man showed up with his pretty, young, white, female helper. She saw them enter trailers in her village and then leave behind a clean dwelling with those inside healed of whatever malady they possessed. She confronted people afterward, but they had no recollection of his visit.

"What do you mean you don't remember?" the woman asked them. "He walked right through your front door. It's the same door whose screen is now patched."

"It didn't have a hole in it," the woman who lived inside argued.

"That door's had a torn screen for years Mattie!" the woman retorted, but to no avail. "What about Melissa?" she pointed out. "Melissa can walk Mattie and even talk! Do you even recall a day when this sweet little girl ever uttered a word?"

"You get out of here and bother someone else," Mattie argued with her.

The gray-haired woman experienced a similar story three times that week. She used to know some of the previous residents of Rollo, but did not like them. When they suddenly moved away, their hurried departure puzzled her. Still, she did not miss them. Yet, she feared the new people who took their place. They behaved rather strangely. Too many changes took place in a short span of time with no one asking questions.

"…and where is the law?" she wondered. No County Sheriff's cars patrolled through Rollo or her village any longer. They usually arrested someone from her village once a week for public drunkenness. She had not seen a single patrol car. "Are they the devil?" she wondered, "or perhaps they're aliens!"

On day four after their arrival, her son came home all excited about something. He hummed about the house. His mood was full of expectant joy in a way she never saw in him. He noticed her brooding. She sat at the kitchen table, staring into a cup of coffee.

"What's wrong with you?" he asked her.

He had seen her in this mood once before when he and his friends caused trouble.

"I can't say," she said as she bit her lower lip. "Why are you in such a good mood?"

"Don't you feel it? Feels like good times in the air ever since the new folks have moved into Rollo," he said with a broad grin.

"Have you seen 'em? Those new people in Rollo, I mean? Strange aren't they?" she asked her son.

"I'll say," her son shot back. "What about the old Chinese coot in that weird truck?"

She glared at him. He was the first person that actually recalled the truck without wondering if she was crazy.

"You've seen him in that truck?" she asked.

"Sure," he told her, "My friends and I think it's funny!"

"Yes, yes… What's he done now?" she asked. She was curious he knew something.

"Nothin…" the teen's voice trailed off. "I just thought he looked funny, that's all."

"Round up your friends – run up and there and spy on them for me," she requested.

"You mean you don't mind if we go to Rollo?" he wondered. In the past, his mother told him never to go to Rollo for anything. The teens used to buy beer at Baker's store and drink it in the fields. "We've been bustin a gut to go!"

"Sure!" she said and waved her arm at him. "Go, explore, do anything you want… only come back and tell me what's goin on!" she demanded.

"Ok," he mumbled as he turned and went out the front door.

She sipped her coffee and brooded over what to do next. Normally, their village stayed quiet during the day, only interrupted by someone's loud-playing radio. When she leaned back in her chair, she distinctly heard the sounds of people talking outside, not just one or two, but a crowd.

She stuck her head out the front door. One of the tall, young, oriental men with broad shoulders and a muscular physique came into village right after her son gathered up his friends. The man stood up in the back of his pickup truck and spoke to her son's group of pals for a long time. After a few minutes, he jumped down, stepped inside his truck, and left. Her son returned home. He met his mother at the front door. He had an expression of shock on his face. She followed him as he plopped down on the sofa. He sat and stared off into space.

"Well? What did he want?" she demanded.

He looked up at his mother and did not know where to begin.

"I thought you'd be curious about what he said, so I came right back," he said with an expression of astonishment on his face. "I just heard something that I've only dreamed of hearing ever since I could remember."

"What?" she pleaded.

"They're looking for help," he casually mentioned. "That big oriental man told us about his group. His name is Zinni… Zanni…"

"What did he say?" she demanded.

Her son blankly stared up at her. "He said they had plans to rebuild Rollo. Seems one of them is a very wealthy. They came out here to start a new community. He wanted men for hire to form a work crew. He asked for anyone strong enough to do construction-type work and wanted a full time job. Said he was willing to pay us every week in cash," he told her. "Cash mother!" he said as he waved his fist. "He said if we stayed on the job and worked through the month, he promised to give all of us bonuses!"

"How much money did he offer?" she asked him.

"Thirty-five dollars an hour to start with forty hours a week guaranteed," he said. "We don't have to pay taxes. He said he would pay our taxes separately. He promised us free health care too!"

"Free health care…" she echoed.

"Mother, that's fourteen hundred a week in cash!" he declared.

"Thirty-five dollars an hour… Are you sure?" she skeptically asked.

"That's what he said," her son replied. "That's more money than anyone ever offered me for manual labor. Mother?" he questioned as she turned away unfocused.

She nearly bit her lip right off and rubbed it after she made it sore. She went to her freezer and took out an ice cube to place on her lip. She sat at the kitchen table and brooded over this news. Her son followed her.

"What should we do?" he asked.

"Did you agree to his terms?" she glanced up at him.

"I wanted to check with you first. The other fellows wanted to say yes, but I told them to wait. Well?" he turned to her.

Her eyes went to the window where she saw the collection of run-down aging trailers.

"Go tell your friends to accept," she said as she walked away.

"Whoopee!" he cried.

He did not catch her reaction. He struck the ceiling with his fist. He ran out the front door to his friends. They all took off and jogged up the highway for Rollo. They were eager to start making some money. The woman sat out on her front porch and waited. However, her son and the other young men did not return until later that evening. The sun nearly set when she saw their group walking up the road. They waved to one another as they broke up. The woman tried to address her son as he walked back into the house. He did not say a word. His face appeared drawn, upset.

"Hey!" she said as she put down the Bible. She was eager to hear what happened.

Brooding, he did not speak to his mother. He went to the bedroom and slammed the door shut. Puzzled she called after him. When he did not reply after several requests, she stormed down the hall. He slept on the floor next to the only bed where his sister slept.

"What did they want?" she asked as she pushed in the bedroom door. "Did they work you hard? What happened? Did they deny you payment? If they did, I'll call the sheriff…"

John spun around and stared at his mother so fiercely that she stopped talking.

"Don't ever say a bad word about any of those people. That's all I gotta say," he said. He pulled his pillow over his head.

"John?" she spoke softer. "Howling wolf?"

He would not answer. He rolled over on his mattress and pulled a pair of old earphones over his head. He turned up the radio to drown out her reply.

"What did I say?" she thought as she came out of the bedroom. She passed her daughter in the hall. She reached out and caught the young teen's arm. "Where have you been?"

"Helping Melissa learn to read," her daughter shot back. She yanked her arm away. "Anything else you want to complain about?" she sarcastically said.

Star Wind's mother backed off. She watched her daughter swing around the corner into the bedroom.

"What's gotten into my children lately?" Running Elk thought.

For those and many other reasons, the Comanche matriarch suddenly felt obligated to the benevolent strangers. She felt she owed them a debt that she could never repay for their kindness. Therefore, she did not mind watching over Rollo during the night. She kept an eye on the road, intent to run off anyone that might try to stop while the strangers slept.

Chapter Thirteen

As did Ruth

By the end of the fourth day, Running Elk finally grew tired of her nightly ritual. She gave up her watch that night and slept in her usual place on the sofa instead. However, she decided to confront this miraculous old man should he show up in her village again. She rose very early the following day and sat out on her front porch. She slowly sipped from a tall glass of ice water. She patiently waited for him to show up. If she had to wait here every day, she was determined to do so.

Not long after sunrise, the silent old rusty truck that defied reason for its ability to function rolled up the highway. No other cars or trucks ever seemed to be on the highway at the same time. She regarded this phenomenon as peculiar. Still, many in the village began to think of his odd truck as a good sign. Since the old man visited, the small village transformed into a cleaner place, free of refuse and full of curious people who grew increasingly anxious about their future.

Running Elk sat up when she saw his truck approach. She wondered which way it would turn. Yet, when the truck turned onto the dirt road, it kicked up a large dust cloud as it bounced in her direction. The air stood still. Yellowish dust hovered in place and obscured her vision.

"Where is that old coot?" she wondered as she leaned over her front porch rail. The dust made her cough and wave her hand in front of her face. As the air cleared, she no longer saw the truck.

"May I help you?" a voice next to her spoke.

Startled, she jumped and jerked her head around.

"What the hell?" she declared.

A short, elderly, oriental man with white hair and wearing plain baggy clothes, stood at the base of her steps. He stared up at her. He had already parked the truck behind him.

The woman peered from under the wide brim hat that shielded her narrowing eyes from the hot, bright, rising sun. She glanced over at the truck. She noticed the young girl that unusually accompanied him on his daily trek was not present. This fact emboldened her to act.

"Yes, you can help me," she said as she approached him slowly. "I'd like to speak with you." Since she no longer considered him a threat without his helper friend, she invited him in. "Would you mind coming inside the house for a private conversation?" she politely requested. "I don't mind speaking to you out here, except this place has many long ears," she added and glanced around her.

"Of course," he said. "I wouldn't mind at all."

He strolled up the stairs easier than she thought he would. She guessed his age as in his late seventies. His voice sounded strange to her. It had a soothing sound, similar to her father's voice. Her father's tribal name was Stumbling Bear. His father gave him that name when he heard the news of his wife's pregnancy and grew dizzy from the news. He thought of a stumbling bear. Her father was inspired during a hunt when he watched a herd of Elk cantor across the great plain.

For a reason she could not explain, she did not feel fear in the presence of this man. Just the opposite, she felt more at home with him than she did with practically anyone she knew. That included her best friends. These sensations threw her off balance, as she was prepared to be cross with him and actually felt elated instead.

She opened the screen door. Its rusty hinges cried out their warning to those inside that someone was coming through the front door.

"Thank you," he responded to her courtesy.

Master Li noticed at once that despite the humble dwelling within, this woman kept the floors clean with the rooms neat and tidy. He did not see dirty dishes in the sink or cobwebs in the corners. He did notice the cramped quarters of the one bedroom house and that this woman probably slept on the couch in the living room. She gave up the bedroom to her children, which he considered a noble sacrifice.

"Would you like something to drink, tea perhaps?" she asked as she led him to the small kitchen table.

"Hmm," he murmured agreement while he stared at one small corner bookshelf.

The old house, the only one present on the property, had the same furnishings for over fifty years. Running Elk was born in the bedroom. She grew up here and never traveled anywhere else except the state capital. She never knew her mother, who died of influenza when Running Elk was a little girl.

Master Li quickly examined the bookshelf in the corner. The top shelf was decorated with knick-knacks. The lower shelves contained many books he did not expect to see, books on history, biology, anthropology, art, Shakespeare, books of poetry, fiction and non-fiction, along with an empty space for the infamous Bible. She kept that book on a small table by the front door.

"Probably self-taught," Li surmised.

"Beg your pardon?" the woman whirled around as she grabbed for the kettle on the stove.

"Nothing," Li replied. He cast a furtive glance in her direction.

He pulled out one of the kitchen chairs and sat down as he took in the surroundings.

The kitchen table had a strip of wide chrome around the edge with an old Formica top, scratched badly from years of wear. In the center of the table, the woman kept some plastic flowers in a small white vase for decoration. The 1940's plywood cabinets had a matted stain finish over cheap wood, worn around the edges.

Still, the woman took pride in her aged home. Li could not find one speck of dried food on any countertop or problems with the antique appliances, such as the 1950's toaster that still worked. It sat on the counter next to an old-fashioned breadbox. To Master Li, these things seemed more like the home he left behind in Harbin than the current homes in Rollo with relatively newer items inside. The interior of this house seemed like something trapped inside the middle of the twentieth century.

Li calmly waited for her speak. For a reason he could not explain, he found it difficult to read her thoughts.

"I've been watching you," she quietly spoke with her back to him.

She reached up and took down a box of teabags. She turned the stove's burner on underneath a typical metal kettle. Li did not object, although he would never buy such a commercial preparation of tea. He preferred his freshly-shipped, loose-leaf green tea boiled in water and then strained. That is exactly how his wife made it for fifty years.

"I don't mean to pry..." she started as she turned around to face him. "Those are my people," she gestured toward the window. "I am responsible for them. My father brought us here to this place many years ago. Since he did not have a son, and no man seemed fit for the role, I took over as tribal leader when he died. My name is Running Elk," she told him.

For the first time, Li examined her kind face. Her skin had only begun to wrinkle around the eyes. He noticed she took great care with her nearly perfect teeth. Her pinks lips and nose betrayed her Native American heritage, though only slightly. Her hair seemed a bit grayer than it should be for someone yet so young in Master Li's opinion. He acknowledged her introduction.

"I am pleased to meet you Running Elk," Li said. He rose slightly and bowed his head. "I am Li Po Chin. My friends call me Li."

"Lee?" she asked.

"Yes," he calmly spoke. "I am the one who should apologize, Running Elk. I did not mean to pry into your personal affairs. I only meant to be helpful."

"Don't get me wrong," the woman said. The small water-filled kettle on the stove started to make noise. "I do not object to anything you did, only..."

At that moment, the kettle screamed, a column of steam shot from its black mouth. Running Elk turned off the precious propane gas that she could scarcely afford. She mostly used the gas to heat the water and her home. She started to make the tea by pouring water over a teabag while Master Li watched with trepidation.

"Do you take sugar?" she asked.

"No thank you," Li quietly replied.

She took the steaming cup in her hand and set it down in front of him. She knew he liked tea. Then it struck her that this was not how he usually fixed his tea. Yet, how did she know that about a person she never met?

"This is not to your liking," she said.

"What makes you say that?" he wondered.

"I don't know," she said. "When I set the cup down, I just had the feeling you enjoyed tea but not how I prepared it..."

"Is she psychic?" Li wondered.

"Did you say something?" she asked.

Li regarded her face for a moment.

"Such a lovely face," he thought, "...so kind... so considerate... so loving."

Running Elk stared back at him. She grew lost in Li's face with similar feelings.

"What a kind face... so generous... so understanding..."

Electricity filled the air between them. Li felt something akin to attraction and quickly dismissed the emotion as he glanced down at his cup. Running Elk turned away and took in a deep breath.

"Why should I be attracted to this old man?" she thought.

"Why should I be attracted to this much younger woman?" Li thought.

"What did you say?" they both spoke aloud at the same time. They both nervously laughed.

"I'm sorry, you go ahead," they both spoke again, which brought more laughter.

For the first time since his wife died, Li relaxed around another woman. He could smile and feel something akin to attraction, a feeling he thought died with his wife's parting.

For several seconds Li did not speak, nor did Running Elk. Rather, they resumed their previous posture and stared into each other's eyes. Li felt his heart beat pounding in his chest. Then his eyes widened with a sudden realization. The psychic spark that attracted them to Rollo as their jet approach came from this woman!

"Oh my God," Li exclaimed. He dropped his cup onto the saucer. "She's psychic!"

That time Running Elk had been intently watching his face. When his words leapt into her mind, she reeled back, terrified. She knew that the man sitting at the table across from her, put a thought directly into her mind.

"You are not Li," she said slowly as she backed up to the sink and shook her head.

"I'm not?" Li questioned. He rose from his seat.

"You are… Master Li," she uttered. The words tore from her lips as she shuddered. She closed her eyes and felt faint.

Li rushed over to her, pulled her up and into his arms with more force than she thought possible. Their faces were just inches apart, their lips nearly touching.

"How did you know that?" he whispered to her. "I must know."

"You showed me… with your mind," she said weakly, unable to stand. She closed her eyes and collapsed in his arms. Her head dropped back which exposed her neck.

For a second, he looked at her in his arms, so vulnerable, so light, as if she weighed nothing at all. Running Elk took in a deep breath. She opened her eyes and lifted her head. She placed her arms around Li's shoulders. She moved her face in to kiss him on the lips. Li's mouth slightly parted, when they both heard a noise.

"Mother?" a young person spoke.

The two adults pulled away from each other. Running Elk straightened her clothes and hair while Li moved around the table to his seat. He picked up his tea cup and gazed toward the hall when a slender teenager dressed in an old pair of men's pajamas emerged.

"Star Wind?" Running Elk called out to the teen. She shot Li a glance from the corner of her eye. "You're up early. Are you feeling alright?" she asked.

"I heard voices," the sleepy teen said as she dragged her feet. "They woke me."

"We have a visitor," Running Elk spoke sweetly.

"Hello," she addressed Master Li.

"Star Wind, this is Mast… uh, Li, a new friend from Rollo," Running Elk introduced. "Li, this is my daughter, Star Wind."

"What a lovely name," Li commented. "A pleasure to meet you," he nodded.

"Did you say Rollo, mother? I thought you didn't know anyone from Rollo," the teenager asked.

"Li is one of the new residents…" Running Elk explained.

"What happened to the old residents? I saw everyone driving off in limousines. Do you know why they left Mr. Li?" the teen innocently asked.

Running Elk and Li quickly glanced toward each other. Running Elk's expression appeared open, as if she would agree to anything he said at that moment.

"Their leaving so suddenly does appear mysterious, does it not?" Li quickly responded when he sensed Running Elk's increasing nervousness. He pulled out his pocket watch and glanced at it. "Perhaps you should sleep a little longer," he suggested.

The teen yawned and then turned back up the hall.

"I'm tired… going back to bed… nice to have met you…" she said. Her voice trailed off.

Running Elk shot Li a harsh stare.

"You made her sleepy!" she accused.

Li gulped as he shoved his pocket watch back into his pants. He did not want to offend her. He nodded and glanced down.

"You can do such things?" she questioned. "You can put such influence on the mind?"

Li listened for the bedroom door to close before he spoke.

"You perceive many things for being uninitiated," he linked directly to her mind. "I did not impose my feelings on you," he added.

Her eyes widened but she did not recoil with fear this time. Instead, she boldly faced him.

"I do not fear you," she linked back to his mind. "Are you going to make me do something against my will?"

He did not respond to her question. He only admired her. Li shook his head.

"You are amazing," he thought to her. "You have incredible natural ability. Did you always possess this trait?"

His thoughts no longer put fear inside her. Instead, they relaxed her and filled her mind with confidence and courage.

"From the time I was a little girl," she thought back to him, "I could hear what some people thought when they were calm and not angry. You are the first person I could speak to in this manner. Yet in you, I sense the ability to do so much more. You have great power," she linked and hesitated. She added with a sense of awe in her heart, "... very great power. So that is why they call you Master Li."

Li laughed in response. He moved over to her again and took her elbow. He gently guided her to a seat.

"Please, will you sit down?" he politely requested. "I need to explain a few things."

Running Elk sat in the chair next to him. She could not take her eyes off him.

"First of all," he began, "I am only Master Li to the others. They are psychic, too. We formed a band in China and came to this country. We seek to form a community of like persons. Our founding member, Michael Tyler, is American. He was born in Connecticut. He is very wealthy. We chose to start a community in Rollo because... well, because of you, Running Elk. You see, Michael and I could sense your presence as our jet approached this area. The location of the town... the addition of your people... everything seemed to suit our purposes. We were very generous to the previous occupants that left Rollo. I'm sorry if we drove away any of your friends."

"I called no man or woman in Rollo my friend," she informed him. "For years we begged them for well-digging equipment. We have only one well and have to share it between seventeen families. We have sixty-eight people in this village! Do you know what it is like to try and take a shower when someone flushes a toilet elsewhere?"

"Scalding water?" he guessed.

"Try no water!" she blurted.

"That must be extremely uncomfortable at times..." his voice trailed off.

She smiled in response and then they both chuckled. They felt at ease around one another, as if they had been friends for years. At that moment, it struck Running Elk that she owed a great debt to Master Li, one she doubted she could ever repay.

"You've done so much for my people... the little girl," she thought to him. "The doctors in Wichita told us she would die. We ran out of money trying to save her. Then we lost hope... you saved her life, as you helped so many others," her thoughts telegraphed in spurts. "You fixed their lives and their houses. What can I do to repay you?" she asked. Her voice choked with emotion.

"Nothing, Running Elk," he told her. He patted her hand to punctuate his thought. "I only offer my power to spread goodwill and kindness in the world. If I accomplish that goal, it is reward enough for me."

"Yes, but you do not understand," she continued. "For so many years we had to beg for everything. Times lately have turned hopeless. I started to pray for help. Then you showed up. I feel you are an answer to those prayers..."

"Rest assured, we are ordinary people who happen to possess special gifts. That is all," Li told her.

"Yet you chose Rollo and not some other place. You helped us from the moment you arrived and never asked for anything in return," she said and took his arm. "No doctor or surgeon could do what you did for that little girl," she pointed out. "You are a great gift to humanity Li," she said. "I will forever be in your debt."

Running Elk bowed her head. She burst into tears. Li discovered that he admired her and yet was powerfully attracted to her at the same time. He could no longer remain in her presence. He had feelings for her that confused him. He did not wish to take advantage of her generosity. He did not trust his own emotions. He might try to use his power to his advantage and could not live with his actions if he ever did such a thing.

"I must go," he said as he rose and pulled his arm away.

She reached out to restrain him.

"Wait please," she said. She did not want him to leave.

She took hold of his hand. Her grip was strong. All at once, energy flowed between them. They made a strong psychic connection that brought their two minds together. He turned to face her and took a hold of her other hand. Their fingers entwined.

For a few moments, the thoughts, desires, and passions of the two aging people intermingled. They cast off their physical bodies. Pure energy flowed between them. Afraid he might injure her and guilty about using his power, Li started to push away. However, her grasp on his hands tightened. She pulled him in and drew them closer together as their energy built to a crescendo. Their arms entwined. Their faces closed the distance between them.

The psychic power that poured out from Li would have overwhelmed the best psychic mind in Rollo. Yet even in this moment of passion, he protected her from its power while it filled her body with an incredible sensation. The two stood together, the air turned golden around them as energy pulsed and throbbed in the room. Running Elk wrapped her arms around Master Li and pressed her lips against his. He could no longer resist her. She held on for as long as she could before she started to collapse from the strain.

"Aiiee!" Running Elk cried out. Her body glowed like the sun.

During their tryst, Li had isolated them inside a psychic shield. For a moment, he held her tight in his arms. Then he withdrew and the energy flowed back into his body. He dropped the bubble around them. He gently sat her in a chair. He wanted to tell her how much she meant to him, or perhaps he should apologize. The whole episode confused him. Had he fallen for another woman? He could not decide or sort through his feelings. He turned to walk away, ashamed for what his unleashed passion did. Running Elk reached out and grabbed his hand. Out of breath, she linked to him.

"Li…" she whispered to his mind, "you did not force anything on me… I wanted you…" she whispered. "We are adults… you have nothing to be ashamed of in my eyes… or his…" she added and glanced up.

"Running Elk…" he quietly replied. "I am so very sorry…"

Li and Running Elk reluctantly let go of their hands. Li turned to the front door and dragged his heavy feet toward other obligations.

"Do you believe in love at first…" she spoke behind his back.

"Sight?" he finished her thought and paused. He wanted to say more. He wanted to confess the love he felt inside. However, he also knew he was a powerful psychic being and the leader of a community. He hung his head. "I must go…" he linked to her. "They need me…"

"I am not far away," she linked back. "Go and be their master… Master Li."

She watched as the screen door opened on its own. Li walked through and then the door quietly closed with only the soft sounds of his feet as they pattered away.

Running Elk rose from her chair. She had not expected this exchange, yet she welcomed this man, this Li into her life. Her eyes filled up with tears as she watched him climb into the truck. She knew that with a word, she could keep him there. Yet, she wanted him to go, to do his duty. She understood his duty better than anyone, for Li allowed her into his most private thoughts, a place no other human or even psychic had ever seen, not even his wife. As he left her presence, she felt his energy leave, too. It drained something out of her at the same time.

She stood in the doorway and watched the silent truck move back to the road. She leaned on the table next to the door and put her hand down on the Bible. She picked up the holy book and glanced down at the cover. She walked out the screen door and leaned against the front post, clutching the book against her chest. At that moment, an appropriate passage from the Bible jumped into her mind as her eyes followed the truck that moved silently up the road.

"…for whither thou goest, I will go; and where thou lodgest, I will lodge: thy people shall be my people, and thy God my God."

Chapter Fourteen

Invasion

A LOUD SOUND, FOLLOWED BY a vibration, shook the house and woke both men from a deep sleep. Sputtering to cast off dreams, both men distinctly heard loud pounding that intruded into their peaceful quiet world.

"What's going on?" Han linked as he sat up.

"I don't know," Li linked back.

Han did not believe Li.

"You? You don't know something? Ha! Circle this day on the calendar…" he sarcastically blurted.

Another loud rap sounded, this time they knew it came from their front door. The violence of that knock forced Han from his cozy warm bed. He glanced over at the east-facing window and stared bleary-eyed at the horizon.

"The sun isn't up!" he declared.

The persistent fist pounded the doorframe so hard that it shook the entire house each time it slammed into the wooden frame.

Han swung his feet around. After all, it could be Michael with some urgent matter.

"I'm coming!" Han yelled through his open door. He heard Master Li rise, too. "What on earth could block Master Li?" Han thought as he pulled his robe shut. He made it to the top of the stairs when the pounding resumed. "For the love of…" he started down the staircase and stopped before he reached the bottom step. Through the white lacy curtains that covered the glass in the front door he could make out a stranger, a person he did not know.

"Who is that?" he wondered.

A woman with an old hat and gray hair pulled back into a ponytail stood outside. She wore a fierce expression on her face. Han gulped, afraid to take another step when he heard Master Li behind him.

"Isn't that the woman with the shotgun?" Han wondered. "She's here to shoot us!"

"Running Elk? Hardly," Li commented as he peered curiously over Han's shoulder.

"What's she doing here?" Han questioned.

"How should I know?" Li retorted.

"Aren't you supposed to be the great Master Li that knows everything?" Han said over his right shoulder.

Li finally pushed past Han. He took the rest of the stairs with more boldness than Han demonstrated. He started to open the door and realized that Han bolted it in two different places. Li shot Han a disgusted expression as he pulled back on one lock and twisted the other. He finally pulled open the door.

"Really Han!" Li said.

He opened the door to find Running Elk staring at his face. She faltered a moment in the prepared speech she rehearsed the entire time she spent walking up the highway to Rollo. For a second, Li thought she would leave. He would have been relieved if she did. She took a step backward. He noticed her struggling to speak in Han's presence.

He did not tell anyone about what happened at the tribal village during their encounter, nor did he wish to. He felt that moment was a private one between him and Running Elk. She pursed her lips together and blurted her words out.

"I'm here to serve you," she finally said.

"In what capacity?" Li pointedly asked.

"I will be your… servant," she mumbled.

"I don't wish to have an indebted servant or a slave," Li told her.

"I wouldn't actually be one… would I?" she questioned.

"I don't know… what did you want to do?" Li questioned from the doorway.

"I want to serve you," she said again. "You helped my people. You brought them out of a terrible state. Now the men tell me that Michael will pay them a salary, my son included. He can take care of my daughter. I am here to look after you… if you'll have me," she said. Her last words were followed by quiet.

"I cannot employ an indentured servant Running Elk," Li began. "I have no means of paying you. Besides, you lead your tribe. You are its spiritual head. They need your wisdom and guidance."

"My son is very wise," she countered. "He only lacked ambition. He has that now. He wants to be crew leader. I started when I was sixteen. He'll be twenty later this year. I can't think of a better way to teach him about being a guide for others… and that makes me free. I am here to serve."

Han watched this exchange with growing interest. He stepped up next to Master Li.

"How would you serve us?" Han spoke up.

"I can clean…" she started.

"Master Li does that," Han interrupted.

"This old man?" she questioned doubtfully.

Han knew that Running Elk must know about them being psychic, yet probably not the extent of their power. He said nothing in reply. He simply put his index finger to the side of his head and winked at her. This threw her off track.

"Yes, very well… as you say, Master Li cleans the house…," she thought. She tried to find another reason to stay. "What about cooking? How do you men cook your food?"

She had both men on that point. Neither Li nor Han knew anything about cooking, nor did they try. Thus far, they ate sandwiches or packaged meals, which were beginning to wear out their welcome. Both men would have done anything for a good, home-cooked, Chinese meal. Yet, Han realized, and perhaps Li did too, that having a woman in the house would change how they did things, such as walking around in their underwear late at night.

"Running Elk," Li cut Han off. "We know your intentions are honorable ones. You feel you owe me something. I feel honored by your acknowledgement. However, despite the fact we could use a cook, I don't really have a place for you to…"

"Stay?" she cut him off. "This is a three bedroom house with two men. I have a one-bedroom house which three of us share. We managed just fine. Can you think of a reason I may not stay in the third bedroom?"

Her eyes searched both of their faces as each man struggled to find some objection and could not.

"Good," she said as she pushed her way inside the house.

Han tightened his robe and stepped back. He thought that Master Li would somehow intervene. Instead, he noticed that Li had the queerest of expressions on his face. Li's reaction puzzled Han.

"Then it's settled. I will be your new cook," she told them. "I don't require payment or a day off. Tell me when you are hungry and you can eat whenever you like. Would you like your breakfast?" she asked.

"I…" Li hesitated and glanced over at Han.

"Nothing for me thanks," Han said and shook his head. "Perhaps, later…"

"Yes later," Li said. He released air from his lungs as if he had been holding it.

As the two men ascended the staircase, they heard Running Elk going through the kitchen. They heard banging and clanging along with her mumbling complaints over the disorganization she found.

"What have you done?" Han whispered to Li at the top of the stairs.

The two men stared down the staircase toward the first floor. Their heads turned together and Li held up his hand.

"When the barbarians are at the gate," Li started, "we must learn the language of the barbarian."

"Truer words were never spoken," Han nodded.

Both men wandered back to their bedroom to dress. A few minutes later both Master Li and Han emerged from their bedrooms, both men stood at the top of the stairs. Neither took a step forward. They hesitated as if the path led to a dungeon.

"You first," Han held out his hand.

Li gulped and put his foot down. The first step creaked. He closed his eyes when he realized he just revealed his position.

"Coming down?" Running Elk called out from the kitchen.

Li took in a deep breath and started down the stairs. Han turned back to his bedroom when Li gave him a poisonous stare.

"Don't you dare!" Li said as he glared at Han.

The other man shrugged and moved in behind Li, when the elder man held out his arm.

"Be careful what you link… she may be able to hear you!" Li warned.

Han suddenly realized that when Master Li arrived home in such a shaken state, he had some altercation with Running Elk. The two men crept carefully down the wooden steps to the first floor. Running Elk proudly stood in the doorway to the kitchen, ready to jump at their slightest wish.

"Would you like some breakfast?" she asked. "I've started a few things!"

Li swallowed hard. He hated to tell her that he usually ate plain yogurt, a bite or two of fruit and a cup of hot tea for breakfast. Occasionally he had a piece of toast with some honey. He could not imagine what Running Elk would fix. If he opened his mind for a second to scan the kitchen, she would be able to read his thoughts and his emotion.

He smiled clumsily and moved toward the dining room table. At the same time he yanked on Han's sleeve next to him so that the twenty-eight-year-old, ex-civil servant could not slip away. Han also smiled and bowed. Running Elk, eager to please, bowed back and turned into the kitchen.

They heard some sizzling sounds and occasionally heard Running Elk say things like, "Garsh darn it," or "Ohhh!" or even "Oops!" Each time Li and Han exchanged glances. Unable to scan, they wondered what would come out of the kitchen.

The first thing she set down in front of them was a pot of coffee – the old fashioned kind that involved putting grounds in the bottom of the pot and boiling water on the stove. Han didn't mind drinking coffee. He enjoyed the flavor of coffee now and then. Li seemed disappointed in this choice, as Running Elk said only the day before that she knew he liked tea. He wondered if she guessed he drank coffee for breakfast.

When Han poured the coffee, the liquid had the consistency of chocolate syrup. He suspected the coffee boiled on the stove for several minutes too long. His eyes widened with a look of horror on his face as he tipped the pot. That was nothing compared to Master Li's face when Running Elk brought out the first plate.

"Here's your breakfast gentlemen!" she declared.

She had two sunny-side-up, practically raw eggs on the plate with a burnt piece of canned ham next to them. The entire plate shined as the food swam in grease.

"Dig in!" she declared. "Han I'll have yours in a minute."

The moment she left the room, Han turned to Li with a look of desperation on his face. He started to link, when Li held up his hand to stop him. Unfortunately, Han did not have time to learn sign language, which the rest of the group memorized in China. Li only had one last move up his sleeve before Running Elk returned from the kitchen.

They heard a loud knock at the front door. Running Elk stuck her head out of the kitchen. Li and Han both smiled at her. She assumed that when they did not move, it was part of her duty to answer the door. She dropped a plate of greasy raw eggs and ham off in front of Han on her way to the front door.

Michael stood outside. She did not recognize him, as he had not been to the village. She could tell he had been running. He anxiously paced back and forth and gasped for air. She cracked the door open.

"Yes?" she asked.

"Who are you?" Michael asked. "Is Master Li in? I need him right away."

"I'm the new cook…" Running Elk told him.

"Cook?" Michael reacted with alarm.

"Yes, my name is Running Elk. Who are you?" she suspiciously asked.

"Your name is… are you kidding?" Michael responded, half-smiling.

Offended, she started to close the door when Master Li hurriedly walked up. He stepped between Running Elk and Michael while he pulled the door open all the way.

"Running Elk meet Michael Tyler," Li anxiously spoke. He introduced the pair and then hurriedly added an explanation. "He sort of runs things in Rollo. Michael, this is our new cook, Running Elk. She's from the village. She'll be staying with us in our spare bedroom."

"Ma'am," Michael quickly acknowledged and politely nodded his head. He turned to Li. "Master Li I need you right away."

"What about Han…" Li softly added and jerked his head back toward the dining room.

"Oh yes, I need Han too," Michael put in. "This is urgent! Come quick!"

"Han!" Li called out. "Pardon me Running Elk. Things are happening so fast around here… must be some emergency. We'll be back later. Thanks for fixing breakfast."

Before she could object, Master Li pushed Michael out the door. He grabbed the tall young man by the arm and practically pulled him down the steps out to the sidewalk. Han burst out the front door as if fired from a canon. He ran after them. The trio turned left around the corner. They walked along the east boundary road, moving north toward Main Street. They turned left at the corner and stopped in front of Michael's house. Michael stared at Han and Master Li with a frown.

"Would you mind telling me why I went to your house at six thirty-eight in the morning?" he demanded. "I have absolutely no clue as to why I knocked on your door and asked for you… for both of you!" Michael angrily stated and stamped his foot.

Han and Li exchanged looks before they glanced up at Michael's frowning face.

"To save our lives," they said together.

"…for which we will be forever grateful," Han added.

"Now," Li put to him, "do you have a loaf of bread to make toast?" he asked.

"…and a tea bag?" Han added, his eyebrows raised with expectation.

Michael did not know what to think as he looked back and forth at two powerful psychics humbled by a very peculiar woman.

Chapter Fifteen

Long overdue

The first tumultuous week in Rollo finally came to a conclusion. The psychic group – while still in its infancy – began the slow work of building a new community out of this obscure tiny town made up of old crumbling houses and inadequate supplies. Thus far they evacuated the town, took over its buildings, and began to interact with local Comanche Village's residents up the road. From that contact, their tribal leader, Running Elk, now lives with the psychic group leader Master Li in a tenuous position at best. The psychic group has made a series of visits via Galactic Central to a variety of planets in order to expand their knowledge related to specific areas.

However, all was not going well, at least not as well as Michael Tyler had hoped when he first envisioned such a community. Seeking to uphold his dream of a unified psychic organization, Michael tried to keep the group's morale up when he called for daily meetings and noted the progress of individuals. He constantly moved about the town and linked with the eight other psychic minds scattered across Rollo in various stages of alertness due to off planet activity. He monitored their gradual progress toward their individual goals and offered whatever support he could supply to hasten that person's achievements.

Michael calmly strolled down the street after a busy morning of rounds. He just left Su Lin at Baker's store and intended to visit Han next for some strategic consultation. About fifty meters before the house he paused when he smelled an acrid strong odor of smoke.

A horrible thought occurred to him that if one of the houses caught fire, they did not have a fire department or even an organized brigade to put it out. While psychics have the power of manipulation, they could not coordinate enough water on a fire before it spread. It was at that moment he noticed black smoke start to emerge from the back of Master Li's house. The longer he stood there, the thicker and worse the smoke poured from the back window.

"Oh, no," he gasped. "Han! Master Li!" he mentally cried as he bolted up the street. "Fire! Help! There's a fire at Master Li's!"

He searched around Rollo with his mind for help. Practically everyone was preoccupied with either browsing Galactic Central's vast database or traveling to some other world. Villi was hard at work under the belly of the jet on the opposite side of Rollo. No one heard his plea.

"Han?" he called as he ran. He wondered if Han was in the house.

As if an answer to a prayer, Michael stopped just outside the back of the house when he felt Master Li's presence coming up the highway in his silent truck. It progressed painfully slow toward Rollo, far too slow for Michael's impatience.

"Master Li!" Michael called out. "Your house!"

"What about it?" Li calmly replied.

"It's on fire!" Michael linked.

"Oh," Li responded with a calm tone. "Is that all," he replied. "Stay right there Michael. Take no action…"

"But Master Li…" Michael protested.

"I'll be right there…" Li linked back.

However, the smoke coming from the back window grew worse. All at once, Running Elk stuck her head out the window and coughed. A huge column of black smoke poured out around her. She waved her hands in front of her soot-covered face.

"I'm coming Running Elk!" Michael shouted.

She did not hear him. From Michael's point of view, it appeared that she withdrew, possibly overcome by smoke, and passed out on the floor.

"Michael, stop, please," Li pleaded as he drew nearer.

Michael was too focused to hear Li's plea. Instead, he seemed determined to rescue the new cook Running Elk. He headed straight for the back door and shoved it open with his foot. The door swung inward so violently that it broke the glass.

With her back to the door, Running Elk screamed. Instinctively, she thought an intruder had broken into the house. She grabbed an iron skillet off the stove and threw it across the room at Michael's head. The heavy black object flew through the air just as Michael used his martial arts training to react. He quickly ducked as the skillet flew past his head. The pan smashed through the upper pane of the kitchen's back window and careened into the yard. It plopped into the grass with a dull thud. Running Elk started to pick up another pan and stopped her assault when she saw it was Michael standing there with a puzzled expression on his face.

"Don't kill me Running Elk!" he declared. "I'm here to rescue you from the fire!"

"What fire?" she said back to him.

Michael glanced over at the stove. Smoke poured from the open oven door. He saw what appeared to be some kind of toasted black meat smoldering in a burnt dish coated with black soot. The room smelled as bad as the sight appeared. Michael coughed. The singed odor filled his nostrils with the irritant.

"I'm sorry… I was outside… I thought…" he said as he tried to recover. He did not wish to offend her.

However, Running Elk could see that Michael was panting. His chest heaved up and down. His body was covered with sweat. Despite the pained expression on his face, she burst out laughing.

"I'm sorry Michael," she said as she walked up to him. "That was a wonderful thing you intended," she added as she patted his shoulder. "I'm glad you thought of my safety. Sorry I threw a frying pan at you. I thought you were an intruder."

"That's ok," he said as he tried to stifle his cough.

She turned around and mournfully looked back at her stove from his point of view. "That is a sad sight," she said as she shook her head. "So much for my meatloaf," she added. She stared at the blacken pan that contained a solid block of charred blackness. "The last time it came out too raw inside, so I turned up the heat. I got busy with laundry and forgot I left the stove on high," she said in a low voice.

She used her apron to pick up the pan and drop it into the garbage. She briskly rubbed her hands together.

"Do you think Baker's have any frozen pizzas left?" she asked.

Michael could not smile. He saw through her façade.

"I tried to stop him," they both heard Master Li's voice as he walked in through the front door. "He seemed intent on saving your life."

"He's a good boy," she said as she turned to Li when he entered the kitchen. She tried to put the best face on. But when Li appeared, she started to unhinge – nearly on the verge of tears. She grabbed a towel to wipe off the smudges of black soot on her face.

"What's going on?" they heard Han's voice call down from upstairs. "I thought I heard something smash and breaking glass. Is anyone hurt?"

No one answered because Li quickly linked, "The situation is resolved."

"Do we have the makings for a sandwich?" Li asked Running Elk aloud. "I would love a sandwich and a cup of tea for dinner," he stated.

Running Elk ran her fingers through her hair and sat down in a kitchen chair.

"I'm such a failure," she started. She brought her apron up to her face and started to sob.

Li glanced up at Michael, closed his eyes, and shook his head. Michael took this as his cue. He stepped backward out the door and felt for the stoop with his foot. He watched Master Li put his hand on Running Elk's upper arm. The pair disappeared from view when Master Li isolated them within a powerful shield. Michael noticed the frying pan lift up out of the yard and float in through the window. Glass shards gathered and re-fused into a window.

"I wish I knew how he does that?" Michael thought before he turned away.

He walked across Li's backyard and easily hopped over the fence between their houses. Inside, he sensed Cecilia in the process of another medical lesson via Galactic Central. As his senses traveled across the town, he found Chou and Zhiwei in a similar state inside their houses.

"One of these days," he thought, "I should take a journey or two."

Michael sensed Villi still at work in the barn on the north end of town. He had converted the space into a hanger for the jet. The barn seemed strange with the jet's tail sticking out of one end covered with olive-green tarpaulin. The group had to remain vigilant with every vehicle that passed if they regarded the sight suspiciously.

For the past few mornings, Villi took an hour or two out of his busy day to take courses from Galactic Central. Villi learned every aspect on the subject of engines. He not only knew how they worked, but he could build any engine from the ground up. In one week, Villi transformed from being a Khabarovsk police officer into the most eminent expert on the art and science of transportation technology. He felt his only limits to advanced transportation were the tools he lacked to set his plans into motion.

As he sat alone in the barn, he began to make conceptual designs, such as ceramic engines that utilized air as a source of energy. He envisioned magnetic inducer coils that propelled spacecraft by using "star energy" outside the atmosphere. He drew so quickly, he literally tore through a stack of pencils and paper in an hour.

A pile of sketches lay on the ground next to him. He was on his fourth sketch pad when he finally pulled back from his latest blueprint.

"That would be nice," he thought as he gazed at his plans for a subterranean hanger complex that included crew quarters. "The only thing missing is the crew..." He threw the pad aside. "Who am I kidding?" he thought. "None of this will ever come to pass," he said as he rose. "What am I doing here? Rollo is a terrible place! Why did I let Michael convince me..."

He glanced out the window across the field. Long before he could see her, he felt her presence growing nearer. Like a ship's sails that rise out of the sea on the horizon, he spied Su Lin's white scarf billowing in the afternoon breeze as she made her way toward him. In the heat of late July afternoon, the slender yet buxom Chinese woman chose to wear a long white silk scarf around her neck that seemed to float on the air. Yet, she wore an open halter-top blouse with nothing else on underneath. Her bouncing ample cleavage was clearly visible to the overheated Russian. She wore some tight jeans that seemed a size too small. Everything accentuated her curvaceous figure that swung its way toward him.

"Working hard?" she linked as she approached.

She had been monitoring Villi's thoughts all afternoon after she returned from her trip to Artane. She watched with increased interest when he discarded his shirt while he worked on the jet's belly. His hairy pectoral muscles glistened as he whipped the aircraft into shape. He had not put the shirt back on. He intended to before he walked back.

The pencil in his hand snapped as she emerged from the tall grass and stood before him like some Asian goddess. He stood still and did not link. He could only stare at her.

"I see you've been busy," she commented as moved closer. She looked everywhere but at him.

He could feel his heart pound in his chest. His thoughts caught in his throat. He could not link back to her. He swallowed hard, afraid to move.

"You could stop for a visit," she whispered to him. "Even prisoners are allowed visitors."

She was so close to him that he could smell her body. She had a clean freshly showered scent. He finally relaxed enough to respond.

"I could make the same request," he quipped back. "Between the lessons on mechanics and creating a temporary hanger, I've been a little busy."

"Yes," she sighed as she moved past him. She ran her hand along the fuselage. "This is bigger than I remembered."

She slyly glanced back at Villi over her shoulder. He turned to follow her as she walked further into the barn.

"We are psychics Su Lin," Villi linked as moved behind her. "Your motivation for coming here is quite transparent. I thought Master Li forbid conjugal visits..."

"Master Li is not in Rollo..." she linked back. "At least, I don't feel his energy nearby. Anyway, Master Li doesn't matter. This is between us. I am an adult female. I have feelings for you. I have a right to express those feelings without my parents or Master Li's permission. I was once a married woman." Her eyes traveled all over Villi's half-exposed body. "I know what it is to be needed and loved…"

She moved up to Villi and put her hands on his arms. He did not try to stop her. She nodded toward the aircraft's interior.

"Let's go inside the jet," she suggested.

"Su Lin…" Villi countered. "Perhaps we should wait as Master Li suggested."

She pushed him backward toward the jet's opening hatch. He did not resist. He allowed her to back him up. She pushed harder and harder each time.

"What are you going to do officer?" she said as she pushed hard on his chest. "The lady is out of line…" she pushed. "Have her arrested…" she pushed again. "You'd better take me in… frisk me… I plead… guilty as charged."

Su Lin then wrapped one arm around Villi's head and pulled their faces together. Their eyes finally met.

"I want this as much as you do, but…"

Her eyes filled with water. She shook her head.

"That excuse won't fly this time… pilot," she said.

Their lips came together. Villi's dirty and sweaty body clung next to Su Lin's clean and chaste one. That changed rapidly as the two adults wrapped their arms around each other in a tight embrace.

"Uh oh," Cecilia thought as she popped up from her bed. She had only just returned from her latest medical lesson when she felt the psychic energy building out in the barn. "I could feel that clear across Rollo!"

The rest of Rollo felt their sexual energy rising too, including Running Elk. She glanced over at Master Li. He was still nursing her wounds over the burnt dinner. He started to create a shield for privacy, when the couple dropped a psychic bubble around them and isolated their movements inside the jet.

"I was wondering when that would happen," Michael thought as he walked inside his home. He sensed Cecilia back from Galactic Central.

Though distracted by Villi and Su Lin for a moment, Zinian had other more important priorities. He had just finished laying out his plans with his work crew. He spent the day training them with the new tools that arrived. He also promised to pay them at the end of the day, "in good faith," he told them.

The Native American men gathered at the front of Baker's store. Michael left a shoebox full of money for Zinian in the general store. The group authorized Zinian to hand out as much cash as he deemed necessary to his workers.

"What if they're lazy? What should I do?" he asked Michael.

"Fire them," Michael suggested.

"I can't do that," Zinian responded.

"Then find a way to motivate them. Otherwise, you might have to crack the whip," Michael recommended.

Zinian simply frown at that notion. He was not that kind of person.

"What should I do if someone takes the cash and heads off to Wichita, Topeka or travels even further away? They might talk to strangers about the Chinese that took over Rollo," he put to Michael.

"Search their minds every night for their intentions. Don't feel as if you are invading their privacy. We have security issues at stake. You must be on guard that these men don't betray our secrecy," Michael instructed.

"I'll do my best, Michael," Zinian responded with hesitation. "But I'm not a police officer. I don't like to enforce these arbitrary rules," he reiterated. "I feel I'm invading their privacy. What if one of them skips town?" he put to Michael.

"Then you must erase Rollo from his mind," Michael told him. "We don't have any alternative."

"I'm sorry, Michael," Zinian told him. "I can't do that."

"You wanted to be master builder," Michael pointed out. "However, your crew is your responsibility. Their safety and any breach of security is also your responsibility."

"I can't watch them twenty-four hours a day," Zinian protested.

"Then Zhiwei will monitor them at night," Michael offered. "If they run, you must decide on a course of action to maintain our security… the alternative is too terrible to consider."

Zinian took in a deep breath and wondered how to handle passing out the cash. His crew stepped out of the two trucks and surrounded him. He held the cash box in his hand.

"I have your pay," Zinian said to them as he opened the box. The men saw a stack of cash.

"That's all right," the crew's leader said as he stepped in front of the others. "You can pay us when we finish a job, just as any employer would."

Zinian stopped to regard the leader for their group. He intended to put this young man in charge of a second crew to work on projects in the Native American village. The young man confused Zinian. For a moment, he could not read his mind.

"I thought…" Zinian said aloud, "I mean look, I have the money right here… honest," he told them.

"We trust you Zinian," John said. "When you and Michael approached us for help, we were glad to pitch in. We know you will pay us. After the old one helped my mother, we decided to stick together. We are here to help for as long as you need us."

"Well, if that's the case then I…" Zinian stopped and looked up the street.

He felt he owed them more than just a paycheck. If they were going to help rebuild Rollo, then they should become a part of this new community as partners. He knew he had not consulted anyone. However, it suddenly dawned on him that Michael was right. He was responsible for his crew.

"I have an idea," he began. "We're only using eight of the houses in town. I see no reason why this crew can't take over some of the other houses. No one is living in them."

The men stirred. A few of them exchanged glances and smiled.

"We want to build a special place here – a unique place," Zinian continued. "I believe I speak for the others when I say that we want to include you in that community, if you'll have us," he offered at the end.

The other men turned to the group leader. John nodded toward Zinian and shook his hand. Each man followed his example. They stepped up to Zinian and shook his hand on the deal. One by one, they hopped back into the truck.

"They all feel the same," John said. "Whatever you decide will be enough."

"Ok," Zinian began. "If you won't take the cash, take some food from Baker's store. You need at least much compensation. The store is open. Help yourself. Later at tonight's meeting, I intend to propose that each man on my crew be assigned a house," Zinian said. "Tell them to move their whole family."

"Thanks Zinian," John said and shook his hand. "I'll drive the men back to the village, and then bring the truck back to Rollo. I can walk back to the village. See you in the morning."

"Wait…" Zinian called to him. "Keep the truck. Since you'll be in charge of a crew, you'll need it."

The men in the truck whispered when Zinian made this trusting offer. Yet, something about the young man puzzled Zinian. Why couldn't he penetrate the young man's mind? How could he block him, unless…

"You mentioned your mother a moment ago. Do I know her? Who is your mother?" Zinian asked the man.

"Running Elk," John answered.

Chapter Sixteen

Intimate Revelations

Villi and Su Lin exited the aircraft, dirty hand clasped in dirty hand. After their exhaustive lovemaking, Villi wanted a moment to share his designs with Su Lin. She looked over his sketches and marveled at the details which he included in the hastily made drawings.

"You're good... very good, Villi," she commented, "...uh, the drawings."

He smiled at her double entendre.

"Drafting was one of the subroutines in my engineering download," he told her. "Along with perspective drawing, artistic design, use of color palate, you name it. Want me to paint you as the Mona Lisa?"

"I believe you," she said as she held up one drawing after another. "In fact, your freehand is better than most polished draftsmen," she told him. "We'll open Villi's design studio," she said as she fanned out her arms.

He picked up one of the sketches, one he made of the underground system. It showed a breakaway opening to the substructure that included details on every floor from where pipes and wires would go along side an elevator system with exhaust ducts.

"A fantasy," he muttered. "It would take Zinian years to complete this," he said as he started to tear it in two. "What's the point?"

"Don't," she said to stop him. "This is art. Don't destroy it. Please." She placed her hand on top of his. Her hand imparted more than touch.

"Ok," he said as he placed the drawing back on the table.

"I'd like to frame them… put them up in your new underground complex," she softly spoke. "Someday… perhaps."

"Someday…" he echoed.

"Do you mind if we…"

"…spend the night together? No, I don't mind."

"Good," she smiled and tugged on his hand.

They left the drawings, scattered about the space where he tossed them, and walked out of the barn for home. For the first time in their relationship, Su Lin completely understood Villi's fascination with engines as he understood her love of education. Their mind link this time was unfettered by any interference. The two rapidly linked thoughts back and forth as they casually strolled for Su Lin's home.

"I've been so caught up with my own problems," he linked to her as they walked along. "What's everyone doing?"

"Zhiwei spends his days diverting outsiders," she told him, "while Zinian has to run after his crew and tell them what a hammer does."

Villi chuckled at this. She knew, however, Villi was jealous that Zinian had a crew.

"What have you heard?" she asked.

"Michael told me that Chou is strung out over this Ziddis thing," he told her. "I saw him yesterday morning. He looked stressed out."

"I'd say you were stressed out earlier," she kidded.

"You took care of that," he said as he squeezed her hand.

"The stress relief was mutual," she said and squeezed back.

As the couple strolled through the field in the dark, nature reflected their lives in its ritual of continuous renewal. The night sky seemed to flourish overhead with a blaze of twinkling lights.

"A starry night for star crossed lovers?" Su Lin wondered as she gazed skyward.

A shooting star cut across the blackness of space. A fragment of rock entered the atmosphere and provided brief celestial fireworks. More meteors streaked across the sky. Their faint trails were easy to see in the darkness that surrounded them.

"That's a good omen," Villi said as he stared up, his arm draped around her waist.

"Perseid," she chimed in.

"Perseid?" he questioned and then saw it in her thoughts. "Oh, the annual meteor shower."

"Seems it's started something," she linked as she indicated the ground.

As if on cue, fireflies began to rise up from prairie grass – their brilliant yellow light flashed on and off. Soon, thousands of spinning tiny yellow dots moved in a ritual-mating dance. The couple stopped to behold their spectacle.

"I've never seen so many stars," Su Lin confessed as she gazed skyward. "Where I grew up, the city lights blot them out."

"I've never seen a firefly," Villi told her.

"Never?" she wondered.

"They spray the countryside with insecticide. It kills them," he explained.

He pointed toward the horizon. The couple watched as a large orange disc slowly crept over the horizon into the night sky, a rising full moon.

"What an amazing night," Su Lin sighed. She slipped her arm around Villi's waist.

"What an amazing place, especially with you in it," Villi concurred as he glanced her way. "I believe I'm beginning to like it here."

"Who would have believed that a little town in southwest Kansas could be so wonderful?" Su Lin commented.

She turned to face him. Her lips were only a few inches away. A blaze of tiny flashing lights swirled in the blackness of their eyes. Their lips touched and they tightly embraced as lovers do. They shared a tender moment with nature which they would long remember.

"What is the time?" Su Lin asked.

"Time?" Villi questioned.

Su Lin pulled it from the mind of a Native American.

"Michael called a meeting… we need to go," she told him.

He was content to remain here the rest of the night. However, duty and obligation called on both of them to prepare for the night's meeting. They had a town to help build. Each member of their group did his or her part. They signed on to that promise and intended to carry it out.

"Coming?" she asked as she pulled on the reluctant man.

"Sure," he said as he withdrew from the starlight ballet.

"Race?" she linked.

Su Lin laughed and took off at a sprinter's pace. Villi easily caught up with her. Like ballet dancers, the lovers sprang through the air over the back steps and kicked off their shoes while they opened the door with their mind at the same time. Both psychics landed inside the house and slid up the hall in their stocking feet. Inside Su Lin's house, they both paused by the full-length mirror in the hall to take in their image.

"Uh, oh," she muttered. "We're a wreck!"

Villi whiffed his armpit.

"We stink, too. I don't believe we should go to the meeting like this," he commented.

Su Lin nodded and motioned toward the stairs with her head. Villi smiled and agreed when he picked up "shared shower" from her mind.

Together, they took the stairs, two or more steps at a time. Bounding to the top, they ripped their clothes off in the process. Before the wretched aromatic articles of clothing struck the floor, Su Lin floated them down to a waiting basket near the back door.

The old washer and dryer that sat on the back porch badly needed replacement. Su Lin could probably order a new machine if Michael approved it – another item on a long list of things to put Rollo on its collective feet. As the foundation of Su Lin's acquired house settled through the years, the entire back porch listed at an angle toward the ground. The previous occupants had to wedge up the front of the washer so that the spin cycle would work.

"You have a nicer shower than I do," Villi commented as he turned on the water. "The bathroom has more room too."

"Then it's decided," Su Lin broke in on his thoughts. "You must move in here...," she offered. She squeezed her bare skin next to his naked body.

"But Master Li said..." Villi started.

She put a finger on his lips.

"I can still link," he grinned.

"Master Li will not separate us this time," she quietly linked. "If he wants us to function normally, he must allow us to live together. It doesn't take a psychic to see that!"

"You took the words right out of my brain," Villi linked back to her.

The two enjoyed a brief amorous time in the shower while they simultaneously cleaned up for the meeting scheduled to start any moment.

"Do you have any towels?" he asked when he stepped from the shower. He shook his lengthening black mane free of water. He had not cut his hair in weeks. He noticed his head in the mirror. His longer dark hair had changed his overall image from the one he had as a nearly bald Russian police officer.

Su Lin laughed when she recalled that she left the towels in the dryer.

"I'm so sorry darling. I wasn't thinking that far ahead. I forgot about fresh towels for us. I'm still adjusting to this buddy system," she half-smiled.

"Well..." he spoke honestly. "Since we're on the subject, we should share domestic chores. I can do the laundry as well as you can, I suppose. I'll try to help out with things like that," he promised. He put his large wet hairy arms around her slender nakedness.

"You would do that for me?" she questioned.

"I would do that and more for you," he said as he bent to kiss her.

Since psychics cannot lie without instantly revealing a falsehood, she knew that he spoke the truth. For Villi, being honest was not just good policy. It was a way of life, long before he became a psychic.

"I suppose we can air dry," he continued as he held her close. "The air is warm enough for the water to eventually evaporate. If we walk slow, our bodies will be dry by the time we arrive..."

At that moment, a towel flew through the door and carefully draped over her shoulders.

"You can go to the meeting naked," she smiled and looked down. "I want to dress."

She pulled away and started to dry off. He stared at her with disbelief.

"Su Lin, you amaze me," he linked. "You have incredible control. I didn't even feel you do that!"

"We have to hurry," she linked as she rubbed the water from her hair. "I sense Michael is waiting for us. Sometimes women act out of desperation."

"I'll say!" he grinned. "You can act desperately around me any time you wish!"

He started to chase her around the bathroom while she shrieked and giggled. Just then a second flying towel struck his face and blocked his view. Villi nearly ran in to the wall, but Su Lin prevented any injury. He yanked the towel down and stared at her. She curtseyed and smiled, did a pirouette, and stuck her tongue out at him. She tore out of the bathroom and ran up the hall. He took off after her as she fled screaming and laughing at the same time. When Villi rounded the corner, five more towels flew up the staircase and pelted him like missiles. She laughed as he struggled to tear them off his face and chest.

"All is fair in love and war!" she called out and ran into the bedroom.

"Just remember that the next time we have a pillow fight!" he called after her.

Michael glanced over when he saw Cecilia standing near the window smiling.

"What's up?" he asked as she had her thoughts blocked.

"Oh, eavesdropping on the neighbors having fun," she said as she turned to him.

He glanced over her shoulder to the house diagonally across the street and caught part of what made her smile.

"I'm glad they're together," he commented. "That will lift Villi's spirits."

"Speaking of which," she began, "we'll have to do something about the rest of the men in this village, don't we?"

Michael could only nod as he turned away. He wondered what would be the major topic of conversation this evening, the fire at Master Li's house or the torrid love affair across the street. Perhaps Zinian would explain why he did not hand out any money to his crew, which Michael sensed when the crew returned to their village with only sacks of groceries. He turned to Cecilia. He sensed that her only concern was the appearance of her house.

"What about snacks?" he wondered.

"Should I make something?" she responded.

"No," he shook his head. "We don't have time. We could open a bag of chips..."

"I don't have any," she confessed.

"Then just be your usual pleasant self," he offered.

"That's easy," she thought playfully to him. She threw her arms around his shoulders. "What do you think about Villi and Su Lin?"

"Wasn't it long overdue?" he put to her.

"Uh, huh," she nodded.

"They'll have to use caution when they romance, just as we do. That stunt in the barn sent a shockwave through the community," Michael thought to her.

She realized what he meant.

"I wonder if the others think about... well, you know," she commented implying Zinian, Zhiwei and Chou.

"Sex?" Michael shot back. "Trust me Cecilia, all young men think about sex, even Chou," he linked to her. "Villi and Su Lin's interactions only reminded them of their isolation."

"Do you believe they are... jealous?" she cautiously asked.

"We can address the mating problems of sexually deprived psychics that start colonies in isolated locations on another occasion," Michael said as he brushed off the subjected. "I have other concerns. Starting this community with so many obstacles may be too much of a challenge for us," he linked. "I have my doubts about our effort here. I've set a daunting task before the group. Somehow I must rebuild a new town from the ground up. Chou is having difficulty trying to convert alien technology to Earth standards. I'm not certain if he'll ever be able to do it," Michael absently linked. "Here's another problem: a group of mostly young Chinese people is trying to adapt to life in an American small town with no access to their former diet or their cultural way of life. They must try to start their lives over with few resources. Perhaps my little utopia is more impractical than I considered. After all, we're only nine people who..."

"Nine very powerful people, Michael," she reminded. "Before you start some blame game to sound off the end to your dream even before it starts, may I offer some advice?"

Michael nodded. He needed some input from Cecilia at this moment and she sensed it.

"Give them and yourself more time," she offered. "We've only been here a week. Look at how much we've accomplished already..."

"Let me see," he sarcastically began. "Where do I begin? The jet is practically out of fuel and stuck inside a barn. The abandon town needs maintenance at every turn – the roads are in bad shape, the power system is inadequate, every house needs an extensive upgrade, the town is littered with tons of unnecessary materials and the every vehicle is about three decades behind in technology. In addition to that woeful list, I have three lonely Chinese teenagers on the verge of running off to the nearest city to find a mate, and that list might include Han but he's being very secretive," he added. "We also have a collection of well-intentioned but hopelessly inexperienced Native American builders whom Zinian will need to train. Finally, Running Elk shows up and has become Master Li's love slave..."

"Michael!" a shocked Cecilia burst into his head.

"Ok, I went too far," he relented. "Only I wish she would not be so head-over-heels into this hero worship thing whenever she's around him..."

"Like someone else I know?" she linked which made him pause.

He stopped to stare at her.

"Do I behave that way toward Master Li?" he asked her.

"At times," she linked back, "yes you do, but without the love part."

He plopped down into a chair and ran his fingers through his hair out of frustration.

"I suppose I am having a crisis of confidence," he thought.

A knock sounded on the front door. Michael glanced over at a pendulum clock on the wall. It read precisely nine o'clock. Zinian arrived first as he was eager to share his thoughts on this new plan he devised.

"They didn't take any money because they refused their pay," he blurted in a link to Michael the moment he walked in. "I felt your probe," he said as he headed for a chair. "I'm starving. Any chips? Good evening, Cecilia."

"I told you about the chips..." Michael started when Cecilia interrupted.

"What did you say about the money?" she asked.

"You were right when you said they would stay out of friendship," Zinian said to her. "They felt a moral obligation after Master Li went meddling in their village."

"I knew it," she responded.

Just then Chou walked through the front door. He did not bother to acknowledge anyone. Instead, he mumbled something about his basement being an inadequate size for a laboratory.

Cecilia watched him carefully as he crossed to take a seat in the circle. She did not like his pale color. She wondered when he last ate. Zinian and Michael noticed too.

"Sorry I'm late," he said aloud.

He did not link. Yet every psychic in the room could hear his thoughts. His mind rambled on as it balanced a whole series of formulas before him as if he were looking at a crowded chalkboard. He would sort them out in order and then shift one to another spot. Zinian opened his mouth to address his concern about Chou's physical condition.

"Don't go there," Michael privately linked, "at least not now."

Zhiwei arrived shortly after Chou walked in. He also appeared fatigued and moody over security concerns. He sat next to Chou and crossed his arms. Before he looked around the room, he noticed how preoccupied Chou seemed to be. He glanced over at Cecilia as if to say, "What's with him?" She silently shook her head and hand signaled, "Stressed."

"Welcome to the club," he signed back.

Master Li and Han followed Zhiwei through the door. Michael thought Li had new lines on his face. He skin seemed pale, older, and he moved slowly, weaker than earlier in the day. Finally Su Lin and Villi walked in. They were the only two with color in their face. The two love birds did not part but headed over to two empty chairs and sat together, unabashedly holding hands. When no one volunteered to speak, Michael rose in their midst to address them. He wanted to say, "Well! This is a fine group of hopeless individuals!" But he kept those thoughts blocked. Honesty isn't always the best policy. He did make an observation.

"This has been a stressful beginning for all of us," he said as he glanced around the room. "I know everyone is trying hard considering our resources. I commend you for your effort."

He paused and looked over at Chou quietly mumbling. Master Li noticed Chou's condition, too. He had been watching Villi and Su Lin.

"After his encounter with Ziddis," Michael continued, "Chou has begun to create some new technological wonder…"

"An alignment device with the capacity to manipulate an energy stasis field that can rapidly build connective lattices on a subatomic level into complex molecular forms…" Chou said as he started to link the details.

"You don't have to explain," Michael tried to cut him off.

"…minute quantities when fused in a controlled reaction held in magnetic stasis can produce a powerful energy field that can break the bonds of subatomic particles…" Chou continued.

Michael wondered what he should do about Chou's ramblings. No one linked or said anything to help him. All at once, the young man stopped and looked up with an excited face.

"I need the basement enlarged!" he suddenly blurted.

"What?" Zinian sat up.

"Yes… I must have the dimensions increased by this much," Chou said as he fumbled with a piece of paper he produced.

Zinian reached over, took the paper from Chou, and briefly looked it over.

"I can do this," he said, "if I can have the right kind of equipment."

"You promise?" Chou put to him.

"Sure," Zinian told him. He hated to say anything that might discourage Chou as the young scientist seemed so fragile.

In the silence that followed, Michael seized the moment to change the subject.

"Zinian has some news for us," he linked. "He felt obligated to offer his crew some of our recently acquired housing."

"You heard that exchange?" Zinian spoke up.

"You live in a psychic community," Michael replied. "Unguarded thoughts are passed quickly around town," he said as he smiled at the master builder.

"I didn't mean to exceed my authority…" Zinian confessed.

"No one is saying you did," Michael politely cut him off. "Running Elk's son, Howling Wolf, who also goes by the name of John, roused the other men's spirit of fair play," he explained. "They have ambitions and dreams, too. It is John's desire to not only rebuild Rollo, but his village as well. Zinian felt he could stay in touch with his crew easier, if they lived here."

Han cleared his throat. He felt he had to speak up on this matter.

"Do they understand who we are?" he asked them. "What will happen the first time you think of a tool and it floats across a construction site to your hands? Will they run screaming from Rollo? Will they turn against us? Will they consider us the devil or aliens?"

"If you mean, do they suspect we are strange or unusual, only a blind man would not notice. Master Li left a tremendous impact on the village," Zinian spoke up. "On his first day, he completely cured a dying girl in a Biblical sense. He gave her the ability to walk and speak for the very first time in her life. Believe me when I say that this incident alone left a profound impression on them. Had any of them cell phones, they would have broadcast that news all over the world. They were ready to make Li the second coming, when Running Elk wisely intervened," he told them.

"So, do they believe we are saints or witches?" Han started.

"On the night before Running Elk showed up at your door," Zinian explained, "she brought everyone in the village together for a special meeting.

She told them her intention to move in with Master Li and why. She also told them that we are gifted people – special people. 'We are to respect them,' she said. She also told them that we are willing to share our benefit with them and that they should be prepared to cooperate. An argument broke out in their group, not over the money, but how they would share our vision. They wanted to know our aspirations. Running Elk convinced them in an impassioned speech that we intend to help out humanity…"

"Now where did she get that idea?" Cecilia asked as glanced over at Master Li.

"I did nothing to her mind," Master Li protested. This answer did not satisfy either Cecilia or Han.

"Is she…" Zhiwei started to ask.

Master Li realized he needed to explain a few things.

"She's not one of us," Li linked to the group. "She has an exceptional psychic acuity but she possesses no portal," he explained. "She cannot level. She cannot link with Galactic Central. Not now or ever. She can hear your thoughts if you use an open link. You'll have to exercise caution in her presence," he told them. "She… she gleaned our intent from my mind… I believe."

"How did you find this out?" Villi asked Zinian.

"I saw it in John's thoughts," he answered. "Psychic ability may run in their family."

"I'd better keep a close watch on them," Zhiwei promised.

"On the housing matter… the question is up for consideration," Michael addressed them. "Should we give them access to the remaining houses in Rollo? Is there unanimous consent?" he asked. The group instantly responded with their mutual approval. "Then it's settled," he continued. "The Native American men and women can move into Rollo's remaining houses. Han, you know their condition. Why don't you meet with the crew and decide which of the remaining houses they should occupy. They usually arrive at the general store very early. Zinian will help you."

"I'll go over our inventory sheets tonight," Han told him.

"Onto new business," Michael continued. "We've heard from Chou about Ziddis and we heard from Han about his trip. We haven't had a chance yet to share some of the other off world trips. Perhaps the rest of you travelers would like to share your journeys with us."

"I have been to seven planets," Zhiwei started. His blanket statement turned every head in the room. "They were brief visits. The voices showed me security systems on seven different planets. In nearly every case, the use of stealth seems to work best where psychics form a distinct minority of the population. Unfortunately, we have very crude technology when it comes to masking our appearance," he pointed out. "Keeping vigil over this village is a full time job," he reminded them. "We are most vulnerable at night. Any suggestions?"

"Your concern over the night vigil is already too late," Master Li spoke up. "The county sheriff's department drove right up Main Street a few days ago when reports of evacuation surfaced in nearby communities," Li conveyed. "They've been back twice since. I diverted their minds each time. However, on the last visit, I decided to go ahead and plant a diminishing suggestion. I sent it out as a ripple that spread in a three hundred mile radius."

"A three hundred..." Han exclaimed as he stared at Li. This did not surprise anyone else in the group.

"As far as the sheriff's departments are concerned – or anyone else from the farms that surround Rollo – this little town is a fading memory to them," Master Li told them. "The memory implant should start a gradual decay process. We shall become a ghost town that will one day cease to exist. Hopefully, we can come up a camouflage device within the next six months," Li said as he glanced over at Chou. "Otherwise, the sight of Rollo will reinforce previous memories and my effort will be for naught."

The other psychics stared at Master Li. Han had his mouth hung open.

"See? That's just what I mean!" Zhiwei linked in. "We need a camo... a cam... what did you say?"

Michael realized that he had overlooked many aspects of security on his to-do list. He turned to Zhiwei.

"We'll go over how we can beef up our security together," he tried to reassure him. "I'd like to return to the subject of off world visits. Su Lin," he said to change the subject. "I understand your journey is particularly unique. I'm certain all of us would like to hear about your journey. Please share," he asked her.

Su Lin sat up and let go of Villi's hand. She brightened to tell her story.

"What can I say about the city of Artane," she linked as she continued. "It has been around for many thousands of our years. Gigantic monumental architectural wonders made from carved stone rise up like mountains dedicated to knowledge instead of to warriors or conquerors: physics, mathematics, music, art, architecture, history, cosmology, chemistry, literature, biology, medicine, botany, zoology, entomology, ornithology... the city has hundreds of these giant buildings," she told them. "As the hills rise higher toward the center of Artane, so too does the magnificence of each building. As we walked higher up into the hills of the inner city, I saw that Artane's architects adorned each structure with more elaborate statues and reliefs. Each one told the history of some world in the collective. One for Earth is not yet considered."

As the librarian walked along in Su Lin's memory, each psychic in the room could feel his footsteps on the stone pavement. They could see out his eyes as he glanced around at the stonecutter's paradise where artists like Michelangelo or Donatello would feel perfectly at home. The alien finally paused before a great carved gate covered with stone flowers that sprung from stone fabric draped over stone wood. The alien gestured toward a large structure atop the highest hill in Artane.

"I cannot go beyond this point without an appointment," the host linked. "At the pinnacle of Artane resides the most respected being on Xiltil, the Principle Curator named Yuii (you-ee)," Su Lin's Stigan guide pointed out. "He is supposedly over three thousand years old."

Su Lin interrupted the flow of her memory to comment.

"Until Master Li came along, Yuii was considered the most powerful psychic in the galactic collective," she informed them. Master Li simply shrugged his shoulders. Su Lin continued her memory.

"Both Xiltil and Xititli revolve around the same star. Yuii was the first envoy to arrive from Xitili," the Stigan explained. "He helped the people of Xiltil set up Artane. Once a year, Yuii makes a pilgrimage across Xiltil in a great caravan. He cures the sick, settles disputes, brings gifts and spreads goodwill along with knowledge among the ordinary citizens. He also searches for any new pre-psychic candidates. However, the highest honor on Xiltil is not to serve in Artane but to be a farmer or so Yuii tells them."

"Did you go inside any of the libraries?" Chou asked her.

"Yes... yes, I did," she told him. "You would have loved them Chou..." she began when she suddenly stopped. Su Lin could not speak or link. Her mind was a mix of wonder, awe, and sentiment.

The group of psychics exchanged glances. No one knew what to say or link.

"What did you learn from your visit to Artane?" Han finally spoke up.

"Everything!" she declared as she started to choke up with emotion.

Villi reached out and took her hand. He had no idea she went through such an elaborate journey and could not wait to hear about it with even greater detail when they returned home that night.

Su Lin felt guilty she did not finish her story. She tried to make a second attempt in relating her experience when Michael smiled and shook his head. The group joined his sentiment. His thoughts softly broke into this moment of awkward silence.

"Artane sounds like the kind of place we should all visit Su Lin, as its affects on you are proof positive. Anyone wish to add anything else?" Michael wondered. "If not, good night."

The group drifted their separate ways, except for Villi and Su Lin. Master Li did not voice his objections to their cohabitation.

"How do you think our group has progressed?" Michael asked Cecilia as he helped return the chairs to their places.

"As well as can be expected," she said with a yawn. "Everyone appreciates what you're doing Michael. You keep us focused on task."

Michael stared at her. She blocked his probe. She smiled back at him. As he stood before her he began to notice how circles under her eyes and bloodshot sclera betrayed a recent lack of sleep. Without speaking or linking another word, he gently guided her toward their bed, tucked her in and went to brush his teeth.

"Everyone appreciates what you're doing..." her words echoed.

"Strange," he thought. "Less than two months ago, I set out from New York City with no idea what I would find."

As he stood before the mirror, he thought on what they had accomplished since their arrival, the potential goals for their future and if he possessed sufficient wisdom to lead this group of highly gifted individuals in a way that he hoped would form a very unique community.

He stared up at the ceiling.

"I could use a little help here," he quietly whispered.

Chapter Seventeen

A Most Magnificent Dream

Master Li spent the last few minutes of this very long day in bed staring at the ceiling. His mind went blank. He had nearly exhausted his level of psychic energy when he assisted the Galactic Central voices in the manipulation of funds, sent out an elaborate psychological implant, and finally arranged for delivery of Chou's outrageous list of items. Despite Michael's assertions, the voices needed Li's assistance in where and how to obtain these precious rare ingredients.

"Do you believe he has the ability to create the fusor?" they asked him earlier in the day.

"Chou has a very keen mind," Li replied. "However, the best scientists on the planet have worked for decades and spent billions on the problem of fusion with little to show for their effort."

"The best minds on your planet do not possess Chou's current knowledge level of physics, chemistry and mathematics," the voice reminded.

"True," Li acknowledged. "We shall see what develops."

Master Li took in a deep breath. His heart went out to these Rollo psychics. They were trying very hard to adapt to this new way of life. He nearly agreed with Michael after the first week – that perhaps putting down roots in an isolated place like Rollo with few resources was a bad idea.

A family in a station wagon approached Rollo on the highway. They were on their way home from Oklahoma. He reached out and refreshed his energy level while diverting their attention away from Rollo. It reminded him how much they would need the Native Americans.

"Speaking of Native Americans..." his thoughts rambled to include Running Elk.

He longed for a taste of simple Chinese home cooking. He wished he could rise, walk up the street to the open street market back in Harbin and be greeted by his old friends, familiar faces he knew for years. He would sit in repose, drink hot tea, and discuss the troubles of the world. He missed his life in Harbin. America with its emphasis on cars, shopping, packaged food, and watching television did not appeal to him. This was not his way of life.

He questioned those so-called American values: Where is America's culture? Where is her literature? Where is the art? Are the only safe havens for such things in large cities? Staring at a rectangle with pretty flashing lights brought none of these things to him. What happened to people's imaginations?

"Life is more about living than what is on television," he thought. "Although... I've never been to a baseball park," he added. "I might like to watch a baseball game. Then, I suppose if I ate hot dogs and drank beer, I would have a fat belly, too."

He had too many distractions that kept him awake. He tried to close his eyes and sleep. With hardly a month's worth of experience to draw upon, Li had already accomplished many things. Yet, he knew he had more work to do when he woke up. He had confidence in Michael, and in the other's abilities to create their own village in time. Still, he lacked something in his life... something he could claim as his own.

"Li..." a voice called to him.

He knew this voice. It first spoke to him at the park in Siping. It guided him in China but only spoke to him and not the other psychics.

"You must come with me," the voice responded.

Given sufficient psychic energy, Li could create a non-corporeal and yet visceral body that was capable of traveling outside Earth's confining atmosphere, if he desired. Within a few blinks of one's eyes, Li's psychic body rushed outward away from the planet, the solar system and the galaxy. He crossed the vast reaches of space and time that separate great star systems from one another. He zoomed past other galaxies, nebula and gargantuan clouds of cosmic dust that stretched out for light years, undetected in the cold vast reaches of space.

A spot of swirling light mixed with a group of other swirling lights appeared first as a dot and then a group of galaxies that widened in distance until Li's body streaked toward one disc-shaped mass. Within this great conglomeration, the stars began to separate while Li kept his focus on just one star with its planets faintly visible from the distance. Finally he passed down through the atmosphere of a large forest-covered world with a giant silvery spire that thrust upward from the ground, high into its atmosphere.

His body passed through its shiny outer walls and inside the great structure. A cheer went up from the voices at their stations while Li rushed toward its pinnacle to where one creature perpetually rested inside a special chamber designed to hold it for a comparative eternity. Here, it channeled all psychic thought that flowed in and out of this complex system.

Li's head throbbed with the beating of his own heart as time passed slower and slower. He began to feel the changes taking place. He sensed the valves of his heart open and close, the red blood cells giving up carbon dioxide as they squeezed through arteries in his lungs, and the mitochondria in his cells converting ATP into energy, until time stopped. He wondered how he could maintain a link to his body on Earth.

"This is your station," he wondered.

"My home," a gentle voice answered. "You have never been in this place," the voice told him. "They call me the (director). I channel all thought from every psychic in the universe to stations below us."

"Then you must be very powerful," Li said respectfully.

"I have no particular power per se," the director linked. "I am what I am, an organic device attached to this complex mechanism. They constructed me to integrate with the machine," it spoke to Li's mind. "I have no emotion. Yet I have understanding. I cannot explain how I work in the idiom of language."

"Believe it or not," Li chortled, "I actually understand."

"I invited you here for a purpose," it told Li. "As you can see, time flows here at a different rate relative to any other place in the universe. What amounts to a second of your time, is for me nearly an eternity. Observe," it gestured with one of its many mechanical tentacle appendages.

Li noticed a streak of bright light that headed toward them. He first saw this as a small round ball that elongated, compacted back into a ball and then back to a streak. It grew closer and closer. Li found the intensity of color striking.

"What are those?" Li wondered.

"Quanta," the creature observed.

"Particles of light?" Li questioned.

"Light is a particle and yet not a particle, as you see," the creature pointed out.

"We see each other... I do not see quanta bouncing off you," Li observed.

"That packet is magnified so that I may analyze it before I break down its components and send those to various stations," the director stated.

It used its appendages and made a few gestures before it sent the "quanta" on its way. Li marveled at the process. As more quanta continuously entered the chamber in a stream, the creature directed each packet of information to its intended destination. Yet, Li noticed the creature performed this function as easily as one takes a breath or blinks without effort.

"Those are not simple packets of light, are they?" Li enquired.

"No… they are part of the psychic energy that we use, the unseen light that slips through portals in the minds of humans and (unintelligible) beings you call voices. That energy is amplified many times. I process it here and send it through translators. It arrives at their stations in less time than it takes you to blink your eyelashes," the director explained.

Li stared about the chamber with a sense of wonder.

"I have a revelation for you," it addressed Li again while it also performed its functions. "Each system… each world… each area of space operates both together with all the others and yet separately, just as quanta can be two things and yet act as one. We call these unique places timelines. Only via this chamber can one access timelines. The timeline for Earth consists of its history and all its past. Its future does not yet exist and is contingent on what transpires during its present. Travel into the future is impossible, since it is comprised of infinite probabilities. However, travel into the past is not only possible but also very tangible. You can interact with the past in any way you deem fit and you will not alter the present. The past's outcomes have already been determined. Do you understand?" it asked Li.

"Where is this timeline?" Li enquired.

"You must regard space not in three dimensions, but as a flat plain that flows like a continuous river. When you picture this in your mind, step onto this place. It will expand around you. Then you will begin to understand. You may travel as often as you like into the past Li," it addressed him. "Your power and great mind permits this. Regarding or considering the future, on the other hand, takes energy from this chamber and diverts its use to contemplate probabilities. Stare at the future too long and you will stop the flow of time for Earth. To do so, even temporarily is not good. It will impact other systems around your planet's star. Remember, a second of time here is an eternity to me. Now… take your first step. Face the inner crystal as it spins… see the interaction of all space and all time within… take a step forward… and…"

Li turned to regard the enormous spinning crystalline substance at the heart of this vast complex system. Within its complex matrixes the power that emanated created a powerful enveloping bubble that slowed time within the great spire, especially within the directors shielded chamber. As he heard the words of the director, he saw other worlds open. He traveled inside an atom, inside an electron and then inside a string that determined what kind of quark it was. He watched filaments change as he slipped even further between them until…

Li's non-corporeal body left the confines of the chamber. The creature and the room in which it performed its marvels vanished. He floated in a vast star field where he could not focus on one galaxy or system. He rotated with no up or down. His mind started to rip from his skull as he tried to make sense of this place.

"No!" the director's voice broke in. "Logic does not apply here. You are not in some location of space. Your field of vision only appears to you that way. You are beyond space and time. Those tiny bright dots around you represent not stars and galaxies but countless forms of the present universe," it explained. "Li! Listen to me! You must focus your great power to create the divide between realities. Focus on the event horizon… it bends the universe back on itself. Time flows from it like a ribbon… a river that brings order to the universe… look for it!"

As Li applied his power, the field around him stopped spinning. He realized as the director told him that these points of light were illusions and the blackness of space was an illusion too. A line began to form that cut through everything, a long thin line that formed a horizon.

"That's it!" the director reassured him. "I knew that of all the psychics in our collective, you would be the one who could perform this function. This is proof for me at least, that you, Li Po Chin are the…"

"Stop!" Li protested. "I am a human. Nature provided me with the ability to manipulate psychic energy. That is all I am and nothing more."

"Li no one has done what you have just accomplished… ever… in all recorded time," the director told him.

Li did not wish to dwell on the director's words. He watched with fascination the event horizon expand as a thickening line that cut through the space in front of him. It stretched left and right to infinity, he presumed. From this horizon, millions of tiny straight filaments began to flow toward him as a focal point. Along each line, he saw movement. When he regarded them, he saw many things that took place. He recognized at once that they represented the many possibilities of the future. As the lines grew closer, the images in each grew similar. The lines converged on one point beneath him. He found he suddenly stood on that spot. It felt solid. He knew this to be an illusion.

"Those lines represent the future," the director told him. "As fascinating as they seem, do not look at them for any length of time, or the line upon which you stare will begin to draw you inward on your own thoughts. It will continue to pull you into a thread of probabilities where your thoughts will be lost in a Mobius reality – time that rips away from the universe and bends into itself," the director warned. "If you fall into that reality, I do not believe that even I can rescue you. You would live the same moment in time for an eternity with no resolution ever possible... only the same probably of a single outcome that would repeat over and over, a living hell, to borrow a religious reference," it said.

Li immediately glanced away from the compelling light.

"Better," the director indicated. "Look down beneath your feet human," it told him. "That gravity well you feel is the present time in the present universe from which your body is anchored. See how the flow of time has stopped. That is also an illusion. Time flows slowly, yet it is consistent. With your ability, you can leap to certain points in the present. The greater the distance, the more energy you will consume. If you try to travel too far, you could perish," the director informed him. "The greater the action, the more energy it absorbs from time – a paradox of the present. Now, turn around to observe the unified woven ribbon that flows away from the present. That is the past."

Li turned around on the wide band that formed beneath his feet. Behind him, a wide flat band constantly flowed away from him. He began to see a series of historical events. Curiosity drew him forward. He started to take a step when the director's voice sounded an alarm.

"Stop!" it warned.

Li halted his actions and waited.

"If you step toward an event in time, you will enter the past," it told him.

"Time travel?" Li questioned.

"Time observation," the director indicated. "Remember, you cannot change that which is set. The moment you put your foot down onto the ribbon, the band will pull you into that reference. Since all of the past is recorded, you have the power to run the recording back and forth with your mind by accessing one moment independent of others."

Li thought about ancient Egypt and bent forward to examine the ribbon more closely. The pyramids appeared new, as if its workers had just finished their construction. They shined in the hot sun like brilliant mighty stones shapes of perfect geometric configuration. A great plaza surrounded them with irrigation channels of water that fed date palms and small green fields of grain run by the temple priests.

"Gifts for the gods," Li thought as he watched the amazing scene.

He then thought of ancient China and witnessed the emperor's court at the height of his power. The emperor wore long flowing and beautiful woven silk garments. Thousands of minions cheered as they surrounded the mobile elaborate throne that moved emperor through the great palace square.

Li stood up erect and the images in the ribbon blurred.

"Excellent!" the director declared. "I knew you could manipulate the ribbon," he told Li. "The rest will be up to you. Feel free to satisfy your curiosity with Earth's past. Indulge your mind Li," the director told him.

"If I interact with the past, won't I change outcomes?" Li wondered.

"Outcomes have already occurred. You can not affect the future, even if you shoot your younger self in the past," the director explained. "The moment you leave, everything will revert to its former state."

"How do I return to my present form?" Li wondered.

"That is easiest of all," the director informed him. "Simply think of the present and where you were when you started your journey," it explained. "Your memory of that place will pull you out of this chamber and back to your real time."

"How long may I spend in the past? Will the present continue while I am gone?" Li asked.

"You may spend as long as you like in the past," the director explained. "The present continues but at a much slower rate compared to where you are in time. Say you spend a week in the past, only an hour or two of your time in the present will pass."

"A week?" Li thought. The implications astounded his brain with possibilities.

"One final warning," the director cautioned. "You are vulnerable wherever you travel. Interactions with figures from the past are real. A bullet is still a bullet. It can penetrate your manifested body and kill you. If you are punched, you will feel it. If you die in the past, your body in the present will perish. Travel with caution," it warned.

"I understand that I can travel through time and must use caution," Li repeated. "Can I interact with my past self?"

"You can," the director told him. "You can travel to the past and shake your own hand. However, your past self will not recognize your future self. To your past self, the future Li will always appear strange and unrecognizable."

"What about the timelines of other worlds?" Li inquired.

"Your life is entwined with planet Earth," the director pointed out. "You do not have the capacity to manipulate other timelines in the universe. No living creature has that power."

"You said I was the first being that could manipulate the timeline. Perhaps I could manipulate others," Li wondered.

"You are powerful Li," the director stated. "Yet, the universe has other great beings whose power goes back to the origins of time. To them, we might as well be an amoeba."

Li did not bother the director with any more questions. Instead, he changed his focus back to Earth's timeline. Li thought about the ancient

Greeks. He saw the Acropolis and the Parthenon as new structures with people milling about. He started to place his foot down, when another more intimate thought occurred to him.

He thought about his namesake, the great poet Li Bai (also known as Li Bo). The timeline shifted to ancient China. He saw a young man in his mid-twenties who sat under a tree next to a river. A full moon shone overhead and a small fire crackled nearby. A jug of wine rested in the grass next to him. Li stepped down on the fluid ribbon. He fell forward and nearly toppled over when his foot struck something solid. He materialized into the past as if he walked out of a mist.

"Who might you be?" the anxious young man asked as he glanced up from his parchment. "I did not hear you approach."

Li glanced down at his body. He wore the clothes of a peasant. He had primitive sandals on his feet with his hair pulled up into a tight bun and stuffed under a broad straw hat. His face sported a short, shaggy, beard.

"My name is..." Li hesitated before he fully answered, "Chang."

"Where are you from Chang?" the young man persisted.

"From beyond those hills," Li gestured to the north.

"Is your home far away?" the young man continued.

"Yes, very far. I have walked a very long way. What are you writing?" Li asked him as he gestured toward the parchment in the young man's lap.

"I write of everything – the air, the water, the tree – they all mean something to me," the poet replied.

"I would consider it an honor if I could read what you have written. May I?" Li asked as he moved closer.

"You are not some bandit here to rob me," the young man declared. "I have no money."

"Nothing of the sort," Li reassured him. "I am only curious of your words."

"Do you read?" the young man questioned. "You appear a peasant yet you must be educated if you can read."

Li quickly invented a lie.

"My uncle... a government official... not in favor... taught me," he told the gullible young man as he moved closer. He felt compelled to read the parchment.

"It is an attempt at best," the humble young man said as he gave up the work.

Li took the parchment paper in his hands, almost fearful of what he might recognize. When he read the young man's symbols scribbled with a hurried hand upon the crusty old parchment paper, he realized he read one of Li Bai's most famous works. How ironic the timeline chose this moment for him.

"A cup of wine, under the flowering trees; I drink alone, for no friend is near..."

The poem was still in rough form, but Li recognized "Drinking alone by the Moonlight" at once. The special moment in time moved Li to tears. He closed his eyes and took in a deep breath. He tried to control his overwhelmed emotions. Having been a professor dedicated to poetry and English for over fifty years, and then to be in the presence of China's most distinguished poet at the moment he wrote his greatest work, shook the elderly man. The parchment in his fingers trembled.

"I had no idea my words would have such impact," the young man stated as he watched Li's reaction.

Master Li's confidence in his power and ability that he gained from his experience over the past few weeks melted away. Only the simple poetry professor remained – a man overcome with feeling. He looked up from the paper at the young man's face. He saw a face so innocent, so pure, so clean.

"Words can mean a great deal from certain writers... perhaps they can move mountains or old men like me to tears..." Li suggested.

The young man laughed and took back the parchment.

"Would that be the case," he said and still chuckled. "I cannot find anyone to read my work. I try and try but they only tell me to keep writing! A man cannot live on the good wishes of others."

"I would consider it a great honor if you wrote something for me," Li asked. He had to clear his throat with his voice on the verge of choking.

"By all means," the young poet eagerly replied. He reached into a knapsack and produced another piece of parchment. "Quills, ink and parchment cost money. You would not begrudge a poet to ask for some inspirational drinking money. Would you?"

Li smiled. He wanted to grant the young man his wish. He reached into his pocket and felt a solid round object. The costume and his appearance surprised Li when he first landed, as if the cosmos intended for things to happen this way. When he pulled out his hand and offered the object to the young man, he did not bother to look at it. The young man whistled. Li had given him a gold coin with a royal seal on it, both extremely rare and very valuable.

"You would give me your family fortune for some words scribbled on paper?" the poet asked Li.

"I would give you all there is to give for those special words," Li replied.

The young man regarded the coin in his hand.

"Tempting," he said as he stared at it. "No, I cannot take it. No poem is worth that," he protested and tried to force the coin into Li's hand.

Master Li backed away.

"Any poem you write is worth an emperor's ransom," the elderly man declared. "Besides, I would spend this money on a woman too young for me. You put it to good use."

Li Bai turned the coin over in his hand. He tossed it into the air and caught it. He then stuffed it into his pocket.

"For such a sum I shall write you an epic poem," the young man jested.

"All I ask is that you dedicate a few words to... Li," the psychic requested.

The young man's face twisted into a puzzled expression.

"I thought you said your name is Chang. You have my name?" the poet wondered.

"I have that honor," Li bowed.

"Then this is indeed a happy day!" Li Bai declared. "I have a new friend that has my name and is very generous with his money. By all means," he said with a sense of pride. "Give me a few moments sir and I will write you something from my heart. Then I will dedicate it to Li!"

Time had no meaning to Li. He only knew ecstatic joy from being this close to his idol. The two men sat next to the river and talked for hours. They drank wine and discussed poems to Li's contentment. They fried the fish on a clay slab that the poet carried in his knapsack. Li discovered he had salt in another pocket, an item as precious as gold.

Soon the moon began to sink and the two men ended their evening in conversation by the dying fire. They drank rice wine from the poet's large gourd jug. The wine warmed Li but did not intoxicate him, as he feared it might. Exhausted, the young poet eventually yawned and handed the finished paper to Master Li. The elderly man fell asleep under the tree next to Li Bai with the treasured piece of paper clutched to his breast.

Master Li took in a deep breath and blinked. The early morning sun flooded in from across the hall. His mind searched for Han until he recalled that Han rose early to meet with the work crew and Zinian. Li's eyes squinted as sunlight streamed into his room and fell across his face. He reached out with his mind and closed his bedroom door. In the comparative darkness, he glanced around his bedroom. Nothing had changed. He wore the pajamas he had on when he went to bed.

He sighed and thought, "I never left this room."

He sat up in bed and realized he was in the same place where he finally fell asleep last night after he stayed up so late and contemplated Rollo's fate. He shook his head and felt a tinge of disappointment.

"The director... the crystal... the timeline..." he muttered. "Nothing happened. It must have been a dream."

A booming voice shattered the stillness in his room. It startled the elderly man.

"Search inside your pajama pocket," the voice offered.

Li recognized the voice of Galactic Central's director. His hand slid down across the fabric until he felt something underneath in his breast pocket, a folded piece of paper. He pulled out the plain parchment paper and quickly opened it. On the paper, he saw the scribbled Chinese characters that flowed down the page, signed by Li Bai at the bottom.

"But how is this possible?" Li pondered.

"You have the power to bring back objects from the past," the director took the time to explain. "Treasure that would be lost to time has no relevance to the past. You can bring such objects with you back to the present. No other creature has this power human. Your ability is unique. You may walk the timeline when you choose."

Li fingered the valuable piece of paper in his hand that appeared new, although now its comparative actual age was quite ancient.

"I thank you for showing me this marvel," Li told him.

"Visit often," the director's voice echoed. "We value your presence."

Master Li leaned back into his mattress and stared up at the ceiling.

"What a most magnificent dream…"

Chapter Eighteen

Altering Rollo

Southwest Kansas in late July can be a very warm bleak place. When you add the dry plains to an even drier southwest wind, the breeze does not bring relief, only a fine brown dust that settles on everything and makes lips parched. Despite having a work crew for assistance, Zinian stressed over the manual labor he and his crew poured into a hopeless situation. As he sat outside Baker's store at the western end of Main Street and looked around at the collection of old houses, any sense of optimism slipped away from his mind, carried away on the dry southwest wind.

"Why do I feel as if I'm the only one doing any work around here?" he thought to Michael as the two men shared cold drinks. He glanced down at his rough, dirty, and cut-up hands. He struggled with his thick fingertips to pull out a fine wooden splinter wedged tight under his skin.

"Use your mental power," Michael suggested.

"Ha!" Zinian laughed with bitter sarcasm. "If you thought my crew might run when they saw their pay, they'd never show up for work if I started to make objects fly."

"A splinter won't matter," Michael stated.

"Yes, but if I made that tire strike you in the head it would!" the big man declared.

Michael understood Zinian's frustration better than his crew did, as he could feel it.

"They'll find out eventually," Michael spoke quietly.

"Then let them find out eventually," Zinian answered. "But for now, I need every man I have. We've too much work to do. None of these people has ever built a house! I have to teach them everything!"

The two psychics sat on the bench in front of what once was Baker's general store. Only a gutted heap of rubbish remained. Zinian's crew tore down the old store to make way for a new single-story building that Michael hoped would become Cecilia's clinic. Zinian's crew moved out the large cooler and freezer to another house that currently acted as the community food storage, open and free for anyone to use. Michael stored their meat, milk, cheese, eggs, bread, butter, oils, flour, sugar and other stables in them. He had shelves for dry goods, and another cooler for just fruit and vegetables. He checked the storage twice a day and had replacement food delivered in bulk on Tuesdays and Thursdays.

This hot August afternoon, Michael stopped by to bolster Zinian's deflated morale, not to pick a fight with him.

"I feel your frustration," he told his friend. "This isn't supposed to be a marathon," he said as he glanced around. "I suggested you and your crew take some days off. You have two teams working nearly ten hours a day. When did you plan to take a break?"

"We have so much to do," Zinian spoke half-hearted. "I have plans…"

"Excuse me for interrupting," Michael linked. "I'd like to share with you what is going on in the rest of this village. Villi has plans, too. He is trying to overhaul the jet engines inside a hot barn. He has some notion about 'tweaking their performance ratios' or some such idea. I haven't measured the ambient temperature, but it feels like a hundred and twenty degrees in there," he gestured over his left shoulder. "This is a man raised in a part of the world where a heat wave is a day over sixty degrees. When I walked in on him the first time, he was completely naked except for his boxer shorts, and those were saturated with sweat," Michael relayed. "Trust me, it's a picture I'm not eager to share."

"I appreciate that," Zinian mumbled with sarcasm.

"In addition to making those sandwiches for your crew, Su Lin is playing nursemaid with every snot-nosed kid in the region while trying to set up teaching plans in the process," Michael pointed out. "Remember, most of the children have only watched television. None of them can read or write! If it's any consolation, she isn't using her power to do this," Michael pointed out. "She claims it might frighten the children, whom she regards as Rollo's future."

"I didn't mean to complain…" Zinian began to apologize, when Michael cut him off.

"Chou is slaving away in his basement from dawn to late at night. He hardly sees the light of any day," Michael told him. "He doesn't eat. He doesn't sleep. No one understands the formulas he repeats in his head. They sound more like mantras. He is trying to build the following: a control board from scratch, a program to run his control board, a robotic arm, and a complex mechanism that resembles an atomic car wash. He has no help and no one to talk to."

"Michael, I…" Zinian tried to speak when Michael held up his hand.

"Han is helping John to clean up the tribal village," Michael went on. "He refrained from using his power while he physically dragged old moldy worn carpeting and dusty old drapes out of these old trailers. I don't think he's worked that hard in years," he added and pushed on. "Master Li works daily on a variety of fronts from the moment he rises from his bed until he closes his eyes late at night. I've never once heard the seventy-five-year-old complain," he told him.

Zinian did not try to stop Michael. He simply listened instead.

"Cecilia is preparing to turn this horrible pile of rubble into a medical clinic once you give her four walls and a roof," Michael pointed out. "She performs house calls every day on the sick and injured. Some people have incurable diseases that are so far advanced that not even Master Li can help them. She works painstakingly close with patients to stop their advancing cancers in hopes she can reverse the process. She can only hope to make these patients comfortable as she struggles against their march toward death."

Zinian sat in silence and stared at the ground.

"You didn't mention Zhiwei," he thought.

"Oh, you don't want Zhiwei's job," Michael jumped in. "Yesterday he had to alter one hundred and twenty-three minds that passed by on the highway. That was in the morning. Travelers, business people, vacationers, farmers, and truckers who observe a little too much about Rollo need mental manipulation. He's becoming quite the expert at draining psychic energy while he alters their memories at the same time. He does it so quickly, I worry he'll accidentally alter our brains in his sleep by mistake!"

Zinian stared at him with alarm on his face.

"Oh, don't worry," Michael said as he dismissed the builder's concerns. "I told him if he has any sensations in that regard to start with your mind, his friend and next door neighbor."

"What?" Zinian declared as Michael stood up.

"See ya!" Michael said as he casually walked on to the next person on his list.

Zinian gave Michael's departing back the universal sign of displeasure.

The days flowed by, one into the next as Rollo gradually stood on its own – a fledgling community that experienced the pangs of growth. Zinian insisted that his crew refrain from addictive substances such as alcohol or drugs like marijuana. This was very difficult as some crew members used the stuff to fight boredom after work. He sought out Cecilia to help the afflicted with their recovery from addiction.

Zinian's crew consisted of fourteen people, twelve men and two women, all Native American Comanche from the tribal village. They ranged in ages from sixteen to thirty-six. In about a week, most of them managed to move from the village into some of Rollo's fourteen remaining vacant houses. Some men brought their girlfriends or wives with their children along. They gladly left their cramped trailers behind.

A few of the single younger men who desired a house of their own, chose to live together. A sixteen-year-old male named Steven moved in with two young single men aged nineteen and twenty, Christopher and Matthew. The two female crewmembers, Emily and Chloe both nineteen, took over one small two-bedroom house. They surprised Zinian by working as hard as the men did. Side by side, job to job, they performed the same strenuous physical tasks with no complaint.

As Michael suggested, Zhiwei scanned the memories of the Native American crew every night. He removed anything "unusual" from their memories in regards to feats of psychic prowess that they saw Zinian or any other psychic perform in front of them. Finally, at the urging of Master Li, he stopped manipulating their memories. Eventually, the Native Americans began to take for granted that the nine were unique and not devils, monsters, or aliens.

Clearly, the mood of the Comanche Native Americans changed considerably during this period. They seemed content with the new direction their lives had taken. They expressed willingness to keep an open mind in regards to Rollo's rather peculiar residents.

Finally, as Michael promised, the well-drilling equipment arrived along with new electric trucks to help move construction equipment and building supplies. Zinian directed John to put them to good use in the Comanche village right away. John drilled four new wells, placed water pumps and storage tanks at various locations, and finally installed new septic systems.

One morning, Zinian drove up Main Street with his crew toward a site on the eastern edge of Rollo, when a young man stepped out in front of his truck.

"Zinian!" Chou yelled as he ran into the street. "You promised!"

Zinian slammed on the brakes to avoid hitting his friend. He ran a hand down his face. No one had seen Chou for days. He fell into the background. Zinian forgot to help Chou with his "basement" project. So much had happened recently.

"We'll be there in one hour!" Zinian shouted to him. He gestured to his crew in the back of the truck. "Take everything out of the basement that you can carry," he instructed. "We'll help Chou dismantle the rest and divert the furnace along with the water heater to another room in the house." Then privately, Zinian linked his apology, "I'm very sorry about this Chou."

In about three days, he and his crew gave Chou about double the square footage. Zinian offered to help Chou assemble the fusor when the parts arrived.

"How will you do that?" Chou wondered. "I don't even know how it's going to look myself!"

Deliveries began to arrive with parts for the fusor's actual construction. Zinian's crewpersons carried in sections of black metal pipe, large pieces of black metal configured in strange shapes, rolls of thick shiny yellow metal wire, generators, compressors and other large pieces of equipment. They filled up the space until Chou could barely move around his expanded basement.

"What's this heavy wire?" one of workers asked, as it took two of them to lift the rolls.

"Solid twenty-four karat gold," Chou nonchalantly answered. He was too busy checking off his list to look up.

One worker laughed, "Right! Sorry I asked." He paused for a moment to contemplate the reality it might be real gold. "I beg your pardon," he politely asked Chou. "What does a person do with four spools of solid gold wire? Each one of those must have cost..."

"Six hundred and forty three thousand dollars," Chou said with a straight face.

The two workers stopped and stared at Chou with their mouths open.

"You wrap wire in tight coils around a superconducting magnet," Chou explained. "Then you pass some liquid nitrogen through the inside and apply current. Voila! You've created one beeeeg magnetic field!" he said expanding his arms. "I tried to get platinum wire but I could not find large quantities," he complained. "You see Maxwell's equations in electromagnetism were false in regards to..."

"Easy doc," one worker said backing up. "You're way over my head."

Chou advanced on the man until the worker backed out of the door. Then Chou slammed the door shut. The man tripped over the edge of entry and fell backward. His friend who stood nearby laughed.

"Did you hear what he said?" he blurted to his teammate. "That nerd just spent over four million dollars on four spools of metal that he's jus gonna twist around those black funny shaped things!"

The man who stood next to him, nervously glanced around, and bent lower.

"Keep your voice down!" his friend said as he reached down and helped him to his feet. "Let me ask you this… Do you like you're your new house, that fat paycheck and all the other things you've got?"

"Yeah, well…" the confused worker started.

"Then, you'd better leave those people alone and not question what they do or they'll sick Master Li on you," the other one warned. "I like the way we live now, or have you forgot what livin in a trailer was like?"

"No, I just thought…" the man stammered.

"These people are different," his friend said as he cut him off. "That's why they're here. They came to this god-forsaken place because they're just like us, they don't fit in with the rest of the world," his friend explained. "Personally, I'm glad they came… and you should be, too! Now, shut up about the things you see till we get home. We've got work to do," he said. He grabbed his friend's arm and pulled him away from Chou's new entry ramp.

Zhiwei observed them from a distance. He chuckled at one young man's speech. He was grateful Zinian's crew developed that kind of respect for them. Still, he removed from their mind anything they saw in Chou's basement, including the delivery.

The following evening, Chou heard a knock at his new basement entry.

"Who is it?" he asked as he yelled at the door. "I'm a little busy…"

"It's me, you fool," Michael put into his mind, "so stop shouting. You're supposed to be psychic. Or have you forgotten how to use your ability?"

"Sorry Michael," Chou answered. "My mind is swamped with a thousand things to keep track of lately. What is it?"

"Open your door and find out," Michael linked as he walked away.

Chou opened his new side door to find a metal box lying on the ground with a nuclear symbol on the top. Judging by the weight when he tried to lift it, he knew the radioactive materials he requested lay inside the lead-lined container. He started to open the box when Chou realized he had not pulled energy in several hours.

"If you knew what I had to do to retrieve that," Michael said as he ran to his next errand.

"Michael I've been waiting for this!" Chou linked to the fading figure.

"You're welcome!" Michael linked back.

Chou reached out to the Native Americans and pulled in needed nourishment. The psychic energy rejuvenated him. He pulled his goggles down over his eyes, put on a flexible shield over his body, and special gloves on his hand. The box unsnapped. Chou reached in and took out two vials of clear liquid, one with a green top, the other purple.

"You have the potential to destroy mankind or save it," he quietly whispered. "Which will it be?"

Chou sensed the radiation levels streaming from the two tubes. He put them back in the box. He quickly took the box to his workbench and slid a portable shield around it. He took off the protective gear and then touched his control panel.

"I hope our test runs work," he thought as he pressed the first sequence.

A robotic arm swiveled around, opened the box, and grabbed one vial.

"Ever so gently," he thought as he moved the first vial into position.

He had to reduce the concentrated substance down to its most element particle. He did not have an accelerator. However, his last physics lesson from GC gave him an idea. He could bounce tritium atoms back and forth off between two magnetic plates until they achieved the speed and velocity needed to impact the formulation of deuterium he would next prepare. He chuckled in a way that would have made any other human being very nervous.

"I'll either achieve a controlled stasis field or…" he thought. He knew his calculations were correct, or so he hoped. No one on the planet ever tried what he was about to attempt.

Zhiwei quietly watched Chou work. He waved at Michael as the young man passed his home. To forestall an unintended invasion from the public while the residents of Rollo slept, Zhiwei installed motion detectors around the perimeter of the village and across the streets which entered the town from the highway.

To his delight, he no longer had to work alone. The Comanche village had an abundance of wayward teens on the verge of leaving what they considered to be a trap, a hell hole, and a dead end. Two bored sixteen-year-old young women from Su Lin's new school, not interested in construction, volunteered to help Zhiwei with security. Their names were Jennifer and Selena. They offered to respond to Zhiwei's alarms while he slept. Instead of a separate house, Zhiwei opened up two bedrooms on the second floor. At first, some in the village balked at the idea of an eighteen-year-old boy cohabitating with two sixteen-year-old girls – until Master Li intervened on his behalf.

"This young man is above reproach," he told them. "I personally vouch for the girl's integrity," he told all those concerned.

Zhiwei appreciated Li's vote of confidence at the open forum. From the time he agreed to his conversion, he was always open and honest with every member of their group. Li saw that level of integrity in him from the start. So the village allowed the two teenage girls to move in with Zhiwei. That is how Jennifer and Selena came to work in the security division.

One morning when he rose early to jog, Zhiwei hurried from the house to join the others in this daily ritual. He opened the back door of his house with his mind. Unfortunately, the wind caught the door and it started to slam shut just as Zhiwei started to walk through. He accidentally used his lightening fast reflexes and literally shattered the wood into thousands of tiny splinters by combining his martial arts and psychic energy focused into the palm of his hand.

"Whoa!" he declared. He stopped and stared at three small pieces of wood still attached to the hinges that swung back and forth – all that was left of the door. "A combination of psychic energy and a power move, focused a powerful blow into the palm of my hand," he thought. "I must remember to keep my senses in check or I could hurt someone."

The two young Native American women seated in the kitchen watched with amazement when Zhiwei made his explosive move. When he turned and examined his hand, they were not concerned the young man hurt his hand. They knew something else transpired in that moment that transcended reality. They silently and mutually agreed that Zhiwei had extraordinary power. They rushed to his side.

"Teach us," Jennifer and Selena pleaded.

He thought about what this might mean to their relationship. They would have to work close together. They would physically strain and these actions might make their relationship more personal. He mentally checked with Master Li before he gave his approval. The elderly sage considered Zhiwei's predicament.

"You may train them," he told Zhiwei. "However, you must guard your emotions."

"I will Master Li," he promised. He turned to Jennifer and Selena. "We'll train twice a day, before and after your school lessons with Su Lin," he told them. They quickly agreed.

Zinian passed along his advanced knowledge in construction to his workers. By the middle of August, they raised the medical building. At Cecilia's request, Michael brought in medical equipment and supplies to the new clinic as soon as Zinian's crew finished it. Prospective clients filled her waiting room from the first day. After the clinic opened, she and Michael only saw each other late in the evening.

While journeys off world seemed a noble pursuit, most psychics were too busy to take them any longer. Han pitched in to help move many of the families from the village into Rollo. He took a personal interest in their lives. He often went to Michael with requests for new clothes and new appliances. Michael made every attempt to purchase what people needed. Trucks practically made deliveries to Rollo on a daily basis, with both Michael and Master Li busy as they diverted suspicions about the changing community.

Villi's work in the barn ground to a halt. He did not have adequate space to work on the jet or the physical ability to perform all of the tasks. He was determined to find some help, even if that meant walking to Dodge City and drafting two mechanics from a shop. He headed across town to find Michael when he saw a group of Native American men standing in front of Cecilia's clinic in a heated discussion. As he started in their direction, Master Li pulled up beside him with his magical truck.

"I sense from their discussion that John needs your help," Villi informed Li. "He says there's an emergency in the..." he started.

"Hop in!" Li told Villi.

"Actually sir," Villi tried to explain, "I was on my way to see Michael and discuss..."

"No time," Li said. "You must come at once!"

Villi felt Master Li's force practically push him into the truck. As the truck moved its way painfully south toward the village, Villi noticed a column of black smoke ahead that gradually turned white and then vanished. He reasoned he could have run faster than the truck.

"I understand you need help in hanger," Li finally commented.

"That barn is hardly a hanger," Villi muttered. "How did you know... oh, yeah, I keep forgetting that we're all mind readers," he sighed and leaned back in his seat. "What's going on?" he asked about the smoke.

"When we come into the village, keep your eyes and ears open for an opportunity," Li advised. "You'll know the opportunity when it happens."

The truck pulled into the old dirt road with its deep pot holes. Villi noticed a crowd standing around one trailer that was completely gutted. Nothing but a smoldering heap remained.

"Two young teenagers refused to participate in school or help with the building project," Master Li privately linked as his truck rolled up behind the crowd. "They moved into one of the abandon trailers and usually spent their days smoking marijuana, watching television, and drinking. They've known each other since birth. They never did mix well with other people," he explained to Villi. "This afternoon, one of them started a fire while cooking on the trailer's stove. The trailer burned before they could pump enough water from nearby."

Villi and Li stepped from the truck. A couple of men held the two teenagers. They were deciding their punishment when Master Li walked through the back of the crowd. A hush fell over the gathering.

"What would do to these boys?" Li asked them.

"They started a fire..." John started to explain.

"I know," Li cut him off. "I ask you again. What is to be their punishment?"

"Beat them!" one woman yelled.

"Beat some sense into them!" a man added.

The boys did not resist when the men who held them, yanked them around. The crowd started to strip the young men of their shirts when Li stepped between them.

"I have a proposition," he said to them. "True, these boys were reckless and showed disregard for the village," he said aloud, yet in his calm quiet way. "You all know Villi," Li said as he gestured to the tall Russian. "He's repaired every car and truck in this area. He never asked for any favor in return because he loves his work."

Villi realized his opportunity and walked over to where Li stood. He turned around and confronted the angry faces.

"Some of you know me," he said with all the command he could muster. "I used to be a Russian police officer. I was a cop. What better person among you knows more about rehabilitating a criminal?" he put to them. No one made a comment. "I'll take these two," he said and grabbed the backs of the boy's shirt collars. "They'll learn a thing or two about discipline when I get through with them!" he declared.

John started to object when he glanced over at Master Li and saw a twinkle in the older man's eye. He decided it was best to say nothing. The crowd backed away as Villi pulled the two young men toward the truck. He motioned for them to climb in the back. Li had to practically bite his tongue to keep from smiling. Li nodded to those present and made a parting comment.

"Zinian and his crew will be down this afternoon to help clean up this mess," Li told them. "We'll take over the boy's welfare for now and keep you informed as to their progress."

"Thank you Master Li!" someone shouted.

"Thank you Master Li," the rest mumbled.

Li and Villi climbed back into the truck and departed.

"You have your help," Li said as the truck rolled up the highway toward Rollo.

Villi glanced back over his shoulder at the two scowling faces that stared back at him.

"I wonder who will be helping whom?" Villi answered him.

Li dropped them off at the edge of the field before he returned to discuss the situation with Michael. Villi marched the two teenagers over to the barn.

"This is what I need," he said when the two teens sat on crates inside the barn. "I need help working on this jet," he said as he gestured to his left, "as well as the cars and trucks we use in Rollo. I'll train you as mechanics. You can live here in the barn," he told them and glanced up at the loft.

"Up there?" one teen spoke up. "It must be a hundred degrees up there!" he complained.

"I'm not goin up there," the other teen said. "I'm leaving and you can't stop me. If you touch me, I'll say you tried to molest me have you brought up on charges!"

He and his friend started to leave when they both stopped – frozen in place.

Villi smiled slightly as he walked toward the two teenagers.

"You're right about the heat up there," Villi said.

He glanced up at the loft. It was a dirty filthy spot that he knew needed to be prepped before he would allow the two teens to spend the night in it. He pointed to one end of the loft.

"We could use a little ventilation," he said.

He made a gesture, although he did not need to, and one section of boards broke loose and shattered. Its debris blasted outward into the surrounding field. Villi allowed the two young men the movement of their heads to follow his action. However, from the neck down, they remained frozen to the spot. After they saw what he did, their eyes grew wide with surprise and fright. They turned their heads back toward Villi.

"Would you like to see what I can do to a human body?" he put to them.

Both young men shook their heads.

"Then lets you and I head up that ladder over there and start cleaning out the place where both of you boys… er, young men will live. I promise to make the place hospitable. For starters, I'll have Michael purchase a large screen television, video game console, your own refrigerator, a comfortable sofa and two full sized beds," he told them. He looked them up and down. "You could use some clothes too, and a bath!" Villi punctuated.

The two teens glanced at one another and half smiled.

"But I have conditions," he told them. "You'll have to learn mechanics and work for me," he added. "I need your help. I can't do this alone, Edward… Victor," he personally addressed them. That he knew their names surprised them too. "I'll also promise never to lay a hand on you," Villi told them as he held his hands up. He slyly added, "as you can see, I don't have to."

He released them and the two teen exchanged glances.

"You weren't just saying that about the TV and stuff?" Edward asked.

"Yeah," Victor chimed in.

"I really do need your help," Villi said sincerely. "If you're going to live here, I plan to make the place hospitable. If it were my home, this is what I would want. Do we have a deal?" Villi held out his hand.

Again, the two teens exchanged glances.

"Beats livin in that trailer," Victor commented.

"What trailer?" he friend responded. "You burned it down!" He looked down at Villi's hand and then grabbed it hard. He did not expect Villi's strength in return. "You got yourself a deal," he said wincing.

True to his word, Villi joined the effort with the two teens to clear out the loft. Their first night was uncomfortable. However, before the boys bedded down, they sat with Villi and Michael to go over a list of items that would transform the loft into a decent place to live. During the first few days, they made one additional attempt to run away. Villi knew they would. Zhiwei alerted Villi that he stopped the teens in the field outside the barn. When they tried to fight him, he simply used his mind to deflect them. Zhiwei used his power to lift the surprised teens into the air and floated them back inside the barn. After that incident, they gave up trying to escape. The following day, Michael arrived on the back of a delivery truck with furniture, an air conditioner, a portable generator and a refrigerator, along with the other items the teens requested. Michael also purchased laptop computers for Victor and Edward so that Su Lin could give them lesson plans to take home.

Working with his new crew, Villi created a workspace to perform maintenance on the engines and the rest of the jet. The three cleaned out the barn, painted the floor and walls, put up insulation and wallboard to make the place a cleaner environment. In less than two weeks after the teens arrived, Villi and his two-man crew converted the barn into a larger and roomier hanger for the jet. Zinian's crew replaced the entire entrance to the barn, put in a larger doorframe and added a motorized door. Villi and his helpers set up a fuel storage tank that Michael supplied. They placed it in a fire zone in the field away from the barn. Later a truck delivered aviation fuel.

One afternoon, a large truck arrived with Michael riding in the passenger seat, the driver seemed in a daze. Michael jumped out. The teen smiled at his approach. They knew that the only man in the village capable of challenging their boss was the man who walked up to him. They had seen Michael and Villi spar during their off time in the field. In as much as their respect and admiration for Villi had increased over the past two weeks, Victor and Edward knew that Michael was the man who delivered the goods.

"Here comes Santa," Victor whispered to his friend as the two teens raked the ground.

"I don't think this is for us," Edward added and moved over to stand behind Villi.

"I brought you a present," Michael said. He slapped the side of the truck. In the back of the big dump truck, Villi noted a backhoe. He then saw a grater underneath the truck's base for leveling the ground.

"You know what they say," Michael said with a smile, "if you want anything done... I thought you'd appreciate being able to make your own runway."

Villi shook his head while his helpers stood with mouths gaped open.

"Can they drive?" Michael asked. He jerked his thumb in their direction.

"You know me," Villi replied to Michael. "I do the driving," he noted.

The driver stepped down out of the cab and then walked over to the side. A chair floated out from the barn. The man sat in it. Victor and Edward poked each other as they watched Michael in action.

"He'll keep until you're done with his truck, although I believe he'll be late for dinner," Michael told them. "I'll think of an excuse by then."

"Won't the highway crew miss their truck?" Villi wondered.

"Zhiwei already took care of that for me," Michael smiled.

"Let me work the backhoe," Edward asked as he stepped up to Villi.

"This will only take me a moment," Villi said.

He gathered energy from his two power-emitting crewmen and then floated the heavy vehicle out of the truck's back end. Once on the ground, Villi explained what he wanted and put Edward to work. Victor then helped Villi level the ground by first measuring and then placing stakes to the side that gave them reference marks.

Two hours later as Villi and his teen crew rushed to finish before the end of the day, Zhiwei confronted Michael as the leader made his way to the next project.

"It didn't dawn on me until this moment," he said as he approached the tall young man. "Do you realize what you've done?"

"What security protocol have I violated now?" Michael replied. He grew exasperated by Zhiwei's continual protests.

"You've identified us by satellite. A new runway? Homeland Security will believe we're smuggling drugs!" the head of security complained.

Michael glanced skyward. Zhiwei made a good point. He forgot about satellite surveillance.

"I'll check with my voice Zhiwei," Michael interrupted.

He tuned out his surroundings to contact Galactic Central. Zhiwei watched anxiously as Michael nodded a few times. After a minute, he reengaged his psychic head of security.

"My voice said that no communications or military satellite has focused on Rollo in the past two weeks. However, they've scheduled another routine pass over this area in two days. Does that give you enough time to camouflage the runway?"

"I'll see what I can do," Zhiwei replied.

"You might want to monitor the NSA and other government agencies," Michael suggested.

"I've done that since the second day we arrived!" Zhiwei shot back.

Zhiwei's female helpers were all too eager to meet the changed Victor and Edward (whom they previously despised) when the security chief put all four to work. The four teens spent one whole day painting the new runway to match the terrain around the airstrip. Villi came upon the scene in the afternoon as they drew to a close. He watched with consternation as they finished.

"What will you do when the grass turns green in the fall?" the skeptical Villi put to Zhiwei.

"I'll think of something else by then," he replied.

Villi wasn't happy that Zhiwei chose this time to camouflage his runway while Villi made an off-world journey to learn more about flight. Zhiwei was supposed to watch Victor and Edward, not put them to work or socially introduce his two teens to Zhiwei's girls. He wanted to monitor that situation. He wondered if Victor and Edward were ready, as they exhibited sociopathic tendencies in the past. He had to admit they did a good job with the camouflage. He was also surprised at how well the boys behaved. He gazed over at the freshly painted strip that seemed to vanish when only a few meters away.

"How am I supposed to judge the location of the landing strip when landing the jet," he linked to Zhiwei as he took in the camouflage work.

Zhiwei looked inside a large bag of spray paint he carried for touch ups. He pulled out a can and then walked to the end of the runway. He then made three wide bright pink stripes on the ground.

"Knowing you would object, I had that in mind," he linked as he sprayed out the brightly colored phosphorescent paint.

In the days that followed, Michael delivered on his promises to the Native American who came to their aid. Supplies arrived at every household in Rollo – new appliances, electronics, clothes, linens, cookware, glassware and a variety of other household items needed by most homeowners. Zhiwei and Master Li scrambled on a daily basis to cover up Rollo's existence while Michael and Han worked to erase the paper trail. A month had passed since the psychics arrived in Kansas and life had changed radically for both the psychics and their new friends.

"My only fear is that with their pockets full of cash and new vehicles in the driveways, someone doesn't try to slip away," Zhiwei brought up in the usual nightly meeting.

His fears were well founded.

Chapter Nineteen

Friendship Betrayed

Rollo gradually began to change its outward appearance when Zinian's crew made improvements to the interior and exterior of houses as well as changes to the town's appearance. Rollo trimmed down its size. Several old buildings came down. Trash heaps disappeared. The medical clinic went up on the western end of Main Street. Zinian rolled out the plans for the new school. The residents forged new friendships during this period. They learned to cooperate on a variety of projects. Yet, even as their mutual standard of living rose, not everyone felt content with the arrangement of living with those who possess otherworldly power.

The most restless were the younger people in Rollo. Some of them wanted to spend their new fortunes in the city. Others were content to stay but sympathized with the plight of their friends. Traveling in style, seeing the sights, or just plain having a good time were aspirations shared by deprived people who had lived in dire poverty for most of their lives. Rumblings of rebellion moved through their ranks. The young Native Americans decided to secretly meet one evening in the home of Christopher and Matthew, the two twenty-year-olds who befriended their roommate sixteen-year-old Steven.

"It's bad enough we can't leave this place," a young man named Ethan spoke up. "I check with supplies. Michael refuses to order any wine or beer. We can't drink a beer now and then? What harm will that do?" he questioned.

No one responded. That was not the most sensitive topic. Too many in the room had alcoholic mothers or fathers. Still, his words rang with a familiar chord as others had the similar feelings regarding a different aspect. The idea that someone dictated terms on how they should run their lives – what they could eat, drink, and whether or not they could leave, left many with the feeling of being trapped – a feeling common to everyone present, and perhaps a few silent adults as well.

"Instead of meeting in secret, maybe we should bring our complaints to Master Li," a young woman named Sophia said.

"Yeah, he would listen," Emily echoed.

Sixteen-year-old Steven, who had been moody for the past few days, took his can of soda and threw it against the wall. He immediately garnered everyone's attention.

"What a sad pathetic group we are!" Steven blurted as he glared at the forlorn faces. "You're all sitting around here, moping, acting like a bunch of whipped kittens…" he started.

"Did you sneak some hooch from the village?" Victor asked him.

"I don't need hooch to know how dull this place is. A little hooch would…"

"Put you in your dad's place," Selena jumped.

Steven fiercely stared at her. He could not deny her accusation.

"Steven is right about one thing," she went on. "It would be nice to go out somewhere… anywhere…"

"I mean I'm just asking for a date!" Steven declared. "Why can't they let us have just one weekend in Wichita?" he protested. His friends saw his point. "I just wanna sit in a bar and drink with a few ladies…"

"Oh, that's a bright plan," Sophia quipped. "I thought you wanted to sightsee or go shopping…" she added.

"Where will you say you got such a big chunk of change?" Christopher spoke up. He reached into his pocket and pulled out a wad of hundred dollar bills. They all had them. Zinian had paid everyone with cash. "You think they'll believe you? An injun? Besides, what if you get picked up by the police?" he put to him. "You don't have a driver's license. How you gonna order a beer? If they find out you're underage… you could be arrested."

Jennifer was tired of living this lifestyle within Rollo, too. She wanted to see the world. She decided that if given the chance, she would even go as far as betraying the citizens of Rollo in exchange for her freedom.

"I'm not sayin I wouldn't join you," she said as she addressed the group. "At times, I'd like to skip town, too. I would like to meet a young man my age. We could go out, perhaps have dinner together. Who knows? But do you think the old man will let us leave after what we've seen and heard? Sure they pay us well," she paused. "But there's people out there who'd give us millions to know about them…" she stated in a whisper.

"That's what this party is about?" Edward questioned. "Coming here to complain about people who have helped us? I don't know about you," he said as he moved around the room, "but I had no prospects a few weeks ago. Nobody wanted me or Victor," he said as he pointed at his friend. "... and no one cared what happened to us. You wanna drink? My old man was an alcoholic. Yeah, you can learn a lot from a drunk! I was strung out on anything I could get my hands on grass, pills, beer, wine... until the day Villi showed up," he added. The room grew quiet. "He's the first person in my life that didn't try to hit me or force me to do something I didn't want to do," he paused and considered how Villi froze their movement in the barn. However, he recalled that Villi simply restrained them, not with his fists but with his mind. He turned on his friends, Steven and Jennifer. "Go ahead and rat on us," he gestured toward the highway. "Go on! Go to Wichita... blab it all over town about Rollo, get your moment of glory on television," he said with a sneer. Then he moved in close and stuck his finger near Jennifer's face. "But keep an eye out over your shoulder," he added, "cause if I find out that anyone in this room ruined my chance at making something out of my life... I swear I'll come after you myself..."

"We don't need to threaten each other," Matthew spoke up. "It's like Zinian, Zhiwei, Michael, and even Master Li told us. If you don't like it here they've said, we could leave at any time, plain and simple. I believe them. They said they'd take care of you if you chose to move out there. So like Edward said, if you want to go to Wichita, fine. But ask them first," he said with a calm voice. "Believe me. If you bolt out of here and try to turn us over to the authorities, it won't be Victor or Edward or Chris or me who comes after you," he said to Jennifer and Steven. "You'd better worry about them," he said as he pointed out the window. "I would not stab them in the back for all they've done for us."

"Think about something else," Christopher added. "If you tell the authorities and they alert the government, do you believe they will reward you and just let you go scot free for being so warm hearted," he said with cynicism. "You don't know nuthin about the world. The government would stick us in an internment camp and question us morning, noon, and night. You think you're freedom is limited now... wait till the government gets through with you. You'll never see the light of day. Why do you think they came to Rollo? Why do you think they want to keep their existence a secret? Don't you get it?"

Everyone in the room muttered their thoughts to each other. Christopher struck a chord.

"Do you think the government would do that to us?" Jennifer asked. "I never thought about that."

"You're probably right Chris," Victor added.

A hush fell over the room as each person began to feel as if they were trapped for life.

"I thought this was supposed to be a party," Edward said as he raised his voice. "Let's have some fun and stop talking about being in prison or betraying our friends."

"Yeah, put some music on," Selena suggested. "Anyone care to dance?"

Most of the others in the room mumbled agreement. However, too many fears were expressed this evening. Every young person had more to think about that night after they left the party than when they arrived.

Unfortunately, Steven decided he had enough of this sanguine life. He wanted out. He didn't care about the others. He had never tasted a beer. He knew that men went to bars and met women. He just wanted to enjoy his newfound wealth in a way that no delivery service could provide. He didn't want to be told what to do any longer. He was leaving on his own accord.

As soon as the party ended, he shoved as many personal affects as he could into a backpack. Michael recently blessed the young man with a new motorcycle, a present Steven personally requested with an ulterior motive. Despite knowing his motives, Michael gave him the gift anyway. He wanted the young man to show he was trustworthy. To be safe, he alerted Zhiwei who kept his eye on Steven.

Around one thirty in the morning, the young man crept outside and silently pushed his motorcycle north of town nearly a mile before he started it and took off for Kansas City.

Jennifer woke when she heard the proximity alarm go off. She glanced out the window in time to see Steven pushing his bike north on the highway.

"Good luck Steve," she whispered. "I hope you make it."

She heard Zhiwei behind her. She turned to see his face. She thought he would be cross or angry. Instead she realized he seemed sad. He had a duty to perform that he did not like.

"You still don't understand Jennifer," he said to her. "By running away with no driver's license, Steven could be arrested. If that happens, he will put all of our lives at risk."

"I'm sorry… I didn't realize… What are you going to do?" she asked.

"It's alright," he told her. "Unfortunately, I must take care of Steven in our way. I won't penalize you because you neglected your duty this evening and didn't wake me Jennifer. I heard what you said at the party tonight. Your betrayal hurt me. You should go to sleep. I'll take over your watch."

"Zhiwei…" she started to say.

"Not now," he told her. "We'll discuss your position here tomorrow."

Zhiwei had monitored the party. He reached out with his thoughts to the north of Rollo. He reluctantly entered the young Native American's mind and altered Steven's memory. He found the entire process hateful. He regretted having to delete references to Steven's previous life. Zhiwei felt guilt and had to speak to someone. He knew that Master Li and Michael appeared overly fatigued at that evening's meeting. Zhiwei couldn't disturb those men. Instead, he reached out to his best friend.

"Zinian," he called next door via a mind link.

"What?" the young man sputtered as he sat up.

Zinian was the most tired man in Rollo. He worked longer hours than any member of the psychic group. However, Zhiwei felt less guilty waking up an old understanding friend than he did any of the others in their group.

"Zinian!" he called.

Zinian looked around for a second before he realized it was Zhiwei. He yawned and glanced over at the clock.

"Do you know what time it is? What's wrong?" he linked back.

"We have a runner," Zhiwei linked to him. "It's Steven. He took off so fast… no warning. I had to erase his memory before he moved out of range. I'm sorry, Zinian. I cannot risk him spreading the knowledge of us to others," he linked.

"Poor Steven," Zinian stated as he lay back on his bed. "I suppose I'll need a download in adolescent psychology next."

"You can't blame these teenagers for being bored," Zhiwei told his friend. "Some people just want to spend some of their hard earned cash on a good time. Can't blame anyone for feeling that way. At any rate, Steven wanted to see the world. I only hope the world treats Steven with an even hand. He's a decent person. I'll notify Michael and Master Li in the morning," he said. "I don't think anyone else is running away tonight. Go back to sleep. I wanted you to know because you rise early and he's a member of your crew."

Steven rode like a man possessed all through the night. He went clear across the state, passing through Dodge City and Wichita before he arrived in Kansas City just past dawn. He could not recall anything about Rollo or even what motivated him to drive for such an extended period. When he arrived in Kansas City, he stopped to refuel. He reached into his pocket to pay and pulled out a round wad of hundred dollar bills held with a rubber band.

"Whoa!" he thought. "Guess I can afford to get a room somewhere."

He stopped up the highway at a very reputable hotel chain. However, without a driver's license or some identification, they would not rent a room to him no matter how much cash he said he had. The moment he left that hotel, the clerk intended to call the police, except that a customer who wanted to check out distracted her. Steven drove further into the city until he found a cheap motel in a not-so-reputable part of the city where he thought no questions would be asked.

Steven practically begged the clerk for a room when the man asked for identification. He said he was very tired and had been up driving all night.

"You'll have to pay up front… in cash then," the night desk clerk demanded.

"Oh, that's alright," Steven said, relieved he could finally rest. "I have it right here."

When he brought out the large wad of hundred dollar bills to pay for his room, the night clerk's eyes flashed. He had not yet been relieved of his shift duty. The moment he saw Steven's roll of bills, wheels in man's head turned. He quickly rented a room to Steven. As soon as Steven walked up the hall to his room, the clerk called one of his notorious friends, a thief by trade.

"Bring Bridget," the clerk suggested.

"Who?" the voice on the other end questioned.

"You know, Lisa, Fifi, whatever her name is this week… just bring the one with the big… yes, that's the one. Bring her," he told his friend. "This kid is loaded. I want my usual twenty percent… and no cheating. I saw how much he has… that's right, he'll probably be up after six, then you can ambush him… outside the hotel."

He hung up the phone and looked over at the clock. He had to sleep as well. He hoped that later, his crooked friend would stop by the hotel to arrange a meeting with… what's her name and Steven.

Zhiwei finally slept when Selena came to relieve him around three.

"What are you doing up?" he asked as he struggled to stay awake.

"Guilty conscience," she mumbled as she shuffled through and rubbed her eyes. "Jennifer told me when she came to bed. I'm as much to blame for Steven running as Jennifer is, I suppose," she told him. "I should have spoken to Steven last night."

"No one knew he would run," Zhiwei muttered.

"You did," she said as she started a pot of tea. "If you're going to speak with Master Li, you'd better get some sleep. I'll watch for a while."

He looked up at her and started to question her motives when he realized he had to trust her – they had to trust one another.

"Ok," he relented, "but wake me by seven."

At 07:30, he was walking up Main Street toward Michael's house with a hot cup of tea in his hand. He found out he did not need to reprimand Jennifer. Selena did that for him. She laid into her friend pretty hard, which made her cry. Zhiwei decided not to interfere. However, right afterward, Jennifer came to him and apologized. Now he had the unpleasant duty of reporting on Steven to Michael. He found the tall young American at the breakfast table. Michael sensed Zhiwei coming up the street and did not bother to pick through his thoughts. Judging from the emotion he felt, he knew it could not be good news. Zhiwei walked into the kitchen with a haggard expression from both stress and lack of sleep.

"Look at what the cat dragged..." Michael stopped smiling and then moved out a chair with his mind for his friend to sit. "I'd offer tea but I see Selena made you a tall cup."

"Huh? Oh, yeah," Zhiwei said as he sat. "I had to make a quick decision last night," he said as he stared at his cup, "against my better judgment." He took a sip of tea. He couldn't reiterate the events that led up to Steven's hasty exit from Rollo. He simply replayed the associated memories in his mind for Michael to observe.

"I was so afraid this might happen," Michael said. "I must contact Master Li at once." He rose and stopped next to Zhiwei before he walked out his back door. "You performed your duty. No one can fault you for that, my friend."

Zhiwei did not follow Michael to Li's house. He had duties to perform today. He and Michael silently parted. Michael quickly crossed the distance between back doors. He reached out for Master Li and halted before he entered the kitchen. Running Elk was trying her hand at muffins. Han was starting a shower. Master Li should be... Where was Master Li?

"Master Li?" Michael tried to link. "Master Li..."

"Why a triangle, or rather a pyramid?" he asked of the builder.

"It is the shape of the fulcrum, lord," the man humbly spoke. "Is it not? The fulcrum is the center of the universe. It forms the focal point to balance all that there is..."

Li marveled that this concept should be so universal. He sought the answer to why pyramids should show up in so many disparate cultures separated by oceans and continents. He traveled back to ancient Egypt and sought out one of the first tomb builders to find the answer. He did not believe that aliens landed in spaceships. He knew better than to pursue that path.

"The fulcrum you say," Li responded. "It would be as basic a tool as the wheel," he considered.

"It is also a strong shape lord," the man continued. "If you think about stacking stones to create a hollow place underneath for a tomb," the builder said, "a cube is subject to side pressure, a pyramid is not. It is as durable as it is strong."

"As I suspected," Li thought, "an innovation created by man, not aliens."

"Master Li..." a voice echoed in his head.

"I must go," Li told the builder.

"You grace us with your presence lord," the builder said.

The mysterious Lord held out his hands and closed his eyes. The builder and his servants bowed their heads. When they raised them, the deity had vanished.

"I am curious as to why a god should wonder why you chose this shape?" his assistant asked.

The builder walked over to the side of his platform that overlooked Kufu's tomb. If a god bothered to check his progress, then he knew he must be doing something right. He smiled down at the laborers, stonecutters, and masons. He waved a green flag at them three times, a sign he was pleased with their work.

"Extra rations of grain today," he told one assistant, who rushed from the platform to spread the good news. He then turned to the assistant who posed the question of their visitor. "It is better never to question the motives of the gods," the builder said. "Rather, accept their gift."

"What gift?" the assistant asked.

"Inspiration," the builder answered.

As the clerk predicted, Steven finally rose around six o'clock that afternoon with the sun low in the sky. When he first sat up, a nervous chill ran down his spine. He quickly glanced over at his clothes to see if they had been moved. He wondered if he only dreamed he had all that money he noticed at the gas station. He sprang from the bed and went through his pockets. He readily found the large roll of bills. He breathed a sigh of relief when pulled out the large roll of currency. He went to the shower and stood in the warm water as he wondered about the feeling he had a moment ago.

"How did I come by such a large sum of money?" he wondered. "For that matter, who am I? I mean, I know my name is Steven… and I think I'm sixteen," he thought. "But where did I grow up? Do I have a girlfriend?"

He realized that he had huge gaps in his memory. He remembered playing in the yard behind his parent's trailer when he was little. He remembered bits and pieces of images if he concentrated hard enough. Toweling off after the shower he glanced out the window at the parking lot. He walked over and looked down from his room at his motorbike in the parking lot.

"A new bike," he thought as he appraised its appearance. "Did I buy it or steal it?" his thoughts rambled.

As he pulled his clothes back on, he knew that his backpack held few possessions, mostly clothes. Earlier this morning when he stopped by the first hotel, he discovered he had no driver's license. For that matter, he realized that he had no legal papers with his name on it or proof of ownership for the motorbike either. He knew all of that seemed wrong. He should have those things.

"I suppose I can pay cash for what I need," he thought as he prepared to leave. "I'll look for a store after I go… but first, the reason I'm here is because… because I wanted to go… out to… to… a bar?" the thought sprang into his mind. "I'm here because I want to go to a bar and meet a pretty girl," he remembered. "That's right!" he grinned. Yet, that seemed to be all he remembered as to why he was in Kansas City.

In the parking lot, the night clerk's shady friend pulled into the parking lot at six. His black leather vest, inky arms, and pierced body parts indicated his social leanings. He was not a rock and roller or an artist. He stole things for profit. He had a long record with the authorities to prove it.

The thief was amazed the young man had his curtains wide open, as if he had nothing to hide. He sat in his car and watched Steven's room while he smoked a cigarette. He saw the young man come to the window with only the sill blocking the lower half of his body. He saw how Steven looked in the direction of the bike. He realized that he was probably leaving the hotel soon judging from the way he toweled off his hair and quickly pulled on his clothes. He decided he would put his plan into action as soon as he saw the kid emerge from the back. The way the night clerk describe Steven, the man knew the naïve kid would be no problem to hustle for his cash and that new bike in the parking lot. He lit another cigarette, leaned back in his seat, and alerted the young woman in the back seat.

"Tell me if you spot him comin out," he told her.

"Sure," she uttered back. "Gotta another one?" she asked as she indicated his cigarette.

"Get your own," he told her.

When he wasn't stealing, he "pimped" his girlfriend for "tricks." After the girl contacted a "john" he would intervene at the last moment and "rolled" the victim before they exchanged sexual favors. The criminal world has an abundance of quaint colloquialisms.

"There he is," the thief's girlfriend suddenly spoke up.

The man took a long drag on his cigarette and flicked it out the window. He looked the young man over for a second.

"Easy pickins," he smiled. "Go take him babe," he told her. "Start slow," he added. "You might be this kid's first time…" he chuckled.

Before Steven could cross the parking lot to his bike, the voluptuous young woman "accidentally" ran into Steven as he moved between two parked cars.

"Excuse me," he said at first.

Her artificially enhanced cleavage hung out from her skimpy outfit that clung to her body and revealed every sensuous surgically-created curve. She overwhelmed the teenager with her blatant sexuality.

"Ooo," she cooed. "Excuse me," she added as she pressed against him.

"Oh, that's alright," Steven blushed.

"You stayin at the hotel?" she asked.

"Uh, sure," Steven muttered. "You?"

"No..." she told him. "I was looking for a friend. She told me to meet her here. I guess she's late. She wanted to go with me to a bar," the woman said as she moved closer to Steven. "I'm awfully thirsty. Would you buy me a drink?"

"Gee, it's like you knew what I was thinking," Steven smiled. "I'd love to go to a bar and have a drink... with you," he added.

"Ooo," she cooed again. "Sounds delicious," she licked her lips. "But I came with a friend," she said and nodded with her head. "Can he come along?"

Steven glanced over and saw a tall thin man dressed in black leather standing next to an older model car. The man smiled at Steven as Dracula must smile before he bites his victim.

"Sure," Steven said when the girl ran her hand over his back.

"He can give us a ride there," she offered as she pushed on Steven's back. The girl took Steven by the arm and introduced him to her "friend."

After introductions, they drove Steven to a nearby bar and ordered him the strongest drinks. Within an hour, they completely intoxicated the poor young man to the point he could hardly see. It was only one hour before midnight, but dark enough to suit the thief's purposes. He and the girl filled Steven's head with the idea that he could be alone with the tattooed girl in his motel room.

"You sure you don't mind," the young man slurred.

"He don't care..." she whispered in Steven's ear. "This is between you and me, honey."

Steven nearly fell over when he stood up, so the couple practically dragged the staggering young man from his seat. They pretended to take Steven to the restroom. In the hall, the thief signaled to the girl, "back door." Outside the back of the bar, something hard struck Steven's head and he fell to pavement. A few hours later, he awoke on a street that was blocks from the motel with no possessions and no cash. Nothing looked familiar. He had no clue how to find the hotel. Despondent, Steven looked for help from people who walked past him. However, no one took pity on the drunken young Native American or believed his story.

"Please," he begged a man that walked past, "please I just need a few dollars..."

The man would not look his way.

"Please lady," he begged the next person, "all I ask is for a couple of bucks."

She walked faster to get away from him.

Michael finally informed Master Li of Steven's exodus when his psychic signature mysteriously appeared in his bedroom. Michael did not question where Li had been. He only wished to keep him informed about Steven. Li thanked Michael for the information.

"We don't want a repeat of this to take place. Make certain Zhiwei has the resources he needs," he advised before Michael moved on.

Li said nothing else to the young psychic. However, concern for Steven's safety in a strange town worried Master Li. Of all the people in Rollo, experience taught him how quickly one could find trouble in a city. He reached out to monitor the young man's progress. He quietly waited and watched Steven all day with detached disdain as Steven made one wrong decision after another. Finally that night, when he saw the wicked group stand over the unconscious youth, rifle his pockets for the cash, and then take the keys to his bike, Li knew he must act. Despite the hour, he found Villi still working in his shop.

"Villi," Li linked across town.

"Master Li?" Villi responded.

"How soon can you make the aircraft flightworthy?" he asked.

"Now?" Villi wondered.

"This is about Steven…" Li began.

"I heard he left without permission," Villi responded. "Shame about Zhiwei's course of action… the lad forced his hand, I suppose."

"He's in trouble Villi. We don't abandon our own. We'll have to fly to Kansas City and retrieve him. Is the jet up to it?" Li wondered.

"I can have it fueled and ready in about an hour," Villi told him. "Will that be soon enough?"

"Yes, Villi," Li linked. "Thank you." He turned his focus next to Michael and Zhiwei in a combined link. The two psychics were already in bed. "Michael… Zhiwei… we have a sort of emergency," Li linked. The two young men roused from sleep, responded to Li at once when he used that urgent word. "I've been monitoring Steven's activity," he informed them. "I'm afraid the young man is in trouble. We need to bring him back to Rollo."

"Master Li," Zhiwei started to object. "We can't force someone to live in Rollo that doesn't wish to be here."

"Zhiwei," Li said with controlled patience, "Steven is a confused young man. Perhaps we need to try harder and address the concerns of our citizens before we drive them to the wolves. I don't mean to cast blame. As a group, we should have seen this coming. Therefore, I have decided we must change our approach to the problem. First, we must bring Steven back. For that, I need your help. Meet me at the airstrip in one hour."

"Ok," Zhiwei linked. "I didn't mean to…"

"Please," Li interrupted. "You did your best. I respect that Zhiwei. One hour."

"Yes Master Li," he said and signed off.

While Michael kept the link open, he did not add any thoughts. He waited until he felt the connection with Zhiwei go cold.

"I don't mean to question your judgment," Michael started. "Steven represents a threat to this community," he asserted. "He could drum up anger and resentment toward us."

"Being closed-minded represents a threat to this community," Li countered.

"Master Li," Michael protested. "That is not fair."

"I wasn't accusing you," Li said. "Or don't you glean intent from thoughts any longer. I'm afraid I must insist on Steven's rehabilitation… not just from Zhiwei or you, Michael," Li told him. "From everyone… every person in this community is our brother and sister. We are our brother's keeper. If we don't look out for each other, we might as well be cavemen."

"Point taken, Master Li," Michael responded.

"I need one more person, and then I'll see you at the airstrip. Li out," he linked.

"See you in an hour," Michael replied. He wondered about the other person for only a second, before he realized the wisdom in Master Li's choice.

Steven walked down a street in Kansas City with no particular destination. The sky turned dark and threatened rain. He heard rumbling in the distance. He wished his mind was not so confused. He could not recall the hotel where he stayed. Nothing looked familiar to him. He was lost, in a strange city, with no friend, no help, broke, and in pain. His head ached from the blow and no one would even stop long enough to speak to him.

"What am I doing here?" he wondered as he made his way up the street. "I lost my bike, my money… I don't even have enough money to make a phone call… and who would I call?" he mumbled as he walked aimlessly along. "I'm not sure where I'm going…"

A police car slowed down as it approached him. He saw the uniformed men and felt fear in his stomach. He knew that if they stepped out of their car, he would try to run away, and that would only make matters worse. He closed his eyes and swallowed. He wanted to drop to his knees and beg for help.

"Excuse me!" a voice called out to him.

The voice was too high to be a man's voice. He opened his eyes, afraid to look up.

"Steven?" a woman asked. "Is that you?"

"Huh?" Steven muttered as he slowly raised his head.

A large four-door car silently pulled over next to the curb. A beautiful blonde-haired young woman waved her arm from an open window before she stepped from the car, which Steven noted had some other people in it.

"Steven!" she declared, "that is you!" She walked over to him. "What are you doing in Kansas City so far from home?" she asked him.

"I… I'm not sure," the young man hesitated. "Do I know you?"

"Know me?" she responded. "I live next door to your parents. I just spoke to your mother. She's worried sick about you."

"She is?" the confused teen asked.

"Are you ok?" she asked. "You don't look well."

His face was pale and the world seemed dizzy to Steven. The pretty young woman seemed too nice to resist. It was the only thing the drowning man had left to cling to for support.

"I don't feel well…" he said with a low voice.

"You'd better come with me," she told him as she tugged on his arm.

Steven suspiciously looked at the car. He had walked into a trap earlier. It made him shy and weary of trusting strangers. Yet, this clean-cut girl seemed more like an angel of mercy than the other girl's appearance as the epitome of temptation.

"The car is safe," he heard the words echo in his mind. "You are safe with the girl."

"Yeah, sure," he finally agreed as he allowed her to lead him.

Unlike the previous vixen who led him astray, he trusted this young woman, although he could not say why. He climbed into the back seat of the car with her. Steven noticed that a tall dark-haired man drove the car, and in the front passenger seat was a much older man with white hair. The older man turned around and smiled at Steven as the car pulled away from the curb.

"I know you are confused," the older man said. "I know life has been rough lately," he went on. "We are here to help put things right for you once more." He turned to the driver, "the airport, Villi, posthaste."

"Yes Master Li," Villi replied aloud.

"Li…" Steven said as he tried to shake out the cobwebs from his thoughts. "Why do I know who Master Li is?" he wondered.

"Because all the best people do," Li said smiling as he turned his focus back to Steven.

Li's comment brought a big smile to Villi's face. Yet, the teenager seemed too trouble for any humor.

"I've a feeling I did something terribly wrong," Steven began, "and was punished."

"We can build on those feelings and sensations," Cecilia said next to him. "They are part of the first step on the road to recovery," she told him. "With our help, you will eventually recall your previous life… your life in Rollo, that is."

"Rollo?" Steven questioned.

"You are from the small town of Rollo," Cecilia told him. "As we return on the plane, I will try to help reconstruct some of those fragments of memories you still have of the place. Then we will address the root problem that drove you from your home… a sense of adventure, one that Michael and I share with you. Nothing wrong with a young man wanting to leave home and explore the world," she told him. "We will address those concerns and other unspoken problems that have been ignored for too long."

"For now," Li suggested, "we want you to sit back and relax. You are safe with friends. Try to remember your life in Rollo."

"Life in Rollo…" Steven echoed. All at once, he looked at the other three people in the car and started to cry. "I'm so glad you found me. I did a terrible thing last night… I…" he struggled to speak. His mind was torn with anger and despair. "It's so good to have friends…" he said and broke down.

He buried his sobbing face in Cecilia's chest. She put her arms around him and patted his back as she looked at Master Li's kind eyes.

"You have friends for life, Steven," she repeated. "Without judgment… just support… friends for life… the cure for all that ails you."

Chapter Twenty

Preparations

Shortly after Steven's misadventure in Kansas, rumors of how and why he returned to Rollo from Kansas City quickly spread throughout the Comanche community. Running Elk knew Steven well, as she knew all of her people. She knew their needs, their hopes, and their desires. When she began to hear private mumblings of "feeling trapped" and "fear of psychics," she knew of one voice in the village who could address those concerns – a friend, a kindred spirit, a person who knew her feelings better than she did.

Just after breakfast, when Master Li opened the front door of his house. He looked down the front stairs to find...

"Good morning," a large wide brimmed hat spoke to him.

The hat tipped back to reveal the woman underneath. He took one step down and sat next to Running Elk on the front steps. She slipped away from the kitchen to speak privately with Li. He knew why she waited for him and what she wanted to say.

"I know why you are here..." he began.

"Before you start rattling off what's on my mind," she cut him off. "I'd like to say it so I can tell, that's what I'm thinkin!" she told him with her rudimentary English. He said nothing further, so she continued. "They admire you very much," she began as she referred to her tribe. "I know you can sense that. Yet, the one thing that all of you are missing, is that they are ordinary people, Li, with ordinary needs and desires," she told him and turned one eye his way. "They're grateful for all that you and the others have done for them. Who wouldn't be? I mean, we had nuthin until you came along." She shifted her posture toward him. "But this is the first time in their life they have money, real spendable money. They can't fly off the planet and go visit Mars like you do," she said.

Master Li knew that Running Elk could occasionally penetrate the thoughts of psychics around her. She must have sensed some of their off world conversations.

"Mars isn't one of the destinations," Li calmly said. "It's rather barren..."

"You know what I mean," she cracked. "You've got to let them out... go to town... spend a little dough," she told him. "Know what I mean?" She faced him to judge his reaction. "Freedom of spirit is how we are, deep inside. That's the human condition."

"I believe we can arrange an out of town visit," Li told her.

"You mean it?" she asked.

"I'll speak with Michael and Zhiwei," Li said.

"Thanks," she replied with a sense of relief. "It'll mean a lot to everyone."

"I see you are still looking out for the tribe," he added.

"As you look out for yours," she put in.

Running Elk's face hardly broke a smile, similar to Master Li. She kept a straight face all day long. However, when Li gave permission for an outing to Dodge City, her face brightened so broadly, it seemed as if her skin would crack. She put out her arms.

"You know what I'd like to do," she said and lowered her voice.

Master Li pulled back as he glanced around them.

"Please, Running Elk," Li answered in near whisper. "I'm sorry. We mustn't..."

She turned away and nodded her head. Regrettably, she realized that on the front steps of the house, in plain sight of anyone passing by, for Master Li to show personal affection might compromise his position. She relented to his request and kept their public persona on a professional basis. Besides, she knew it was harder for him to show his feelings after being married for over fifty years. She had never married, and only lived with a man for less than ten years before he committed suicide.

"Thanks," she softly spoke as she rose and returned to her household duties.

Master Li left and went in search of Michael. Yet for a moment, Running Elk's thoughts lingered in his mind, as did his thoughts linger in her mind. As she entered the kitchen, a tingling sensation started in her fingers and toes until it gradually ran through her entire body. Had another psychic been present, Running Elk's body would have taken on a golden glow. She stopped to catch her breath as the glow faded.

"A little warning would be nice," she said aloud as she brushed back matted hair from her moist forehead. She took in a deep breath and thought to Li. "I'm beginning to appreciate your long distance style of romance," she blushed. Although he did not answer her, she knew that Li could hear her. "That was much better than the hug I intended. Feel free to do that anytime..."

Although Running Elk held deep personal feelings for Master Li, she managed to conceal them from the rest of Rollo. The other psychics had their own unspoken suspicions. Li would only reveal his true feelings to her in private moments like those she experienced in the kitchen. They chose this life, this type of romance, this distant interaction as their way. Neither Running Elk nor Master Li felt any shame in these exchanges. They were, after all, adults. For the remainder of the day, Running Elk practically skipped from task to task.

A few days later, Cecilia and Su Lin spearheaded the effort to escort groups of ten on day trips to Dodge City. This helped everyone feel "a little bit of freedom" as they needed to express their desire for social interaction. This was a first for most of the village – to have a disposable income and purchase frivolous items, such as: music, books, magazines, games, or videos. Some people shopped with their money to buy clothes or jewelry, while others ate in restaurants. Some went to shows, attended sporting events, bowled a few lines, or played miniature golf.

Zhiwei, Michael, Han, and Zinian quietly monitored their activity to prevent anyone from revealing Rollo or thwarting suspicious minds about "them injuns" from prejudiced locals. Fortunately, everyone kept the subject of their town mum without psychic interference. After the success of the first trip, it was decided they would go once a month via caravan to Dodge City. This improved relations between the Native Americans and the psychics more than any gift Michael could bestow.

Work progressed on rebuilding Rollo. As the psychic team labored daily to start a community, those days soon turned to weeks, and the weeks passed to months – July turned to August, and then August moved on into September. The arrival of fall brought with it the promise of new hope to Rollo as the town began to take shape – houses had new siding, the school and clinic opened, most people had new washers, dryers, refrigerators, air conditioners, and so on. The psychics gradually established close working relationships with their Native American crews.

Having specialized in particular areas, these highly intelligent and gifted individuals began to shine in each of their chosen fields: Zinian with his building projects, Villi and his motor pool, or Zhiwei's security concerns. Michael and Han volunteered to help everyone else. Su Lin struggled to start a school. Yet, Cecilia especially stood out when she established a medical clinic that met everyone's health needs including trauma from accidents on the work sites. The villagers came to trust the little blonde teenager with her incredible medical talent. She saw patients in her new clinic and performed practical medicine. She could not duplicate the dramatic and miraculous transformations that Master Li performed on the first day. Still, she treated sprang backs, joint pain, persistent cough, fevers, chronic headache, chills, or minor injuries such as setting broken bones. She delivered a baby (supervised by Li and her off-world professor at the time) and even occasionally made minor surgical repair in the same way any physician would.

After Li made his rounds and inspected the latest changes in the tribal village one last time on this warm September morning, he returned to his house in Rollo via the rusty truck with no motor. Despite Michael's insistence on a trade-in, Li kept the truck as a reminder of their beginning. He decided to take the rest of the day off and relax. He went inside and made his way to the back room of the house that had a fireplace, the room Han referred to as the library. He pulled down all the shade blinds before he sat in one of the nine large chairs arranged in a semi-circle around the hearth. The psychics made this room their official meeting place. Running Elk anticipated his return as she prepared a fresh pot of tea and added a plate of cookies taken from a commercial tin. She placed the tray next to him and backed away.

"Thank you, Running Elk," he sighed as the cozy lifted into the air and the pot poured out a steaming cup. A slice of lemon lifted over the cup and twisted while a small glob of honey rose out of a crock, gently dropping into his cup. "Cecilia was right about living in the suburbs," Li recalled. "They'd accuse us of witchcraft if they saw what I did through an open window."

Li looked over at the cold, dark fireplace. With a thought, an illusionary fire sprang to life. The flames cast their flickering orange light about the dim room.

"That's better," he thought as he wiggled back into the seat.

Despite the early September heat that lingered from summer, Li enjoyed staring at the flaming vision. The fire did not burn or give off heat. In Li's mind, the vision soothed his tired eyes. He could relax and meditate while he maintained the illusion as easily as breathing.

"If only others could enjoy this life," he sighed as he leaned back in the chair.

A thought occurred to Li that his busy life in Rollo had distracted him from one of his original intended duties, to monitor the status of the world's pre-psychic candidates. He promised Galactic Central he would. Lately, he had neglected that particular duty. He knew of several candidates outside Rollo, although most of these people were not ready for conversion for one reason or another. He turned his attention to a strong psychic force that pulled him eastward. He remembered this same sensation from that first day when they arrived on the jet.

Crossing the Atlantic, Li's mind traveled to Paris. It was early evening in the big city, its ornate monuments brightly lit, its grand avenues and exquisite shops all aglow. He traveled across town to a busy townhouse in the middle of a city block. An attendant opened the wide wooden front door for arriving guests. Li's mind swept in like a cool, fall breeze. Pale, yellow drapes hung in perfect straight lines around a wide front window in the terraced living room, filled with a variety of formally dressed guests. Large, bold, original works of art adorned white walls and sculptures mounted on black tables sat in the room's corners. This was no gallery. This was the living room of a wealthy art patron. The party's revelers drank expensive wine, munched on small hors d'hoeuvres, and barely spoke above a hush while they awaited the start of the evening gourmet feast...

"This is a strange gathering," he observed, "an odd mix of intellectuals, the world of finance, politicians, artists, writers and..." Li's eyes narrowed on the source of the strong psychic energy, "that woman!"

A tall, slender, beautiful, young woman wearing a sleek, shimmering gown stepped into the room. Unlike the curvy sensual shape of Cecilia or Su Lin, this woman had the elegant straight lines of a model with the regal bearing of a queen. Her small pink mouth betrayed no sense of bitterness. Her sparkling eyes seemed to catch the glow from the nearby flickering candlelight. Li held his breath as he embraced the lovely vision of intelligence, beauty, and charisma emanating from perhaps the most captivating woman he had ever seen. Everything about her, the way she gracefully moved, the way she purposefully gesticulated, how her face showed just enough emotion, and the sound of her musical voice, mesmerized Li with an enigmatic power that extended beyond charm. He forgot his mission, for he could not take his focus from her. When she moved into the room, she did not walk, she floated among the guests she called friends.

"I pity any man not in this room on this night," Li thought.

He watched her kind, yet sharp piercing gaze as she took in every detail and aspect of those around her, a calculating introspection behind such a soft and gentle gaze. All at once her aspect brightened when she noticed the proximity of two particular people. The first was a young, broad-shouldered, and very distinguished black man who clumsily stared down at his drink in quiet contemplation. The other person was a young, gregarious, black woman with bronzed skin and flashing bright eyes. This African woman wore a sleek cocktail dress that accentuated her fine robust figure. She had her hair pulled back from her face. Li thought she resembled an Egyptian queen.

He simultaneously read all three minds. He noted that the shy, young, black man hid behind his drink, although he possessed a brilliant mind with an established career in medicine and virology. He sensed that the black man wanted to meet another woman for companionship, yet he felt inadequate as to what to say or do. Despite his great physique, he seemed humbled by social encounters.

"Unbelievable!" Li exclaimed. "He is so brilliant and yet so shy. Even stranger – those two are from the same country in Africa – Mali! It's as if they were…"

His thoughts trailed off as he watched the young black woman work her way through the crowded room. She wasn't simply being sociable. This was practice for her intended avocation – hospital administration. She felt quite comfortable being able to hold her own side in practically any conversation, as she could speak French, German, Italian, and English in the multinational gathering. She did not take notice of the shy black man. He did not impress her as someone worthy of her attention. In fact, no one spoke to him. His withdrawn demeanor put aside the party spirit and seemed repugnant to those around him.

"She is Filla, and he is Salla," Li surmised from their thoughts.

Salla could only sigh and stare at his drink. His thoughts wandered with imaginary scenarios, where he was popular and could easily converse with other women. Social situations like this baffled the physician turned scientist. He felt at home in a laboratory or in the hospital with his test patients. Having to mix in a party with strangers and be spontaneous with his wit challenged his intellect and lack of social skills.

Li suddenly realized that the host brought these two to this party hoping they would meet. She figured that since they were from the same country, they could become friends.

"Good luck with that idea," Li thought. "Why am *I* here this evening?" his thoughts wandered. "I remember sensing them months ago."

He recalled that when he went to Galactic Central nearly three months ago, he requested information in regards to their voices. Yet, he also sensed urgency in their conversions. When he evaluated their present condition, he knew he nearly arrived on the scene too late.

"Good gracious!" Li thought. "These pre-psychics are on the verge of self-transition!"

If they converted on their own, they would lack the necessary discipline to control their psychic ability or to communicate with Galactic Central psychics. That same mental state warped his cousin's way of thinking. The idea of having unlimited power over ordinary people drove that psychic to madness. Li knew he had to intervene and soon.

"I must help them convert tonight or they could go rogue," he surmised.

Li felt the power of the Frenchwoman. She emanated the most energy of the trio.

"She could give Michael a run for his money," he thought when he sensed her level of natural ability. "I will return later and supervised their conversion."

As Master Li held his mental lock on the trio and simultaneously read the minds of all three psychics, he also accidentally bonded them together for a moment. This freakish exchange of psychic energy gave all three at the party the sensation of being openly linked. They stopped what they were doing and stared back and forth at each other as psychic energy passed through them, leaving an indelible impression.

"Salla… Filla?"

"Filla… Camille?"

"Camille… Salla?"

Li sensed the mistake he made and withdrew his probe at once. The French woman named Camille, shaken from her poised social bearing as the party's host, headed to the hallway guest bathroom. The woman shook all over as sweat broke out on her face. She sought privacy and a moment to recover from the sensation. The young, black woman glanced over at the young, black man not far away. She watched him as this man looked over at the host of the party, who struggle with her emotions. For a few seconds, she could sense his concerns and knew that he had more to his character than she surmised. She had misjudged his appearance. In that moment, he turned his body and their eyes met. They held that gaze as they moved closer together.

"Well," Li thought wistfully as he withdrew, "she certainly sees him now."

Li sensed an immediate attraction between them. He pulled his awareness back to Rollo and glanced up at a clock on the mantle above the fireplace. He noticed the time – 12:30 pm.

"Eight hour time difference," he thought "would be eight-thirty in Paris. Later this evening, I must pay those three a visit… about six hours from now," he noted.

Master Li took a sip of tea and closed his eyes.

"I've seen the tribal council's progress today. I wonder how our group has adjusted to conditions lately?" he privately wondered.

He set his powerful senses on short range. His mind first crossed the yard to the house located diagonally from his back door.

"Chou is trying to modify the blueprints he derived from Ziddis," he remembered. "I wonder how his work is progressing..."

Master Li saw a basement crammed with equipment. At one end Chou constructed a large cubic shaped object made from sturdy metal pipes, each pipe wrapped with thick, gray, insulating material. Those conduits passed through amphorous magnets tightly wound with gold wire. The pipe tubes hissed and moaned as pumps maintained the liquid nitrogen at high pressures. Inside the cubic, a suspended platform held a mixture of the nuclear isotopes. Generators hummed at one side, while heavy black cables ran along the floor to a central control panel that had two rectangular screens. One panel displayed power outputs, while the other screen showed sixteen distinct magnetic fields focused at the center of the cube. The young Chinese scientist watched the scene through the tinted window of a thick barrier on wheels.

At that precise moment, Chou increased the power to the superconductors. Li sensed an enormous magnetic field pulse from the frame which exerted tremendous force on the suspended isotopes. Chou attempted to manipulate these fields when a strange blue light appeared inside the cubic configuration as controlled fusion took place. The new energy field fluxed but could not quite hold the form Chou hoped to achieve. His eyes widened with excitement. The whole room throbbed with energy as the unstable blue field inside the giant cube sparkled and tried to come alive.

"That's it… keep going!" he practically pleaded as his hands furiously worked his control panel.

Without realizing the mistake he made, a hammer that he left on the top of his workbench leapt into the air and flew across the room into the center of the field. It instantly turned into a ball of floating metallic goo.

"No!" Chou shouted. He turned to his control panel. The perfect sine waves that he had so meticulously formed into a harmonious pattern began to distort. "No… please…"

The interior bluish field made a loud snapping sound. White sparks shot out. The field vanished and all activity in the chamber stopped. His emergency cut off switch automatically activated to prevent an accident. Chou started to curse in Chinese. The hammer reformed, though quite misshapen, and dropped to the floor with a loud dull thud that surprised Master Li.

"I hope that wasn't a setback," Li said as he winced sympathetically.

Master Li could not bear to observe Chou's disheartened moment of failure.

"I'll look in on Cecilia next" Li thought as he changed focus. "She opened her clinic last week. I wonder how she is fairing."

Cecilia was working on her first major case. One of Zinian's workmen cut a deep gash into his left leg when he accidentally pushed a power saw's blade through a wooden brace. The crew picked up the young man and hustled him to the clinic located next door to the schoolhouse currently under construction. Cecilia recognized the young man being carried on the human litter.

"Steven!" she said as he came through the door. "What trouble are you in now?"

The young man smiled when he saw her.

"It's bleeding bad, Dr. Beaton!" he gulped as he stared anxiously at the young blonde.

Using supplies from an emergency medical kit at the work site, Zinian had the quick presence of mind to hold a thick stack of sterile gauze over the open, bleeding, wound. Despite the pressure he applied to slow the bleeding, Cecilia noticed Steven's blood had saturated the gauze, the red fluid dripped down over Zinian's hand. The excited crew tried to crowd into the new clinic that they finished building only a few weeks ago. Others, waiting to be seen in the clinic, strained their necks as they wondered what the little Canadian girl could do for such a deep wound. Cecilia calmly took the whole incident in stride.

"Bring him in here," Cecilia commanded. "Set him on the exam table."

Cecilia had not just one, but the lifetime experience of many physicians in her brain. She only had to put that knowledge to use.

"This isn't a sideshow!" she said with a commanding voice. "I'll let you know when I'm done," she told the curious group as she herded the people out of her examination room. She turned to Zinian, still holding the young man's leg. "You too," she told him. "Steven will be fine. I'll link when I'm done." She pushed the door shut. "Now, let's take a look."

She first floated a number of supplies over to a side table. Steven smiled at first when she did that. Sterile gloves magically slid onto her fingers. She pulled back the gauze after she poured a sterile solution of normal saline over the wound in case the gauze stuck. She inspected the wound's damage and depth.

"Good, a clean cut," she thought, "easy to repair."

"Is it bad?" Steven anxiously asked.

She could tell the sweating young man was very nervous.

"You missed the big arteries, so you won't need a transfusion," she told him. "I'll have this closed in no time."

Her biggest concern was blood loss. Rollo did not have a blood bank. She could not type and cross without a laboratory up the hall. She had to do everything on her own. She was relieved to find that no major arteries were severed. She only had to close the wound. She laid out her new surgical instrument pack and grabbed stacks of different sutures. She disinfected the wound's interior and anesthetized the area.

"Let me know when you can't feel that," she said as she poked a needle into his flesh.

The young man winced and hissed. Cecilia went to her cabinet and took down an ordinary clay pot jar. She pulled off the lid and applied a gooey green salve around the wound's exterior before she started to sew his leg closed. Cecilia's Galactic Central voice downloaded a program that allowed her to make natural antibiotic preparations that also assisted the wound in healing faster. She found the natural substance extremely helpful, although it had to be replaced often due to its short shelf life.

She set the clay pot to one side. She heard the door creak and people whisper behind her when she applied the green goo. They shook their heads and doubted her skill.

"This young man needs his privacy," she demanded with a finger pointed at the door.

The door clicked shut. Cecilia thoroughly scrubbed her hands before she opened her instrument pack to start repairing the torn ligaments. The fear inside the mind of the young man rose when she revealed the numerous shiny metal instruments.

"Perhaps I should go to a hospital," he gulped. "That's pretty deep, doc."

Cecilia nodded and kept a straight face.

"You're right. We should call an ambulance and ship you off to a surgical center," she commented as she mentally activated special magnification glasses down over her eyes. "It might take another eight hours before you saw a doctor," she continued. "By that time, this wound will be infected and you might lose your leg. If you relax and allow me some elbow room, I can close this wound in less than ten minutes," she said as she pointed to the group of tiny instruments laid out on a sterile towel. "The choice is yours."

She stood still with the instruments in her hand. The apprehensive young man swallowed hard and finally nodded his approval to proceed. True to her word, Cecilia surgically repaired the ligaments and connective tissue within minutes. She not only repaired the injury with amazing speed and dexterity, the young man watched with fascination as she quickly closed the wound and stopped all the bleeding. Within minutes, his leg began to feel better. The color returned to his pale foot. Blood flow returned to the venous system as she performed an anastomosis on the severed veins and minor arteries with microscopic precision. She did such a thorough job that he never had any internal bleeding once she closed. As she wrapped the area with a bandage, she read his intention to walk and cautioned him to rest for a few days.

"My leg feels good, doc," he said wiggling his toes. "I got the feeling back in my foot. Can I go back to work?" he asked her.

"No," she said while she pushed blonde hair off her face with her forearm. "You cannot stand on this leg," she informed him. "Any increase in local blood pressure might cause some of those delicate stitches to burst in the next twenty-four hours," she explained. "Your friends will carry you home. You must elevate the leg and keep it up for at least three days. Under no circumstances are you to lower that leg," she told him. "I'll be by later to check on you," she said. "No showers! Do not get the bandage wet!" she emphasized. "I'll also stop by in the morning to check the dressing. Take one of these pills every eight hours for pain," she instructed as she handed him an envelope. "If the pain worsens during the night, call me at once."

She opened the door and the whole waiting room was on its feet trying to see into the examination room. Steven smiled and waved at them. A general sigh of relief passed through the room.

"Doctor Beaton, I'm telling you, my leg doesn't hurt!" Steven objected.

"I'm glad to hear that," she answered with a slight smile.

She motioned for his friends to come into the room. They seemed relieved to see their friend smiling.

"Carry him home," she told them, "and don't drop him!"

Steven's friends laughed.

"Seriously, he's not to put any weight on that leg or lower it down. Do you understand?" she requested. "If he does, I want you to call out my name, Cecilia. Trust me, I'll hear you."

"Yes, Doctor Beaton," the group humbly replied. "Thank you, Dr. Beaton…"

She watched them through the window as they hoisted their friend up high in the air. They bounced him as they moved off up the street. "Uh, oh, almost dropped you!" they kidded. She could hear them laughing and poking their friend as they carried him home. She opened up the window and stuck her head out.

"If you drop him you'll have to deal with me!" she called out through the opening.

"Yeah!" Matthew scolded, "you heard Dr. Beaton!"

The men all laughed again. She smiled and closed the window.

"Dr. Beaton," Cecilia thought as she shook her head, "…and you said I would make a good teacher or a secretary, mom."

She turned toward the Dutch door that opened to her examination room. Cecilia stared disheartened into the waiting room full of people anxious to see her. She longed to be with Michael, but knew she had a long day ahead of her.

"I could probably use an assistant one of these days," she considered. "Who's next?"

Those in the waiting room saw the gash and blood when they brought the young man in, and they noted his improved condition when he left. This one act inspired general confidence throughout the community in the young girl's abilities.

"You'll be a great doctor Cecilia," Li considered. "They believe in you. That's a relief," he thought. "I'll move on to Su Lin."

An empty lot separated the new clinic building from an old house that no one wanted due to its poor condition. Zinian's crew gutted the insides. They decided to convert the house into a new school for Su Lin. They were still working on some areas when the accident happened.

Su Lin stood inside the makeshift classroom next to a hastily erected blackboard. She had a large piece of chalk in her hand and wrote out a group of words. She called on a student to read what she wrote.

"Melissa," Su Lin addressed the slender girl, "would you mind reading that?"

The same girl, who only three months earlier hovered on the edge of death, stood up and stared at the board. She read the words aloud that Su Lin wrote.

"that that is is that that is not is not is that it it is," she said. "Ms. Yuk," the little girl asked, "it doesn't make any sense."

"Please call me Su Lin," she told her. "I wrote this to demonstrate the value of punctuation," she explained. "If you watch closely, I want you to see how it makes sense after I add punctuation," she told them. She quickly placed some commas, periods, a question mark and an exclamation point.

"Go ahead, Melissa," she instructed the pupil, "read it now."

"That, that is, is. That, that is not, is not. Is that it? It is!" she softly spoke.

The children screamed with delight. Su Lin offered cookies as a reward to anyone who could duplicate her effort. She instantly had ten volunteers.

"Let's see what Villi's up to," Li commented as his psychic senses moved to the north end of town.

Villi had an engine's cover open. He and his assistants poured over the complex device with expert care. Villi carefully tested the metal blades with a special device that read metal fatigue and stress levels. Li noticed that Villi recently removed the cover of the other engine. After he had extensive downloads in engine technology, Villi decided to overhaul the aircraft's engines with the help of his two new assistants. Li listened as the three worked together on the second engine.

"See this design," Villi said as he held out a drawing he made, "with these changes, I can increase power output by twenty percent," Villi commented to his young crew. "Of course we'll have to make other adjustments to the controls when we make the jet go faster," he added. "I've made the engine capable of increased thrust, though it will burn less fuel. I believe I've added about six hundred miles to its range," he said with a broad grin that faded. The two teenagers exchanged glances and hesitated to speak. Villi searched their troubled minds.

"Villi," Edward finally spoke up, "do you know Zhiwei?"

"Yes, I know him," Villi answered. "Why do you ask?"

"He is teaching Jennifer and Selena karate," he stated. "We… we…"

"Do you know any martial arts moves like Zhiwei?" Victor blurted when Edward hesitated. "We saw him practice in the field and we've seen you and Michael…"

"Moves like this?" Villi said.

He leaped backward, took the screwdriver in his hands, and threw it between his legs with so much force that it deeply embedded into one of the barn supports.

"Whoa!" the two amazed teens said.

He walked over and pulled the screwdriver from the post. "This engine is our first priority," Villi told them as he slapped the mesh of steel and aluminum. "I want to incorporate this new design before we need to use our jet again."

Villi saw the disappointment on their faces.

"Listen, I'd like to run some field tests once we finish our work. How would you like to receive lessons in flying?" he asked them.

"Could I?" they spoke up together as each teen tried to push the other out of the way.

"He meant me," Victor commented.

"He spoke to me first," Edward threw back.

The two young men started to argue over who would fly the jet.

"If you pay close attention, complete your work, and do well in school… I'll start martial arts training and flying lessons with both of you," Vill told them. Their heads eagerly bobbed up and down.

Pleased with how Villi ran his operation, Master Li moved on to another member of their psychic group.

"How is our construction engineer doing these days?" Master Li wondered.

He not only found Zinian, but he also discovered Zhiwei with him. Zinian needed his friend to assist with a delivery that took both men to the south end of Rollo at Zinian's new construction-site supply area.

A large fuel tanker truck arrived at the site to fill a new storage tank.

Zinian and his crew had just placed the tank in its new cradle. After the tanker transferred the precious fuel, they would have sufficient capacity to last roughly fourteen months, Zinian conservatively estimated. Two assistants guided the truck while Zinian placed the hose for the transfer. Zhiwei put cash on the man's clipboard and wrote on the bill, "paid in full." He then worked on the driver's mind. Master Li helped Zhiwei refine the memory manipulation technique without the blunt changes Zhiwei previously practiced. Meanwhile, Zinian directed his team to finish off-loading the fuel.

"Have your team cap off that tank and then send the trucker on his way," Zinian directed. He turned to his friend. "Thanks for your help, Zhiwei," he privately linked. "See you later."

"I wonder where Han is," Li asked as he pulled his thoughts back.

He brewed on the problem for a second until he located the psychic's signature in one of the newly refurbished houses. Han stood in a new kitchen surrounded by four of the married Comanche females.

"Cooking with stainless steel is easy," Han demonstrated. "You'll use less energy and cook faster," he told them. He tossed an onion into the air and sliced it as it came down catching both halves at the same time. "Don't try this at home," he smiled.

The women applauded Han. The older married women also giggled and flirted with the single man. He tried to avoid looking at their thoughts as he was certain some of them would have dropped their overweight husbands in a heartbeat if he made a pass. He pressed on with his demonstration.

"Keep your knives sharp with this," he said. He ran a simple device down the edge of the blade. He pulled out a flexible chopping surface. "If you cut using this technique, you'll save your fingers and countertops from harm," he said as he briskly chopped the onion. "Plus, you can bring the vegetables right to the pan…"

Master Li again pulled his thoughts back. He contemplated one last place to observe.

"That only leaves… Michael," Li thought with great affection.

Master Li found Michael sitting inside an ex-storage barn that Zinian's crew expanded and converted into the town's food storage system. Michael sat on a stool while he looked over lists of inventory. He counted items on hand and ordered supplies with a satellite-connected notebook computer. Master Li noted that Michael was in constant contact with his Galactic Central voice to guard against government traces. He quickly manipulated funds while his voice covered their tracks, a combination the two used to establish Michael's first financial front in New York – whose assets he eventually gave away to charity. Li overheard Michael quite plainly as he dictated with fluent Chinese, business memos to his Asian contacts.

"...transfer seventeen million yuan from our bank in Fushun to our investment house in Guangzhou. Buy eight million shares of..." Li heard Michael dictate.

"Very tricky," Li commented. "Too honorable to be a pirate, too polite to be a thief, too kind to be a gangster, and too clever to be caught," he threw in as he observed him.

"...and too aware of his environment not to feel the presence of his master," Michael shot back.

"You must give bank regulators fits," Li added.

"That and a memory loss," Michael quipped. "I see you are tooling around town and eavesdropping on everyone's condition." He closed the lid on his computer. The action automatically paused his dictation to a business computer in Hong Kong. "How are you this fine day Master Li?" he inquired. "How is your health?"

"I must remember to use more stealth next time I intrude," Master Li interjected. "I am fine Michael. I would say the group is progressing well... considering our circumstances."

"Then you are pleased with our progress?" Michael asked.

"I shall continue to be hopeful," Li told him. "We should postpone tonight's meeting. I have other urgent business. Three new pre-psychics have emerged in Europe."

"Three? In Europe? We don't need to fly there and convert them?" Michael asked.

"This case is unique. My own negligence has forced my hand. If we flew at top speed, we would not arrive in time. I must perform this conversion from here," Li told him.

"When will they join us?" Michael wondered.

"I doubt they will for some time," Li told him. "Our Rollo group formed a supportive network because we had all the right elements to make it work. I doubt that combination can be duplicated elsewhere any time soon. We may have to allow other members complete autonomy. These psychics in Europe will be a test case. I believe they should stay and independently interact with their environment. Not everyone is suited to leave their life behind and form a community like ours," he stated.

Michael did not question Li's wisdom in this matter. Rather, he constantly looked to Master Li for guidance.

"Then I wish you well Master Li and... good luck tonight with the conversions," Michael added.

Li returned to his own thoughts. He had his work cut out for him. He had to cross over three-hundred million parsecs of space to the planet of Galactic Central and locate the voices for the three pre-psychics in Paris. Perhaps he also had time to visit the past. He closed his eyes and drew psychic energy to him from the Native Americans before he set out on this complex course of action.

From the darkened hallway outside the library, a lone figure silently watched Master Li as she sensed him take psychic energy from those around her. He never took any of hers, nor did the rest of their group take their energy from her. She realized that most of them treated her as an equal, although she could not perform the magical feats they did.

To borrow energy from a fellow psychic was considered an assault. She knew that the main purpose of her Comanche – in addition to supplying manual labor – was to fortify the psychics' with the energy they needed to perform their fantastic feats. Therefore, Running Elk never told the other tribal members about this secret. For the past twenty years she had served as their leader. Now, she had but one master.

"It seems you need us as much as we need you," she whispered. She silently watched as Master Li's body began to fade away, although she knew that if she plunged her hand into that vacant space, she would feel his body. She turned up the hall toward the kitchen. "When you return you will be famished," she thought. "May your journey be a pleasant one, my dearest Li."

CHAPTER TWENTY-ONE

THE VOICES ARRIVE

AS THE EVENING PROGRESSED AND Han returned to the house, he discovered Master Li in an odd situation. Li sat with a cup of tea staring at a roaring fire, logs burning brightly with orange, glowing coals that filled the grate. Han noticed the elderly man appeared lost in thought.

Within a second of his arrival at the hall doorway, the fire vanished – no traced of it remained – only the cold, black, empty hearth. A nearby lamp turned on. Han wondered for a moment if he imagined the fire, and then knew better. He realized the illusion was probably one of Li's designs.

"It's very warm outside," he questioned as he sat. "Why a fire?"

"I like to contemplate ideas while staring at a fire," Li informed him. "I find the process disciplined and restful."

"Dinner!" Running Elk announced from the dining room. She heard Han come through the front door.

The two men closed their eyes. The prospect of another Running Elk disaster from the kitchen did not move either man.

"You first," Li offered Han.

Han took in a deep breath. He hardly had time to relax before being involved with some other stressor. He rose and shuffled reluctantly toward the dining room.

"I finally learned to make meat loaf!" Running Elk proudly stated as she stuck her head out from the kitchen.

Han shot Li a look of consternation as the two men prepared to sit down.

Han struck up a private comment of camaraderie with his housemate when Running Elk returned to the kitchen.

"At least we don't have to worry about gaining weight," he linked to Li.

Master Li held up his finger to his pursed lips and shook his head to signal Han that Running Elk might hear his thoughts. He could not be certain if she could perceive them or not. He only knew that when he contacted Galactic Central about her psychic ability, he discovered what he suspected to be true, that she did not have a corresponding voice. Therefore, she did not have the capacity to open a portal, an important development to further advancement. She somehow possessed a level of rudimentary psychic ability that allowed open communication with advanced psychics only. Li could not explain her anomaly.

"Perhaps she represents a failed line of psychic deviation from nature, just as hominids developed along different lines," Li once commented to Han.

The kitchen door burst open with Running Elk full of accomplishment. She carried a large steaming pan.

"I finally learned how to make meat loaf and not burn it," their cook proudly stated. She brought out a large lump of brown cooked meat on a platter that resembled nothing appetizing to the two men. She ran back and next plopped down a large bowl of boiled potatoes next to the platter. "Dig in!" she eagerly declared.

Both men fixed plates, cut up their food and pushed it around.

"I know you mean well Running Elk," Li finally told her. He saw her face drop. "I've had a very busy day. To tell you the truth, I'm not that hungry. I'm going to turn in early," he told her.

"Me too," Han said. Han was not as hungry as Master Li. At least he ate samples of food when he demonstrated his cooking class. He rose and practically ran to his bedroom.

Running Elk took her food back to the kitchen. She braved a bite and could not stomach the taste either. She threw all of it away.

"What's wrong with me?" she brooded. "I just want to please them..."

She felt exasperated and disgusted with her own choice of menu. She wanted to cry but that was not her style, not after running an entire village for the past two decades and raising two children with less than adequate means.

"I wish I knew the answer..." she thought as she turned out the kitchen lights.

Running Elk decided her best course of action this evening would be to turn in early.

The old wooden clock that rested on the mantel for the past thirty years struck seven – the perfect hour for Master Li to work his magic. He walked into the room and closed the sliding doors shut with his mind.

"I do not wish to be disturbed," he linked to both Han and Running Elk in such a manner that they took those words seriously. Han retired to his bedroom for the night with a novel. Running Elk closed her eyes and drifted off to sleep.

Master Li gathered up a large store of energy before he ventured off to the other side of the world. He leaned back in his chair, closed his eyes, and opened the special psychic portal in his mind. He contacted Galactic Central without the aid of his non-corporeal body.

"I must locate the voices assigned to the three French psychics," he openly called to any voice in the tower.

Thousands of voices with varying levels of rank immediately interrupted their contacts. They eagerly responded to any request from Master Li. Other psychic members from the planetary collective wanted to join after they felt Li's presence via their voice connections. Li quickly dismissed all of them. He knew better than to divert the important resources of Galactic Central to his trivial problems. He would find the three corresponding voices with only one or two of the tower aliens to assist him.

Unfortunately for Li, Galactic Central's bureaucracy scattered these specific three voices to different departments at opposite ends of the vast complex. Li did not have the time to run that kind of search. Instead, Li rapidly jumped from voice to voice and changed each contact with lightening speed. His speed startled and amazed the voices as he appeared to split his psychic connection into hundreds of directions at the same time.

"Master Li!" the voices cried out their cheery sentiment. The director collectively cleared its throat and demanded a return to the tasks at hand. Fortunately, the earth-bound psychic quickly found the voices assigned to the three intended conversions. He paused to consider his next course of action.

"What will you have us do?" they asked of him.

"I've thought about this predicament for hours," Li began. "We cannot apply the usual protocols in this instance. We must proceed with their conversion without prior approval. I sense that these three secretly desire it," he relayed to them. "The French woman's ability is already very strong. I intend to make her level four. The other two have rudimentary capacity. Start them at level two. Begin your conversion now," he instructed the three voices.

Since no one at Galactic Central challenged the wisdom of Li's decisions, the voices carried out his request. Three Galactic Central voices opened portals on their side and entered the minds of the three receptive people as they slept in their Paris beds. An hour later, two voices had finished their complex series of alterations and adjustments. They opened a quiet yet subtle interactive dialogue to help prepare the involved subject before they woke up.

In the case of the French woman, the transformation included the infamous DNA alterations. Her voice required the help of others. When the young woman in question finally woke from her sleepless night, Master Li's non-corporeal body hovered nearby. He could not unleash her powerful being on the world uninitiated. Instead, he traveled from Rollo using his alternate body form so that he and the woman could easily interact. He waited for her mind to regain consciousness by sitting on the cedar chest at the foot of her bed. A few minutes after the voices completed the conversion, he half turned to glance back over his shoulder.

"Good morning Camille Ossures," he said.

The stranger's voice jolted the young woman awake.

"What? What is it?" she asked into the dark room as she sat up in her bed.

Her white satin gown that usually draped loosely around her slender figure, clung to her body like a wet gunnysack. The surprised CEO rose from her soaked sheets and went to her vanity settee across the room. She did not need a light on to see as she made her way through the familiar darkness of her very expensive Parisian townhouse bedroom. Two nightlights provided enough illumination.

"What on earth happened to me?" she wondered. She wiped off her sweating forehead with the back of her hand. "I must be ill," she spoke as she neared the large mirrored vanity.

She did not notice the glowing, greenish, form of Master Li as he sat on the cedar chest at the foot of her large four-poster bed. However, as she approached the mirror, she caught sight of Li behind her. She whirled about and stifled a scream. For some odd reason, the ghostly shimmering image of the elderly Chinese man sitting cross-legged on her cedar chest did not frighten her – his image only startled her. He acknowledged Camille with a slight bow of his head and smiled. She started to bow back when she realized that she could be dead.

"Are you a ghost?" she asked afraid to hear the answer. She squinted her eyes to see his translucent form better.

"No more ghost than you are Camille," he said. "This is my energy form."

"Good… I'm glad I'm not dead," she wondered.

"Far from it Camille Ossures," Li said. "You are alive and quite well."

Dressed in casual clothes, the little thin man's face held a knowing expression that offered her peculiar comfort considering the circumstances. Camille could barely see the details of his face illuminated by the outline of his pale greenish-yellow light. She distinctly heard his voice when he spoke her name, yet his face remained motionless. His lips did not move.

"You know my name?" she asked.

Again, she wiped the sweat from face. Her hair still dripped perspiration from her scalp down onto her face and clothes. She fidgeted as the wetness felt extremely uncomfortable to the compulsively clean and fastidious young woman.

"I know many things about you," he replied as his figure rose and moved closer. "I know of your company. I know of your parents. I know about your hopes, your dreams, and your ambitions. I even know about the history of your personal life. Everything about you is abundantly clear as your mind is completely open to me."

"Yet, I know nothing of you," she responded. Her anxiety increased as he drew nearer.

"I am rude," Li relented. "Please forgive me. Introductions are in order. My name is Li Po Chin. I am a retired Chinese professor. I currently live in Rollo, Kansas where I moved recently."

"You live in America?" she pressed.

"We started a colony of psychics…" he started to explain.

"Si… sidekicks? Who are you?" she interrupted. "Are you an illusionist with the circus?" Her fear rose with each step he took. She thought he might attack her.

"No, you misunderstood me. We're psychics, Camille," Master Li corrected. "You must have heard of psychic people. We're the silly creatures that read minds?"

"Oh, psychics," she thought. "What have psychics to do with me?"

"Do you recall the metallic voice that spoke to you as a teen?" he asked her.

For the first time since she woke, his words distracted the French woman. Her mind drifted back to her teen years. Those were difficult years, full of strife and confusion.

"How can I forget?" she replied. Her words took on a far away quality as she wandered into terrible memories from her troubled past. She snapped back to reality and resumed her composure. "My father only wanted what was best for me. Naturally, he felt that the voice I heard was some sort of malady. He sent me to the best psychiatrist in Europe at the time, a man in Zurich."

Li detected the painful adolescent memory in question when she tried to brush off the recollection as best forgotten.

"Last night something happened to you before dinner – in the living room with your friends," Li interjected. "Do you remember?"

Again, Li's words triggered frightening memories in her mind. Who was this person? He knew too much about her. She looked with uncertainty upon his ghostly figure.

"I know that I held the best party of the season," she started.

"You cannot deny the mental connection between you, Filla, and Salla," Li said.

Camille stared at Li and held her breath. How did he know her darkest secrets along with her profound fear of insanity?

"What the hell is going on?" she demanded. When Li did not respond, she turned back to the vanity and buried her face in her hands. "This can't be happening to me," she cried. "This is a dream. This can't be real. I can't go insane. I can't. Father told me I was cured!" she said as she brushed away the sweat from her face with the damp sleeve of her satin gown.

"That moment last night during your party was a harbinger of fate," Li's voice broke through to her. "Your voice has returned," he continued. "You are not insane and this is not a dream."

His figure walked toward her. He no longer glowed with weak pale light but with a growing glow that lit up the room like daylight. Camille glanced up into the mirror and saw Master Li ablaze with glorious white light. She turned around and cowered.

"You are an angel," she whispered and lowered her eyes.

Master Li let out a belly laugh.

"Far from it," he linked. "Please, look at me. Do not be afraid," he told her. "A wonderful thing has happened to you Camille Ossures. Your mind, your body, everything about you has changed. You are different. You are a new being – a powerful being – capable of reaching out to the stars," he said as he moved in close.

He touched her trembling hands. Li's power and warmth flowed into her body. His cascading energy stripped her fears and worry away. Li opened up some of his thoughts to her. She saw faces – kind smiling faces that welcomed her – the faces of Michael, Cecilia, Villi, Su Lin, Zhiwei, Zinian, Chou, and Han. She was not alone with this conundrum. They had all confronted the same dilemma, the same fears. Tears streamed from her eyes as she gazed into Master Li's kind eyes and this realization filled her mind.

"I'm beginning to understand," she linked to him.

The ability to mentally link came to her so naturally that it caught her off guard. The sensation made her giddy. She laughed and giggled at the same time.

"I can… link with you," she realized.

"Yes," he calmly answered.

"I've had this power for awhile. I've been so silly," she thought to him.

"Much better," Li agreed.

The bright light around his body dimmed. He let her hands go, returned to the cedar chest, and resumed his previous posture. Camille sat in front of the vanity. The two psychics faced each other from across the room.

"I want you to be of calm mind," he spoke softly. "We have much ground to cover. First, I want you to realize that you are not insane. You had no malady when your father sent you repeatedly to Switzerland for hearing voices, nor do you now. You see me as a figure of energy because you are supremely gifted. Should an ordinary person walk in, they would not see me at all. The voice you heard in your head is not a delusion. It is an off-world alien that is trying to make contact with you, so that it can help you. Each of us hears these voices. They can assist us at times in ways you will learn. The same voice you once feared, converted your mind last night by creating a special area within your brain," Li explained.

Camille spun around to look in the mirror. She ran her finger tips along her temples.

"I don't see any manifestation," she commented.

"I can assure you, it is there," Li told her. "Since your conversion this evening, you are no longer an ordinary human being. You possess abilities that make you one of the most unique individuals in the cosmos, let alone the planet Earth. Welcome Camille to the universe's most exclusive club. You are now one of us," he told her.

Camille stared with disbelief at the shimmering image of the old man.

"I don't know what to believe," she thought. "My senses don't usually lie. But alien voices? Psychics? Exclusive clubs? You have to admit, it all sounds very peculiar… and what did you mean when you said I am no longer human?" she demanded. "By the way, did I ask you to make this change in me?"

Li paused as he weighed his response.

"Under normal circumstances the usual protocol is to explain the change before we ask permission," he began. "However, the world around us is changing in ways we cannot stop Camille," Li stated. "Ordinarily, I would consult you. Things have changed and so will the protocol. Even without conversion, sooner or later you would begin to use this power without restraint. Inadvertently you would begin to disrupt society and change the course of humanity. Soon the humans would discover this difference. We'd be hunted down, and what started as a marvelous adaptation, a breakthrough in evolution, would be lost forever to extinction – its uniqueness drowned in turmoil and terminal conflict," Li pointed out.

"You make a powerful argument," she told him.

"When you considered being psychic in your dreams, you privately expressed a desire to possess this power," Li stated. "Despite your alarm over resurrecting the past, you marveled at its potential and even toyed with the idea tonight as you prepared for bed."

Stunned that he knew so much detail of her inner thoughts, she could only nod her head and stare at him.

"Oh boy, do you know me," she replied. "Did you probe all of my private thoughts?" she wondered.

"I did not probe your mind to invade your privacy," Li reassured her. "I only wanted to confirm your personal preference," he told her. "I had to convince the voices of Galactic Central that you really desired this change. Frankly, I wanted to be certain of Camille the woman. Generally, we do not force this change on anyone. After a few observations, I believed you to be an excellent candidate."

"I don't know… I am so busy…" her mind aimlessly ran on, "I'm responsible for my father's corporation… the research lab… we recently acquired the university…"

"I believe you will find that a psychic definitely has her advantages," Li said with a knowing smile.

"What sort of advantages?" Camille wondered. "Can I advance my company's stock or find out the secrets to my competition?"

"It isn't like that," Li said with a tinge of disappointment. "We do not use this power for personal gain. This is the greatest responsibility of your life," he told her. "Our kind must operate by a special code of ethics. I don't believe I have to spell out what constitutes evil. Use your ability wisely Camille, for the benefit of humankind."

"I have to run a business," she flatly stated.

Li saw the conflict in her eyes.

"We do not restrict a person's measure of wealth, just don't get carried away," Li threw out casually. "We psychics can accomplish great things, if we put lofty goals above all other things as a priority. This is your opportunity to help your country and the world as well as your stockholders. Your ultimate aim should be mutual."

"I'll try…" she hesitated. "Perhaps with the help of my friend Pierre, I can sort through this psychic business…"

He cut her off.

"We have a few simple rules to which every new psychic must adhere," Li explained. "Never reveal to a non-psychic your ability, not tonight, not tomorrow, or ever. Make no exceptions to this rule. Do not even tell your closest friend or lover. This ability is too powerful and unique. We can trust no one outside our circle with its knowledge."

"I see…" she said.

"I'm sorry but we have further restrictions," Li told her. "You may not use psychic power in public that will raise suspicion, especially if the explanation is some invisible force," he pointed out. "We consider these basic rules sacrosanct. Violating them may result in the revocation of your power, permanently. If these demands are beyond your capacity, if you feel your restrictions conflict with your lifestyle, or if you simply need help, call out my name by saying 'Master Li.' I will hear you," he linked in his usual calm manner. His image began to fade.

"Wait!" she called out as she rose from her seat. "Li... er, Master Li! You cannot leave me like this. What should I do?" she begged.

"Contact your voice in Galactic Central," his voice echoed in her mind as his image faded away. "It will help guide you through the basics such as how to block, thought transference, absorbing energy, and moving objects."

Camille stood still for a moment, uncertain what she should do first. She fought the impulse to hide. Yet the idea of being psychic felt too new, too personal, and too wildly imaginative to grasp as reality, despite Li's convincing demonstrations. She turned and looked at her image in the mirror with her nightgown saturated in sweat.

"Something happened to me," she thought, "or I wouldn't look this. I'm a wreck!"

She hesitated to contact this "voice." She thought of taking a shower first and then speaking to these aliens.

"I suppose I should get this over with," she thought.

She relaxed and thought of nothing.

"What's supposed to happen?" she wondered. "Hello? Galactic Central? Are you there?"

"Camille Ossures!" the grinding voice broke into her thoughts.

She closed her eyes and gritted her teeth. Li was right – the same voice from her teen years. She loathed the sound. Yet, she promised Li she would cooperate.

"I need your help... voice," she reluctantly requested.

"Good to hear from you, Camille," it began. After it spoke a few times, she found its tone strangely soothing. "Shall we begin," it continued.

Within thirty minutes, Camille and her voice engaged in a banter that soon found the young CEO relaxed and growing with confidence. They covered such primary concerns as blocking, inter-human connections, how to absorb psychic energy, how to apply energy to manipulate the environment. They also informed her on how to create a psychic bubble, utilize downloads, and so on. Although she could not create a psychic bubble, her intensive crash course resulted in a new psychic agenda. Her voice indicated it was available day or night to answer any question.

Satisfied she could attempt the processes, she absorbed energy from passing pedestrians on the street below. New vitality coursed through her body. Psychic energy tingled her in places she never thought possible.

"I could get used to that feeling," she confessed.

In the shower she made the shower gel container rise. It flew against the shower wall a few times. However, she soon learned to focus her power and to conserve its use.

"So Salla and Filla have this power, too," she thought and grinned like a Cheshire Cat. She practically skipped around the room as she prepared to greet the day. "This day will be very interesting," she thought.

Her senses stretched out from her room. Her house servants just arrived. They would start in the kitchen by making coffee and fresh pastry. She felt like tea this morning. Just thinking the suggestion, her chef put the coffee away and took out the tea.

"Strange," she thought. "I never drink tea, such an English custom… or an oriental one."

She half-smiled as she made her bed with her mind. After ruffling blankets and sending the pillows across the room, the bed finally smoothed out. She reached across Paris and sensed her friends waking up inside their apartments. Their initial reaction was as shocking as hers was, though the experience traumatized Filla less than Salla. She spoke to them for a moment via their first link and clarified the vision they had in their dreams. She tried to act as a liaison in the same way Li did for her. She invited her friends to breakfast at her home. Before they arrived however, she had one last thing on her mind.

"Master Li?" she called out.

She found that her mind instinctively reached out. Her thoughts acted as a beacon that pierced through a thick fog.

"Yes Camille…" Li responded.

"I simply wished to say… merci beaucoup," she told him.

"For what?" Li asked her.

"For being so kind, so considerate, so thoughtful, and for being – well, I understand why they call you Master Li – but," she paused.

"Yes?" he wondered.

"Do you mind if I just call you Li, for a while at least, until I become used to this master title?" she timidly asked.

"Welcome aboard, Camille," he replied good-naturedly. "I look forward to having many conversations with you. Now, I must rest. Good morning," he said as he severed the link.

"Goodnight, Li," she said as she felt the link with him go cold.

Camille wanted to jump into the air and shout for joy, not her usual sense of decorum.

"Look out Paree," she said as she reached for her bedroom door, "the new

Camille Ossures has just arrived and nothing about my world will ever be the same again!"

Chapter Twenty-Two

Awkwardness

Although Rollo's houses had crumbling foundations and leaky roofs, Zinian decided he would tear down and replace each house on the same site until he eventually remade the town. With winter approaching, he would not be able to start this undertaking until next spring.

However, the tribal village presented a greater challenge for the inexperienced construction crew. First, they removed the last of the old trailers and place most of the tribe into Rollo houses. John's crew worked hard during this period to construct one new framed house with a foundation. Zinian had to teach them how to set a foundation, how to form walls, make joists, supports, and so on. He took individuals aside and taught them the basics of electrical and plumbing systems. Meanwhile, John put in two new wells and added septic systems at the same time. The tribe members expressed their desire to live on the land they owned.

"It's only one house, but it's a start," John confessed in one of the Native American Council meetings. "Next spring, we plan to start construction on five additional homes, all the funds paid for by you-know-who," he said to them. The tribe members knew who John meant – the Rollo psychics. Master Li promised the tribe they could occupy that land if these wished. After he made that promise, any thought of desertion halted.

Lately, Rollo's psychics seemed so focused on their personal tasks that no one questioned Chou's absences from the last few meetings, except Zinian. He and Michael usually checked on Chou every day without fail. However, even Zinian missed checking on Chou the past two days.

"I'm sorry," he apologized. "Is he ok?" he put to everyone around the room.

No one responded. Everyone was too tired. They had put in long days and had other concerns to share than concentrate on Chou's troubles.

"Well, I know he's alive," Zhiwei finally linked in. "I saw him through the basement window last night, pacing back and forth."

"Master Li?" Michael asked.

"He's alive," Li responded. "Like most of us… stressed, probably more so."

Feeling guilty about his friend, Zinian flashed Michael a few quick hand signs: "Go to him. See if he is ok."

Michael nodded his reply. He saw the fatigue on Zinian's face. He felt just as tired. They were all worn out. Yet, he had neglected Chou the past few days. Perhaps Zinian had a point. Michael dragged his feet over to Chou's house after the meeting. When no one answered the door, he walked in and headed for the basement. He could feel the energy in the air before he hit the bottom step. The hair on his arms seemed to stand up.

At one end of the basement, an enormous cubic structure crackled with energy while a sparkling blue field struggled to take shape at its interior. Chou was so focused on his control panel that he did not sense Michael walk in behind him. Michael noticed plastic forks, knives, foam plates, and pieces of food scattered around the workbench – Chou no longer stored any loose piece of metal in the room.

"I wanted you to attend tonight's meeting," Michael told him as he drew near.

Finally, Chou sensed him but would not divert his attention.

"I'm sorry Michael," Chou responded in a link. "I can't leave my experiments… I'm on the verge of… of…"

Chou turned slightly to look at Michael. His skin suddenly grew pale. In trying to link, he used up the last of his psychic energy. Michael stepped forward and caught Chou before the young man fell backward. His glasses skidded across the floor. Michael lent Chou some of his energy before the young scientist lapsed into unconsciousness. He half-smiled his gratitude as he glanced up at Michael. The blue field inside the cube sputtered and vanished. The control pane automatically shut down the powerful magnets. Michael manipulated the glasses back onto Chou's face.

"I suppose I could use a break," he weakly spoke.

"First, you're going to eat something," Michael insisted.

He led the bespectacled young man up the staircase and down the hall to his kitchen. Michael refrained from commenting on the mess he found. He sat Chou on a nearby stool while he peered into Chou's cupboards. He found some instant soup and popped the concoction into the microwave. After a few minutes, Michael pushed a bowl of the Asian noodle preparation in front of Chou. When Chou could not form his chop sticks, Michael offered him a spoon.

"Even in China, I had trouble with these growing up," Chou confessed. He tossed his chopsticks behind him and picked up the spoon. Despite the ease he had taking in a mouthful, the act of chewing and swallowing seemed like hard work.

"You need some sun on your face," Michael advised.

"I'll try to fit that in tomorrow," Chou mumbled back.

"Tonight you need to take a shower and get some rest," Michael told him. "Give me your clothes."

The nineteen-year-old did not put up a fight. Instead, Chou's face took on a grateful expression. He slurped down the remainder of his soup and stripped. After he finished, Michael helped him into the shower. He threw Chou's clothes into his washer along with his bed sheets while the young man cleaned up.

Not just the kitchen, the entire house was a mess. Michael pulled in some power and then quickly went through the house, straightening things. He did the dishes and transferred the laundry to Chou's dryer once the scientist stepped out from his shower. Chou shivered and shook all over. He was about to collapse a second time when he pulled in some needed psychic energy. He linked with Michael busily cleaning his house.

"Thanks Michael," he weakly linked as he toweled off.

"You're going straight to bed," Michael ordered from the bottom of the staircase.

Chou did not protest. He patiently waited until Michael pulled the sheets from the washer. Michael pulled out every drop of moisture before he wrapped the sheets around Chou's mattress. Chou gratefully crawled under his covers.

"Promise me you'll be at tomorrow's meeting," Michael whispered to the fading Chou.

"I'll be there," Chou whispered. He fell asleep before Michael reached the door.

The following day, Cecilia's clinic was packed. Zinian had problems down in the tribal village when an improper support collapsed. Michael met a delivery truck with supplies. Villi had aircraft parts arrive. Su Lin helped two students, who had shared a spoiled lunch, after they threw up all over her classroom. Han assisted Zhiwei divert passing curious minds. He lost count after the two hundredth vehicle. Master Li aided Michael in manipulating trust funds. Chou did not seem any closer to his stable field than he was the day before. Michael finally called the evening's meeting to order around eight at Han and Master Li's home.

"Where's Running Elk?" Zinian asked Villi, as she usually set out a tea service for them.

"No one has seen her," he replied. "Look..."

The room turned to witness a pale and haggard Chou as he dragged his tired body into the room and plopped down into one of the nine chairs while he mumbled incoherently.

"Don't ask about the fusor," Michael privately warned the others in the room. "I haven't a clue if or when he will ever see results. I would not be surprised to learn he gave up on the project any day now. I don't understand it and I doubt any of us could help anyway."

The moment Chou walked in, Cecilia noticed his ragged appearance, the circles under his eyes, his pale skin, gaunt expression, and foul mood. The physician made a beeline to him.

"Mind if I sit next to you?" she asked.

He shrugged his shoulders. She sat next to him. The young man beside her was not the same eager young man she remembered from their arrival – nor was this the same excited Chou who traveled to Ziddis and then returned with such enthusiasm. His mind constantly ran formulas. He had no regard for anyone around him.

Cecilia looked across the room. The whole group gave her the signal to proceed. She leaned over and whispered into his ear.

"Su Lin made wonton soup. I know it's late, but we're invited to stop by her house after the meeting..." she softly spoke and punctuated the end with a wink when he looked up at her face.

Chou took in a deep breath as he looked into Cecilia's eyes. For a moment, he resented the young, blonde, eighteen-year-old physician's intrusion into his rumination. "How can you understand anything!" he privately thought. "What do you know?"

Although when he considered his age, plus all of that vast scientific, engineering, and technological knowledge he had accumulated, he had yet to produce any tangible device. While in just the past few weeks, Cecilia's reputation as a healer spread throughout the village to the extent that even Chou in his isolation heard of it. He regarded her warm, kind, smiling face as a gesture of friendship and yet he still resisted her offer.

"I'm kind of busy," he finally whispered back.

Cecilia tried not to show outwardly her disapproval of his haggard appearance.

"As your physician I am advising you to go," she further stated. "According to Master Li, I have the authority to shut your project down and put you into bed for a week. I won't do that if you'll come over for some soup and promise to be good company."

Chou leaned back and gave Cecilia a side-glance. She smiled back and raised her eyebrows. He found the energy to chuckle slightly in reaction to Cecilia playing her trump card.

"Actually, now that you mention it, the soup sounds delicious," his dry voice cracked. "It's been a long time since I had homemade wonton soup. I won't try to fight you Cecilia. I'd lose that battle even with all my strength at normal. I'll be there. I promise."

"Good," Cecilia said. She placed a protective arm around Chou.

The meeting passed quickly… Villi, Zinian, and Zhiwei put in their reports of progress. Master Li updated the group regarding the induction of Camille Ossures and her two companions, Salla and Filla.

"How wonderful they sound," Su Lin put in. "I'd love to go to Paris and meet them."

"Perhaps… soon," Master Li told her.

After the brief meeting, the group dispersed. Michael headed directly over to Chou. He insisted on helping Cecilia escort Chou to Villi and Su Lin's house. He stood on one side of Chou with Cecilia on the other. Together, they practically carried the young man to Su Lin's front door. When the trio arrived, the front door magically opened on its own. Chou's face lit up to find the entire psychic group gathered around the dining room table, as if they had held a surprise party in his honor. Su Lin covered the table with a feast spread out for Chou.

"What is this?" Chou asked as the couple led him through the door.

"A conspiracy," Zinian shot back. "Come, sit!"

Every head had turned his way and smiled at him. The cheerful mood lifted his spirit. He smiled back as he beheld the beautiful banquet his host arranged.

Su Lin prepared a grand table with lit candles, fine linen, porcelain china, and small teapots all around. She fixed two covered bowls of "grain" – one large bowl at the table's center held rice, while another large bowl next to it had fresh noodles with trays of grilled vegetables at both ends.

However, the first course was wonton soup. Li sniffed the air with anticipation, as he and Han also showed signs of stress after putting up with Running Elk's horrible series of disastrous meals.

"Real wontons," Han said as he rubbed his chopsticks together. "I can hardly wait!"

The group practically drooled when Su Lin brought out a tray of steaming soup bowls. For the Chinese members of the group, too much time had passed since they ate a true home-cooked meal. They rubbed their chops sticks back and forth as if they were sharpening knives. The festive atmosphere cheered the young scientist and lifted his downtrodden spirits. He watched poor Master Li as the elder man's hands trembled when he picked up his cup of tea.

"I thought I was in bad shape," Chou said to Master Li.

"A couple of months living with Running Elk can drive a psychic to drink!" Li quipped back which brought chuckles around the table.

Michael glanced over at Cecilia. They signed to avoid using a link.

"Su Lin should cook more often," he signaled.

"What a morale booster!" she signaled back.

Moments after Su Lin served each person a bowl of soup, she sat down to join them. Before anyone could take a first bite, they heard a gentle knock at the front door. Master Li dropped the wonton from his chopsticks into the soup with a kerplunk! He turned to Han.

"Oh no," he said as he closed his eyes. No one moved. They heard a second knock.

Finally, Villi rose and went to the door. Running Elk stood outside with her hat in her hand. She peered over his shoulder as eight faces turned her way.

"Something smells very good," she said softly.

"Won't you join us," Villi cordially invited. He stepped aside for her to enter.

"I don't mean to impose," she said. "I wondered what happened to Li and Han when I returned..."

Everyone at the table stood up when she entered the room. Villi gently put his arm around Running Elk's shoulders and guided her to his seat at the table. Su Lin went to the back porch and found a tenth chair to place at the table for Villi. She then brought out a fresh steaming bowl of soup for Villi at his new place next to her.

"I apologize, Running Elk," Su Lin said as she sat back down. "I should have invited you."

"Oh that's alright," the woman answered. "I understand. Your group came over here after the meeting." She saw many of them holding wooden implements. "I can't use chopsticks," she told them.

"Neither can I," Cecilia confessed. She nodded toward the spoon next to Running Elk's bowl.

"Let's eat. Shall we?" Villi offered.

The others were dying to taste Su Lin's soup. They waited for Running Elk to take the first bite. She collected a wonton on her spoon and placed the bite-sized morsel into her mouth. No one made a sound as the group collectively held its breath. The middle-aged tribal leader glanced around and smiled.

"Tastes pretty good," she declared. "I wish I could make it."

She nearly spoiled their appetite when she added that last comment, as everyone's focus shifted up the table to Master Li. However, Running Elk dropped a bomb with her next comment, one that even surprised Li.

"I have a lot to learn about working in a proper kitchen," she commented as she fished for another wonton. "Perhaps Master Li could send me to cooking school…"

Every eye remained fixed on Master Li. He stared at the wontons in his soup. He put his chopsticks down and closed his eyes. The psychics felt his energy level drop. Michael and Cecilia exchanged glances as did the others. No one moved or linked. Even Running Elk paused to see what Li was doing. He nodded a few times and finally raised his head. The silence seemed to stretch on forever.

"You are now enrolled in a cooking school," he spoke to Running Elk.

"That was fast," Han murmured. Li's pronouncement stunned him.

"Fortunately, I found Camille still at home," Li explained. "Despite the distractions around her, she held the link with me until she snuck away under a pretext," he told them. "It's settled. She and I will make all the arrangements. On Saturday, Villi will fly you to France. I want Cecilia, Michael, Villi, and Su Lin to accompany Han and me to help create the psychic bubble. I'd like the rest of you to remain and watch over Rollo." He turned toward Running Elk. "Camille will arrange for you to take an apartment in Paris. She said she will use her influence to enroll you in the Parisian Cordon Bleu School of Cooking. The Tyler Trust will pay all of your expenses. Now… if there are no further pressing matters…" he wondered as he looked about the room. "May we please eat this soup before it grows cold?"

Cheers and congratulations broke out as Running Elk forced a smile on her lips. Everyone dove into their soup and came up with a shared joyful experience. Compliments flowed across the table to Su Lin on her excellent preparation. She watched with pride as Master Li seemed to savor every morsel. After they finished the soup, Running Elk tried to object about the cost of her trip and schooling. When that did not work, she tried to object because she could not speak French.

"I can't speak a word of French!" she protested. "How am I supposed to understand my classes?"

"The Cordon Blue School enrolls cooks from many nations. They have interpreters. Besides, many people in France speak English Running Elk," Han explained. "You'll survive."

"The language will come with time," Su Lin reassured her.

"But I won't know anyone there," she went on. "I won't have a friend…"

"Camille promised to look in on you. You'll make friends at the academy," Master Li offered.

"Who will cook for Master Li?" she finally asked as Su Lin and Villi cleared the empty soup bowls from the table.

No one had an answer to that one. Running Elk lowered her head. She was deep in thought when Master Li cleared his throat.

"What about your daughter?" he suggested. "She could live in Rollo instead of your old house with John."

"Star Wind is welcome to stay with us," Su Lin spoke up. "We have two unused bedrooms and another bathroom upstairs," she told Running Elk. "Villi and I use the bathroom in the master bedroom down here. Why don't you ask her?"

This time the group regarded Running Elk expectantly. Did she trust them with her daughter? The mellow gray-haired woman nodded her head.

"Actually, that's a good idea," she spoke quietly. "I'll ask her tomorrow."

"That only leaves one unfinished task between now and Sunday when Running Elk leaves for Paris…" Li openly suggested. He purposely left off the end of his thought. He glanced up the table in Cecilia's direction.

"What is that?" Cecilia spoke up.

However, all the sound in the room died. For a second, she could see nothing but Master Li's kind face. He tilted his head to one side, but she did not understand. Finally, it dawned on Cecilia what he meant. She turned to Michael with a broad grin on her face. She hugged and squeezed him so tight that it nearly choked him.

"I've been waiting for this day far too long!" she exclaimed.

Michael pulled her arms off. He realized what Li meant. He faced the young woman that he first encountered in Canada on a warm summer morning – the world's second true psychic. During their journey to find Li, he fell in love with her. He never stopped loving her.

"I've been waiting too," he said as he took her hands.

Li cleared his throat and gazed over at Su Lin. She turned and looked into Villi's eyes just as he caught her thoughts. Disregarding the other psychics in the room, a powerful rush of emotion passed between them initiated by Su Lin.

"I suppose the feeling is mutual," he calmly linked to her onslaught.

"I suppose so," she replied.

The two simply stared at each other quietly for a second before they sprang from their chairs and embraced in front of the group. The two lovers exchanged a big long wet and passionate kiss. Zinian poked his friend Zhiwei in the side. The two friends smiled. Even Chou brightened at this announcement. The color at last returned to the young scientist's face when he blushed and glanced toward Han who shrugged back.

"Congratulations," Han offered. He leaned toward Chou and whispered; "now if you could only make that alien contraption work!"

"What did you say?" Chou whispered back.

"I said if you could only make that thing…" Han started.

"Yes, I heard that part. But you called it an *alien* contraption," Chou echoed as he tipped his head and closed his eyes. "Alien… alien… Oh, my god. I've been so stupid," he muttered.

Before Han could respond to Chou, Running Elk stood up from the table and placed her hands on her hips. She practically beamed at the two couples. This was indeed a joyous occasion.

"Does this mean what I think it means?" she asked as she glanced about the room. "A double wedding! Whoopee!" she declared and waved her hat over her head like a buckaroo.

"We shall make it formal," Master Li stated as he rose to his feet. His calm and steady voice drew the group's attention. The two couples held hands and turned to face him. "On Friday, Cecilia and Michael along with Su Lin and Villi will become united in an official ceremony. Are we agreed?"

"Agreed!" the group echoed in unison.

"Yes," Running Elk added, "but do we have enough time to get ready?" she questioned.

"My dear Running Elk," Cecilia said while she smiled broadly, "once a psychic makes up her mind, just try to stop me!"

Even Running Elk had to smile at that comment.

Chapter Twenty-three

An excuse for harm

Han lay awake in his bed. He stared at the ceiling, unable to sleep. Several things kept him awake. His mind reflected over recent events. First, he felt grateful that the dilemma with Running Elk ended on a positive note and that she made the suggestion for cooking school rather than the other way around. He also knew that Zinian would probably put the town's building projects on hold while the two couples prepared for their wedding on Friday. This would become the group's top priority. The night's meeting ended on such a high note that all of the other problems they faced dimmed by comparison. Despite goodwill all around, an odd feeling still kept Han awake, as if he had an irritating hard crumb of food stuck between his teeth.

"What is it?" he wondered as his busy mind seemed to fight off sleep.

He contemplated his life since his conversion in China. Although he enjoyed the power granted to him by Master Li and the voices, he still felt alone with no one to share his life. Unlike Zinian and Zhiwei, who already flirted with women in the tribal village, he had no such attraction. He wanted to find a woman more like him – Chinese and hopefully, an intellectual. He thought about traveling around America to visit places that he only read about. Perhaps he could meet a person of the opposite sex as he traveled and then he could form a relationship.

"After all," Han thought, "I'm still a young man. My wife would want me to remarry. I have much to offer... and yet, this new power might complicate any relationship."

He started to roll over when he experienced an overwhelming feeling of sadness nearby. The emotion did not emanate from some distant galactic source. Han felt this sadness within the house. He rose, put his house shoes on, and slipped into one of Master Li's long silk robes that his elder friend gave to him.

"This is quite exceptional," he thought as he briefly admired the fine needlework in the full-length mirror. "I wonder where Master Li found it."

The air took on a seasonal chill at night recently. He must remember to present Michael with a list of winter garb that included a heavier jacket, since he did not bring many clothes from China. Han quietly stepped out of his bedroom into the hall. He clearly heard Master Li sound asleep. He noticed Li seemed very tired the past few days.

"Well, if Li is fast asleep," Han thought, "then who..."

He went to the top of the stairs and saw the yellowish kitchen light stream across the bottom of the staircase. Han quietly descended the stairs and moved around the bottom banister through the dining room toward the open kitchen door. Running Elk sat at the table alone. She sobbed into a dish towel to muffle the sound. He sensed she did not wish to disturb anyone.

She did not look up or even notice Han when he walked in. He sat down in the seat next to her, and then put his hands on top of her hands. Before he could speak, she quietly muttered to him.

"Is he going to pack me off to Europe to be rid of me?" she whispered. "He didn't even say he would miss me."

Han understood at once that she referred to Master Li. He also sympathized with her feelings, as Li could be rather direct on occasion.

"He is trying to help in his own way Running Elk," Han answered her. "I believe he cares for you as much as you do for him," he told her.

"Ha!" she said and blew her nose into the towel.

"That is...we all care for him," Han continued. "He is the wisest, most generous man any of us has ever known."

She lifted her head. He could see that her eyes were red from crying.

"I'm not learned like he is," she blurted and gestured toward the ceiling. "I know I have no education. I'm just an old 'injun' woman. He won't think about me two hours after I'm gone."

"That's where you're wrong," Han said in trying to lift her spirit. "If he wanted to, he could say goodbye here. He doesn't have to fly to France. He's going along to make the transition easier for you."

She sniffled and stared at Han for a moment. Her eyes blinked with new awareness. She searched his face for a grain of truth in what he said.

"Do you think so? Really?" she wondered.

Han nodded. He offered her an embroidered silk handkerchief that he found in the robe's pocket. She glanced at the precious object in his hand and shook her head. She then blew her nose on the dishtowel once more.

"Ok Han, I believe you," she finally said as she wiped off her face. "It's just that... well, I want to please him... both of you... and I..."

All at once, the ground around them started to hum and vibrate. Small knick-knack ceramics on the kitchen windowsill jumped up and down from the vibration. They fell to the floor and broke. The rumbling sound grew until it filled the air with a roar as loud as a jet airplane's engines on takeoff.

At first, Han suspected Villi might be testing his engines. Yet, when he glanced up at the clock, he realized the hour seemed too late for that. Villi would have more consideration. He noticed Running Elk's eyes widened with fear.

"Earthquake!" she cried out. She flew out of her chair and ran from the kitchen toward the stairs. She sprinted like a woman possessed. "I'll get Master Li!" she called out as she reached the stairs. "Run for your life!"

Han tried to call after her. However, the sound rapidly built to a crescendo that was so loud, it drowned out his reply. The entire house shook with a deafening roar. Han heard breaking glass as windows began to shatter. The kitchen ceiling started to collapse.

"Master Li can protect them," he considered.

He took Running Elk's advice and fumbled his way out the back door and down the steps. Once out on the lawn, he found no safe haven. The ground shook just as hard. He ran toward the side of the property and looked over at the street. Li's old truck bounced up and down. He could see great waves of energy as they passed through the soil like ripples across the surface of water.

He wondered about the other members of their group. He could see between houses as Villi and Su Lin ran from their house. Cecilia and Michael joined them from across the street. Han spun back around in time to see Running Elk and Master Li walk away from the house. He then wondered about Zinian and Zhiwei. He could not sense them. As he turned in their direction, a flash of light caught his eye.

He noticed brilliant white light that rapidly flashed on and off, coming from Chou's basement windows. At that moment, the power failed and the area fell into darkness.

"Creak!" he heard loud metallic sound.

Han watched with eerie fascination as a tall, metal, light pole bent toward the technologist's house.

"What's going on?" he shouted via a link. No one responded.

He noticed Villi, Su Lin, Cecilia and Michael as they waved their arms and used sign language. Yet, they could not see the basement windows that Han saw from his perspective.

"Chou's house!" he shouted and waved his arms. He pointed toward the basement windows.

With amazing agility, Han leapt over his fence and ran toward Chou's basement. He slowed down when he realized that Chou could be dead inside and that he might expose his body to radiation. Michael watched Han leap over the fence and run toward Chou's house.

"It's Chou," Michael openly linked. "Something's happened. Be careful."

Zhiwei and Zinian ran out just in time to see Han leap over the fence. Zhiwei did not hesitate. He bolted across the street straight for Chou's front door. When Villi caught sight of Zhiwei running, he sprinted as well. Han slowly approached the basement windows when the bright flashing light turned into a strange multicolored light for only a few seconds and disappeared. The vibration stopped followed by a high-pitched sound akin to someone singing, a harmonious pleasant sound.

Chou's voice suddenly cried out in the form of a contorted, terrible scream. The sound traveled through each psychic as if it stabbed into his or her brain.

Zhiwei and Villi reached the front porch at the same time. Villi did not have time to undo Chou's locks. Instead, the two like-minded martial arts experts jumped into the air and extended their legs. Chou's front door shattered into pieces as the two men sailed through the opening, side by side. By the time Han made his way around to the front door, he found he was the last to arrive on an incredible scene.

When he reached the bottom of the basement steps, he could not help but notice the large, bulky, hissing machine whose presence startled him. The cubic-shaped contraption filled one end of the expanded basement. Steaming pipes crackled with energy as powerful forces rippled through the structure. Han could feel the device steadily pulse like the constant pound of an intense heartbeat.

Chou stood facing his control panel. He wore a pair of thick, dark, goggles. His black hair stood on end. He pulled down on the elastic band so that his eye safety gear hung down around his neck.

Within the center of this throbbing machine, a plain, solid, gray cube hovered in the air. It slowly rotated in place while it seemingly defied gravity. Around the object, a cloud of bright blue gases sparkled with a million tiny points of light, as if a miniature universe revolved within that space. Chou moved closer to the giant frame that surrounded the blue sparkling field with the floating object inside. Simultaneously, he laughed and cried several times.

He turned to the concerned group that stood huddled together at the bottom of the basement steps. No one seemed willing to move any closer.

"I'm so sorry to disturb you this late," Chou began. "I didn't realize the fusion furnace would ignite quite like that. Once the reaction started, I couldn't stop the field formation until it stabilized," he tried to explain. "It sort of took on a life of its own after the formulas fell into place," he told them. "I took a chance on a new mixture when I factored our gravitation, elevation, atmospheric pressure, and planetary rotation. All at once… well as you can see, the results are quite spectacular. Don't you agree?"

The exhausted psychic before them could no longer link. His hoarse voice was choked with emotion. He rubbed his eyes. The group could see the fatigue clearly visible on his weary face. They all exchanged glances, yet no one offered an opinion. Finally, Michael stepped forward.

"What is that Chou?" he quietly asked.

"Ladies and gentlemen," Chou said and bowed. "I give you the fusor…"

Michael gestured toward the strange glowing field.

"I meant the cube," he corrected.

"Oh… that," Chou half-smiled.

He then mumbled an order in code to a mechanized arm that stood next to him. The sophisticated robotic device responded to his verbal command. It moved its arm around with such rapidity that eyes could not follow it. The arm plucked the cube from the field with both speed and precision. The arm swung back and dropped the seemingly dense opaque cube into Chou's waiting hands.

The group expected the young man to fall over from what appeared to be the sheer mass of the object. Instead, he lifted the perfectly shaped meter square block of material as if it had no weight. He tossed it into the air, and once more, both laughed and cried simultaneously when he caught it. Cecilia – alarmed with the spasmodic expressions on Chou's changing face – wondered about his current mental state. She made a suggestive gesture to Michael. He stepped closer to Chou.

"What did you create?" Michael asked him.

Chou stopped playing with the large cube and turned to regard him.

"Nothing on this planet compares to this material," he said as he held it up. "This is most incredible substance any human being ever created, Michael," Chou addressed him. "This could be the walls of our houses, the floor you stand on, a chair, a table, or even the fabric of your drapes. You can build the strongest bridge with this or make the softest cushion. From one formula, this substance can resemble practically any material… cloth, wood, metal, *anything*… and it would last forever!"

Cecilia moved closer as she wanted to examine the block. She wondered how something so seemingly light would have any strength.

"May I?" she indicated the cube.

"Sure," Chou responded.

He started to hand over and instead, tossed the object into the air. She flinched but caught the lightweight cube as Su Lin gasped.

"This is amazing Chou," Cecilia observed. "It doesn't have any weight. How can it be strong enough to hold up a house?"

"If you could see its internal structure, you would wonder how the atoms can remain together, let alone have cohesion," Chou pointed out. "That cube mostly consists of atoms converted to hydrogen and then fused with carbon in chains that form a huge matrix. They were forced together into layers of an incredible lattice made possible inside this powerful stasis field," he pointed to the center of his fusor.

Chou turned around and opened up a toolbox fixed to the far end of the workbench. He reached in and took out up a large hammer. He held it out for Cecilia.

"Don't let go of it," he warned at first. "Take it firmly in your hand," he said as she grasped the hammer. "Now, go ahead, try to make a dent," he dared her. "Hit it as hard as you want. Its surface is impermeable and impossible to penetrate by any force or chemical."

She took the hammer from his hand and placed the cubic material on the nearby workbench. She came down hard on the object. Surprisingly, the hammer did not rebound off the surface. Instead, the cube absorbed the impact of the hammer, yet the blow left no mark.

"Let me see that," Villi said.

He put the hammer away and pulled out a hacksaw from the toolbox. He tried to scrape one of the edges and snapped the hacksaw blade in the process. He put that broken tool away and started to take down a power saw attached to the wall, when Chou reached over and stopped him. The expression on Chou's face instantly changed to a serious one.

"Please do not try to use that," he requested. "My motto has always been, 'safety first.' The power saw's teeth will grip the edge and jerk the saw from your hands," he warned Villi. "You could be injured."

Villi obliged Chou's request. He took his hands off the power tool.

"What about radiation?" Han spoke up from the back of the group.

Chou referred to his control panel and petted it like an obedient animal.

"When the stasis field formed, the radiation levels dropped to zero," he told Han. "You might say you were responsible for this. I owe this night to you," he added.

"Me?" Han meekly responded.

"Yes," Chou said as he struggled to speak. "It was what you said at Su Lin's dinner party."

"What did I say?" Han wondered as he tried to recall the conversation.

"I had been so blind," Chou started. He wanted to explain his inspiration to his friends, despite his hoarse voice. "Building the fusor was never about creating stuff, but adapting mathematical formulas that the aliens on Ziddis included with the overall plans to this device. Once I adapted the formulas to Earth's rotation and gravity, I applied the new equations to the control panel and the fusor formed a stabilized stasis field. I fed some dirt into the feed slot and applied the built-in code," he told them.

The group looked over at a pile of dirt on the floor with a shovel in the middle and a tall ladder next to it. Their eyes traveled up to the "feed chute" that dropped the material into the center of the enormous pulsing cubic-shaped fusor.

"With the stasis field stable, the control panel could properly adjust the injection and consequent reaction," Chou continued. "The stasis field reformed the atomic structure and created the lattice. In about a second, the block instantly formed." He chuckled and then half-cried. "Isn't it beautiful? I was so stupid. I'd been trying to adapt alien environments to Earth, when all I had to do was plug in our own numbers."

Chou stood there unsteady for a moment as if he ran out of air and could no longer breathe. He started to keel over when Michael stepped in and embraced him.

"I suppose we would say… congratulations Chou! You've done it, my friend," Michael said as he held Chou in his arms. "Using that brilliant mind of yours, you brought alien technology to this planet. This dwarfs any accomplishment by our group."

As Michael embraced Chou, the enormity of the moment finally sank into the mind of the young Chinese scientist. The others crowded around and congratulated Chou or shook his hand.

Han watched this scene unfold with a sense of awe. Everyone in the room laughed and hugged each other. An incredible buoyant feeling of joy swept from person to person. At this moment of triumph, a somber note fell upon the proceedings when they all sensed Master Li and Running Elk make their down the basement stairs.

The group's merriment died down when they felt the gravity of Master Li's power actually dwarf the device. Everyone stepped aside including Chou, as Master Li moved into the room. His eyes beheld the fusor and flashed as he stared at the dazzling stasis field inside the machine. He walked right up to the edge of the fusor and held out his hands. For a moment, Chou thought the man would be foolish enough to reach inside the stasis field. Yet, he knew better than to interfere. Master Li held out his hand to judge the content and power of the sparkling blue field. When he turned around, he glared in Chou's direction. The young technologist squirmed under the piercing gaze of the great psychic.

"What can this device create, Chou?" he asked.

"I can create anything Master Li," Chou boasted.

"You?" Li nearly accused. "Are you so certain? *Anything* is a big boast for an earthbound psychic," he commented. "Please clarify the meaning of your words. What do you mean exactly by anything? Do you mean… everything?" Li wondered. "Can your fusor create new life?"

Chou swallowed hard as Li's probing power bore down upon him. He had to be truthful to the man able to see through the falsity of any statement.

"Not new life, Master Li," Chou softly spoke. "However, once I install the reader, this fusor – if given enough raw material – can manipulate atoms into any atomic or molecular lattice," he told him.

"Living material?" Li asked firmly.

"I believe it could make organic substances, eventually," the young man proudly spoke.

"Human DNA?" Li put to him like a trial lawyer.

"Certainly!" Chou eagerly replied.

The rest of the group understood Master Li's line of reasoning at once. In that moment, Michael realized that someone could play God with this thing. Cecilia closed her eyes when she saw how easily Chou fell into Li's word trap. No one in the room understood the ramifications until now, not even their strategist Han. However within a few seconds, Master Li made its dangers all too clear to everyone present – the fusor had the potential to bring about the end of the human race.

"Zhiwei," Li openly linked to their head of security. "I want this mechanism under the tightest security you can devise," he cautioned. "No one, and I mean no one but Chou is allowed into this lab. Security of this device is to be your top priority. Understood?"

"Yes Master Li," Zhiwei linked. His thoughts clearly betrayed a mind that raced with fearful possibilities.

"Chou?" Li turned back to the nineteen-year-old without missing a beat. "As soon as it is possible, I want you to install the reader device that you mentioned and begin to formulate the fusor's output to create security devices that will assist Zhiwei's job. I want them rolling off the production line and placed all over Rollo. Go to Ziddis at once. Explain our security situation to them. Zhiwei will give you whatever assistance you need. Tell them you want the best security devices they can provide. If they will not help us, then tell them that Master Li knows twenty-eight other worlds in the IPC who will receive top priority when we begin to transmit code. That should make them cooperative," Master Li added, and then he reconsidered that approach.

"Before you storm in with a demand from me, tell them what you've achieved first," he suggested. "That will certainly surprise them. It surprised me. It surprised Galactic Central," Li half muttered. "Ask for the most sophisticated security devices they possess and say we need them on an emergency basis." Li openly linked. "None of us predicted that when you turned on an unshielded nuclear device, the surge of radioactivity may have alerted the US government to our position. They may send someone to investigate." Li turned toward the fusor. "In the wrong hands, this could be the most deadly weapon on the planet. Therefore, it is time for Rollo and your machine to disappear," Li said as he turned to face Chou. "Do I make my meaning clear?"

"Yes Master Li," Chou soberly replied.

"Please don't misunderstand," Li continued with a softer tone. "This mechanism is a great breakthrough," he commented. "We are very proud of your accomplishment. However, we must look at the bigger picture beyond the boundaries of our little western town. The security of the world is at stake," Li emphasized, "not just Rollo's, but that of mankind." He quietly added, "Surely you understand those complications, Chou."

"I do now Master Li," the humble young man said as he hung his head.

Master Li glanced over at Zhiwei. He did not link any specific thought or make a special gesture. However, the expression on Li's face spoke volumes to the youthful head of security.

Zhiwei quickly scanned the area and did not find any Native Americans in the proximity except Running Elk. He wondered why the sound and vibration had not roused them. Master Li linked to his mind as he followed Zhiwei's train of thought.

"Don't worry about our Native American friends," Li linked. "I isolated Chou from the rest of our community. They are asleep, unaware of what happened. I repaired most of the damage to the houses. Only Running Elk is to know about the fusor," he told him.

Zhiwei wondered why Li allowed Running Elk access to this most top-secret device.

"Running Elk is one of us," Li privately linked to everyone in the room except her. "If not in body, she is one of us in spirit. She is bound by the same oaths and vows that we have pledged to uphold. Consider it so as of this moment."

"Yes Master Li," the entire room privately responded via links.

Chou stood before Master Li stunned. Until this moment, he only thought of the good things he could accomplish after he created the fusor. He did not build the fusor to duplicate a human body. After Li's questioning, he realized the fusor needed additional safety protocols.

"How soon can you install the reader?" Zhiwei asked Chou.

"Excuse me, what is the purpose of the reader?" Michael interrupted.

"The reader is a general scanning device that breaks down any substance into its molecular construction for the purpose of replication," Chou explained. When he saw Michael's eyes lose focus, he half smiled. "I know this is highly technical, but I'll try to keep it simple. The fusor will use the scan from the reader to make a blueprint. Once introduced into its matrix, the fusor will replicate the object perfectly, right down to its flaws unless you remove them."

"Yes, but in the case of this cube…" Villi spoke up.

"That is a formula," Chou explained. "It has no equivalent in nature. Ziddis is a planet that specializes in many formulas and codes. Codes can also build machines. I can buy them, but Ziddis never gives them away. Only one formula came with the general blueprint."

"What about tools or devices?" Zinian asked.

"Any tool or device requires a specific blueprint made up of code," he explained. "I must barter for all coded items," Chou added.

"I see…" Zhiwei said as he moved closer to the control panel. "You can use the reader to make devices from coded blueprints and substances from formulas, but stuff like plants or an inorganic substance such as spring water requires the reader to scan it first, because no one else has that code. Is that it?"

"Now you understand," Chou explained.

"How much does a reader cost?" Su Lin asked.

"I don't know," Chou replied. "I've never exchanged code."

Zinian was the last person to hold the cube. He stared intently at the substance. His mind worked as quickly as the builder's vivid imagination could envision.

"Going to erect a new city with that stuff?" Michael posed to Zinian which diverted the group's attention.

Zinian dismissively tossed the material onto the workbench and glanced around at the expectant faces.

"I hate to break this to you, but I can't use that stuff," he replied. His answer stunned everyone, even Chou. "How can I nail a board made from Chou's formula?" he asked. "We can't even pierce its surface. This is harder than diamond. If I tried to stack it, the substance has no weight. A light wind could blow it right over. It's useless!"

Chou chuckled at his friend's lack of information.

"They don't use nails on Ziddis," Chou informed him. "They use tiny droplets of a liquid that behaves like atomic glue. Set two pieces together and they permanently bond. Naturally, they fix that to a foundation..."

"Yes, but what if I..." Zinian started to protest.

"...get the glue on your hand or in your eye?" Chou finished his thought. "The application device is not that crude. No one on Ziddis has ever suffered an accident from using it," Chou stated with confidence in his tone.

Zinian turned his nose up to the gray colored object.

"Does it come in colors? I hate to think we'll be living in the gray city!" he asked over his shoulder.

"Uh huh," Chou replied, "unlimited number of shapes too," the inventor added. "As I said before, I can make it resemble any kind of material, with different surfaces that are soft or pliant but completely incorruptible."

"Fine! Fine! Let's start building!" Zinian grinned at Chou. He reached out and put his hand on his shoulder.

"First, Chou and I have some work to do," Zhiwei spoke up. He moved to stand next to the technical genius on his opposite side from Zinian.

For a second, Zinian's grin was infectious. All three men exchanged smiles, the pallor that Master Li cast on the room a moment ago melted away to thoughts of gleaming towers. Yet, the stressed and fatigued Chou wavered in his stance. He leaned against Zhiwei and closed his eyes. He let out a long sigh as if his last breath left his lungs while he nearly fainted.

Cecilia quickly stepped between them. Her powerful, obtrusive psychic energy clearly dwarfed Zinian and Zhiwei's levels.

"I don't mean to burst anyone's bubble," she said as she took hold of Chou. "Being a physician, I recognize gross mental fatigue when I see it. My word is law at the moment gentlemen," she said. She slipped her arm around Chou's shoulders to support him. "Chou has worked long enough today. He needs some rest," she spoke firmly. "Come with me, I'm putting you to bed."

"Cecilia, I've so much work to do..." Chou weakly protested.

"You suffer from lack of proper judgment, chemical instability, involuntary muscle spasms, inability to focus, loss of balance," she rattled off the signs she observed. "What if you made a mistake and blew us up instead. Can you afford to make such an error, simply based on not getting enough rest? You constitute a danger to yourself and others. I am acting on the community's behalf. Does anyone care to argue the point?" she asked and glanced about the room.

No one moved or said a word.

"Good!" she said aloud and then turned to Chou. "You need rest... not tomorrow, not in the morning, right now, tonight. Let's go," she said. She gently led him toward the steps.

Zhiwei started to protest. He glanced over at Master Li hoping for intervention. Li shook his head and hand signaled not to interfere. Reluctantly, Zhiwei backed away. However, Cecilia's pronouncement upset him. He could only watch with mounting frustration while she guided Chou up the basement steps to his bedroom.

Zhiwei glanced over at Michael who signed back, "Smart move." Privately he added, "Trust me when I say, you would lose any psychic duel to that woman!"

"The hour is late," Master Li spoke up. "I suggest we all get some rest. Goodnight," he gestured toward the stairs.

As the group turned to leave, Li privately signaled Zhiwei. Michael caught part of his message. Li was not content to leave the basement unguarded while Chou slept in his bed upstairs. He leaned over to Zhiwei's ear and spoke in a very quiet voice.

"...guard over this house with your life if necessary..." he heard Master Li whispering to Zhiwei.

Slowly the group ascended the stairs and returned to their homes. Each psychic mulled over the possibilities for future applications of Chou's device. As he strolled across the moist cool grass, Han noticed that Running Elk and Master Li move their heads close together. Although he lagged only a few paces behind them, he could not sense the private conversation that took place between them. Han figured Li offered calming reassurances after her bout of uncertainty in the kitchen.

The following morning when Han rose, he felt completely rested. He stretched as he turned to note the time on the bedside clock. The numbers said nine in the morning. Han felt he had overslept.

"Oh, it's late!" he mumbled as he rolled out of bed. "I must have been very tired," he sighed. He pumped his arms up and down, ran in place, and took in deep breaths before he reached for his clothes.

He almost stumbled down the stairs after he glanced across the hall and found Master Li's bed made. He hoped he slept in his bed last night... alone! He did not know how the dynamics of their relationship would change if Li and Running Elk started carrying on an affair. When he entered the kitchen, he noticed Running Elk had a certain spring to her step, which worried him further. She hurried about, saying she was eager to leave the house. After that, she did not speak to Han and exited right after he sat down. He noticed that she left a note addressed to him.

"Dear Han, I made some muffins and a pot of tea. p.s., I'll be over at Cecilia's if anyone needs me. RE"

He noticed that Running Elk left a covered teapot for him. Han wolfed down a few bites of muffin and quickly sipped his hot tea and milk. The moment he stepped out the front door, he sensed something peculiar about their little town. He felt a strange sensation in the air that he could not quite place. Some element to the usual had changed during the night. He sensed an intangible difference about Rollo. He glanced around for anything out of the ordinary, but nothing stood out.

Han heard a semi-truck approaching as it barreled along the highway at full speed. Usually the trucks slowed down when coming through Rollo, although the highway did not intersect any city street directly. The truck roared past the town.

"That's dangerous," Han commented.

However, only a few minutes later, a car coming from the opposite direction did the exact same thing. It zoomed past Rollo at a high rate of speed.

"If I didn't know any better…" he began as a line of logic.

He turned the corner and walked along the street that formed the town's eastern boundary and then turned left up Main Street until he passed between Michael's house on his left and Villi's house on his right.

"I don't see anything unusual here," he thought.

He sensed the two brides-to-be: Su Lin and Cecilia with Running Elk and Star Wind inside Cecilia's home. The four women had their heads together discussing wedding plans. Han continued to walk down Main Street. As he strolled past Chou's house, he noticed that someone had replaced the front door.

"That was quick," he thought.

Although he recalled a statement Li made last night about repairing damage. He probably did not notice it when he left last night. As he passed the front of the house, he glanced over at the side basement door where workers had earlier unloaded piles of dirt for the feed chute. This was the raw material that Chou used for the fusor. Both had vanished.

He walked through the side yard to have a closer look and noticed something else on the ground, a small black box that was not there yesterday. As he stooped down to touch it when the box vanished. He backed up and the box reappeared.

"Now I know Chou had a basement door a large pile of dirt here last night," he thought. "I must be seeing things. Perhaps I should drop by Cecilia for a check-up."

"No need for that, Han," Zhiwei's voice broke into his thoughts. "I'm monitoring any activity around Chou's house. I sensed you there and followed your actions. You aren't seeing things."

"Would you mind explaining?" Han requested as he held still. "I am all… ears."

"Chou awoke around three in the morning after about four hours of sleep," Zhiwei told him. "Well… actually, I roused him…"

"What about Cecilia?" Han asked. "Didn't she object?"

"I'm getting to that," Zhiwei explained. "Anyway, Chou journeyed to Ziddis while I monitored his link. Fortunately, he timed his landing at midday break hour. He informed his recipient of his breakthrough while I stayed in the background. Suddenly, they were very cooperative and interested in anything else Chou might invent. Master Li was right. Chou's discovery not only surprised everyone at Techno-world, they elevated Chou's contact to a level four manager, beyond what we hoped."

"Li was right to take the second approach. Go on," Han said, curious.

"The manager turned out to be extremely generous," Zhiwei told him. "He said that Ziddis' connection to Earth was now a *treasured* one," he emphasized. "Seems everyone is curious about the planet that produced Master Li, as we have some secret ingredient in our water!"

Han smiled at the rumor.

"We downloaded the blue print codes to security devices and advanced tools, including an advanced reader that can eventually assemble organic molecules," Zhiwei informed him. "Chou took the complex code and created the reader. After he ran some tests, he attached it to the fusor. The first thing he made after that was the power cube…"

Han started to question when Zhiwei cut him off.

"Let me finish," he continued. "Chou said he needed power sources to run devices. He made several power cubes before he started making holo-projectors. We placed them around Rollo's town limits. Presently, no one outside of Rollo can see us."

"How do we appear to outsiders?" Han asked.

"They only see fields of empty grasslands or farmland. They cannot see structures of any kind. The village of Rollo no longer exists," Zhiwei told him. "We've vanished. Even if they accidentally drove off the road into Rollo, they would not see us."

"This is amazing Zhiwei. Does Michael know about this?" Han wondered.

"I contacted Michael the moment we returned from Ziddis," Zhiwei explained. "He thanked me for waking him… said he wanted to see Chou create the reader. He quietly slipped away to avoid waking Cecilia. After Chou explained the mechanisms to us, Michael and I activated the first projection devices early this morning," Zhiwei stated.

"What about the Native Americans coming from the village?" Han asked.

"We mentally guided them into Rollo this morning," Zhiwei further explained. "Zinian told them that we had 'camouflage Rollo' and took DNA samples from them by scraping the inside of their mouths. Chou put the information into the resonating filters. The samples altered the holo-projectors so that when our friends look at Rollo, the emitters do not affect their vision. He said he already had our DNA on file."

"I'd say you've been very busy," Han commented.

As he stood in Chou's yard, Han finally saw Zhiwei as he walked up the street toward him. He wondered why Zhiwei did not appear tired.

"Are you serious about this? Are you saying that Chou actually created these devices and activated them that quickly?" Han asked dumbfounded.

"I take security very seriously," Zhiwei replied. "Master Li told me to guard the fusor with my life. It had to be done."

"Yes, but Chou was tired. Cecilia demanded he not be disturbed," Han pointed out.

"Chou is asleep now. He'll be fine," Zhiwei told him as he crossed the street.

Zhiwei's efficiency in this matter impressed Han. He told Han that he acted on the group's behalf, doctor's orders or not. He performed his duty as Master Li requested. First, he ran back to his house, grabbed a caffeinated drink from the refrigerator, and then waited inside Chou's house until three.

He had no trouble waking Chou after four hours of sleep. Chou had operated on less sleep over the past few weeks. However, Cecilia knew that Zhiwei would probably pull a stunt like that, especially when Michael alerted her to Master Li's directive before they went to bed. She allowed Michael to believe she was still asleep when he left the house. She dressed and followed behind him, timing her entrance into the basement right after Chou started to attach the reader to the fusor.

"Rested?" she asked when the three men spun around, surprised by her visit.

"Cecilia, I..." Michael began.

"Forget it," she said as she dismissed his puny excuse. "Is that the reader?" she asked Chou.

"Uh, huh," he said as he balanced on the ladder near the feed chute. "If you want, I can go to bed right after..."

"...right after you make those security devices... right, Zhiwei?" she put to him.

Zhiwei smiled and nodded. She turned her attention to Michael.

"Why don't you and I fix breakfast for these two before you and Zhiwei run around Rollo setting up those devices?" she suggested.

Michael liked her offer. Zhiwei traded places with Michael holding the ladder while the newly betrothed couple headed for Chou's kitchen.

"I really didn't fool you this morning, did I?" Michael asked as they ascended the stairs.

"This doctor is no one's fool," she quipped.

"Well," Zhiwei said as he finished his story to Han, "Cecilia and Michael cooked breakfast for us while Chou tested the reader. He started making those power cubes right after that," the young man concluded.

"Did you say power cubes?" Han questioned.

"They are the most amazing devices," Zhiwei pointed out. "Consider them the ultimate battery."

"Yes but when I tried to touch the cube…" Han spoke up.

"It has a built in holo-projector to protect it from tampering. Its true location is hidden nearby," Zhiwei pointed out.

"Cecilia allowed Chou to do all of this?" Han wondered.

"Oh, she watched him like a hawk all during breakfast," Zhiwei grinned as he recalled her attitude. "She did not interfere. I was surprised. She calmly waited until Chou made working copies of everything we needed. Then she pulled him away and announced that Michael and I would activate all the projects. She put Chou back to bed. Once he showed us how to operate the devices he created, Michael and I proceeded to place them all over Rollo. When we returned, Cecilia sat on the steps of Chou's house. She wanted to speak with me."

Zhiwei revealed to Han the conversation he had with Cecilia about two hours ago.

"Fusor-type devices are known throughout the Intergalactic Psychic Collective," she informed Zhiwei. "The fusor can also create drugs. The medical experts on Tegixil are not as stingy as the technologist on Ziddis when it comes to sharing information. They have begun to experiment on human shells anticipating Chou's breakthrough," she explained. "Some of the drugs they hope to develop many eventually cure all Earth-borne diseases – some may even prolong life, or so they inform me. I'm forced to be optimistic with Chou. I see only positive things coming out of this invention. The head of security should be careful, even be cautious in protecting Rollo from outside harm, yes. But do not become paranoid, Zhiwei," Cecilia advised. "A simple thing like fear can develop into mania and bring about the end of the most ardent empire."

"Well," Zhiwei quickly replied, "I appreciate your concern for my mental fitness. However, I can be vigilant and sane for both of us. Believe it or not Cecilia, I see the potential for good as much as you do. I will do as you suggest and remain positive… for now."

Two days later, on Friday afternoon, the wedding came off without a hitch. Everyone crowded into Rollo's largest space, Cecilia's waiting room. Cecilia and Su Lin wore white gowns bedecked with diamonds created by Chou's fusor. The two couples exchanged vows and Master Li presided over the ceremonies. Afterward, the psychics stood back as their Native American friends broke out musical instruments and rocked the place with an old fashioned hoedown. Running Elk had to show Michael and Cecilia the two step, but the newlywed couples danced at their wedding. Even Master Li partook in the high spirited event.

Chapter Twenty-Four

Departures and Arrivals

"Stop!" Chou cried out.

He sat up in bed. He breathed hard as if he had run from one end of Rollo to the other. He glanced about him and saw nothing in the darkness. The clock next to his bed said four thirty in the morning. The wedding finally festivities ended only five hours ago. The newlywed couples decided to retire early due to their flight in the morning. Chou took in a deep breath. It upset him that he could not sleep.

"This is much too early to rise," he quickly reasoned.

He fell back in his bed. He started to close his eyes, when a terrible thought occurred to him.

"I sense a stranger in the house," he thought. "A prowler searching for..." He slowly rose and scanned the darkness. He sensed that the basement door to the lab stood ajar, which puzzled him. Zhiwei installed proximity alarms in the yard, at the doors and windows, but especially to the lab door. "Why hasn't the alarm gone off?" he thought. "They're after the fusor!"

Chou flipped back the covers and headed for his sandals. He quickly slid them on his feet and took careful long strides to the stairs. The house seemed too quiet, the air too still, as if a dampening field hung over the house that suppressed every sound and every movement.

Wearing only his boxer shorts, he tiptoed as quietly as he could to the open doorway that led to the basement stairs and tried the light switch. Nothing happened when he flipped up the control. The basement lights did not work. He flipped it up and down repeatedly but nothing happened.

The basement had several overhead lights connected to this switch. Not all of them could be out, he reasoned. He swallowed hard. His pulse throbbed in his neck. His heart pounded in his chest as anxiety and fear took over his mind. He slowly descended the long staircase.

When he reached the bottom of the basement stairs, he noticed that none of the little robots he made over the past two days moved. They seemed frozen in position. Chou looked over at the fusor. He could see the bluish sparkling field of the fusor in the dark. The stasis field constantly hovered inside the huge cubic shaped device that filled most of the far end. He reached out to feel along the wall. The other light switch at the bottom of the stairs did not work either. Then movement caught his eye.

Off to one side, Chou noticed a dark figure stood next to the fusor's control panel. For a moment, he sensed that this lone human figure seemed intent to destroy the very object he worked so many long hours to create. After the countless downloads that he endured, the rejected start-ups, reconfigurations, missed calculations, and failures night after night, he finally created a stable field that could manipulate atoms to duplicate any structure. Now this person wanted to destroy his creation? He started to use psychic manipulation. Yet, he knew that the presence of radiation diminished psychic potency. Instead, Chou silently crept into the room toward his toolbox. He reached in and grabbed a heavy non-magnetic tool. He clenched it in his hand. If he had to stop the person by force, then he would use violence.

"What are you doing?" he angrily shouted at the figure. "Get away from that!"

He started to leap across the room when the figure turned to face him. In the dim light of the magnetic field, the stranger's face came into view.

"Master Li!" a surprised Chou exclaimed as he pulled up short. "Sir… what are doing?"

Li turned his face away from Chou. He stared at the interior stasis field – once turned on, the stabilized configuration can no longer be turned off. Its stability depended on the pulsing magnetic forces that held it in check. Chou absently dropped the tool on the floor with a clunk. When Li heard the sound, he gave a short glance backward at the object on the floor and then returned his focus to the field. The heavy tool floated through the air and back into the toolbox.

"Master Li," Chou wondered as he slowly advanced, "I'm sorry… I didn't mean to… it's just that… well, you surprised me. What's wrong?"

"This… it bothers me…" Master Li quietly spoke. "The ramifications are… beyond what we can possibly imagine. In all of the futures I envision for us, I never once pictured something that could impact our world with such profound vicissitude. The future has been altered. Now, I am overwhelmed with a flurry of choices."

Chou timidly stepped forward until he stood next to Master Li.

"I feel... fear coming from you," Chou quietly linked as he looked at Li.

"Imagine if someone used the fusor to create duplicates of me," Li said as he openly explained his fear to Chou. "They could create an army of Master Li's. We could conquer every world in the universe. Nothing could stop us." He looked over at Chou. "What have you done Chou? What have you done?"

Chou's face did not reveal concern but instead his posture and expression instantly relaxed.

"That's your fear?" he calmly replied. "I hate to burst that imaginary bubble you've created but they can't." His link became confident. "No one in the universe can do that. It's impossible."

Li realized the young man held a secret in his mind that he had not revealed. Chou did not easily give it up.

"Why can't they?" Li asked as he cocked his head.

Chou smiled to Li. He leaned back against the workbench and for once, felt as if circumstances to possess great all-knowing power were reversed. Chou was the one giving the lecture for a change.

"It is true that a fusor can perfectly duplicate a person," Chou began, "You were right to be concerned when you questioned me. Other worlds have tried and succeeded in creating duplicates. However, they, like you, forgot one tiny, important detail," he stated. "I could easily make a thousand Li Po Chin's," he pointed to the fusor, "but not one of them would be Master Li. Only one such person can exist. The reason I know this, is that someone already tried thousands of years ago," Chou explained.

"Over four thousand years ago, the engineers of Ziddis experimented with the first fusor. Some of these trials ended disastrously," he explained. "While many people on their planet began to evolve portals to Galactic Central, they were greatly outnumbered. However, the people of Ziddis did not treat the new arrivals as those on Earth would treat us. They offered to help. They devised a plan to create greater numbers of psychic people. One of the new psychic leaders volunteered. Their scientists very carefully made many copies of him. However, none of them – not a single being – possessed psychic power. In fact, the duplicates had no impulse to do anything but stand there. As hard as they tired, the engineers could not motivate a duplicated being to move. What was the reason, you might ask?" Chou said with a smile. "We are the sum of what we are from birth, every moment from the cuddling of our mothers to the rocking we receive from our fathers, affects us. Our life experience imprints on us who we are. The duplicates would not budge, not because they could not walk, but because they had no reason to walk. No one taught them. They had no concept of walking or what walking could do for them. They stared straight ahead with empty minds. The fusor duplicated the person, but not the memories. Yet, even with training, the duplicates did not exhibit psychic ability. It was as if that aspect – the portal that connects us to Galactic Central – defied replication," Chou told Li. "Without the conduit necessary for a connection to Galactic Central, none of the cloned beings could be converted."

Master Li stood perfectly still and listened as Chou continued his explanation.

"The Ziddians felt tremendous guilt over those experiments," Chou continued. "In the end, they had to destroy every duplicate they created. After that, they altered fusors to prevent anyone from using the devices to create duplicate life forms. To this day, only about ten percent of all Ziddians have psychic ability. Those with that ability are assigned to head up the research and development teams."

A wave of understanding spread across Master Li's face in a way that made Chou very proud he did his homework before he attempted to build the fusor.

"Honestly Master Li," Chou added. "I would never create anything in my lab that would have a negative impact on humanity. I also changed the fusor control panel so that it cannot create weapons or duplicate people, even if someone figured out how to run it," Chou stated as he gestured toward the control panel. "To help put your mind at ease, I took your advice and added some security features. If you tried an unauthorized access, my fusor would have automatically protected itself with an incredible electromagnetic shield. Watch."

Using his mind, Chou opened toolbox and flung the heavy tool across the room right at the control panel. In a blinding instant, the tool vaporized.

"Would that have zapped me?" Master Li weakly asked.

"No, it won't destroy humans," Chou said with a grin, "but it would definitely sting if you tried any unauthorized access!"

"Whew! That's a relief!" Li declared. "You've taken a great weight off my mind Chou. I'm very grateful we have you as our technologist," he linked with a yawn. "At last, I can sleep."

"It's nearly five," Chou said to him. "In an hour we leave for Europe. Don't we?"

Li spun around and fiddled with a pocket watch he had. He pulled it out and blinked.

"Good gracious!" he declared. "Do you know how long I've been standing over there?" he asked Chou.

"Half an hour?" Chou guessed.

"Try four..." Li told him.

"Four hours! But how..." Chou started.

Li took in a deep breath and put his watch away.

"What were you thinking about for four hours?" Chou asked.

"Every terrible thing that humanity is capable of doing," the elderly man sighed. "Now that I have that out of my system, I must go and pack my things for Europe," he said as he walked past Chou.

An hour after he left Chou's house, Master Li, Running Elk, and Han rode in the old, silent truck over to the hanger-barn on the north end of Rollo. Villi backed the jet out of the barn and parked it at the end of the runway. While he carefully inspected the outside of the aircraft, Edward refueled the jet. Zinian, Zhiwei, and Chou showed up to say their goodbyes. The September air had the first chill of fall on it. The cold made their breath clearly visible in the early hours before dawn. The moment Edward finished fueling the jet, he ran over to Villi.

"Topped off sir," he told him.

"Thanks," Villi said. He took hold of the young man's shoulders. "Watch over things with Victor until I get return. Don't let anyone else in the hanger. I'm counting on both of you."

Zinian's crew converted the upper part of the barn into an apartment for the two boys. A light came on in the new window above the hanger door. A sleepy Victor waved to Villi who saluted back at him.

"Edward showed up early," Han commented as the truck pulled up.

"Villi encouraged the boys to make the place their own," Master Li linked to Han. "They have two beds, a hot plate, a sink, a refrigerator and a shower. Oh yes, Villi gave them a gaming system – everything two teenage boys need to get by. Zhiwei installed fire detectors, smoke alarms, and carbon dioxide warning sensors for their safety. Villi trains them every day in mechanics and the martial arts. He wants to make them black belts by the end of next year he told me. Ah, I see the jet ready for us. We should board," he linked as he opened the truck door.

"How will we get the jet to Europe on one tank of fuel?" Han wondered.

"Villi altered the engines to extend our range," Li first explained. "Plus, I believe he scheduled one fuel stop," Li commented as he helped Running Elk from the truck. "I trust him implicitly. You should too."

Villi planned one stopover at a private airstrip in southern New Jersey before he attempted to cross the Atlantic. He wanted to avoid high traffic areas along the east coast, if possible. He took a short flight to test the improved engines with his helpers. He brought Su Lin and Michael along to help him form a temporary bubble while they circled Rollo. The engines perform well for the test at least.

Running Elk and Han went to the back of the truck and brought out their luggage. As they reached for the bags, the heavy objects floated up out of the truck and over to the cargo hold.

"Thanks Master Li," Han linked.

Star Wind and John arrived to say goodbye to their mother. This was the first time they would be separate from their mother. Running Elk gave some last minute instructions to her daughter Star Wind on what to cook for Master Li and Han during her absence.

"… they drink green tea," she reminded her daughter, "with honey and lemon. Let Master Li put it in."

"Yes mother," Star Wind replied as she kissed her mother's cheek.

"…and no meatloaf," Running Elk whispered into her ear. "They don't like it."

Star Wind pulled back and smiled at her mother.

"That's good because I don't know how to make it," the teen said.

"I don't either," Running Elk added.

"This is the first time you've ever left me…" Star Wind started.

"Don't remind me," Running Elk said. She took her daughter in her arms and held her tight. Both women started to cry.

Villi finished his inspection of the plane and turned to walk under the wing when he ran right into his new wife's arms.

"File a flight plan?" Su Lin kidded.

At first her presence startled him. He had been so absorbed with his pre-flight check and refueling the jet, he did not feel her presence just a few feet away. He put his big arms around her waist and planted a kiss on her lips – their first official night of nuptials still fresh in both of their memories. She eagerly reciprocated his actions. She only broke away when she realized that Michael and Cecilia stood nearby waiting for them to board. The other couple smiled and shook their heads.

"You'll have plenty of time in Paris…" Cecilia threw out.

"Yeah, let's get this show on the road," Michael added.

Su Lin and Villi reluctantly pulled away from each other. Su Lin cleared her throat.

"I went over the list of everything that we packed in the cargo hold," she said to her husband. "After today, you will have flown over the two largest bodies of water on the planet. Any words for your adoring public?" she offered.

"Yes," he joined in, "it is better to have company when you fly, if you plan to employ a psychic shield."

"Works well for a honeymoon in Paris too," she added as she noted one more duty before she boarded the jet.

Zinian, Zhiwei and Chou stood together outside of the hanger. Each wore a heavy jacket against the morning chill. Their combined breath formed a hovering cloud of mist in front of them. They said goodbye to Villi first. Su Lin walked over and kissed each of them before she boarded.

"Where did you get these?" she asked as she indicated the jackets. They did not resemble any ordinary jacket one could order. "Don't tell me, you've been busy with the fusor," she indicated to Chou. "Those jackets probably do everything but fly. Am I right?"

Chou sheepishly nodded, "Close."

"He's been busy," Zinian spoke up, "inventing things on the side."

"We'll have to keep an eye on him," Zhiwei added. "He's like a kid in a candy store, filling up his basement with all kinds of devices."

Su Lin laughed at the trio. They had become good friends. She wondered if Zinian, Zhiwei, and Chou would get carried away creating new technologies. Villi waved toward the jet and then pointed to his watch. Su Lin took the hint. Michael caught up with Cecilia who added her goodbyes to their friends. Michael followed suit before he boarded, when he checked with Zhiwei, Zinian and Chou one last time in regards to Rollo's security.

"I knew this trip would be stressful on you," Chou linked before Michael could express his concerned. He stepped up to Michael and pressed a small, flat, black card into his hand.

"What is it?" Michael asked.

"I gave one of these to Master Li," Chou explained. "Press three fingers on the surface," he showed him. "The rest is self explanatory. You can contact me anywhere on the globe with that. I'll keep one on me at all times should you need me. Zhiwei and Zinian have one too. I'll make one for the rest of our group when you return," he added.

"You *have* been busy," Michael noted as he fondled the device.

He slipped the card in to pocket as he stepped onto the jet.

"Will we have enough people to make the bubble?" Cecilia asked Li while Su Lin showed Michael to his seat.

Han addressed Cecilia directly via his mind.

"During all those medical downloads with GC, did you notice the ease and speed of your absorption rate each time you added a new packet of knowledge?" he asked her.

"Now that you mention it, I did notice the sessions were shorter each time. I thought they gave me less to absorb," Cecilia answered.

"A librarian from Artane informed me that my power level increased with usage," he shot back.

"You spoke with a librarian?" Su Lin asked.

"You aren't the only one interested in increasing their knowledge," Han replied. "Anyway, this librarian noticed power fluctuations in all of Earth psychics. He said our power had increased significantly since they started to monitor our species. As we use our ability more frequently, we gain knowledge and experience. Like exercising a muscle, we're developing our psychic ability," he pointed out.

"I wondered about that," Cecilia relayed.

"Do you move things around your house?" he put to her. "Do you link with Michael continually throughout the day, or Su Lin? Naturally, your skill has also improved with the same measure. Master Li's ability has not incrementally increased, his power has exploded exponentially. Soon, he could probably form the psychic bubble on his own without our help," Han said as he glanced over at Li.

Cecilia leaned back in her seat, buckled her seatbelt, and linked with Michael. He had his eyes closed while he privately recalled last night.

"Oooo," she cooed, "Paris is going to be fun!"

Chapter Twenty-Five

A Troubled Flight

Sound can travel great distances on Kansas' flat plains, especially during takeoff. To prevent arousing any curiosity as to its origins, Villi requested the bubble prior to take off.

"Master Li," he openly called, "we need the psychic bubble."

"Very well Villi," Li replied. "Send us the signal."

"Now," Villi linked.

The psychics aboard the jet combined thoughts and created the unified form of energy that saved them from the Chinese military three months ago. With the shield in place, Villi revved up the engines and prepared the aircraft for flight. The jet roared down the runway, rose into the air at a steep angle, and headed due east. He figured at their present speed, it would take about two hours to reach the private airstrip in New Jersey. He noticed immediately that the strong presence of this bubble around them offered the jet less wind resistance. Use of the bubble improved their fuel efficiency and increased their top speed.

"Less stress on the wings, too," Villi considered.

"What's our airspeed?" Li inquired.

"About 700 knots!" Villi informed them.

"That's very fast for a jet of this type," Li pointed out.

"I reinforced the wing structure to withstand the stress," Villi linked as he patted the console.

"Are we leaving a bow shock?" Li asked.

"I can't detect one Master Li," Villi indicated as he made a mind sweep.

Li turned his attention to Running Elk. This was her first flying experience.

"How are you feeling?" he asked her out of courtesy.

"I'll survive," she whispered back, although she fixed her eyes on the retreating ground.

Master Li kept his conversation with Running Elk private while the aircraft rose higher until they cruised along above the clouds into the jet stream. As long as they maintained the psychic bubble around the aircraft, they were invisible to both tracking systems and by sight. However, the wedding night of celebration exhausted Su Lin, Michael, and Cecilia. They decided to enter a meditative state, which allowed them time to rest while they contributed to the formation of the bubble – a technique taught to them by Master Li as a way to conserve psychic energy. Villi wished he could join them but had to stay focused flying the plane instead. Han read from a 5th century Chinese text by Faxian that Master Li gave to him yesterday. He learned not to question Li's extraordinary gifts. Time passed quickly for the preoccupied group.

"Master Li," Villi eventually cut in. "I'm starting my approach to the airfield in New Jersey. Can you clear the landing strip?" he requested.

"Give me a few minutes," Li replied. "You brought us too close to the Naval Station near Lakewood. The traffic is heavy."

"The private strip is the only one in this area with a runway long enough to handle our landing," Villi explained.

Master Li cleared most of the air traffic in the area before the jet set down at the private airport. Villi found he still had nearly a half tank of fuel on each side. Still, he wanted full tanks before he crossed the Atlantic. As soon as he paid for the fuel using a bank transfer, Villi took off and headed due east for France.

"That wasn't too difficult," Cecilia observed as they lifted off over the ocean shoreline and headed out to sea.

After making certain Running Elk was relaxed, Li addressed the group.

"I want you to save your psychic energy," he informed them. "We can release the bubble once we pass beyond the two hundred mile limit."

"What about visibility?" Michael asked.

"According to air regulations, we're no longer considered a threat by the American military. Besides, we'll be in international air space. European air traffic controllers can track us and even follow our progress. However, we will disappear before we come close to French airspace," Villi informed them.

"Tell us when we reached the limit," Han asked.

"Just now," Villi informed them.

"Release the bubble." Master Li ordered.

With the bubble off, Villi noticed a difference in flying the jet at once. The atmosphere pressed down on the outside of the fuselage. He had to fight the controls to keep them on a straight course. He decided to cut back on speed, which eventually smoothed out the flight.

"That's strange," Su Lin commented as the aircraft cleared the cloud deck. She detected an energy spike off the right side of the aircraft. She felt the energy as a distant contact, far away from them to the south. "What is that?" she asked as she turned in her seat to look out the window. "I've never sensed so much energy."

"You've only had your psychic ability three months Su Lin," Cecilia broke in. "Perhaps because you lack experience…" she started to remark. She paused when she felt the same spike of energy. "I apologize, Su Lin. I sense a growing threat."

"It's a large storm system," Michael said as his mind reached out. "Big thunderstorms in New York used to mess with my mind," he told them.

"Kansas has had a few large storm systems pass through this summer," Han added. "The lightening always bothered me. But this… this is atypical, Michael," he pointed out. "Could it possibly be a hurricane?" he linked to the pilot.

"I'll check the geostationary weather satellites," Villi linked. "Excuse me," he piped back to them. "I don't mean to alarm you. NOAA just broadcast a warning to all flights in this area. The storm is a Category 2 hurricane located northwest of the Bahamas," he observed on the screen. "Su Lin, isn't that unusual for a hurricane so developed to move that far north?" he wondered.

"Not really," she spouted. "Historically speaking, the most recent hurricanes have occurred in the Caribbean, Florida or the Gulf of Mexico. A major hurricane of significance hasn't struck the east coast since Isabel," she told them. "The last major hurricane to strike New York was the Long Island Express in 1938 – a deadly storm that rose up without warning and took over 600 lives."

"How much time before we enter French airspace?" Master Li asked Villi.

"Around six hours," Villi linked back.

"Then I suggest we nap for the remainder of the trip," Li requested. "Villi will keep us posted on the weather." He turned to his nervous passenger. "I contacted Camille Ossures last night," he whispered to Running Elk. "She has a private landing strip outside Paris for corporate jets. Ossures Pharmaceuticals owns a large cargo hanger where we can park the jet."

"I believe I'm starting to feel excited about Paris," she half-smiled.

Li slipped his hand over hers for a moment. They briefly intertwined their fingers. Running Elk stared out the window. Li detected lingering doubts in her mind whether or not she could succeed at cooking school. He did not try to influence her thoughts.

With the group resting and the cabin quiet, the six hours seemed to slip past quickly. When the jet crossed into French airspace, Villi woke the group and requested they raise the bubble around them.

"We're about one hour from Paris," he alerted them.

"Paris," Cecilia and Su Lin sighed.

"Paris," Villi and Michael grinned.

When they neared the airport, Li arranged to clear out the runway so they could land during a brief gap in traffic. When Villi touched down, Camille immediately directed his path into a large private hanger. Safely inside, Master Li closed the hanger doors behind the jet. Camille watched as the large aircraft pull into her hanger. She could not yet form the psychic bubble with the same level of success as those on the jet.

"We're clear," Villi called out so the group could release the bubble around the craft.

Su Lin went to the cockpit to exit the plane with Villi.

"Vous parlez Francais?" she winked at him.

"J'ai faim!" Villi replied as he rubbed his tummy.

"You're always hungry. Come on!" Su Lin yanked on his arm.

Camille parked a large specially made stretch limousine across from the jet.

"I've never seen such a beautiful limousine, much less ridden in one of that stature," Cecilia excitedly linked.

"I haven't either," Su Lin noted as she looked out the pilot's windows.

"I believe all that is about to change," Li linked to them.

Villi opened the jet's door. Camille used her mind to push over a special platform that made it easier to disembark. Running Elk helped Master Li down the steps, though he really did not need any assistance. Han, Michael, Cecilia, Su Lin and lastly Villi followed Li out of the jet.

A chauffeur opened the limo door for Camille. The others in the Rollo group had not made contact with the new European psychics. They could not reach around the globe the same way Li could.

A fine pair of fashionable high heels slid out of the shadow attached to a long pair of slender legs. A woman of incredible, stunning beauty extended a hand for the chauffeur to take as he assisted her from the back seat. She stood tall and regal next to the black stretched limousine. She kept her chin parallel to the floor as a person of royal birth might. She wrapped her long auburn hair into a perfectly coiffed style and wore haute couture complimented by accessory jewels. She pulled her sunglasses away to reveal a brilliant blue-gray gaze that flashed in their direction. Her psychic energy pierced each mind so swiftly that it belied description.

The group unanimously regarded her as if she were a Parisian model and not the head of a pharmaceutical conglomerate. Michael sensed she had significantly more psychic power than other members of their group, while he made no comparisons with his own power. He wondered why she had not formed a psychic bubble.

"Probably from lack of experience and practice," he reasoned.

"Camille Ossures!" Li exclaimed and smiled as he nodded.

"Li," she replied. A smile crossed her lips that did not create one line on her face. Cecilia wondered how she did that. "What an honor and a pleasure that we finally meet," Camille added.

She spoke her last words aloud as she moved forward. She extended her hand to Li. The elderly man lightly touched the palm with two fingers, bent forward, and let his lips come close but not touch her skin. When he rose, Camille bowed her head ever so gracefully to him.

"Where are Salla and Filla?" he asked as he searched the car with his mind.

"Salla is developing a new anti-viral serum," Camille explained. "Filla is nearly finished with her dissertation. After that, she must prepare for final exams," she told them. "I'm afraid you won't see much of them during your visit."

"Why don't they simply…" Cecilia questioned.

"Go to Galactic Central?" Camille responded. "They want to continue their work traditionally. Is this everyone from Rollo?" she questioned. "I understood there were nine in your group?" she wondered as she glanced over Li's shoulder.

"We had to leave a few behind for the sake of security," Master Li briefly explained. "I would like to introduce you to the man that started all of this…" Li said as he turned and made a sweeping hand gesture. Before Li could link the next thought, Camille stepped forward.

"Michael Tyler," she linked directly to him.

Her personal link carried with it such resounding respect that Michael stood perfectly still – stunned by her strong mix of emotion and sincerity.

"I am certain you have heard this from the others," she said to him. "After everything that Master Li has shared with me about you, I am truly honored to meet you at last."

Unlike the level of respect that the group showed to Master Li, Camille bowed and curtsied to Michael as if he were royalty. At first, her manner threw the young American. However, in a brief moment of rare honesty for Camille, she opened her mind to a man she regarded as kindred spirit.

Michael immediately empathized with her plight and reciprocated. Within only a few ticks of a watch, the two psychics – nearly matched in ability and level of power – shared a common bond that transcended language, culture, and familiarity.

"The honor and privilege are mine," Michael countered after the brief yet revealing exchange. "Master Li often mentions you with great respect," he added.

Camille's face broke into an uncharacteristic grin, lines included. She casually placed her arm around Michael's back and turned to the rest of the group.

"I am so happy you have come to visit me," she said. Her demeanor seemed quite natural with no artifice. "Welcome everyone," she declared. "Welcome to Paree!"

As they stepped forward, Master Li introduced Camille to Han.

"Ah! Rollo's master strategist!" she responded.

"This is Cecilia..." Li introduced.

"I hear you have become quite the doctor. No?" Camille said as she warmly extended her hand.

"This is Su Lin," Li went on.

"Someday you must come and teach at my university," Camille offered.

"I would feel honored," Su Lin replied as she accepted Camille's hand.

"...and this Villi," Li continued, "our head of transportation and an excellent pilot."

"I am insanely jealous of Su Lin," Camille linked. "Congratulations on your nuptials."

Villi actually blushed before he felt Su Lin's elbow firmly nudge him.

"Finally, this is... Running Elk," Li finished.

Camille paused before Running Elk. The woman's mind puzzled her. Camille sensed a rudimentary level of psychic ability compared with the others.

"Can she hear me?" she asked Li.

"Yes I can... some," Running Elk stated aloud.

Camille wore one of her polite faces that she would use with a client.

"Li speaks kindly of you Running Elk," she said to her. Camille took her hand and shook it. "I believe you and I will become good friends. Welcome to Paris," she warmly added. "I do hope you will enjoy your stay here while you attend the cooking school. I've tried to make your rooms as comfortable as possible."

"Rooms?" the older woman questioned. She glanced over at Master Li.

"Oh, my dear, you have a lovely apartment," Camille declared. "When you are my guest in Paris, you must live in style... No?"

"Yes!" Cecilia declared. She gradually inched closer to the open limousine door. She could not wait to see the inside. She tugged on Michael's arm as she wanted in first.

"Go ahead," Camille signaled.

The chauffeur gestured toward the open the door. The sophisticated level of luxury inside the vehicle impressed the entire group with soft leather seats and a multitude of electronic extras.

"Is fuel very expensive in Europe?" Han asked.

"Yes," Camille answered. "That is why we converted this vehicle to magneto drive," she told him.

"Is that where the car passes over chargers built into the road?" Han asked.

"That's right," she said. "As we drive along certain roads in Paris, the car completes the circuit and gains in charge. Otherwise, this vehicle is completely electric. I contribute 200,000 carbon credits weekly to maintain the fleet of vehicles for the corporation," she told him. "I donate another 800,000 to charity. France uses these credits to help the poor and indigent."

"Oh Michael," Cecilia broke in as she ran her hands over the interior. "Could we have one?" she asked with her eyes pleading. "It's like owning a piece of history," she cooed.

"They do have that reputation," Li said as he followed Running Elk inside. "The American's have yet to build the necessary chargers in their roads."

"Chou will take care of that," Cecilia shot back. The level of luxury enamored the ingénue. Cecilia took the command seat surrounded by a myriad of electronic devices. Once everyone moved inside, Camille instructed the driver.

"Proceed on our planned route Charles," she spoke to the driver through a monitoring device.

"Are we staying at your townhouse?" Li asked as Camille mostly kept her thoughts blocked.

"Oh, no, my friends," she said. Her face showed almost no expression. "I have a permanent suite at the Paris-Ritz for special out-of-town guests."

Cecilia's eyes widened considerably.

"We're staying at the Ritz?" Cecilia excitedly spoke.

"Cecilia," Camille said when the driver pulled away, "once you've been to Paris, all other places will seem dull in comparison," she stated with a calm relaxed manner and expression.

"Camille," Villi linked in. "I could go back to Rollo right now and be impressed with *this* much of Paris."

Camille actually blushed when she realized Villi's meaning. She addressed Su Lin, "How do you control this Russian bear, my dear?"

Su Lin squeezed Villi's hand in a loving way.

"You have a family fortune," Su Lin replied. "I was lucky to find Villi."

"My friend," Camille linked back, "to be lucky in love beats all other forms of luck."

Chapter Twenty-six

Paree

The late afternoon sun slanted through the parting clouds as the limousine drove into the heart of the city. Although the trip only took eight hours, the Rollo team lost time as they traveled east. With the remaining hour of daylight, Camille decided to take the long way to the Ritz. She instructed her driver, Charles to take the Champs Élysées and pass by the Arc de Triomphe de l'Étoile'. This route also took them around the Eiffel Tower. Thankfully, Camille pulled back the covering on the expanded sunroof which allowed the tourists a chance to look up at the great ironwork landmark. Cecilia craned her neck the entire way. Su Lin leaned her head on Villi's shoulder.

"Can you believe this? I'm on my honeymoon in Paris!" she sighed.

Villi glanced over at Michael. The two friends exchanged smiles and shook their heads. With their wives so enamored, the men looked forward to the evening rather than the scenery.

The limousine made its way to the heart of Paris, the location of the Paris Ritz Hotel.

"Many famous people have stayed at the Ritz," Li whispered to Running Elk.

"Now they can add the name of Master Li to the list," she smiled in return.

When the limo pulled up to the front door, the hotel staff rolled out the red carpet treatment at Camille's behest. An army of handlers escorted the guests and their luggage to their rooms. Curious heads turned to see who would step from the flashy limousine. Naturally, Camille stepped out first. Some people took her photograph. Strangely, those same people abruptly turned away right after that.

"Nice move Li," Camille linked as she sensed his handiwork. "You certainly killed my entrance," she quipped.

"Sorry, we don't need unnecessary publicity," he linked to her mind.

Master Li cleared the lobby as well. By the time the entourage stepped into the elevator, they were practically alone except for the hotel's staff. The bellhop, who brought the luggage on a caddy, stared blankly ahead as if he stood in a fog. Their elevators arrived at the same time. In the hall, the chauffeur fell in behind them with a briefcase he brought from the car. As they prepared to enter the room, he handed it over to Camille and promptly left.

Camille opened the doors on a magnificent room replete with ornate relief wall decorations, moldings trimmed in gold, rich Persian rugs on the floor, and faux Louis XIV furniture. Brightly colored bouquets of fresh flowers adorned special tables near the walls and a large basket of fresh fruit sat on a coffee table in front of a splendid chaise lounge. Sheer drapes covered tall glass double doors that led to a wide terrace outside.

"Oh, Camille!" Cecilia declared when she entered the magnificent suite. "This is too much!"

"This is a hotel suite?" Running Elk declared. "This looks like a palace!"

Cecilia and Su Lin grabbed an arm on either side of Running Elk nearly pulled her in two directions at once. The trio brushed through the suite to inspect their new accommodations. Michael and Villi stayed close to Master Li and Han. However, the opulent ambience managed to impress everyone. Once the baggage handler spread the luggage to their appropriate destinations, he made a quick exit. Camille watched as Master Li hastened his exodus.

"Saves on tips," she shrugged.

"I'm certain you'll see he is well compensated," Li droned.

With their privacy ensured, she opened the briefcase that the chauffeur brought.

"Gather around," she beckoned. She pulled out seven official-looking documents and spread them out. "These are your French passports," she declared. "Once I knew the dates of your visit, I contacted my voice in Galactic Central and had these rushed over. I realized that security would be a problem. Thank goodness Zhiwei sent me your photographs."

"Can't we just bubble our way around?" Han asked.

"The European Union requires identity cards when its citizens travel, even walking about in Paris. You must take these along if you venture out these rooms. Security is very tight since the terrorist attacks two years ago. The police will not allow you into museums without identification. Naturally, as my guests, I expect the authorities to give you the VIP treatment," she smiled.

Each person reached in and took their new identity card and passport, including one for Master Li. He glanced down and noticed his name was now Mr. Fong with the picture slightly askew from his actual face.

"What's this?" he linked.

"That is how you must present your form to them," she instructed. "So you'll have to maintain a bubble around your head at least part of the time. Once away from authorities, you could remove it. It was Zhiwei's idea, so that the government will not have an exact replica of your face on record."

The group examined the passports and took turns using psychic bubbles around their heads to alter their image to match the photograph. Camille watched with interest as they performed this complex form of psychic manipulation. She had yet to make a psychic bubble that could last longer than a few seconds. Rather than disrupt the current proceedings, she continued with her itinerary.

"Since it is too late for lunch, I would like to treat you to an early dinner at my restaurant," she offered. "I have arranged a special tour of our kitchen for Running Elk. I understand you are a gourmand Su Lin. I hope you enjoy the cuisine. In France we say, *bon appétite*!"

"J'attends avec intérêt votre cuisine (I look forward to your cuisine)," Su Lin replied.

"Good accent," Camille noted. "Then it's on to the restaurant," she told them. "After that, I leave the rest of your time here up to you."

"I can't go out looking like this," Cecilia said. She tried not to sound too peevish.

Camille returned one of her knowing nods as if she knew something.

"Oh, I nearly forgot," she hesitated. "I thought with all the running around, you searched through your wardrobes," she said as she indicated their rooms. "I purchased a few odds and ends for you, knowing that you had little time to shop for clothes since you landed in that dusty little Kansas town."

Su Lin and Cecilia regarded each other for only a second. They bolted into their perspective bedrooms Shortly after, the group heard shrieks from those rooms. Michael and Villi started to rise when Camille reached out her with her hand and shook her head.

"Give them a few minutes," she said.

They heard Cecilia's shower start and then Su Lin's.

"It may be more than a few minutes," Camille added. She glanced Running Elk's way. "I left clothes for you too. I hope I have the size right."

Running Elk performed a silent, "Me?" as she indicated herself. She rose and went into her bedroom.

Master Li glanced back at the room with two double beds where he and Han were staying.

"Any new clothes in my bedroom?" he asked with a contorted face.

Camille used the same light laughter that she did in the hanger when they first met.

"I did not expect a man of your caliber to have such a sense of humor," she chuckled. "I did put warm robes for both you and Han inside," she indicated, "and a few day outfits, plus some evening ware."

"Villi and me, too?" Michael perked up.

"Yes, you too!" she said as she gestured with a wave.

The four men rose and went back to their rooms. They discovered that Camille filled their rooms with many treats. Each dresser contained sweaters for the evening, underclothing, socks, matching ties, also shirts, trousers and jackets in the armoires. The men changed as the women emerged from their showers and dove into the cosmetics and jewelry that Camille laid out in front of their vanities.

The room's doorbell rang. Camille answered it. Two women dressed in white wearing aprons and a belt that held a variety of items such as combs, scissors, and spray bottles seemed impatient to begin.

"Through there," she pointed.

The two young female assistants split up. One went into Cecilia's room while the other headed into Su Lin's. Within ten minutes, both women came back out. Their speed belied their age. They nodded and gave Camille a knowing smile. Camille then nodded toward Running Elk's room. They both went in this time and came back out ten minutes later. Camille offered them an envelope with cash. They took it and left.

An hour after she made the first suggestion, the group re-emerged back to the main room, completely made over. Camille beamed at them like a proud parent.

"Very nice," she said to each as she gesticulated for them to turn around. "I am quite pleased."

"You picked out these clothes?" Cecilia asked.

"I tried my best. Master Li gave very detailed links regarding all of you," she informed them.

"This is a perfect fit," Su Lin excitedly said. "I've never had clothes fit me so well!" She swept around and ran her hands down her sides with Villi admiring her.

"I…I've never worn such fine clothes," Running Elk stammered from her doorway.

In the excitement, everyone forgot her. She emerged from her bedroom a completely transformed woman. She no longer had her homespun appearance with the gray ponytail and blue jeans. Instead, they saw a woman of European mold, face made up, hair perfectly coiffed, both stylish and sophisticated. She stood before them and blinked her eyes.

"Do you like it?" she asked Master Li. In her humility, she cast down her eyes.

Master Li's face lit up. Running Elk glanced up in time to see his reaction. When their eyes met, he blushed. The other psychics could not guess what passed between them. Li made certain no psychic in the room could sense their thoughts.

"You are beautiful Running Elk," Camille commented. "Now we are ready," she declared.

The improved ensemble returned to the limousine just as it pulled up to the front entrance. No matter what Li did, the unusual car naturally attracted attention. Most people thought it was a celebrity. Once more Camille instructed the driver to take the scenic route to the restaurant. She offered suggestions along the way of the sites they should visit the following the day.

Camille then treated them to dinner at her Solé restaurant located in downtown Paris. Instead of arriving via the front door, they entered the building through the back. She brought Running Elk and the others through the immaculate kitchen and introduced the Native American to her chefs. They were all graduates from Le Cordon Bleu.

"Here is the next parfait chef," she exclaimed, to which her kitchen responded by giving Running Elk a round of applause.

Running Elk whispered into Master Li's ear, "Thank goodness they never tasted my meatloaf!" to which he tactfully remained silent.

Camille seated the entire party in a secluded private dining room. Running Elk asked Han to explain proper table manners to her. She knew to unfold her cloth napkin and place it in her lap. He indicated she should start with the outside tableware first and that the little yellow ball was lemon ice meant to clear the palate between dishes and not dessert.

Michael and Villi could hardly take their eyes off their transformed wives. Michael had never seen Cecilia look as ravishing. She definitely rivaled Camille in that department. Even Han noticed how much the change in hair styles, clothes and make-up transformed the ordinary women of Rollo into glamorous beauties.

Hardly anyone but Li noticed Running Elk's level of anxiety rise when the waiter brought the first course. She stared down at the crackling cheese atop the French onion soup served in small individual ramekins. The cheese crust perfectly browned with its wafting aroma reminded the Native American how woefully inadequate her standards were as a cook. Tears welled up in her eyes. Every person at the table felt her swell of emotion and turned to face her.

"I've been so..." she started to say "stupid" and stopped. Her emotional state nearly drove the normally stone-faced woman to tears.

"Just a moment," Master Li interrupted her internal rant. "Before you belittle your ability to cook, know that this bowl contains more than just onion soup," he said to her. "It contains the knowledge of many years working as a professional cook. You can't possibly compare your level of experience to theirs. That is why you are here, to learn. You must trust the wise old man in this judgment," he spoke kindly to her.

She fought away her emotions and managed to recompose her face into a slight smile after Li's self-effacing remark. Camille immediately noticed the intimate interaction between them. She tactfully withdrew any intrusion into their thoughts as did the rest.

"How do you like Paris?" Camille asked as she quickly turned to the newlyweds to divert attention.

"Who would not like this version of Paris?" Cecilia said with an almost wistful sigh. "The limo, the room, the clothes..."

"You've certainly laid out the red carpet," Michael commented. "I can't begin to show my appreciation," he told her.

Camille gracefully smiled. She still tried to avoid any attention toward Li and Elk.

"Su Lin?" Camille turned to her.

"Villi and I are overwhelmed at your generosity Camille," she told the young French heiress. "You've made our stay perfect."

"You may stay as long as you like," Camille told them, "go see the Palace at Versailles... or tour Notre Dame... walk along the Left Bank and take in the art... or stop by a café and drink café au lait while you munch on a croissant. It is what all the tourists do. Perhaps the women would like to spend some of that large Tyler Trust on a dress or two?"

Cecilia's eyes brightened at the thought of owning an original French gown – one made specifically for her that no other woman in the world had. Su Lin also glanced over at Michael. She wondered if what she heard was true. Michael chuckled and shook his head. He resigned his fate to the fact they would behave as tourists for a few days. He looked over at Villi who shrugged and went along.

"I can arrange a private fitting," Camille suggested.

Cecilia and Su Lin were practically giddy.

"You know... Running Elk," Camille finally addressed the forlorn Native American, "Li could arrange a course in the French language. Couldn't you Li?"

"I can make that arrangement," he said as he changed his focus. "You would be able to understand your instructors and communicate better," he suggested.

"I will," Running Elk nodded. She poked at her food with her spoon. She broke through the crust of cheese and cubed French bread. The onion soup oozed up through the baked topping. She took a small bite with a surprised reaction.

"This is delicious," she declared and took another, larger bite. "I could get used to this," she said. Her comment helped the rest of the group relax.

"I could too," Li quipped.

The others waited for Running Elk's reaction. She glanced at Li and softly laughed. The others joined the laughter.

When the waiter served the main course of boeuf bourguignon, everyone marveled at the presentation. They closely watched for Running Elk's reaction. By this time, she had relaxed and began to enjoy the meal. Camille ordered some of the finest wine from her cellar to be poured out around the table. Yet when she offered a toast to her guests, she noticed that everyone smiled and set their glasses back on the table. No one drank any wine.

"Is something wrong with the wine?" she wondered.

Several at the table dabbed their mouths. They turned to Li for an explanation.

"We feel that alcohol will interfere with our perception," he half explained.

However, Camille looked up the table toward Michael. She felt that this had something to do with him. Michael stared at his glass. For a fleeting second, he thought of taking a drink. Cecilia worried that it would be the first time he drank wine since he "went on the wagon" over a year ago. The whole table could palpate his tension. Instead, he reached for his glass of ice water, closed his eyes, and took a long drink. As the cool liquid slid down his throat, he recalled the taste of wine. He remembered drinking bottle after bottle on that railroad track in Mississippi. He used to pray that the next wine bottle would make him forget about his parents. Everyone at the table watched as he downed the entire glass of water. They felt how he longed for the wine he missed. When Camille picked up on his thoughts, she tactfully withdrew any thought of mentioning the wine again. The conversation around the table died off.

Master Li tactfully linked to everyone except Michael to resume their meal. He purposely moved Michael's knife off his plate. The noise brought the young man back. Distracted from the meal, he pulled a pen from his jacket pocket and doodled on a piece of paper he brought from the hotel. He took a download in drawing months ago and quickly sketched out an idea he had mulled over recently.

"Is that the Vatican?" Su Lin asked as she peer over at his drawing.

Michael simply grunted and put his pen and paper away. When Camille offered dessert, the entire group declined. Most were tired and ready to retire for the night. With the meal finished, the evening came to a close. Camille alerted the chauffeur who appeared moments later at the room's entrance ready to escort the party back to the car.

Camille stayed at the table and watched them go. Despite Master Li's private assurances to the contrary, she felt she had intruded into Michael's painful past. She stared at the empty glass of water that Michael downed when he thought about drinking wine. As a Frenchwoman, she experienced a very awkward moment. Wine is practically the national drink. She glanced down at her glass of wine and knocked it over with her hand.

"The stuff is overrated," she said as she rose and headed for the kitchen.

Chapter Twenty-Seven

Event Horizon

THE TOP OF THE HOUR screen opened with bold graphic letters, "HURRICANE CRISIS." Various shots of extreme weather in quick succession appeared behind the three-dimensional letters.

"This is breaking news from News 55, New York's finest twenty-four hour news cast," the announcer stated. The camera swung down to reveal a man seated behind a sculpted desk. "Here is Josh Brogan," the voice-over spoke.

"Good evening, New York," the straight-faced newscaster spoke directly to the camera. "Here is the latest on Hurricane Estelle. The President and New York's Governor are in a special meeting at this hour to decide on which course of action the government will take. To bring you up-to-date, we have reporters standing by at the State House in Albany, outside the White House in Washington, and out on Long Island, where hurricane forecasters predict Estelle will strike with full force."

As he spoke, the screen next to him split into smaller and smaller boxes. Each box showed a reporter waiting to speak his or her turn. "First, we'll start with our own weatherperson, Miriam Jenkins at Hurricane Central in Atlanta. Miriam has the latest update on Hurricane Estelle. Miriam?"

The picture switched to a young woman standing in a control center surrounded by men and women as they sat at their stations. On the wall behind her a large screen spewed out the latest hurricane information with a screen split between satellite, radar, infrared, and other current displays.

"Thank you, Josh," Miriam said as she took over. "Well this is the hurricane that many scientists have predicted and dreaded would happen.

The storm has picked up heat from the warm Gulf Stream and has begun to build in size as a result. Estelle's eye is currently parked about 200 miles off the coast of Maryland and headed nearly due north. The gulf current is moving further north and is believed responsible for New York's mild winters in recent years."

While the weather woman stood next to a wall, graphic animations demonstrated her point.

"Because of this phenomenon," Miriam continued, "we believe Estelle should follow this current and grow in strength before it impacts New York City in about three days, by which time it could be a Category 4 or even a 5. At that strength, it would bring a storm surge that tops off at nearly eighteen feet…"

The screen animation showed the southern end of Long Island from Fort Tilden to Fire Island under water from the surge, coastal homes destroyed, freeways jammed, and many parts of New York cut off from the rest of the world. The camera then switched back to Josh Brogan in the studio.

"You can see why the President is in a special meeting with New York's governor…"

"Master Li? Master Li?" a soft voice spoke. A hand gently prodded the elderly psychic.

"Uh, what?" he sputtered when he opened his eyes.

"Did you fall asleep out here?" Han asked as he stood next to Li's chair. He noticed that Master Li had put his feet up on one of the terrace chairs.

The morning air seemed refreshing and not too cool, although both Li and Han wore the thick, plush, monogrammed robes that Camille provided.

"I couldn't sleep, so I came out early right after room service opened at five," Li explained. He hesitated to add more to what recently transpired.

"What time is it?" Li asked.

"Six o'clock," Han told him.

"Would you like a cup of tea?" Li offered as he gestured toward the cozy.

"Not just yet," Han commented as he stretched and stifled a yawn. "I noticed you were not in your bed. When I walked through the suite, I saw you on the terrace," he said as his eyes traveled over the table and lighted on a black playing card-sized device. "What's that?" he asked.

"Chou's communicator," Li replied.

"That's a communicator?" Han wondered.

He picked up the paper thin yet rigid object and held it in his hands.

"Place three fingers on the front," Li instructed.

Han lightly place three fingers from his right hand while he held the flat card in his left.

"Recognize Han Su Yeng. Awaiting command," a voice spoke.

The screen instantly expanded in his hands to a larger size. Han saw a picture of Rollo in three dimensions. Han turned the flat device in his hands. The perspective changed.

"Nice!" Han smiled. "Do I get one?"

"Chou pressed this into my hand before we left," Li explained. "I can only assume we shall all have one soon."

"How do I…" Han asked.

"Put your fingers back on the front, say or think 'end,'" Li told him.

Han did so. The card turned black and shrunk in size. He placed it back on the table.

"You spoke to Chou this morning?" Han asked. "That would make it about…"

"Ten o'clock at night there…" Li stated.

"So you did speak to him…" Han inferred.

"Uh, huh," Li muttered. He added nothing else.

Han could sense Li's unease at some problem he'd been considering. Rather than press the matter, he changed the subject.

"I like the robes Camille bought for us," he linked as he rubbed his hand up and down one sleeve of the soft material. He glanced over at Master Li. The elderly man appeared distracted. "Something *is* troubling you. I didn't hear you stir."

"I tried not to disturb you," Li responded as he rubbed his eyes. "The two couples stayed up long after we retired. They made every attempt to remain discreet while they erected a sphere around them. I noticed it did not affect either you or Running Elk. I had difficulty sleeping with their bedrooms only six meters across the main room. In Rollo, they live much further away. However in this close proximity…" his thoughts trailed off. He glanced over at Han's accusing face. "Look, I tried every kind of distraction I could to keep my thoughts isolated," he confessed.

Han raised a questionable eyebrow as he stared at Li and realized he must have been inadvertently privy to every detail last night.

"It never occurred to me that with the range of your power and them being so close…" Han linked. He stopped his train of thought and reached to prepare a cup of tea instead.

"I did not watch them make love, if that is what you are thinking," Li threw out. "I went to Galactic Central and eventually had tea with King Usl," he told his friend.

Han saw that Li spoke the truth and that he had not witnessed their nuptial bliss.

"How is the king?" Han queried as he had met with Usl on three previous occasions.

"Fine," Li said with an abrupt manner. "He sympathized with my plight and kept me distracted with a discussion on teaching young psychics control. I actually picked up a few ideas," Li told him. "I think you should look in on him before too long."

Han took this as a warning, for being king shortened the lifespan. Li rubbed his eyes and took in a deep breath. Han could see that his friend badly needed rest. He decided to change tact.

"How is everyone in Rollo?" he asked and took a sip.

"Busy in Chou's basement," Li quickly shot back, "as you suspected."

Han smiled at this suggestion as he had not openly discussed it with Li.

"Do you think we should stay a whole week?" he asked.

"Camille would like the two couples to explore Paris. I'm inclined to agree," Li replied. "I see no pressing need to return at this time. How is your French?" Li asked Han.

"Je le parle bon," (I speak it well) Han told him.

"Vous parlez Français bien pour entré Chinois," (You speak French well for being Chinese) Li commented.

"Merci," (thank you) Han stated.

"Je vous en prie!" (You are welcome!) Master Li replied.

Just then, Villi walked out onto the terrace from his room. He wore only his boxer shorts as he yawned and stretched his limbs. The movement at the table distracted his reverie on this morning's continuation of his honeymoon. He turned his head and saw the two men dressed in robes and drinking their tea as they looked his way. He glanced down at his state of undress and made a half-grin before he clumsily bowed and apologized. Yet, before he withdrew, he quickly read from Li's mind the older man's state of fatigue and knew that he must be at least partially to blame.

"Master Li," he quickly spoke, "I must apologize for… our activity. I promise that Su Lin and I will be more… discreet."

Master Li nodded back. "You are adults on your honeymoon and not children. No one expects you to be celibate in Paris. However, I would appreciate a modicum of decency," he said and indicated Villi's underwear.

Villi blushed, ducked back into his room, and pulled their bedroom double-doors shut. Ten minutes later, the two couples emerged wearing their robes. They joined Han and Master Li on the terrace for breakfast. Running Elk took a shower first before she arrived at the breakfast table. She told them she was not that hungry and only drank juice instead. She was fully dressed and ready to start her tour of Paris.

"I'd like to get an early start!" she declared as she rubbed her hands together. "Who's with me?"

Surprised by her entrance, the others gulped down tea and part of their breakfast before dashing off to dress. No one understood how Master Li changed so quickly. Yet Han did not spend much time either as he changed in the bathroom at the same time. Eventually, the two couples made their way into the main room. Han, Li and Running Elk stood by the door. They were growing impatient and were ready to leave.

True to her word, Camille provided a different limousine for a private tour of Paris. This time they had a commercial driver – a talkative fellow who insisted on describing everything around them.

"Zis ees thee Arc uf Treeumph," he declared in his best English, which as Su Lin described, *was not too good*!

The group smiled at her joke and tended to ignore the driver's rambling speech. The driver turned down the Champs Élysées, drove around the Arc de Triomphe de l'Étoile′ and the Tower Eiffel before they moved on to Notre Dame Cathedral. They eventually managed to avoid any further driving to squeeze in the Palais de Chaillot and Versailles on the same day.

Han and Su Lin seemed to enjoy the history more than Villi or Cecilia. Michael didn't express an opinion one way or another. He seemed content to hold Cecilia's hand and glance her way now and then. Without the medical clinic as competition or some list to fill, he relaxed around his new bride. Master Li gave Running Elk a private tour of Versailles as he seemed very familiar with the place. Although during their previous conversations, she recalled that Li claimed he never left Harbin.

"She stood over there the night the messenger delivered the message," he pointed out. "Her face turned white as she read the shocking news that…

"I thought you said you and your wife never left Harbin," Running Elk wondered. "You seem to know a great deal about this place – who lived where, what they ate, how they dressed and so on."

"Do I?" Li tried to mask his reaction. "I probably read it in a book somewhere…" Li said as he turned his head to cover his half smile.

Running Elk shook her head. She did not yet know about his ability to travel through time, though she guessed that he probably knew a great deal more than he revealed to her. Li held out his arm for her to take.

"I see the hour is late," he said. He started to reach for his pocket watch when Running Elk placed her other hand on his arm.

"None of your tricks," she told him. "I agree. The hour is late. Let's go."

Li and Running Elk missed an opportunity to have lunch with the others and grew eager to dine out in Paris. Li contacted Michael to rendezvous at the limousine. Once the group reassembled and piled into the commercial vehicle, Li called Camille's office to request arrangements for a late supper. She surprised him by breaking in on the line.

"How do you like Paris?" she asked him.

"Everything is splendid," he told her.

"Made any plans for this evening?" she wondered.

"We thought we would return to the hotel and clean up first before we went out," he put to her.

"Don't bother," she told him. "I'd rather you tell your driver to head straight for the Louvre. I have a little surprise for waiting for you."

Camille had to make her phone call short. Her private secretary arranged a special private tour of the Louvre instead. The guide turned out to be a member of the Louvre's staff acquainted with every work of art in the collection. She was also a friend of Camille's. She took them on an extended tour that included many anecdotes and finished at the museum's most famous work of art. She allowed the psychics to dwell before the Mona Lisa as long as they wished.

Afterward, Camille met the group for a late dinner at the Solé. When the waiters brought out the first course of seven, the group unanimously sighed with welcome relief.

"Bouillabaisse!" Camille declared as they uncovered the steaming bowls.

This came as a welcome surprise for the oriental psychic members, as seafood played an important role in their diet, whereas Midwesterners Running Elk and Cecilia cautiously tasted the strange and different meal. The young physician smiled broadly when she tasted her first sample of lobster and other seafood culinary delights from the platter accompaniment.

"You'll have to add scallops braised in brandy and butter to your lists," she directed to her husband. "This is quite yummy," she sighed.

"Su Lin will have to teach us how to make seafood dishes," Michael pointed out.

"Such variety," Running Elk commented. "As if the ingredients were on a palate…"

"…and the cook, an artist – mixing, blending, until the right balance of flavors and textures creates – voila! Magnifique!" Camille completed her thought.

"You do have a way with words," Running Elk told her. "But I couldn't agree more, Camille… magnificent perfectly describes this meal."

The kitchen had created a series of dishes in smaller portions for the group to taste. Camille did this as a favor to Running Elk. However, as the meal progressed toward its end, she could see that everyone gradually lacked sharp focus.

"It doesn't take a mind reader to know this has been a long day," she linked. "Perhaps we should skip dessert, no?"

"No!" the visiting group chorused back. They recalled missing last night's creation.

Running Elk enjoyed tonight's cuisine more than last night's. Each dish represented the kind of art to preparation and taste she secretly longed to express. She asked many questions about how the chefs prepared the food and the ingredients they used. Finally, Camille invited the cooks to the table where they interacted with the Native America. Camille took that moment to link with Michael.

"About yesterday…" she began.

"I should apologize," Michael spoke up.

"You? I am the one who is sorry," she told him. "I was so clumsy Michael."

Despite their open minds at the airport, Michael did not share the most sensitive part of his life. He rarely shared that with anyone except Cecilia and Master Li.

"How could you know? How could anyone know?" he retorted. "It's difficult to share my history. Master Li told me I must be honest about my past. In time I suppose, the pain will become bearable," he told her.

"To be honest, I didn't completely open my mind. If we are truly to be friends, then I must share with you some my very private memories," Camille confessed.

She took that moment to share with Michael the trips to Switzerland with her parents and the cruel way her father threw her at one particular therapist who boasted a solution for the teenager. She described how he put her through one different therapy after another to cure her malady and the infamous voice that would never abate. During this period she lost her friends and the chance of ever forming a relationship. Her tribulations culminated with the death of her father and the fight to gain control of his company, her inheritance.

"Does any of this ring true for you?" she asked.

"All too familiar," Michael retorted.

"Funny how fate can seem so cruel," she added. "In the end, the corporation is stronger now than under my father's tutelage."

"Perhaps you are right Camille," he said. "I feel very fortunate despite my earlier circumstances," he said as he glanced at Cecilia.

"Fortunate indeed," Camille echoed.

The dinner ended on an upbeat note. Running Elk went to the kitchen where the chefs helped her make a Béarnaise sauce without it separating on her first attempt.

"I did it!" she exclaimed when she showed the others her creamy preparation. "I made my first sauce!"

The chefs who stood around her chuckled and applauded. Master Li looked on from the back of the group and sighed with satisfaction that she would fit in. The entire kitchen staff cheered her on, which boosted her confidence. One chef leaned over to another and whispered.

"She learns quickly," he pointed out. "Perhaps she does have certain natural abilities," he considered.

By the time the limousine returned the sightseeing group to the Ritz, it was time for bed. Master Li said goodnight to Running Elk. He and Han immediately retired. The two couples parted to their rooms. Master Li did not bother to block anyone tonight. He was too exhausted to think about that. He started to meditate and then fell into a deep sleep.

Michael and Cecilia retired to their room. As Michael stood before the bathroom mirror and brushed his teeth, Cecilia sensed him brooding over some underlying problem. He hurriedly left the bathroom made for a corner of the room where he produced a sketchpad. He worked on a detailed perspective drawing that showed a large structure with a piazza in front and an elaborate fountain in the center of the piazza. Atop the enormous five-storied structure, Michael added some final touches to a dome with nine ribs that extended down from its top. Nine statues faced outward around the base of the dome. She smiled when she recognized her face in miniature.

"What is that? I don't recall seeing that on the tour today," Cecilia inquired as she looked down at the pad. "Is it a palace?"

"Not yet," Michael linked back. His words only proved to confuse Cecilia. He pulled the top of the pad over to cover his work.

The following morning the group decided to split up and go separate ways. Han had more museums and galleries on his agenda. Right after a light breakfast, he took a taxicab from the front of the hotel and headed out on his own. Master Li and Running Elk decided to shop for some necessities that she might require for her stay. Li wanted to buy her clothes and accessories or whatever struck her as something she wanted. After shopping and lunch, they intended to drop by her new apartment. Camille handed over the keys to the apartment during last night's dinner. Everyone grabbed from stacks of cash that Michael arranged through the hotel's bank, left out on one of the tables. No one bothered to count it. Money meant nothing to them.

"Cash is always acceptable wherever you wish to spend it," Li commented.

Since money was no object to wealthy Michael Tyler, the newlywed foursome explored the world of Parisian women's fashion much to Villi's adamant objection. He could think of a dozen other things he rather do than shop for women's clothes.

"Is this absolutely necessary?" he objected privately to Michael as they approached the limousine. "Can't we go to a football game or something else?"

Michael chuckled a Villi's naïveté. "It isn't that bad, Villi," he informed his Russian friend. "They have places for men to sit. The models are very beautiful..."

"Models?" Villi perked up.

"Yes, this isn't like going to an American department store," Michael told him. "They actually bring out the clothes for the women to see before they buy them..." Michael pointed out.

"Models?" Villi repeated.

"Beautiful models," Michael added, "who sometimes wear lingerie."

"He's going," Su Lin said as she grabbed his arm and shoved Villi into the back of the limousine.

Despite the enticements, the whole day dragged for the Russian. Shopping for women's clothes completely bored Villi whether they had pretty girls or not. Although, he enjoyed the lingerie display the best, he had to behave next to Su Lin. Michael tried to divert him several times with stories about Rollo that Villi may not have heard.

"... it turned out that Steven's father was actually her cousin, a fact that no one..." Michael halted in the middle of his story.

As the men waited for Su Lin and Cecilia to try on the twentieth outfit, Michael sensed Master Li was in some sort of trouble. An odd chill passed through him, as if the temperature suddenly dropped without explanation.

"Did you feel that?" Villi spoke up as he turned to Michael.

However his words arrived too late. He noticed Michael on his feet. His skin seemed pale. He felt a sense of urgency in his friend.

"I hate to cut this short..." Michael began in a link to Cecilia.

"We're stripping now. We felt it too," she linked back. She and Su Lin hurried out of the dressing room. Each woman carried three outfits on each arm.

All four psychics sensed that Master Li needed them immediately. After Michael paid out a hefty sum for the Paris originals, they headed out of the renowned clothiers with stacks of boxes and called for the waiting limo.

"Do you plan on shopping for any more clothes today?" Michael asked Cecilia as they walked up the street.

"I don't think so," she linked back.

"Good," he said. "Here!" he called to a homeless man on the street.

A downtrodden beggar stared down at his chest with no interest in passersby, when a stack of 500-Euro notes fell into his lap. Startled, the man looked up to find the same type of people walking by, the same people who ignored him as they usually did day in and day out. He picked up the stack and ran his thumb through them.

"I'm rich…" he began. "I'm rich!" he said as he struggled to his feet.

With rotten teeth bared in a fanatical grin, he discarded the trappings he had dragged around Paris for months and headed to the nearest restaurant.

"I'm not eating out a dumpster tonight!" he declared as he marched up the street.

"That was sweet," Cecilia linked to Michael as they arrived at the limo. Michael opened the trunk and started putting in the dress boxes when Han's thoughts broke through to them.

"What's going on?" he asked. "Did Master Li try to contact you?"

"No, we sense he needs us," Michael linked back. "We're heading for the hotel as fast as we can."

"I'll catch a taxi and be right there," Han linked back. "I can visit the gallery of modern art another time."

The foursome loaded their things in the trunk and instructed the driver to head quickly for the Ritz. As the driver turned onto the street, Michael slammed his fist down on the privacy window control to cut them off from driver. He found he could not link with anyone. He opened his mouth to speak but nothing came out. As he turned his head he saw Cecilia, Su Lin, and then Villi roll their eyes and pass out. The last thing he remembered was the blue sky outside the window and how untroubled that world seemed. Then his world went black.

Chapter Twenty-Eight

Crossed Wires

"I wondered if someday..." she posed as they watched the scenery pass, "will we travel to other cities?"

"I suppose," he nonchalantly replied.

"I hope you won't be too old..." she thought. She kept forgetting he could read her mind.

He chuckled and grasped her hand. His touch settled her anxiety for the moment. She knew that when they began their long distance separation, she would have trouble adjusting.

Master Li and Running Elk sat alone in the privacy of the limousine's back seat, while the driver took them across town. They spent the morning casually walking in and out of shops, tasting tidbits in cafés, and taking in the culture of Paris. In just the past twenty-four hours, she had picked up a few words of French, enough to be friendly – please, thank-you, hello, and the like. Finally they made their way to her new home for the next three years. The limo driver pulled up to a beautiful old refurbished building. The pale yellow stucco structure stretched up three stories high above the street with a full basement. Strategically placed tall bushes and a recently painted black wrought iron fence surrounded the secure entrance.

"Are you sure this place is my apartment?" she asked Li as she looked out. "It's too much space for one person. It would take me a week to clean!"

When the driver did not move, Li indicated the door handle. Running Elk stepped out first. Her eyes traveled up to the windows.

"This is the right address," Li told her as he closed the door. He stood outside the gate beside Running Elk as she continued to stare up at the great structure. "She is quite wealthy," he added. "I believe she owns many buildings."

Running Elk stepped forward and tried her key in the large black gate. It worked. The gate slowly closed behind them as they ascended the front stoop. Three front steps brought them to a large, carved, wooden door with a great elaborate brass knob, a polished brass plate with Ossures on it, and the door frame flanked on either side by tall, narrow, frosted panes that had trimmed trees in planters placed in front of them. Running Elk noticed an electronic security panel, which seemed out of place compared to the elegance of the building's old-world charm. From their perch, they noticed Camille's limousine parked on the side of the building in a private drive.

Li started to knock when the door opened.

"Hello?" a small voice asked.

"Hello," he started. "I am..."

"You must be Mr. Li," the voice continued as the door opened wider. A beautiful young black-haired girl appeared from behind the door. She wore the uniform of a domestic and looked the couple up and down for a second before her face erupted in a wide smile.

"You must be Running Elk!" she declared. "Welcome to your home," she said and nodded her head.

"...and who might you be?" Running Elk asked her.

"I will be your assistant," the young woman said. "My name is Danielle."

She curtsied and moved back just as Camille walked up the hall toward them.

"Well? Do you like it?" Camille asked them.

"I... I...," Running Elk struggled to speak as she looked around.

"I see you've been remodeling," Li noted. He considered the fact that Camille probably sunk a million or more Euros into the place and had intended to sell it. He would help compensate her losses through the Tyler Trust.

"I appreciate the gesture, but I can't accept anything this nice," Running Elk said as she noted the highly polished wooded floors, oriental rugs and other fine furnishings that surrounded them. "I left the tribe behind in near poverty conditions. I would feel ashamed if they knew I lived in such a refined place."

Before Camille could speak, Master Li stepped in.

"Your path through life changed when you gave up leadership of the tribe to your son and chose to serve me," he told her. "You recall our agreement?" he put to her.

Running Elk could not speak. She lowered her head and nodded. Camille chose not to interfere, as she was not certain of their relationship. She only watched their interaction with fascination.

"Since you wish to devote your life to servitude," he continued. "I have some rules regarding that service. The first is that you must accept my guidance when I give it freely. Are we agreed?"

Running Elk hesitated and glanced between the two women. Then she looked over at Master Li and nodded, "Agreed."

"Very well," he continued. "We discussed that cooking school would help both of us. I've never felt that servitude included having to wash floors on your hands and knees. Please allow Camille and me to provide what we feel you need to attend school. Trust me when I say, you will not recognize Rollo when you return. No one will be living in poverty," he told her.

Camille chimed in agreement. "You should listen to Master Li." That was the first time she honestly addressed him as his title, "master."

He took Running Elk's hand. She gazed into his eyes. She did trust him. She knew Li would make everything right.

"Ok… I agree to your terms," she replied. She began to look at her surroundings. She gently laughed as she took in the place. "I know Paris has plenty of them, but you didn't have to give me a palace," she said. "I would have settled for a plain and simple apartment."

"We start with plain and simple here," Camille pointed to her head. "When we finish, we have a palace." She added a smile and a wink at the end.

Everyone laughed, when all at once Master Li clutched his chest as if he were having a heart attack. He fell backward against the wall as he tried to catch his breath. He appeared to be in extreme pain.

"Li!" Running Elk cried out as she moved to him. "Camille, help me…"

When she turned, she noticed that Camille appeared in distress too. Camille staggered around, trying to catch her breath. She reached out for the wall and held it for support.

"What's going on?" Danielle cried.

"Go get some help!" Running Elk practically demanded.

The French maid ran toward the kitchen to phone for emergency help.

Master Li gasped for breath as did Camille. He broke into a sweat. His hands trembled.

"Negative energy waves impacting the environment of such magnitude," he uttered. "I've never felt so much terror. This feeling is new to me… I need time to think," he said between gasps for breath. "I need some air," he said as he moved toward the door. "Block," he linked to Camille, "block all of your thoughts."

Camille fought to regain her composure. She struggled to stand up straight. Uneasily, she walked up the hall toward the kitchen. She took the phone out of Danielle's hand.

"I am Camille Ossures," she spoke into the phone. "We're fine. Danielle is simply excited. We do not need help at this time. Thank you."

She hung up the phone.

"Get me some cold water please," she asked the maid.

Danielle ran to the kitchen's refrigerator for a glass of ice water while Camille changed her position to look up the hall toward the front door. She saw Master Li heading outside. She took the glass from Danielle and drank a few deep drafts before she handed the glass back to her.

"I feel better now," she said to her. "I want you to return to your duties," she instructed. "I will see to our guests."

"Yes madam," Danielle said. She reluctantly took the back staircase up to the second floor laundry room where she had been folding linen.

Camille did as Master Li suggested, she blocked all of her thoughts. That seemed to help more than the water. She reached for a tissue to dab off her moist forehead before she headed for the front door.

Running Elk stayed by Master Li's side as they walked down the stoop, through the gate, and out to the street. When Camille's chauffeur saw Li's stressed face and watched as he staggered, the conscientious man ran inside to check up on Camille. Master Li did not stop at the gate. He kept walking up the street as if drawn by some force.

"Where are you going?" Running Elk asked as she walked along beside him.

Master Li could not speak. He waved her off and kept an unsteady staggered pace up the street. He struggled for air while people walked around them and ignored his distress. He continued along until he reached the first intersection, where he stopped outside the local corner café. A nearby newsstand drew his attention to the headlines.

"DÉSASTRE DE NEW YORK IMMINENT!" it read in large French capital letters.

"Pardon me," he said as he laid out a bill and reached to take a paper. His eyes rapidly traveled down the page. He closed his eyes and wrinkled the paper in his hands.

"What is wrong?" Running Elk asked.

"This hurricane," Li noted. "A major disaster… I had a feeling this might happen…"

"What might happen?" Running Elk wondered.

The couple turned to see Camille with her head erect as the determined woman marched toward them. Her driver slowly tailed her progress from the car on the street.

"Would you mind explaining what happened back there?" she practically demanded. She suspected Master Li's power may have influenced the environment.

"Don't you have people that keep you informed?" he asked. He held up and shook the paper in her face.

"I've been busy," she replied. She frowned when she took the paper from Li and read the front page. "What does this mean?" she asked after she glanced over the paper. "How can a hurricane two thousand miles away affect us?"

"This hurricane isn't just any hurricane," Li pointed out. "This storm is now a Category 5 and may become the most powerful Category 5 hurricane in the history of weather. Don't you realize what will happen if this thing strikes New York City with its full force? It could spell worldwide financial collapse. If New York is destroyed or non-functional for even a week, it will affect markets around the world. It could plunge the business world into chaos."

"Li… is that possible?" Camille stared back at him, aghast.

"More than just a possibility Camille," he said as he took the paper back. "The markets will begin to reflect those fears. Panic selling will spread from one market to the next."

"Perhaps I should sell too…" Camille considered.

"…and add fuel to the fire?" Li shot back. "Besides, you've plenty of cash on hand. Hang on to your stock," he advised. "You may be able to scoop up some bargains in the next few days. We have other considerations. I need my team to help strategize. Can I hand Running Elk over to you?"

"Of course, she can stay with me until her apartment is ready," Camille offered.

"Good," Li said. "I've a feeling this will require our entire group from Rollo."

"Would you like our help? Salla and Filla can join us?" Camille stated.

"You should remain here in case the government needs your company to start making mass quantities of antibiotics or other medicines for America," Li suggested. "I must go to the hurricane."

"What will you do?" Camille asked him.

"Try to stop it," Li focused on her. "Meanwhile, intensify your blocking technique," he advised. "Instruct Salla and Filla to do the same. I'm sorry to leave you like this. Please excuse me."

With that remark, he stepped between the newsstand and a parked van just as a bus pulled up to the corner. It formed a three-way wall that cut off anyone's point of view except the two women. In that instant, he vanished into nothingness right before their eyes. Camille could not follow his psychic presence. Running Elk gasped at his sudden disappearance.

"Where did he go?" she wondered. She had seen Li fade once, but never instantly vanish.

Camille backed up and swallowed hard. She was unaware that any psychic had that kind of power. However, she knew that Li would not use that ability unless a situation required it.

"He had to leave," she muttered.

"That's impossible," Running Elk countered. "He stood right there. How did he..."

Camille shook her head. "Running Elk, you should know that Li is no ordinary man. We must leave this place. Please come with me," she said. She motioned for her driver. "I must find Salla and Filla. They're probably in need of some advice right about now."

Across town, Villi, Su Lin, Cecilia and Michael tried to recover from the onslaught of negative energy bombardment which they experienced in the limousine. Fortunately, the blackout lasted less than a minute while the limo was still en route. Upon waking, Michael wisely requested that everyone block while they absorbed additional energy.

"That includes any communication," he added.

Han had been shopping in a store. He rushed into a nearby restroom and immediately put up the strongest block he could erect. He had acted out of instinct, which saved him the embarrassment of passing out. With few public telephones available, he finally found one inside an old restaurant and was able to trace Michael's psychic signature to the mobile phone inside the limousine. After a few vain attempts, he got through, and listened as Michael described the group's experience.

"We'll meet you at the hotel, Han," Michael requested at the end.

"I'll join you shortly," Han told him and hung up. He started to leave the corner restaurant when he sensed Master Li's presence. He headed for an isolated booth and ordered coffee from a passing waiter before he spoke to Li.

"Master Li?" Han called out with his senses.

"Han," Li answered. "Listen...the hurricane we sensed as we crossed the Atlantic has become a Category 5 storm and is headed straight for New York. We're feeling tremendous negative energy from its impact on the populous," Li explained. "The entire group must block against its effects. Spread the word."

"We're one step ahead of you," Han responded.

"Good," Li's voice echoed. "Go to a book store. Buy the most detailed geographical maps they have of New York," Li instructed. "Strategize! Look at this problem from every angle and seek solutions that might have seemed impossible to you four months ago. Please Han," Li implored. "You must act quickly."

"Is that possible?" Han questioned. "I mean, is it possible to stop a Category 5 hurricane? The power inside that storm must be...."

"Remember Han," Li broke in. "The hurricane must not reach New York. If it does, it will be the end of everything, and that includes our plans for Rollo, not to mention the deaths of many innocent people. Meet me at the hotel. I'll be there shortly."

"You'll be..." Han questioned. "Isn't Running Elk with you? Where are you?"

"Where no ordinary human being can possibly go," Li commented. "Tell the others to pack."

"Yes, Master Li," Han replied.

The moment he stepped from the restaurant, he searched with his mind for a novelty shop or bookstore until he happened to look over across the street.

"Ben's and Taylor's!" he exclaimed, seeing the famous book chain's sign. "If they don't have a map, then I'm Master Li... and I'm not!" he thought as he sprinted through the sparse traffic.

Across town, Michael and the others approached the Ritz as quickly as the driver could safely take them there, despite their urges to go faster. Just as the limo pulled in, Michael heard his master's voice.

"Michael," Li's voice called to him.

"Master Li," Michael responded and allowed the others to hear. "It's funny. We started to use blocking technique because..."

"I hate to interrupt Michael," Li broke in. "You must listen to me. I don't have much time. Han is gathering some necessary information. We have a situation. A Category 5 hurricane is headed for New York City and will make landfall in the next day or two. We are their only hope of stopping that force."

"Master Li," Michael weakly protested. "How can a handful of psychics stop such an immense weather system?"

"I want the group to decide the best course of action..." Li told him.

"We can't create a psychic shield large enough to divert a weather system like that," Villi spoke up.

"We can affect many things Villi," Li advised. "Work through this problem on the way to our rooms. Villi, I want you to head straight to the airport. Prepare the jet for takeoff, so that the moment we arrive, we can depart. We will meet you there as soon as we can."

"Where are you?" Su Lin asked.

"Su Lin, please pack Villi's things. I will be with you soon," he said. They felt his connection go cold.

"Category 5," Michael muttered. "If New York is destroyed, it could cause the collapse of the entire banking system!"

"Tyler Trust goes bust," Cecilia commented.

"Along with nearly every fortune in America," Su Lin added. "The ripple effect would travel through Russia and China, too. Even German bank stocks would plummet. This is a lose-lose situation."

"This is not good," Villi put in.

The others stared at him and shook their heads.

"It's fine to think of money, but think of the cost in lives, disrupting the families," Cecilia linked. "Terror and panic is spreading through that city even now," she expressed her feelings that the others shared. "That is what we are feeling… this horrible negative wall of fear."

"Unfortunately, some people won't believe the media until it's too late. I'll wager every bridge and road off Long Island is in grid lock," Su Lin added.

"A break down in law and order…" Villi commented. "Innocent people hurt…"

"You heard Master Li," Michael interrupted their train of thought. "What will affect weather systems, people," he linked as the limo pulled up. "We need a solution that has an immediate cause and effect on that storm. Think about it!"

On the way up the elevator, the four racked their brains as Villi began to make a mental list of what he needed to do to make the jet ready for flight in less than an hour.

Master Li stepped through the giant crystal lattice into a place where time did not flow and space had no dimension. He focused his energy on the phenomenon known as the event horizon. This action created two distinct sections within the realm of reason dictated by a single black line that had no known end. From this horizon, millions of time lines converged on a point beneath his feet. Their sparkling images called to him like sirens to sailors fighting to find their way through a mist.

He dared not gaze down at these beckoning future events until the lines finished forming. He kept his eyes on the horizon and used his energy to form the ribbon of time.

"Do not focus on the future…" he recalled the director's voice, "or it will trap you forever."

Li lifted his foot and watched the flow of time under his feet. That was the present back on Earth. He saw Han as he rushed from a store with maps wrapped up inside a bag that he had tucked under his arm. Li switched over to the image of Michael with the other three as they rose in the elevator. He saw Camille in her limousine with Running Elk. She was on her cell phone trying to locate Salla and Filla. Li mythically inhaled a deep breath, yet this place held no oxygen nor did his body actually exist here.

"Courage," he thought as he looked out at the probable lines of future.

This time he had to look at them, the probability lines, as they angled inward and converged from millions to thousands to hundreds until the possible choices for a future finally merged into the present with no chance for change in the last brief milliseconds. Each line scenario differed slightly until they grew closer and closer. As they merged, their images grew similar with fewer variations. The converging lines started to sparkle brighter with golden glints along their edges. Their quality drew Li's attention to linger. His mind dwelled on the bright colorful images.

"It's so beautiful…" he thought.

All at once, the lines began to sing to him, as if a great chorus of time called out. The lines drew his mind inward as he watched with fascination the destructive forces of the largest hurricane in the history of the planet move with deadly force upon the world's biggest financial center.

"Li!" the director's voice called to him.

However, Master Li did not hear him. He could not turn his gaze away. The more he looked deeper at the lines, the more detail he saw of the future. It pulled at his mind and drew him in. His eyes fluttered. He began to fall forward.

"Li!" a great shout erupted in his mind. This time the director called up every voice in Galactic Central to cry out and save their prophet. The enormous outpouring of energy shook him awake. He fell backward and the event horizon nearly vanished. "You cannot stop the flow of time!" he heard the director say. "Each second you spend in the future is like an eternity to me…" the director's distinctive mechanical voice echoed in his mind.

All at once, Li felt drained of energy. He wondered what would happen next. He had seen several probable outcomes for New York. He knew that once he returned to the present, he would begin to recognize certain signs around him that would eliminate many of those choices he witnessed. Yet he could not reveal his knowledge of the future. He knew that would be a terrible mistake. He glanced down and saw his destination for the present. Just before he stepped back into the present, he thought about the group's potential choices for action.

"Which future will they chose?" he wondered.

Chapter Twenty-Nine

Flight to Hades

Practically every person who lived on the eastern seaboard and owned a television remained fixed on the constantly changing situation. While nurses and doctors continued their never ending service, police continued their never ending patrol, and the military continued it's never ending vigil, the rest of humanity took the day off. Governments cancelled school, closed offices, and sent the populous scurrying for their lives. An ocean liner unable to flee in time, became trapped inside the storm, swamped and sank. Rescues at sea were tantamount to suicide runs after two Coast Guard cutters sank along with two helicopters. All aboard perished. The nation helplessly watched the situation, horrified as newscasters listed the dead. The storm already claimed more lives than any hurricane had in a hundred years. Every east coast city from Charleston to Boston was affected with destruction.

The hurricane especially impacted those who lived in towns and cities located along the coast between Delaware and New York, as they evacuated barrier islands and tried to flee inward. Estelle's rain bands stretched out over a thousand miles wide, which made it the most fearsome weather system in recorded history. Not Andrew or Katrina or any other hurricane in recent history compared to the power of Estelle and the potential for biblical-style epic disaster. One weather channel watched with horror during a live broadcast as a giant wave came up out of the darkness and took the reporter and her camera crew out to sea, never to be heard from again.

This was not the kind of hurricane people took lightly any longer. Fear gripped the east coast of America. That is why terror reached across the ocean and tore into the minds of the psychics.

Every television station focused on the story including the networks. All normal daytime programming stopped. Anchors and reporters gave continuous reports throughout the day and night. America buzzed daily about the hurricane. The red arrows on forecaster's maps all pointed toward New York as point of collision, and so an anxious nation watched and waited for the storm to strike.

"...the eye that had remained stationary and building in intensity off the coast of Maryland for a second day has finally begun its threatening move to the north as had been predicted," the weather spokesperson stated. "Estelle pushed the high pressure ridge out that kept the storm at bay," the reporter noted as she pointed to the map. "The Hurricane Center predicts the storm's outer edge will reach Long Island in the next twelve to eighteen hours..."

The image behind the reporter changed to news footage of scenes around the New York City. Huge waves crashed into Long Island's barrier communities.

"Some areas of New York have begun to experience flooding in low-lying areas," the voice continued. "Traffic congestion has clogged all roads from Long Island. The government closed the bridge to Manhattan due to flooding in the lower parts of the city. The Verrazano Narrows Bridge is scheduled to close later today when wind gusts are predicted to make travel on the bridge unsafe. Only freeways that lead north will remain open. The president, in cooperation with the governors of New Jersey and New York, has declared Marshall Law..."

Han burst into the hotel suite nearly out of breath. He did not see anyone at first from the foyer. He heard noise coming from the adjacent room.

"Has anyone heard from Master Li?" he questioned as he came around the corner.

Michael, Cecilia and Su Lin stood huddled together with their packed luggage around them. They watched the room's wide screen television on the wall. From their expressions and the images on the screen, Han knew this was no ordinary storm. Michael turned to Han.

"No one has seen Master Li," he explained. "He contacted us in the limo. He instructed us to pack. We have your things ready," he added and gestured toward some luggage. Villi is preparing to head for the airport. We just turned on the television..." he stopped, when he felt Master Li's overwhelming presence flood into the suite. The group turned in unison toward Villi's room. The door was open. Before anyone could move, they overheard Villi's voice.

"Yes, Master Li," they heard him link. "I will."

Villi swiftly emerged from his bedroom with Master Li right behind.

Su Lin stared at Villi's face. She found a steely determined gaze with a firm mental block that kept her out. She tried to penetrate that block when Master Li crossed in front of her as a distraction.

"What is your strategy, Han?" he questioned.

"I've barely had time to look over the maps, Master Li," Han uttered. Li's urgency overwhelmed the young man with this new task. "I'll see what I can do."

He spread out a map on a nearby table. Villi headed for the door.

"Michael?" Li turned to the tall young man. "Have you given the matter any thought?"

Michael, Cecilia and Su Lin watched Villi leave. All three worried about Li's private instructions to him. Li took Michael by the arm and diverted him to the table where Han spread out the maps. Michael glanced down at the eastern coastline of America.

"I don't see what we *can* do," Michael stated. "New York has never encountered a hurricane of this strength. We could ask Chou to..."

"Too late for that," Li cut him off. "Su Lin? Have you given it any thought?"

The young lady blinked away the moisture in her eyes as she heard the suite's door slam shut. She cleared her throat and turned toward the table. She glanced over at the map. Han had taken a highlight marker and drew a large circle to indicate the hurricane's current position.

"I can only consider two options," she spoke up. "Dry ice or silver iodide seeding is a possibility..."

"The American military tried massive seeding this morning by special order of the president," Li informed her. "It failed. The storm's magnitude is too great. Do you have any other suggestions?"

"The only other suggestion I considered seems absurd," she said. "You could use satellites to focus the sun's rays..."

"Sorry," Li cut her off. "Not practical. Cecilia?"

Cecilia walked away and stared out the window while the others spoke around the table. She gazed up at the growing gray clouds in the sky. She suddenly turned around and marched over to the maps.

"Let's have a closer look at those maps," she said.

Li watched her mind work, but he did not say or link his feelings. She ran her finger out from New York City along Long Island and then peered down at the map.

"What is that dot?" she asked as she pointed to a small brownish dot. "Is that an island?"

"Block Island," Master Li quietly linked as he moved closer to her.

The moment Han heard Li's comment; he wondered why Li answered her so quickly.

"How did you know that?" he asked as he peered intently at Li. "Where were you? How did you end up in Villi's room?"

"I'd like to know that too," Michael added.

"Go ahead Cecilia," Li continued while he ignored Michael and Han. "Tell us the significance of Block Island."

"According to the weather reports, the warm gulf stream water turns here at Long Island and then flows out into the Atlantic," she stated. "The momentum of the storm however, will carry it past this point to the north before it turns," she indicated.

"How do you know that?" Han questioned.

"The news report stated as much before you came in," she said. She closed her eyes. "That far north, the warm water is near the surface. Underneath, the sea contains massive amounts of cold water. If we could divert the water from the depths to the surface…"

"Divert millions of tons of water?" Han intervened. "We can't even divert turbulent air that weighs a fraction compared to that!"

"It doesn't work like that," Su Lin interrupted. "The currents that bring cold water from the north already exist. She isn't talking about diverting the water. She's talking about diverting the current to bring the cold water from the bottom to the surface. The place most likely for those currents to converge would be…"

"Wait a minute," Michael interrupted. "Are you saying that just introducing cold water to the surface would shut the hurricane down?" he questioned.

"Oh, I'm such a fool!" Han said as he slammed his fist down at the end of Long Island. "Block Island is the key!"

"Diverting that current would take a machine the size of New York," Su Lin pointed out.

The knowing smiles faded from their faces.

"What can we do then Master Li?" Cecilia asked.

"Fortunately we do have other members of our team who have been analyzing this problem. They started on it yesterday," Li said as he took out his communicator and waved it to them.

"What is that?" Cecilia asked.

"Yeah, I don't have one of those," Su Lin chimed in.

"You soon will," Li responded and waved three fingers near its front. "I don't know what they have prepared for us. However, I believe we should meet them at our rendezvous point…" he told them, and then added, "on Block Island."

"We haven't a moment to lose. Let's get to the jet," Michael advised.

For a moment, Master Li turned away from them and walked toward the terrace. Only Han had seen Li activate the device. Michael suspected that Li must be contacting Chou. Li spun back around. He no longer held the card in his hand. The group put their bags onto a caddy and took the elevator to the lobby. The commercial limousine waited at the front of the hotel.

"With all due haste," Michael informed the driver after they loaded the trunk.

Before the driver could pull forward, a police officer cut the limo driver off.

"What is the meaning of this!" the driver cried as he rolled his window down.

The police officer stepped off his motorcycle and walked over to the driver. They started to argue in French, when the driver suddenly stopped. He turned around and smiled.

"Seems we are to have a police escort to the airport courtesy of Camille Ossures," he smiled. "You must have friends in high places."

With sirens wailing, the limo cut through traffic and flew out of Paris to the executive airport. Their escort peeled off just as they pulled into the private airstrip.

By the time they arrived, Villi had the jet fueled and powered up. He had the systems on the aircraft ready. He laid the course into the onboard computer – the same course the group concluded as their destination. The psychics scrambled to their seats as Villi hurriedly taxied the jet into position.

Han sat across from Li at the front of the plane. His mind dwelled on their choice of Block Island. He had lingering doubts about their course of action.

"I still can't see what we can accomplish by going to Block Island," he muttered as he buckled his seatbelt.

Master Li ignored his comment.

"Are you ready?" Li put to the pilot.

"I'll need our path cleared," he linked back to Master Li.

"Have you thought about your approach?" Li asked him. "You'll be flying us along the edge of huge storm system."

"Landing on Block Island will be easy," Villi linked back. "I checked the runway. Hurricanes turn counter-clockwise. We'll have to compensate for some wind shear," he stated, "but we'll be ok."

"With all that open water Villi..." Han cautioned. "What about eddies, whip currents, down-drafts, and tornadoes?"

"Those are all possibilities and could very likely occur," Villi acknowledged. "However, we have one advantage that other aircraft do not..."

"That is..." Han questioned.

"A translucent bubble of tremendous energy that is resistant to outside forces and will help guide me in like a swan!" Villi declared.

"The runway is clear," Master Li spoke up. "When you are ready…"

"Yes, Master Li," Villi replied.

The engines roared to life as the jet aircraft moved to takeoff. With the psychic bubble in place, Villi simply headed up the runway in front of him and picked up enough speed until the aircraft lifted into the air. He quickly banked the jet toward the west coast of France and picked up speed. He ignored the location of other aircraft. He knew Master Li took care of that.

"Where is the hurricane now?" Michael asked his well-informed pilot.

"Advancing on New York," Villi reported. "The barrier islands are nearly under water."

"Master Li," Cecilia chimed in softly. "How will we obtain enough psychic energy with land so far away from Block Island?"

"The island has a few residents that chose to remain," he explained. "Granted it will be difficult to draw a large amount of energy from those consumed with emotion," he continued. "Therefore, we must conserve our energy until we land."

"You knew…" Han started to link when Li cut him off.

"Villi, we'll have to drop the bubble over the Atlantic," Li advised.

"Master Li, the jet will be subject to turbulence," Villi told him.

"We'll have a bumpy ride for awhile," Master Li retorted. "I trust your piloting skills."

Su Lin stared at Cecilia. The new physician recognized fear when she saw it on her friend's face. Su Lin feared the storm's impact on their flight.

"I wish Chou was with us," she muttered.

Master Li leaned back into the leather seat and closed his eyes. He could not vanish again and play with the timeline. That would tip his hand. He recalled seeing Block Island in the future probability lines. As that future time approached the present, he could predict the outcome better. Yet that would mean additional trips to the timeline. The director warned Li that he must not gaze upon the future too often, or it would draw him in and he would vanish into an infinite world of endless probabilities without ever finding resolution.

"Master Li," Han privately linked as Villi pushed the jet higher. "I've been thinking about Cecilia's suggestion – changing the sub-current – how exactly are we going to accomplish this impossible feat?"

Michael walked over at that moment. Although the jet still shot upward at a steep angle, he did not feel like sitting in his seat like some obedient child.

"Mind if I join the adults?" he chimed in. "Or did you think that last communiqué was private?"

When Han did not reply, Michael motioned for Su Lin and Cecilia. Su Lin would not leave her seat, but Cecilia joined him.

"Cecilia came up with a great idea," he began. "That is, using cold water to blow out the hurricane. I think it's a great idea too. However, I have to agree with Han. Moving around millions of tons of water will take tremendous energy and a great deal of time. We're speaking of hours if not days. The hurricane will be in Boston by then."

Li sat up. He was visibly tired after his long day.

"I refer you to our resident knowledge expert…"

Every head turned to Han, but Master Li stared over at Su Lin.

"You did visit Artane, did you not?" Li questioned. "You did go through five days of intensive downloads to become as smart as a whip. I'd like you to overcome your fear of flying and start to analyze what will quickly move water. I leave it in your capable hands," he said politely. "Villi! Wake me in three hours!"

Su Lin gazed out the window as the jet leveled off.

"What would move water quickly?" she thought as she racked her brain. "Move water… Oh! Master Li!" she suddenly linked to the group, her eyes wide. "You don't mean…"

"Three hours Su Lin, please!" he interrupted and held up his hand. Master Li placed his seat into the sleeping position and instantly nodded off.

"He's up to something," Han muttered as he turned away.

"You just noticed that?" Michael blurted as he headed to the galley.

Michael, Cecilia, and Han finally persuaded Su Lin to join them at the bar near the back of the cabin. Michael took out his communicator card and showed them its operation.

"Compact size," Cecilia observed.

"I haven't used it yet," Michael explained. "To tell you the truth, I forgot about it."

He placed three fingers on the front and tried to contact Chou, Zinian, and Zhiwei. Each time the card stated, "Contact currently busy."

"Huh, try again later," Han commented.

"Some device," Su Lin pointed out, "sophisticated alien technology and you still can't reach the party."

The four psychics fixed tea, carried on short conversations, or watched the news feed that Villi piped through the screen in the bar. Eventually, they returned to their seats and waited. Three hours gradually dragged by. Finally, Villi had to drop from the stratosphere back into the troposphere to start his approach. Without the bubble in place, the aircraft buffeted up and down occasionally from turbulance. Su Lin ran to the bar and drank a club soda to settle her stomach. She barely returned to her seat, when the jet suddenly dropped nearly a thousand feet in one swift movement. The falling jet sent everyone's stomach and anything unattached to the ceiling. Su Lin could not fasten her seat belt in time. She grabbed the arms of the chair and held her breath.

Altimeter alarms went off as Villi struggled with the aircraft's manual controls. Outside the port side of the craft, a dark weather system filled the sky. Its churning cyclonic action appeared as gigantic swirling clouds and enormous bolts of flashing energy. The jet aircraft shuddered and shook as if giant hands were trying to crush it. Master Li's nap abruptly ended.

"NOAA clocked Estelle's winds at 182 mph," Villi told them as he glanced at the read out. "Barometric pressure at the center of the eye reads minus 928 mb!"

Han closed his eyes to search his historical memory. "That would make Estelle the most volatile hurricane on record..."

He stopped his link when the jet suddenly flipped sideways. The rapid move sent passengers and objects over to one side of the jet. Shaking harder still, the jet plunged downward at a steep angle toward the ocean far below them. Alarms blared in the cockpit as Villi struggled to right the aircraft.

Su Lin screamed just as her head struck hard against the sidewall. She lay unconscious on the side of the airplane's cabin. Her limbs crumpled around her. Cecilia had the presence of mind to buckle her seatbelt. However, Michael joined Su Lin in tumbling toward the side of the cabin. He kept from hitting his head by using his martial arts training and landed on his feet instead. His foot missed striking the window by only one centimeter. The cabin walls of the airplane made a crunching sound, as if the wind were trying to tear the wings off.

"I'm glad I reinforced those wings," Villi muttered.

The pilot started to curse in Russian as he attempted to level off the jet. The wind placed so much cross pressure on the wings that he could not regain control. The nose of the aircraft continued to push downward. Villi's eyes widened as he saw the churning sea appear through the base of the cloud deck below.

Han managed to wedge his foot between two seats to prevent the side force from throwing his body. Master Li struggled to regain his body posture while the force of the falling jet pressed his body over to the right.

"Cecilia... Michael... Han... lend Villi a hand," Master Li linked as he pushed against gravity. "The bubble... Villi needs the bubble..."

The psychics understood the urgency in his link. They poured their energy into erecting a psychic bubble around the aircraft. The translucent sphere snapped into place. Immediately, the pressure on the wings decreased. Villi easily righted the aircraft and pulled the nose of the jet level with only a few thousand feet above the water remaining. Taking in a deep breath, he turned the jet to the north and began to regain some of the altitude he would need for their approach. Cecilia jumped up from her seat and helped Michael catch Su Lin's body before she fell onto the floor. Using her mind, Cecilia scanned her body for injuries.

"She's received a contusion," she noted. She placed her hand over the spot and applied light pressure.

In seconds, she heard a hiss and saw Su Lin's face contort into a pained expression while she drew in a deep breath.

"What happened…" Su Lin moaned with her head in Cecilia's lap.

"Villi hit a pocket of turbulence," Cecilia spoke aloud to her.

"Turbulence?" she whispered. "Oh, my head!" she winced. "That reminds me… the water currents… Li's idea is good, but I've got one better."

"Please be quiet," Cecilia interrupted. "Talking only raises your blood pressure," she cautioned.

"No," Su Lin broke in. "You must listen to me. You made the discovery when you crossed the Sea of Okhotsk with Michael."

"I did?" Cecilia looked down at her friend.

"I'm glad I remembered it," she whispered. "For it just might save New York from disaster," Su Lin added as she gazed up at her friend's puzzled face.

Chapter Thirty

Abandon Ship

"The effects of the hurricane have begun to impact the entire metropolitan area," the television news anchor stated. "This graphic shows at least one possibility of what might happen," he pointed. "When the eye comes ashore, we believe that many structures will be heavily damaged…"

Channel change.

"…this animation demonstrates the potential for flooding in the subways and sewage systems not meant to handle a storm surge predicted at over eighteen feet…"

Channel change.

"…the President believes that the government should concentrate every resource on New York City…"

Channel change.

"… the mayors of several major cities have offered to send recovery teams to the north east to help the victims of Estelle…"

Channel change.

"… the senator believes that the President should declare Marshall Law throughout the region temporarily until authorities can restore order…"

"Would you mind keeping it on one station?" Camille asked.

"Oh, sorry," Running Elk replied. She put down the controller.

The two stood inside Camille's office at Ossures Pharmaceuticals. The large screen on the wall opposite her desk showed the terrible predictions made by the news organizations in America. In another area within the same frame, Camille kept an eye on the falling stock markets around the world. Although unreported to the public, Camille knew through private channels that the New York financial district had spent the past week secretly transferring data files and boxes of precious goods such as gold, diamonds, bonds, rare books, antiques, and paintings onto armed convoys nightly that fled Manhattan in droves.

Camille expanded the radar picture of a monster storm until it filled the large screen. The rain bands – which stretched out for hundreds of miles from the eye – varied from green near the outside tips, to yellow, red, and even purple near the center with estimated totals that boggled the mind. Estelle's gigantic rain-band arms advanced toward the continent like a deadly giant octopus pouncing on its prey.

"Li and the others are heading into that?" Running Elk asked as her voice trembled.

"I'm afraid so," Camille concurred. She was afraid to add anything else.

She glanced over and noticed Running Elk with her eyes closed mumbling. The psychic considered her state of mind and decided not to say anything.

"Perhaps we should all say a prayer for them," Camille thought.

"Will you be able to find Block Island in this visibility?" Li asked his pilot. His concern had grown since their mishap twenty minutes ago.

Villi no longer counted on his instrument panel. He did not participate in the formation of the bubble. He concentrated his energy on the turbulent ocean ahead of them. He found one tiny spark in the distance. He homed in on that signal like a beacon that guided him down in the midst of swirling darkness.

The jet lost a great deal of altitude. The passengers could see the churning ocean pass below them through the torrential downpour. The wind buffeted the aircraft. The wings dipped to one side and then the other as Villi struggled to hold it steady, despite the bubble's protection.

"I thought the bubble resisted outside influences," Han linked.

"We shouldn't be able to fly at all in this wind, Han," Villi commented. "I have the runway in my sights now Master Li."

Michael stared up the aisle toward the open cockpit. He watched his friend concentrate on the blur of gray. He saw no break in the clouds or a runway.

"How can he narrow in on something so small without flight guidance?" Michael wondered.

Han twisted around in his seat.

"I believe we have a leg up, as you Americans say," Han stated. "Look!" he pointed.

Out of the bleak landscape, they saw the Block Island airstrip light up like a Christmas tree. They noted other lights focused on the runway from other sources.

"Someone turned the lights on!" Cecilia observed.

"Or forced someone to turn them on," Michael added.

Su Lin sported a temporary ice pack to her head that Cecilia made from the ice machine in the bar.

"I'm sorry," Cecilia apologized. "It's the best I can do under these circumstances."

"I'm fine Cecilia," Su Lin said as she dismissed her concern. "It's only a bump."

Han nervously stared out the window at the turbulent sea that moved closer. They all heard the landing gear go down.

"Please stay buckled," Villi piped back. "This might be rough. I'll let you know when to release the bubble," he told them.

Despite Villi's apprehension, the jet aircraft sailed in smoothly down the short runway. Villi had to use every meter of its length before the jet finally came to a stop on the wet pavement. He pivoted the craft around and headed back up the runway.

"Whew! That's done it!" he proclaimed as he swung the nose toward a large hanger structure.

No one could see anything through the aircraft's windows. Heavy rain pelted the tarmac in near absolute darkness. Only the power generator at the airstrip provided any local power. The rest of island remained blacked out.

Someone waited in the rain outside the largest building. The moment the person in the dark saw the jet coming, they went inside the building and left the small side door into the hanger open. The group rose and went to the windows on one side of the plane. They saw a person with a lit orange cone wave it to help Villi position the jet off the side of the hanger. The psychics could not sense the person. They assumed that Master Li somehow blocked it.

"Release the bubble," Villi requested.

The moment the influence of the sphere vanished, the sound of the storm pounded down upon aircraft. Villi worried that the surface wind could lift the aircraft off the tarmac.

"Did you persuade one of the locals to pay us a visit?" Su Lin asked her husband.

Villi did not answer. He parked the jet as close to the building as he could without crashing into it. The wind howled around them. Villi shut down the jet's engines and entered the cabin.

"Master Li?" he linked. "Phase one, complete."

"I take it we are down and parked at the hanger," he asked the tall Russian.

"Yes sir," Villi told him. "We are on Block Island at the rendezvous point."

Master Li did not address the group. He reached out and took Villi's hand. He knew that in this wind, he may have trouble with the wet steps. Han jumped in behind them. However, Villi did not release the stairs built into the jet. He simply stood in the open doorway.

"Where are you going?" Han asked. "What are we doing?"

Michael questioned this sudden departure too.

"Are we just going to leave the jet here? What's going on?" Michael demanded.

"We would prefer your assistance," Li linked to him.

Villi opened the side door to the hanger with his mind. The person inside pushed a staircase up to the side of the jet and locked the base into place before he disappeared once more. Master Li's clothes blew sideways in the strong wind when he stepped from the aircraft. Villi helped the elderly man down the slippery wet steps. Li leaned into the wind as the two men headed to the open door. Han shuffled right behind them. Cecilia, Michael and Su Lin scurried toward the open door, too. The wind blew so hard that the rain stung when it struck the skin. They could hardly see as they struggled to walk the few meters to the side door of the hanger.

Once they stepped inside the large dark space out of the weather, their footsteps echoed in the vast space, although the wind and rain made the roof rumble around them. Master Li brushed the rain out of his clothes with his hands and then broke into a big smile.

"About time you showed up," a voice said from the shadow.

Su Lin moved past Michael in time to see Villi throw his arms around a man nearly equal his stature. He gave him a big bear hug.

"Zinian?" she exclaimed. "How did you get here?"

Chapter Thirty-One

Chou's Churners

"No time for pleasantries," Li interrupted. "Chou, what have you discovered?"

"Chou?" Cecilia questioned. She wondered why she had not sensed them. She then realized that Chou erected some sort of force field around the entire building.

In the distance, two figures began to walk toward them.

"Hello everyone," Rollo's technician cheerfully answered. "First, I must protect the jet," he said. He pressed a button on a controller in his hand to extend the force field around the aircraft. "That should hold it," he told them. He manipulated the device in his hand once more. The lights inside the hanger turned on revealing Zhiwei standing next to him. He turned toward Master Li. "Actually, I've made several discoveries Master Li," he explained as he walked away from a large device that towered up toward the top of the hanger behind him. "The best way to calm a hurricane is to take away its heat source. In this case, the Gulf Stream provides a current of warm water that hugs the eastern seaboard and extends much further north than it should at this time of year – all the way to Long Island. It's only a few hundred meters deep and overriding cool water underneath."

"That's a wonderful story," Li's voice sounded strained. "We are running out of time. Cut to the point."

"The Gulf Stream is unstable in this region," Chou pointed out. "Greenland dumps tons of glacial ice water into the sea further north. Once we shut down the heat source, the storm breaks up… in theory, that is."

"Your analysis proved correct," Li commented. "Did you prepare the devices as we discussed?" Li asked.

"Yesterday morning," Chou started. "It wasn't difficult to manufacture them in quantity when Zinian helped. However, moving a rocket to the east coast without Villi around presented a problem..."

"A rocket?" Michael, Cecilia, and Su Lin asked in unison.

Chou shrugged off the surprised reaction. He walked over to a large round object propped up against the wall of the hanger. He picked up a metallic disc that measured about a meter in diameter and tossed it over to Master Li. The man deftly caught the new invention. The gray ring had a twisted propeller whose insides met around a hole in the center.

"What is this?" Master Li asked as he examined the simple construction.

"That's it!" Su Lin exclaimed. "That's what I saw from Cecilia's memory... shaped like the propeller of a torpedo, meant to travel rapidly through dense water."

"Exactly," Chou smiled. "I prefer to call it a churner," he said as he held it up. "It's made from a material that also responds well to psychic manipulation. We should have no trouble controlling them. We came up with a design that will propel these devices within the heart of the hurricane. I also added a mix of osmium so that their density will allow them to sink in the water. As they do, they will bring up water from the bottom... if we act in time."

"Launch the rocket now," Master Li ordered.

Their eyes shifted to the tall object in the far corner of the hanger. Michael started to move closer for a better look when Zhiwei reached out his arm and stopped him as he shook his head. Michael then understood the danger involved.

"I've been protecting it," he told Michael.

Chou fiddled with a remote device in his hand.

"How did you bring a rocket to this island?" Han wondered.

"It took us all day to set it up," Chou innocently explained as he touched the control pad.

"What about the wind?" Han continued to question.

"It can lift off in winds of two hundred miles per hour," Chou boasted. "It uses a powerful solid propellant with an engine design of twenty-four outlets that provide lateral stability. I could send this thing to the moon if we..."

"Chou," Li interrupted. "You have no time to make further explanations. You must launch the rocket now!"

"You'll have to stand back," Chou told them. "Zinian weakened the roof joists in the corner. I'm not certain how powerful this is. We didn't have time to test it."

"Worry about that later. Get that thing in the air!" Li insisted.

"Yes, Master Li," Chou said. "This could have a kick," he warned.

The group backed away into the opposite corner of the hanger.

"How many of those spinners are inside the rocket's payload?" Han asked.

"Nine hundred thousand," Chou informed him, "The payload bay is packed solid with nine separate shafts, three on each level." He paused for a second while he pressed the start sequence and removed that end of the force field. "Here goes!" he declared and closed his eyes. Nothing happened. The wind pounded the hanger. He glanced around at the skeptical faces. "That's the problem with rockets," he told them. "They're very complex devices. I'm afraid I'll have to..."

A rumble shook the concrete floor underneath their feet. A huge column of ignited propellant gases shot from the bottom of the rocket. It filled the entire hanger with smoke. The tall round device trembled and sent out a wave of energy that threatened to tear the entire building apart. The support structure around the rocket fell away as the big cylindrical object quickly began to rise. Master Li opened the front hanger doors to allow some fresh air in as rocket exhaust smoke quickly filled the interior.

"I'd back up a little further," Chou coughed and choked.

The group walked backward out the hanger. The rocket's engines filled the interior with a huge roar. Flame blasted out the bottom as the group watched. Suddenly, a section of the roof flew up into the sky as the tall metallic shaft shot straight up into the darkness. Chou looked down at his pad. His fingers quickly ran over the surface activating attenuator guidance controls. The rocket zoomed off into the cloudy sky and quickly disappeared into the rainy blackness. The force field snapped back into place.

"It worked!" Chou exclaimed excitedly as he ducked to avoid a chunk of flying debris.

With the hanger doors opened and a corner of the building demolished, the space quickly cleared of the burnt propellant gases. The missile continued on its course despite the tremendous wind shear. Chou expanded the screen in his hand. The others crowded around and watched its progress. Side jets shot from the nose of the rocket. The flight path turned and made a sharp cut toward the heart of the storm.

"What happened?" Han linked.

"The missile must pierce the storm," Chou linked back, "and find its center. I believe it has sufficient speed and momentum."

"Will it survive the impact of those winds around the eye?" Su Lin linked to Chou.

"It doesn't have to," Chou linked back. "It only has to punch a hole deep enough to reach the eye where it will drop its payload. I designed the rocket to break up. Those canisters will tumble and spread out in the turbulent water."

Chou watched the screen in his hand as the rocket ignited its second booster and blasted its way inside the hurricane.

"Look at it go!" he exclaimed as he jumped into the air. "It's almost reached escape velocity! I told you I could send this to the..."

"I have three cars waiting," Zhiwei cut him off. "We must hurry. This way!"

"Where are we going?" Cecilia asked.

"Isn't it obvious," Han linked to her. "We must guide the spinner-churners into depth of the ocean."

"With our minds?" she replied incredulous.

"That's the idea!" Chou linked in.

The psychic group passed through the force field and headed toward the three cars lined up on the tarmac. Master Li stepped in front of them and held up his hands for their attention. Despite the wind that whipped his clothes sideways, he stood his ground as he linked with them.

"The best way to coordinate this effort is to be near the shore," he quietly linked. "It will take cooperation to control a group of objects that size. If we can combine our efforts, we should start a process that will bring up the cold water from the bottom of the sea to the surface. This process may not stop the storm completely. However, I believe we can reduce its impact on New York."

"I'm reading winds at 208 near the eye," Chou put in as they stood ready to enter the three cars.

"208!" Michael exclaimed as rain pelted his face.

"The rocket will strike the surface any moment Master Li," Chou openly linked. "When the canisters break apart, they'll spread those spinners all over the place. We must form them into organized groups or they'll be ineffective!"

Li held up the ring he still held in his hand.

"Concentrate on this object," he instructed. "Try to imagine them in groups. We'll need to create large circular shafts of water that alternately rise and fall through water like pistons," he told them. "Villi!" Li linked. "Drive the front car. Everyone should try to absorb energy as we approach the coast. We must move with all haste!"

The group scrambled into the three cars. Cecilia drove the second car and Zhiwei took the third. Michael and Master Li joined Villi in the front car as they sped across the island to the southern shoreline.

"What if these spinners don't work?" Michael asked in the quiet of the car's interior.

"I can't think about the alternative," Li said with his eyes closed.

In the third car, Chou watched the screen in his hand. A tiny yellow dot began to drop closer to the surface. It slammed into the eye wall and took a sudden turn to the right. The rocket plunged into the sea.

"The rocket hit the water!" Chou linked to the others. The large yellow dot on the screen broke into three green dots which eventually became nine tiny red dots that bounced, scattered, and tumbled over the turbulent surface. "It's breaking up!" he declared.

Chou placed gyros and shifting weights within the canisters. Some slowed to a halt, while others bounced across the churning surface as they followed the curved path of the eye wall at tremendous speed. As the cars sped through the darkness, Chou bit his lower lip and anxiously watched the last of the canisters finally fall into the water. They very nearly made a complete circle.

"The churners will break out next," he linked to them. "This canister dispersion is better than I hoped," he added as he watched. "They will drift around without purpose if we don't manipulate them soon."

"Villi, drive as fast as you can," Li urged. "We must organize these devices into groups before the water scatters them too far apart."

The darkness and downpour dropped visibility to zero. Villi had to scan the road ahead with his power. Otherwise, he could not see the road.

"Reach for any psychic energy you can find," Li reminded.

Surprisingly, they found eighteen residents scattered around the island – two for each psychic to draw upon for energy. Fortunately, these residents rested calmly in the comfortable basements of some older well-established brick homes. Li probably arranged for them to stay, Michael reasoned. The main road abruptly ended at the south end of the island. Villi pulled the car up behind a new, large, expensive house that faced the sea. It stood vacant as the last barrier between the group and the sea wall of giant rocks up ahead. Villi parked directly behind the house.

"This is as close as I can get us Master Li," he stated. "We'll have to walk from here."

"It'll do," Li told him. "Michael, head for the base of the sea wall in front of this house."

"What about the storm?" Michael asked, concerned for Master Li's safety.

"Damn the storm!" Li said with dismissive tones in his voice. Then his face softened. "Sorry Michael," he apologized. "I can stand a little wetness if you can."

"We'll face it together," Michael replied as he opened the car door against the wind.

The driving rain immediately drenched their clothes with cold water. Using his mind, Li flung the locked gates open as the psychic group pressed on toward the rocky sea shore.

"You can't just hold up your hands and calm the angry sea, can you?" Villi linked through the howling wind.

"He's missing his staff!" Han quipped as he came up behind them.

Master Li actually chuckled at that moment.

"That power is far beyond me," he linked to them while water dripped off his face.

Huge waves broke against the rocks and sprayed icy salt water on them. Li stretched out his senses and searched the vast stretch of ocean for the tiny metallic fragments scattered about in the churning seas. Another large wave sent saltwater spray all over them.

"Master Li!" Michael shouted. He did not wish to waste his precious energy. "Where are they?"

Li held out his hand to his pupil.

"Michael! I need your help to find them," he called out. "The rest of you, join us!"

The other eight psychics hopped across the rocky surface to stand alongside Li and face the sea. They spread out and formed a line that included Han, Zinian, Zhiwei, Villi, Su Lin, Chou, Master Li, Michael, and Cecilia at the far end.

For a moment, the ferocity of the storm confused Han's concentration. He gazed out over the dark water and fearfully watched the huge waves as they crashed onto the rocky barrier in front of them. He noticed Master Li lean forward into the wind with his eyes closed. He felt the elderly man calmly reach across the stormy sea to seek out the elusive spinning devices. He and the rest of Rollo psychics joined with Master Li to locate the peculiar shaped objects.

"I found them!" Chou linked as he was more familiar with their molecular signature.

"Quickly," Li encouraged. "Follow Chou's psychic energy path. Grasp the spinners with your mind and form them into groups!"

The spinning devices had begun to sink down into the waves. The nine psychics went to the separate groups and began to move the objects into organized patterns. Despite the rain and wind, they concentrated their power and focused on thousands of spinners. They aligned the devices into nine giant separate groups around the eye of the hurricane. Gradually, the circle widened until the churners created a perfect pattern around the circular eye in the center.

"That's it! That's it!" Master Li exclaimed as he watched. "Now! Villi, Chou, Han, and Michael… start your group down!" Li cried out as he joined them. "Sink them fast! The rest of you wait…"

The first group of spinners sank. As they dropped, they forced water up through their spinning forms just as Chou predicted they would. The freezing cold water from the depths of the Atlantic's bottom began to rise toward the surface.

"Cecilia, Zinian, Zhiwei, Su Lin… start your columns down now!" Li told them.

Saltwater spray from the waves stung hard against their rain soaked faces as the wind whipped it through the air. The group had to lean slightly forward against the wind to remain on their feet.

"The opposite… Michael, Chou, Villi, Han… lift your groups," Li instructed. "We must create currents."

The spinning devices seemed to slice through the water easier than air. Soon, thousands sank while others pulled their spinners up from the depths. Several hundred square miles of surface water turned into a great bubbling caldron never seen since the beginning of time when the oceans first formed. Tons of icy cold water rose from the depths of the Atlantic. The nine psychics – strained to the limit – forced the devices up and down in alternate patterns as Li suggested.

All at once, Su Lin began to falter. The head injury she suffered on the plane took its toll on the powerful psychic. Sweat broke out on her face from the strain of using so much psychic power. She could not replenish the supply as quickly as she used it. She grew dizzy as her power levels dropped.

"I can't," she linked. Pushed to the edge of unconsciousness, her head throbbed with pain. Her group of churners started to break apart in the new strong currents. The water that flowed in the vertical shaft she created slowed down. That process affected the flow in the other currents as well.

"Su Lin," Li linked to her. "Pull additional power into your mind," he advised. "Your energy levels are slipping."

It was too late. The beautiful, young, oriental woman with her black hair matted to her face fell backward. Cecilia and the others gasped as her head would surly strike the rock beneath her feet. A figure leaped through the air.

"Steady," a deep voice linked, as a strong arm reached out and caught her.

Su Lin blinked the rain from her eyes to see Villi above her face as he deftly landed next to her and held her in his arms.

"I'm sorry. I treated you too rough back there," he whispered, referring to the mishap on the jet.

He pulled her close and planted a kiss on her lips while he transferred some of his psychic energy to her. The entire group watched Villi's self-sacrifice. Su Lin's color brightened as she recovered a little from the transfer and his loving attention.

"Yep!" Cecilia declared as she and Michael watched. "A kiss can do that!"

Su Lin smiled as Villi helped her back to her feet.

"Now if you two are finished… the spinners!" Li reminded them.

Su Lin returned her revived focus back to her group. Soon the water churned once more with near equal vigor. She pulled additional psychic energy and returned to raising and lowering her group. Chou reached inside his pocket and pulled out his scanner. The surface temperature of the water had changed dramatically. Everyone could feel the wind as it blew over the icy water and its chilly blast struck their faces.

"Good gracious that's cold!" Cecilia cried as fresh spray covered them.

"The churners are working!" Chou shouted to save his psychic energy.

However, Master Li sensed the group waiver in the face of the colder air. Between the icy rain and lack of rest, each person had increased difficulty in applying the necessary force to either lift or sink the spinners through fathoms of seawater. The ocean continued to bubble and boil around the eye of the hurricane. However, as Chou watched his scanner, the rapid temperature change seemed to have little effect on the mighty storm.

At that moment, Han had the presence of mind to glance toward the horizon. Out of the darkness, he noticed a large object rise up out of the sea. A great wave headed toward the southern shore of Block Island – a wave large enough to do considerable damage. Han's eyes widened with apprehension when he realized the speed of the wave. They only had seconds to act.

"Tsunami!" he cried out "Run! Run for your life!"

Master Li did not stop to consider why Han shouted. He trusted his judgment. The others did too. With his last bit of energy, Master Li ran toward the large house as fast as his old legs could carry him. The others turned and followed. Michael and Villi moved up on either side of Li. They picked him with their arms and kept on running. The scene resembled a sprint to the finish line. The nine Rollo psychics cut through the property of the wealthy homeowner and sought refuge on the other side of the sound structure of the house, where they parked their cars.

Cecilia glanced back over her shoulder as the crest of the wave momentarily glistened in the dim light. The top edge of the wave tumbled with white foam just before the huge wave crashed down up on the rocky shore and headed straight for them. The last in the group to reach the back of the house, Cecilia started to turn the corner when the wave hit the front of the property at over a hundred miles per hour. For a second, she lost her bearing. The rain blocked her vision. The impending rush of water threatened to carry her away. A hand reached out and grabbed her shirt. The strong arm pulled her sideways into the huddled group behind the house just in time. She looked up to see Michael's face in front of hers with his arm around her waist.

"I can't lose you," he whispered.

He had used so much of his psychic ability that he nearly drained his level. He pulled her close and protectively wrapped his arms around her. An instant later, the wave blasted past the structure with the force of a fire hose. They could hear smashing glass and feel the percussion of furniture that bounced off the walls inside the house. However, the structure stood against the forces of the sea despite the pounding. The group now stood in about three feet of swirling ice-cold water. For a few minutes, they fought to maintain their footing until the water finally began to subside.

"G-good eye," Li muttered to Han as the group huddled close together for warmth.

The others mumbled their thanks too.

Chou pulled his scanner from his pocket and stared at the screen. He hoped their effort made some kind of impact. He looked for any difference in the readout.

"A-anything?" the frigid Zinian asked as he looked over his shoulder.

"I-I'm af-fraid not…" the disappointed Chou started to link. However, the indicators on his pad began to blink. "W-wait," he added.

All at once, the wind speed numbers around the eye wall began to change.

"173 knots…168… 159… 140 knots!" he called out.

A smile broke out on his wet dripping face as the numbers continued to drop.

Zinian and Zhiwei craned their necks as they tried to watch the screen over Chou's shoulders. Zinian poked his friend with his elbow and winked.

"Then we've done it!" Zinian linked.

"The wind speed in the eye must drop below 140," Chou linked back, "to make a difference. It has a long way to go."

A new phenomenon developed that Chou had not planned. The churning water brought even colder water from the north into the picture. The sensors he placed showed that the current around Block Island increased. Chou's eyes started to fill with tears when he saw the effect.

"…128 knots," his raspy voice muttered.

Between the emotional release and exhaustion, Chou started to pass out.

He nearly dropped the sensor device until Zhiwei put his arm around Chou and held him up. Zinian slipped in on his other side and took the instrument from his hand.

"T-take it easy m-my friend," Zhiwei said to him. "You've had a v-very long d-day."

The hurricane's warm winds swept over the ice-cold surface water. The wind patterns began to break into little eddies. Within minutes, the entire central spinning vortex of the hurricane began to wobble. The eye wall was breaking up.

Han laughed as he hugged the others. "We did it! We did it!" he yelled.

The rest of the group stared back at the one person who was usually the most restrained. They burst out laughing as the rain continued to soak them. Villi gently rubbed the sore spot on Su Lin's head, and then he kissed her. Cecilia reached up and kissed Michael, grateful that he saved her from the wave. Zinian and Zhiwei squeezed Chou between them while the two men clasped hands. Even Han and Li exchanged a brief but meaningful embrace.

Master Li moved over to Su Lin and looked her squarely in the eyes.

"You performed admirably well out there," he told her. "I believe it is time to take care of that injury," he added. He drew some sparse energy from the island's residents. The bruised spot on Su Lin's head completely vanished and the internal injuries disappeared.

"Thank you," she whispered aloud as relief set in.

The rest of the group patted a hand on Su Lin's back or offered congratulations to her.

"Let's get out of this rain," Li motioned to the back door of the house that flung open.

Michael spread his arms wide and herded the group in that direction.

"Ah," Zinian quipped, "relative warmth."

Chapter Thirty-Two

An End and a Beginning

"They're calling it the miracle of the century," the television anchor droned on, "scientists remain puzzled as to why a Category 5 hurricane suddenly broke apart and turned into a tropical depression so quickly. Some religious leaders stated they had the power of prayer on their side. However, scientists were quick to point that the colder water in the north acts as natural barrier to hurricanes in this latitude. New Yorkers still braced for an onslaught of heavy rain expected to drop over a foot during the next twenty-four to forty-eight hours. The President expressed the general sense of relief which was felt throughout much of the nation as the danger passed and he rescinded his order for Marshall Law..."

"Please turn that off," Li requested as he strolled past the rectangle on the wall.

Chou touched the control in his pocket. The screen on the wall went blank. He used his mind to turn the satellite dish back to its previous position. Nighttime nearly ended. During the past three hours, the group rested and used their power to repair the house as close to its original state as they could.

"A man has entered the hanger," Zhiwei linked to the others. "He spotted the jet and then the hole in the roof."

"What did he do?" Su Lin asked.

"He went back to his little building and poured out another cup of coffee while he waits out the storm. He will not be curious about the hanger any longer. He's content to listen to the radio and read magazines."

"Nice work Zhiwei," Master Li stated.

"What now?" Michael asked. "Do we stay and help New York clean up?"

"I can help out at the hospitals," Cecilia offered.

"I can assist with family shelters," Su Lin added.

"We will not do any of that," Li told them.

"Why not?" Villi spoke up. "I could work with New York police officers to restore order. I would easily blend in."

"New York has thousands of people who did not leave with the evacuation," Li informed them. "If anyone saw something unusual, they would photograph it and put it on the internet faster than you could say Rollo. That would start the biggest manhunt in the history of this nation. Homeland Security and the NSA would not stop their search until they found us," Li explained. "No, my friends, until we find a way to publically move about with complete secrecy, we must not be tempted to work miracles in public," Li advised.

"You know something," Han said as he pointed his finger at Li. "Did Galactic Central make you privy to some future event?"

Li stared at Han and realized why they called him the master strategist.

"I have been given a rare privilege," Li confessed. "I wanted it to remain a secret. However, in a psychic community secrets are out of the question."

Li moved into the middle of their group. In the air that separated them, he created the image of Galactic Central's great spire. Li then focused on the pinnacle.

"The creature at the top is known as the director," Li pointed out. "The beings of Galactic Central created this organic device and gave it sentience. It intercepts all psychic energy focused on the tower and channels that energy to the creatures below that we call the voices. Every psychic thought transmitted to and from each planet goes through this being. A few weeks ago, it contacted me and informed me that I could travel through time."

"Time travel!" the group declared.

"How can anyone travel through time?" Michael asked. "You told me it was impossible."

"I presumed it was. I'm sorry Michael," Li linked to him and privately added, "I did not tell you about my breakthrough for a reason – one I will make clear to you in the future."

As he glanced about the room, Michael realized that Li linked that last message to him.

"Only I have the capacity to travel backward in time," Li responded to the group. "I can travel into the past. Travel into the future *is* impossible. However, I can glimpse at future possibilities. When I briefly left you in Europe, I traveled directly to Galactic Central. I can make my Earthly body a transitory one. To Camille and Running Elk, I vanished. Yet my physical body actually never left the planet. I am literally in two places at one time."

"So that is why you disappeared," Cecilia declared.

"And how you reappeared in my room without opening a door or a window," Villi added.

"Exactly," Master Li confirmed. "To address Han's point, I deceived you that morning on the terrace. I was curious about what would happen to us. When I ventured into the chamber, I saw the hurricane as an important event in the near future. The only variable that remained was to have one of you think of the idea. I did not foresee my own interference. However, I knew we could not wait for one of you to come up with the idea. So I decided to act and contacted Chou. He considered temperature right away. When he recalled Cecilia's memory and thought of the shape to move water, as Su Lin did, he shifted the future probability of time to this line."

"That's what you were doing on the terrace that morning," Han observed.

"I apologize for my deception, my friend," Li responded.

"You had our best intentions at heart. We can forgive you for that," Han explained and everyone nodded agreement. "Yet, I've a feeling you saw something else… something further into the future."

Master Li paced away from them toward the large window that shattered only hours ago when the huge wave struck that side of the building. Now, with nearly every shard remolded into place, only a few cracks remained. Li gazed out of the large pane at the much calmer sea. The others exchanged glances with Han. He held up his hands to refrain the others from comment and nodded his head in Li's direction. They waited to see what Master Li would say next.

"You will find this difficult to believe," Li began as he quietly linked. "I have some bad news for you," he said as he turned. They could see his drawn face and knew it was not good news. "As much as we would like, we can never mix with the rest of humanity. If we do, our actions will plunge the world into a terrible civil war, nation against nation when they realize that psychics can render a nuclear weapon useless," he told them. "Agents apprehend and torture a psychic until that person reveals Chou's technology and its location."

"Which psychic?" Chou asked.

"It doesn't matter," Li quickly replied. "Government agents use the psychic as a hostage. They demand Zhiwei's security devices. They want the secret behind our ability to amplify and manipulate psychic energy. Eventually, they kill some of us to get to the others. Once they discover our true numbers, the Rollo psychics become expendable. A world-wide power grab takes over. Governments fall. Massive casualties mount. Devastation and destruction spread into defenseless countries based on fear from psychic retaliation. All this takes place on a scale that would put the maker to shame!"

The speechless group stared at Master Li in a state of shock.

"After all we went through to help them…" Chou began.

"It doesn't matter, don't you see?" Li threw out. "The lust for absolute power overpowers reason."

Michael walked up to Master Li and placed his hand on Li's shoulder.

"What a terrible burden it must have been to carry around that knowledge and not share it with anyone," he quietly commented. "Do us a favor and never do that again. Promise?"

The others saw Li pat Michael's hand. The white-haired man nodded.

"You see why we must be careful," Li softly linked to them. "That future must never happen." He stared into Michael's eyes. His own eyes swam with emotion. "This isn't simply a terrible burden for us. This is a burden that all future psychics must bear."

Han's face took on the expression of determination.

"We have just performed a great service for humanity. Master Li is correct. It is enough," he echoed Li's sentiment. "Let them figure out how to manage what remains. From this moment onward, we can elect to help them in times of crisis. However, they must tackle the every-day challenges that naturally occur and which they have endured for centuries. Only one problem for us really remains."

"What is that Han?" Zhiwei asked.

"Other psychics will emerge soon. Am I right?" he questioned as he turned to Master Li.

The elderly man straightened as he moved over toward Han.

"I see what you're trying to say," Li replied. "As others emerge with this power, they could get into trouble if they begin to perform little miracles left and right. Is that it?"

"That's it," Han confirmed.

"I consistently underestimate your contribution to our group," Li said as he half-smiled. "I commend you Han Su Yeng." Master Li then turned to the others. "Han is correct. The time has arrived for us to create an all-encompassing organization that will monitor the emergence of new psychics and indoctrinate them into our world."

"A World Psychic Organization," Michael aptly named.

"The WPO," Cecilia spoke up. "I like the sound of that."

"They'll have to sign a binding agreement," Zhiwei added. His comment made everyone smile. "Well, they will!" he insisted.

"Leave it to Zhiwei to make it all legal," Zinian added.

"We'll make them sign it in their own blood!" Su Lin kidded.

Only Chou giggled at her comment.

"We have another problem," Villi spoke up. "You saw how that hurricane affected each of us from the moment it started to form. We can't go about our everyday lives and stop cold whenever some natural crisis in the world arises. We must learn to block certain outside interferences. Otherwise, a tremor in Timor or a tidal wave in Nassau could pull us in several directions at once," he pointed out. "I believe we should call it crisis blocking and make it part of the initiates training. We'll all work on the technique," he suggested.

"How will we know when the world needs our help?" Cecilia questioned.

Villi glanced over at Zhiwei.

"We have our security chief for that. He'll monitor the news and satellite data streams," Villi pointed out.

"I can easily do that," Zhiwei put in.

"We have much to share with our new members," Michael commented. "I believe we should inform them of these recommendations as soon as possible. Master Li?"

"I agree Michael," Li replied.

Villi smiled, slapped his hands together and rubbed them.

"Hot damn!" he declared. "That means we'll have to fly back to Paris!" he grinned as he glanced over at Su Lin. The young woman blushed.

"Why are you going back to Paris?" Chou questioned.

"We'll all have to go this time," Zhiwei chimed in.

"All the current psychics will have to meet in one place and decide on the rules for this WPO we've concocted. They'll have certain expectations too," Zinian figured.

"We must return to the one place where we know three other psychics exist," Michael pointed out.

"Our vote with them must be in unanimous agreement just as we voted in our meetings," Cecilia offered. "It wouldn't be fair otherwise."

"One thing still troubles me," Su Lin spoke up. "If our group and the three in Paris suddenly popped up within a matter of months, isn't it likely that more of us will be arriving soon? Perhaps other psychics will show up over the next few months. Master Li?"

"Su Lin is right," Zhiwei added. "Psychics could emerge in countries all over the globe. Master Li, do you sense them?"

"The planet is positively swarming with at least a dozen or so candidates," Master Li put in. "However, I do not sense any on the verge of conversion at this time."

"At any rate," Han broke in. "You'll have to monitor their progress Master

Li and help bring them into the fold, N'est pas? (Isn't that so?)" he added in French. Obviously, Han looked forward to Paris as well.

"I'll agree to uphold that position within our organization," Li responded.

He turned and walked over to the window. Outside the first rays of sunrise broke through the clouds as the tropical storm passed over their position. Fortunately, most of the moisture left inside the hurricane dropped into the ocean as rain before it reached the city. The predicted massive flood did not happen.

The group moved around Master Li as he gazed out over the ocean and watched the sunlight break through the clouds illuminating Block Island. The sunlight seemed to represent a fresh feeling of hope that filled their hearts with exuberance – this was their first effort as a team to help humanity.

"We changed the course of human history today with our interference," Master Li linked to them. "I hope you realize that we cannot go back. In stopping that storm, our path, along with the fate of humanity, is set." The weight of his words nearly fell on them like a yoke. "How do you feel Michael?" Li asked the young man standing next to him.

"Like everyone else," Michael linked back, "I feel good. I look forward to our mission."

"By the way," Villi whispered as he leaned over to Chou. "How did you move that rocket?"

"We moved it in the night. Zhiwei arranged a little help from a military cargo plane based in Oklahoma and three helicopters transports from the nearby base of..." Chou tried to explain.

"All at once, I don't want to know the details," Michael sighed as his fingers entwined with Cecilia's.

"Let's get started," Master Li broke in. "We have a hanger roof to repair and a long flight ahead of us back to Paris. I want everyone to think about what you'd like to see in the WPO charter," he said as he moved toward the back door.

"I, for one, can think of several," Han commented.

He waited until the last of the tired group shuffled out the door. As the last person to leave the room, Han reached over and shut out the lights.

The End of "The Voices Arrive – Volume II" of "The Voices Saga"
Up next, "The Voices Emerge – Volume III"

Printed in the United States
by Baker & Taylor Publisher Services